Weird Fiction in France
A Showcase Anthology of its Origins and Development

Weird Fiction in France
A Showcase Anthology of its Origins and Development

translated, annotated and introduced by
Brian Stableford

A Black Coat Press Book

Visit our website at www.blackcoatpress.com

ISBN 978-1-61227-946-6. First Printing. March 2020. Published by Black Coat Press, an imprint of Hollywood Comics.com, LLC, P.O. Box 17270, Encino, CA 91416. All rights reserved. Except for review purposes, no part of this book may be reproduced or transmitted in any form or by any means, electronic or mechanical, including photocopying, recording, or by any information storage and retrieval system, without permission in writing from the publisher. The stories and characters depicted in this novel are entirely fictional. Printed in the United States of America.

TABLE OF CONTENTS

Introduction

The term "weird fiction" has only recently entered common usage, born of a vague dissatisfaction with such labels as "supernatural fiction" and "horror fiction," long used as generic descriptions of a kind of fiction that required distinction from "realistic" or "naturalistic" fiction and, more recently, from "science fiction." All of those labels seemed effective enough as discriminations in common parlance, but all of them run into difficulties if subjected to rigorous examination.

The idea that "supernatural fiction" and "horror fiction" were almost synonymous reflected the notion that anything outside the routine of everyday experience was horrific, simply by virtue of posing a threat to our understanding of the world. That assumption, however, is undermined by either of two arguments. Firstly, we do not live entirely in the real world, but also in a world of imagination, which accommodates spontaneous dreams as well as conscious flights of fancy. Just as dreams can be pleasant or unpleasant, conscious flights of fantasy can be delightful or fearful, consolatory or horrific. In addition, there is no unanimity in people's understanding of the world. There is considerable dispute as to what is, or can be, "real" or "natural" and what is not or cannot, so questions regarding violations of that norm become confused. That confusion might seem to be horrific in itself, but horror is not the only possible intellectual reaction to confusion, and probably not the best one; it can be regarded as a challenge, a problem to be solved, in which meeting the challenge and solving the problem require a denial or suppression of the primitive response of horror.

The French term corresponding most closely to the modern Anglophone notion of "weird fiction" is that of *contes fantastiques*, used as a generic description by several pioneering writers involved with the literary Romantic Movement for the short fiction they wrote under the umbrella of that movement, primarily by Charles Nodier, who published a seminal essay. "Du fantastique en littérature" in the *Revue de Paris* in 1830. which argued that: "the *fantastique* requires a virginal imagination and beliefs that secondary literatures lack, and which are only reproduced therein following revolutions whose passage renews everything." He went on: "When religions...shaken in their foundations, no longer speak to the imagination, or only bring confused notions to it, obscured...by an anxious skepticism, it is necessary that the faculty of producing the marvelous with which nature has endowed it is exercised in a more vulgar genre of creation, more appropriate to the needs of a materialized intelligence," adding: "The apparition of fables recommences at the moment when the empire ends of the real or conventional verities that lend a residue of soul to the worn-out mechanism of civilization. That is what has rendered the fantastic so popular in Europe in recent years, and what has made it the only essential literature of the age of decadence or transition that we have reached."

In another short essay that introduced a short story published in 1832 Nodier proposed that the *fantastique* could feature in stories in three different ways: as frankly marvelous intrusions, as strange events that remain inexplicable, and as the subjective experiences of characters that lend themselves to alternative explanations of hallucination and supernatural activity. It was the third category that Nodier found most rewarding, and it led him to take an intense interest in the physiology and psychology of delusion and hallucination, which he had begun to develop in one of his earliest short stories, "Une Heure, ou la vision" (1806; tr. herein as "One o'clock or, The Vision") and which he put into practice with increasing elaboration in the latter part of his career.

Several other members of the Romantic Movement took a lead from Nodier, especially Théophile Gautier, who extended his thesis regarding the particular propriety of the *fantastique* in a decadent era—and the two collaborators who signed themselves Erckmann-Chatrian; their further examples helped to ensure that by the end of the century the term *conte fantastique* was in common employment by critics and writers alike as an identifier of core strands of the work of writers such as Catulle Mendès, Guy de Maupassant and Remy de Gourmont, applicable to stories of the frankly marvelous but focused with particular interest and attention on stories that drew their principal imaginative force from their ambiguity. Like other categorizations employed in that regard, it proved problematic whenever it came to defining exactly what the adjective *fantastique* could or ought to signify, but it can nevertheless it can be asserted that a distinct tradition of *contes fantastiques* or "weird fiction" was launched in France in the early years of the nineteenth century, and blossomed in the 1830s, with conscious encouragement in the meetings of the writers associated with the Romanic Movement.

There had, of course, been abundant fantastic fiction written in France prior to the advent of the Romantic Movement, and other subgenres, especially that of *contes de fées* and mock-Arabian fantasies had similarly been discussed and nurtured in salons; that tradition had existed in France since the last decades of the seventeenth century, and the roots of weird fiction extended much deeper, all the way back to the prose romances of the eleventh and twelfth centuries, Decisive changes had occurred in French culture in the aftermath of the Revolution of 1789, however, when it seemed evident to everyone that a new era of history had begun, which was bound to generate a modern literature representative of new philosophical attitudes. The predominant facet of that modern attitude was skeptical, seeking to summarize, perfect and embody the heritage of the eighteenth-century Age of Enlightenment which had been generated in its turn by the seventeenth-century Age of Reason, but glare of that enlightenment inevitably case shadows, and Romanticism, which elected to focus on sentiment rather than stern skepticism, and to being reason to bear on aspects of human nature that seemed to skeptics to be unreasonable, was also one of the most important aspects if that post-Revolutionary esthetic progress.

Although the chosen name of *Romanticisme* acknowledged its affinity with Medieval Romance, representing it as, in part, a conscious attempted to recover and renew a treasured component of that Romance, its exponents also regarded themselves as revolutionary, reacting against an alleged stagnation, in which poetry, drama and prose fiction had all become bogged down by arbitrary formal regulation. The new Romanticism aimed to produce an enlightened, self-conscious and deliberate Romance, radical in its determination to return the sentimental and the imaginative to a central role in artistic endeavor, from which they had been squeezed out by habits and rules of procedure that had become stultified, and also to explore their psychological roots—which, it was soon concluded, had to lie deep in unconscious parts of the mind.

A new attitude to the exotic, including the fantastic, was only one component of that renewal of attention, but it was an important one, and a combative one. The imaginative materials employed by previous generations of writers, from Classical antiquity through the Middle Ages to the period preceding the 1789 Revolution had come to be considered by hostile critics to be "obsolete" or "primitive," attacked on one side from the standpoint of religious faith, which condemned them as pagan, and hence implicitly Satanic, and on the other side from the standpoint of Science, which considered that their falsification as matters of fact had robbed them of any intellectual value. The champions of Romanticism thought both attacks simple-minded, contending that that "pagan" notions contained a great deal of esthetic and symbolic value, capable of abundant further extension and virtuous elaboration, and that ideas that are not strictly factual, in terms of scientific proof—even if the supposed proofs are accepted as indubitable—could nevertheless still be immensely useful as instruments of thought. It was within that intellectual framework that modern imaginative fiction, including its "weird" component, took place and the very concept of "weirdness" began to take shape.

The Romantic Movement was imported into France, as it was into England, from Germany, but writers in those two nations paid attention to different aspects of a German Movement that was itself complex, multifaceted and somewhat confused. The most prolific literary response in England took the form of what came to be called "Gothic novels," the fad for which prompted Jane Austen to satirize it in *Northanger Abbey*, whose heroine asks, of a stack of such novels "Are they all horrid?" with a kind of delectable thrill.

The English critic Nathan Drake attempted to argue that there was a "sportive" aspect to the Gothic as well as a menacing one, and that the inheritance it received from Medieval Romance included a much lighter element, exemplified in the German tradition by the folkloristic pastiches of the brothers Grimm and the mock-Medieval romances of Friedrich de la Motte-Fouqué, but to most of his fellow English writers, as to Jane Austen, "Gothic" meant ominous and sinister, and most of the supernatural fiction produced in England in the context of Romanticism was full of menace; the situation was somewhat different in Scotland and Wales, and a nostalgic "Celtomania" is respect of their heritage of legend and folklore became fashionable, exemplified in the work of such writers as James Macpherson, who produced the pastiche romances of Ossian. When Edmund Burke attempted to define the "sublime" as an esthetic category distinct from the "beautiful," however, in *A Philosophical Enquiry into the Origin if our Ideas of the Sublime and the Beautiful* (1757)—a work much admired in France and in Germany as a key precursor of Romanticism—he was careful to suggest that the sublime always contains an element of horror.

In France, the literary influence of German Romanticism was markedly different, mainly because France already had a much more highly developed tradition of fantastic fiction than England—or Germany itself—which had been interestingly and idiosyncratically problematic. At the end of the seventeenth century, there had been a brief fad in the literary salons of Paris, including those associated with Louis XIV's court at Versailles, for writing *"contes de fées"*: pastiches of Medieval Romances that moved enchantresses to center-stage in preference to knights, with a tacitly feminist agenda. Within three years of the first samples appearing in print, the genre was suppressed, presumably by the influence of Churchmen who considered it implicitly heretical, and during the first half of the eighteenth century such tales had enormous difficulty in obtaining the royal "privileges" required for licit publication. By the 1730s, however, enormous quantities of unprivileged texts were being printed in France, usually bearing false title pages advertising foreign places of publication and sold "under the counter," sometimes all the more popular because they were technically illicit, although only a minority of titles attracted active persecution.

Precisely because they were illicit, latter-day *contes de fées* became an attractive genre for numerous writers of a rebellious turn of mind and, together with the spinoff subgenre of Oriental fantasies pioneered by Antoine Galland's translations and pastiches of Arab folklore, such fantastic exercises became a key element of what Voltaire called *contes philosophiques*: calculatedly extravagant and fanciful tales embracing and promoting world-views formed in satirical opposition to those of Church and State. Ironically, much of what Jakob Grimm tried to pass off as "German folklore," ostensibly embodying the roots of a hypothetical German "soul," was actually recycled from French literary sources. Unsurprisingly, French writers tended to see imported German materials through the lens of their own literary history of reinterpreted romances, and their frequent transfiguration into *contes philosophiques*.

The philosophical component of the German Romantic Movement was enormously important as a backcloth to the writings of such author as J. W. Goethe and Friedrich Schiller, and was dominated by a "German Idealism" formulated in the aftermath of the writings of Immanuel Kant, partly as a continuation of his train of thought and partly as a reaction against it; German Idealism, promoted by Johann Fichte, Friedrich Schelling and, most famously, G. W. F. Hegel, shifted the priority of philosophical analysis from "things-in-themselves" (noumena) to the ideas that people form of the contents of the world via sensory perception (phenomena), defining matter not as substance but as the possibility of sensation. That seemed to many people to be a denial of common sense, a challenge to the solidity and independent reality of the world, but the intricacies of the arguments it produced fascinated many writers of imaginative fiction, who readily became preoccupied by the question of what can or ought to be meant by "real."

In England, considered by the French to be an excessively commonsensical and hidebound nation, most intellectuals were prepared to dismiss the arguments of German idealist philosophy as Samuel Johnson had dismissed the idealist philosophy of George Berkeley half a century before, imagining that kicking a stone was sufficient to prove its solidity—thus missing the point completely— but in France such simplicity of mind was far less fashionable. The English Romantic writers who became fascinated with German idealism, mostly under the influence of Samuel Taylor Coleridge, one of its leading English propagandists, did not process the influence in the same way, mostly remaining far more tentative in its exploration than German writers and French writers. It would be a drastic oversimplification to say that the German writers were typically more earnest and gloomier, whereas the French were typically more frivolous and light hearted—all three nations played host to a wide spectrum of attitudes and approaches—but the generalization is not devoid of a certain justice.

French literary Romanticism was a trifle slow to get off the ground, especially in the field of prose fiction. By the time it took wing, it was not only taking aboard the influence of German Romanticism but also of English literary Romanticism. The English writer of Gothic novels Ann Radcliffe was enormously, albeit rather briefly, successful in France, and prompted several writers to produce pastiches, but by far the most powerful English exemplar was Lord Byron, not merely for his narrative poems, which were very loosely translated, but also because of his supposed lifestyle, symbolized in his dress code, imported into France by his friend George Brummell. Byron's supposed image became the model for the French "dandy" and remained so long after English dandies had moved on. Ironically, the work that left the most lasting imprint in the context of French prose fiction was not by Byron at all, but by his one-time doctor John Polidori, who wrote a resentful caricature of his former employer as *The Vampyre*, which was initially misrepresented in France as Byron's work.

The German writers who had the most influence on their French counterparts were J. W. Goethe, whose lachrymose *Die Leiden des jungen Werthers* (1774; revised 1787; tr. as *The Sorrows of Young Werther*), chronicled the agonies of a young writer too sensitive and passionate to survive in a world that remains stubbornly hostile to his dreams, and E. T. A, Hoffmann, a writer of hallucinatory fantasies whose protagonists often lose their grip on reality and begin living dreams or—more frequently—nightmares. Hoffmann's complete works were reissued in French translation in the early 1830s, just as the French Movement was gaining crucial impetus via the *cénacles* hosted by Charles Nodier, Victor Hugo and Théophile Gautier, as well as the salons of Juliette Récamier and Sophie Gay, in which ideas and arguments were exchanged and endeavors ardently stimulated. Hoffmann, although regarded as a secondary figure in Germany and England, became a central reference-point for French Romantic storytellers throughout the nineteenth century, retaining his influence even when it was supplemented, and to some extent supplanted, in mid-century, by that the American Romantic Edgar Poe, initially unappreciated in his homeland but enthusiastically translated into French by Charles Baudelaire.

The particular fascination that French writers in the burgeoning genre of the *fantastique* had for the hallucinatory fantasies of Hoffmann and Poe echoes certain contemporary developments in French medicine, initially prompted by the enormous success in Paris at the end of the eighteenth century of the German physician Franz Mesmer, who promoted a theory of "animal magnetism." Although highly controversial, and dismissed as charlatanry by an investigative commission set up by Louis XVI before the Revolution, the Mesmeric school of medicine remained popular in France, becoming intricately confused with therapeutic hypnotism, and with proto-psychological investigations of somnambulism and dreaming. France was home to many pioneering investigations and attempted analyses of mental disorders, and its asylums, including Charenton, Bicêtre and the Salpêtrière, became important locations of empirical research and attempted psychotherapies. That research prompted intense interest on the part of many litterateurs, and "asylum manuscripts" became a prolific subgenre of French imaginative fiction, vital to the evolution of the *conte fantastique*.

Hallucinations became a frequent subject of literary investigation wherever the Romantic Movement took root, but the particular parallelism of scientific and literary research in France was graphically illustrated by "Le Club des Hashischins"—as it was called by Théophile Gautier in a celebrated *conte* in 1846—in which the narrator is fed psychotropic drugs in a house on the Île Saint-Louis. Many readers mistook the sorry for reportage, and the house identified with the one represented in the story is still associated with the urban legend. Numerous writers in the coteries associated with Nodier and Gautier, including Gérard de Nerval, Victor Hugo, Charles Baudelaire, Alphonse Karr and Alphonse Esquiros, were reported to have employed psychoactive compounds as a source of inspiration, with further encouragement from Thomas De Quincey, whose *Confessions of an English Opium-Eater* (1821) was rapidly but loosely translated into French by cénacle-member Alfred de Musset. Long after the publication of Gautier's accidental hoax, several French writers deliberately employed hashish, opium and absinthe to induce hallucinations, which they then incorporated into stories. Gabriel de Lautrec was the most vocal of those who advertised his exploits in that regard, but the covert influence of psychotropic substances on the development of French weird fiction extends much more widely than the blatantly drug-induced stories included in the present sampler.

Although the notion that genius is closely akin to madness dates back to antiquity, it reached a peak of fashionability in the nineteenth century, in France more than anywhere else. Doctor Jacques-Joseph Moreau's *La Psychologie morbide dans ses rapports avec la philosophie de l'histoire, ou de l'Influence des névropathies sur le dynamisme intellectuel* (1859) must have been read with interest by the authors he allegedly involved with his research into the effects of hashish—which provided the seed of Gautier's account of an imaginary club— as must *Du Démon de Socrate* (1836) by Louis-Francisque Lélut, long-time director of the hospital at Bicêtre, which had pioneered the retrospective psychoanalysis of writers of the past, analyzing their alleged mental aberrations. Lélut and Moreau were only two of many French psychologists fascinated by the relationship between madness and literary creativity, and the links between dreams, hallucinations, weird fiction and madness. Whether writers of such fiction agreed with such theses or not, they could not be unaware of them; stories dealing with apparitions, hallucinations and other anomalous events could not be uninformed by them, in one way or another. The psychoanalytic aspect of French weird fiction is not necessarily more pronounced than that of English or German fiction, but it has a distinctive slant in spite of its enormous variety, the evolution of which is clearly marked by the stories in the present collection.

As Charles Nodier proposed, the true essence of "weird fiction" is not the inclusion of supernatural elements or the horrified reaction that such intrusions cause in a quasi-reflexive fashion, but the ambiguity of such stories regarding the status of their "unrealistic" intrusions, which reflects a fundamental uncertainty faced by anyone confronted by anomalous events. Is the event real or illusory, objective of subjective? Am I only "seeing things," in the paradoxical sense of that phrase that implies that I am not really seeing them at all? Am I "in my right mind" or am I "going mad?" Doctors confronted with actual cases necessarily proceed from the axiomatic assumption of delusion, but in fiction, it is the author, not Nature, who is the arbiter of actuality, and weird fiction, by definition, does not automatically beg the question, even if the story-arc eventually comes down one side of the argument or the other.

In Tzvetan Todorov's *Introduction à la littérature fantastique* (1970) the author draws a careful tripartite distinction, slightly different from Nodier's, between stories of the *merveilleux*, in which the events of a story remain manifestly supernatural; stories of the *étrange* [strange, but rendered "uncanny" in the extant English translation], in which seemingly supernatural events are eventually given a "rational" explanation; and stories of the *fantastique*, in which ambiguity is preserved and essential to the narrative. Todorov seemed to think, when he published his taxonomy, that stories of the third category were relatively rare and that his identification of them was new, but it would not have surprised any of the Romantic writers of *contes fantastiques* in the least to discover that ambiguity of interpretation was the very essence of what they were doing, and that terminal resolutions into the frankly *merveilleux* or the merely *étrange* were arbitrary, perhaps as likely to spoil a story as to provide a satisfactory sense of completion. Abhorrence of ambivalence is not uncommon among readers, but sophisticated readers readily acquire an appreciative understanding of the intricate esthetics of ambiguity,

Insofar as the stories collected in the present volume illustrate a collective narrative of the evolution of a loosely-knit genre, it is largely a narrative of the exploration of ambiguity, not only in the sense that the stories often fall within Todorov's narrowly-defined genre of the *fantastique* or that they toy deliberately with the boundaries identified by his classification in a teasing fashion, but also in the sense that they consciously explore techniques of literary ambiguity and the esthetics of "unreliable narration." In order to serve as an accurate representation of the genre, the sampler has to include specimens of commercial "popular fiction" as well as more ambitious works of "literary fiction," but in the former, as in the latter, ambiguity remains central to the development of the story, and the narrative voices of the stories, whether personalized or not, often raise explicit questions within the narrative as to the nature of their ambiguity and consequent appeal made to readers by weird fiction.

The Romantic Movement underwent various transformations in the course of the nineteenth century, giving rise to various spinoff movements in France, most prominently the Occult Revival and the Symbolist Movement—both entangled and confused with the Decadent Movement—and with the Surrealist Movement to which they eventually gave birth. The stories in the present collection illustrate that pattern of evolution; most of the writers sampled in the latter part would have identified themselves as Symbolists, and most of the exceptions would only have denied it because their egos would not allow them to consider themselves subservient to any Movement. Although the cut-off date for inclusion in the anthology antedates the publication of the first Surrealist Manifesto by more than a decade, the inclusions also illustrate the extent to which Surrealism was present in embryo, and necessarily so, within the gastrula of early French weird fiction. The Surrealists set out to mine the mother lode of dreams with dynamite, but long before such Nobelesque aggression became feasible, writers interested the stuff of dreams and the matrices of hallucination were chipping away with hammers, detaching rough-hewn gems of all colors, and polishing them with an admirable verve and frequent craftsmanship.

A good deal of weird fiction is not so much fiction about the supposed weirdness of the world, even when it pretends to be, as fiction about the intrinsic weirdness of fiction. Even in its popular commercial manifestations, the *fantastique* is problematically layered, and thus far more interesting than critics who dismiss it as puerile are prepared to concede. Many of the stories in this showcase were, in their day, genuinely innovative in terms of their narrative techniques and strategies, as they were obliged to be by their determination to reevaluate and refresh materials whose ultimate sources lay in ancient religion and exotic belief—the occult, in the broadest sense of the term. They participated in the early phases of eventually-drastic transformations of typical images of such revenants as ghosts and vampires, and ideas of fatality and retributive justice, which continued into the twentieth century and still retain abundant scope for further evolution today.

Weird fiction has long been a Cinderella genre, not only unappreciated but actively maltreated by the ugly sisters of orthodox esthetic evaluation, but its position in the household of literature has improved considerably in modern times, and that modification of status has both permitted and encouraged a reexamination and reevaluation of the genre's history. It is in the nature of history that it has to accumulate before it can be understood, and processes of transformation have to be on the brink of completion before they can be accurately assessed—the owl of Minerva only flies in the twilight, as the great Symbolist Hegel put it—so it is not surprising that it required nearly two centuries since the beginnings of modern weird fiction in the cradle of the Romantic Movement for the concept to be properly formulated, and the course of its development from embryo to imago usefully mapped.

That cartography can now be carried out with a reasonable degree of accuracy, as the present collection, albeit limited in time and space, hopefully illustrates. The ensemble hopefully illustrates too, beyond any reasonable doubt, that fiction depicting hypothetical aberrations in nature or perception is not a necessarily a symptom of aberration on the part of the author, as Louis-Francisque Lélut and kindred spirits once thought, but frequently, and typically, quite the opposite: evidence of a sanity contemplating its own potential limits and uncertainties, in a context that is esthetic rather than diagnostic, and all the more valuable for it. *Romanticisme* is not dead, and is no less preciously modern today than it was two centuries ago, and weird fiction is not the least of its achievements.

Brian Stableford

Charles Nodier (1780-1844) was one of the great pioneers of French Romantic prose; his salon at the Bibliothèque de l'Arsenal, begun in 1824, for which he counted the term "Le Cénacle," brought together many of the key figures in the Romantic Movement and spun off other cénacles in which it was anchored, including Victor Hugo's. A prolific journalist and pillar of the Romantic periodical La Revue de Paris, *his most famous works in the genre of weird fiction include the hallucinatory novella* Smarra *(1821), the mock-folkloristic fantasy* Trilby, ou le Lutin d'Argail *(1822), the surreal fantasy* Histoire du Roi de Bohême et ses sept châteaux *(1830) and the delusory fantasy* La Fée aux miettes *(1832).* "Une Heure, ou la vision" *first appeared in* Les Tristes, ou Mélanges tirés des tablettes d'un suicidé *in 1806; this translation is original to the present volume.*[1]

Charles Nodier: *One o'clock; or, The Vision*

I had a heart full of bitterness and I sought solitude and the night. My walk had scarcely extended beyond Chaillot's gardens, and I usually only began it after eleven o'clock in the evening had chimed; but I was obsessed by such sad thoughts, my imagination was nourished by so many dire reveries, that often, in the state of involuntary excitement that is familiar to souls in pain, I had had to repel I know not how many illusions at which a moment's reflection would have caused me to blush.

One day, I had gone, later than usual, to the accustomed place; and, ether because the more obscure darkness had deceived my design, or because the succession of my ideas, more unequal and more fortuitous, had caused me to lose sight of the goal of my nocturnal course, the bell of the village church was striking one o'clock when I perceived that I was no longer following my familiar route, and that my distraction had taken me into a unknown path. I hastened my steps toward the place from which the sound had come. At a turning in a narrow passage, a shadow rose up before my feet and disappeared into the hedge. I stopped, shivering, and I saw a long stone in the form of a tomb. I heard a sigh; the foliage trembled.

[1] Available from Black Coat Press: *Trilby / The Crumb Fairy* (a collection which also includes *"Bean-Treasure and Peaseblossom," "The Dream of Gold," "Goodman Genie," "Love and the Grimoire," "The Man and the Ant," "Smarra, or The Demons of the Night"*), ISBN 978-1-61227-455-3; *The Vampire*, an 1820 stage play adaptation of John-William Polidori 's novella included in *Lord Ruthven the Vampyre*, ISBN 978-1-932983-10-4; and *"Perfectibility"* (1833) included in *The Germans on Venus*, ISBN 978-1-934543-56-6;.

The following day, preoccupied with that adventure, I sought the same place at almost the same hour; the apparition was reiterated, and the phantom brushed me in passing; its footsteps resounded on the stone; the dry grass rustled behind it, and at intervals, I saw it fleeing, like a dark cloud, between the nearby willows or at the corner of a path. Always following the light and uncertain trace, I arrived at the old monastery of Sainte-Marie; but, wandering from one heap of rubble to another, I no longer found anything.[2]

That dilapidated convent offers one of the saddest sights that can strike the human eye. Nothing remains of the church but large isolated pilasters which bear the debris of a destroyed vault in places. When the moon lets its light fall through those columns and owls ululate on the cornices, as one reaches the summits of the uncultivated terraces and advanced among the high walls, stumbling among the ditches, and descending the broken stairways overgrown by poisonous plants, such as henbane and celandine, one ends up at buildings that are utterly degraded, of which nothing subsists but menacing sections of wall and eaves suspended in an almost-miraculous manner. When one is conducted by hazard to that funereal avenue, which leads via a rocky slope beneath damp arches to the ancient catacombs, and by the light of some dying lamp one can read on the scattered stones the names of the chaste women whose bones were deposited there...there is no human strength that can resist similar emotions. They absorbed all my faculties to such an extent that I forgot, in a way, the strange motive of my research; it was not until the next day that I felt the desire reborn more vividly to penetrate the mystery of the being whose encounter had troubled me, and which had made the great sepulcher a habitation as mysterious as itself.

At one o'clock, holding my breath and walking silently, I arrived at the tomb, and I recognized the specter.

He was sitting, with his eyes fixed on a certain point in the sky. It was a young man, thin and very pale, clad in poor rags, whose unkempt hair fell back in thick waves. On seeing his gaping mouth, his extended neck, his stiff arms and his entire occupied attitude, one might have thought that he was delivering himself to a grave contemplation; but a sob escaped him, and I presumed that he had not seen what he appeared to be seeking.

He perceived me then, and leapt up in order to flee. Then, stopping immediately and looking at me mildly, he said: "What do you want with me?"

"To know you, and perhaps to console you."

"You're a man," he said, "and your heart is made like theirs. I don't like that species; there were some in my early days who were sympathetic to the

---

[2] The ruins of the convent of Sainte-Marie, near Chaillot on the road to Passy, have long been swallowed up by the expansion of Paris, but in the 1820s the area was still rural.

suffering of others; they were noble hearts loved by God; things are very different now."

He shook his head and wiped his eyelids.

"There are still some now," I said. "Don't close your heart to your brothers."

"I no longer have brothers; do the unfortunate have any? Look how wan and withered I am; Look how soiled I am. I'm hungry during the day; during the night I lay my bones in the mud and the water of marshes. God has given me bad days. There are moments when my eyes are troubled, when my teeth join effortfully. My breast rises, my nerves vibrate like the strings of a harp; I sense tears that are trying to escape, a chill that runs through my limbs, and an inexplicable malaise that grips me by the throat. It's said that I'm a maniac and an epileptic, and people pass by, letting a smile of disdain fall upon me. That is what I am."

He sat down on the tomb, and I sat down beside him.

"I can recount to you...," he said, suddenly. "She won't come tonight, anyway. Do you see that black cupola rising up there in the blue depths of the sky? And that star, shining above, floating in such a pure light. Do you see it? She's there, in truth, since she told me so; but she no longer descends.

"I was almost as rich as Octavie, but the heir of a great house presented himself, and her parents refused me. Two days before the wedding, I was walking under the trees of the Luxembourg and I was embracing my dolor. What dreams did I not have! I shall take a sharp dagger into the banqueting hall, I said, and I shall give eternity to my beloved and myself; or I shall throw fear into the temple and I shall abduct Octavie from the midst of her consternated friends; or I shall mingle the horrors of a conflagration with the preparations for her hymen; and in the trouble of that scene of terror, I shall steal her, dead or alive, from the crime of a new amour.

"She passed by. The satin of her dress rustled. I shivered all over; a red cloud obscured my sight; all my blood flowed to my heart. She had recognized me, my Octavie. 'I'll come back soon,' she said to those surrounding her. 'The calm of midnight must be more delightful here. I'll come back soon; perhaps I'll come tomorrow.'

"They resound like such sweet music, the words of the woman one loves. They resound for a long time. All the faculties are gripped by them; the soul identifies with them; it seems that in carrying away her last thought, one is bearing her away entirely.

"I went away repeating: *I'll come back soon, perhaps I'll come tomorrow.* Perhaps tomorrow, she had said. But she didn't come.

"One o'clock chimed. Then a lugubrious bell, struck at long intervals, filled the air with a symphony of death.

"I would not have been able to define the emotion by which my senses were surprised, but it was as if it emanated from the sky. Whatever it was, an

19

action of will of which I had not taken account drew me to Octavie's house; and, cleaving through the crowd of domestics, I stopped at the disarray of the apartment that she occupied.

The windows were open. Behind the curtains, shadows and torches could be seen passing by turns, and I know not what stifled cries were rising from the depths of the room.

"'She's dead!' I cried.

"'No,' replied her father, clutching me convulsively in his arms. 'She's asleep.'

"She was lying on her bed of red damask; there was a candle on her nightstand, a book at her feet; a priest was motionless beside the bed; her mother had fainted on the floor. Eulalie was weeping copiously, and a man dressed in black said with a ferocious sang-froid: 'There's no more hope; I knew full well that she wouldn't get out of it.'"

"I have forgotten the entire year that followed that evening, for I was ill, people said, and my malady excited repugnance and horror. Since Octavie's death, there was no longer anyone who loved me.

"A year later, to the day, I was going up the Rue de Tournon by the light of the illuminations of a public festival; I had passed slowly through twenty groups who afflicted me with the outbursts of their vulgar joy when one o'clock chimed. If the stroke of the clapper had hit me, it would have wounded me less rudely than it did in making that bell groan. Why was that hour—the hour whose last murmur had covered the sounds of your agony—not removed from the cycle of time?

"Then an adolescent with an angelic face saluted me with a moist and luminous gaze, and disappeared into the crowd, indicating the Luxembourg to me.

"I hesitated; I could still see him; a tear slid down his face, glistened and fell.

"I went into the gardens, very emotional—me, who had never known fear—and the dust that rose up in my passage, and the rays of moonlight that sprang forth between the leaves, and the distant tumult of the crowd returning home, all filled me with disquiet and alarm.

"She finally appeared to me, dressed and veiled in white, as on the beautiful evening when we had traversed all the quais of the Seine on foot, and I saw distinctly that she was floating in a vapor as gentle as the dawn. I lost consciousness, and Octavie did not draw away from me. She leaned over my motionless body, and her hot breath warmed my breast. Her kisses fluttered from my mouth to my eyelids and from my eyelids to my hair. Her arms enveloped me softly and rocked me in a region full of light and perfumes. There was a burden of voluptuousness upon all my organs. But when my reassured mind began to enjoy more fully that scene of intoxication; when my anxious eyes sought Octavie around me, I could no longer distinguish anything but the trace of her flight, a pale and trembling furrow that extended all the way to that star, and which gradually faded away.

"I don't know why she no longer comes, but if she doesn't come, I shall go...I believe I shall go," he repeated, in a low voice.

Such was the story that the epileptic told me, and after that, I enquired at length, but fruitlessly, regarding his fate. I had despaired of seeing him again, when hazard informed me that someone similar had been seen in the infirmary at Bicêtre. I went there, and had myself taken to his bed. He was little more than a cadaver, almost totally fleshless, and frightfully livid. His eyes still had a little fire and moved quite rapidly in their sunken orbits, but his gaze made one feel ill.

After having reflected for a few minutes with the air of a man trying to fix confused reminiscences, a bitter smile creased his lips slightly and he leaned gently in my direction

"I knew full well," he said, "that I would go. I shall probably go tomorrow. Octavie came to invite me there, and I've already received a pledge from her of imminent alliance—for it's good," he added, "Octavie's hand, which extends thus toward me at any hour; it isn't a hand desiccated by death. It isn't a black and hideous hand like those of skeletons that have grown old in the tomb; its form is sweeter than the hands of angels. It's true that I can't touch her yet, but when the moment is ready to be accomplished, that hand will seize me and draw me beyond the sky."

As he finished speaking, he started staring at his pillow with a fearful joy, and cried out in a muted and alarmed voice: "There she is, there she still is, and there's her oval onyx with a little circle of gold.

"I shall go tomorrow," he said, smiling.

Capricious aberrations of a vivid or credulous imagination! He did not seem to see the straw on which his head was resting, and the coarse sheet that covered him was depressed by the weight of Octavie's hand, conserving its imprint.

How do I know, an unfortunate they call mad, whether that pretended infirmity was not the symptom of a more energetic sensibility, a more complete organization, and whether nature, in stimulating all your faculties, does not render them more apt to perceive the unknown?

That idea still occupied me when I arrived the next day. I approached the epileptic's bed and I did not see him, but a shroud thrown over him allowed me to divine his body. There was also a little candle burning there, and everything else was as it ordinarily was.

When the evening had advanced somewhat I went to the place where I had encountered him previously and I sat down on the tomb where we had sat together. It had been disturbed, perhaps with the intention of taking it away in order to form the boundary-marker of a field or the cornerstone of a building. I heard one o'clock chime and I calculated that that night would be the second anniversary of Octavie's death.

The sky was not pure; at first, a dull and stormy cloud hid the star where her friend had so often looked for her, but it emerged slowly from the darkness, and seemed more resplendent.

"Poor madman!" I said aloud. "What is the price of your discoveries now, vain science of the earth? There is nothing obscure for you in so many marvels that make the astonishment of sages; and if some cloud has veiled your days, you are freed therefrom, like that star, in order to resume in a new life your primal grace and your original beauty."

S. Henry Berthoud was the signature employed for most of his writings by Sam-uel-Henri Berthoud (1804-1919), a native of Cambrai who collaborated with Honoré de Balzac during his student days in the early 1820s before abandoning a career in public administration in his native city in order to return to Paris in the early 1830s, where he worked as an editor for the radical publisher Émile de Girardin on several publications, including the Musée des Familles. *He pub-lished early prose work by many of the pioneering writers of Romantic prose, including Théophile Gautier and Jules Janin. His career ran into inevitable dif-ficulties after the coup d'état of 1851 but he remained active as an editor and writer, especially in the production of educational material for children and the popularization of science. "*La Délation*" appeared, perhaps for the first time, in* Chroniques et traditions surnaturelles de la Flandre *(1831); the translation was first published in* The Angel Asrael and Other Legendary Tales *(2019).*[3]

S. Henry Berthoud: *The Delation*

> The Judge: Accused, reveal your accomplices
> and the law will send you away absolved.
> The Forger: Condemn me. I prefer the blade of the guillotine
> to the infamous name of Delator.
> (S. Henry Berthoud, *Angoisses*.)[4]

To see her again!

That was an idea that burned his brain, an idea that made him agitate and writhe in the post-chaise.

To see her again! When he has been far away six months for six months; when for six months he has not even heard her name: Clarisse!

If, at least, before quitting her, she had said to him: "Paul, I love you!"

He knows full well that she loves him, that she loves him as no angel in heaven has ever loved; he has read it in her moist yes, in her emotional voice, in the indecisive pressure of her tremulous hand; but she never made him that con-fession: "Paul, I love you!"

---

[3] Available from Black Coat Press: *Martyrs of Science*, ISBN 978-1-61227-229-0; *The Angel Asrael*, ISBN 978-1-61227-613-7; *William's Angel*, ISBN 978-1-61227-875-9; "*A Heavenward Voyage*" (1840) and "*The Second Sun*" (1862) in *The World Above the World*, ISBN 978-1-61227-002-9.

[4] The reference is not to any published work.

Before hearing those words, the words for which he would have paid a year of his life, it was necessary for him to leave, to depart on a long voyage, to depart without seeing her once more.

But it was a matter of the life of a brother; for his brother would not have survived the dishonor, and without Paul's prompt arrival, without the sacrifice of a part of his fortune, his brother would have been dishonored. He could not hesitate, therefore, and he had quit everything, his life as an artist, his old mother, and perhaps even more: Clarisse.

But he is going to see her again, and she will love him more than on his departure, for her generous soul can appreciate such a sacrifice. He is going to see her again! Oh, the sensations that he experiences at that idea almost make him bless the absence.

And the dusty vehicle traverses Lille rapidly. A door opens before it; cries: "My son! My dear Paul!" His mother is in his arms.

She weeps with joy; she hugs her son; she hugs him again; she blesses him, she calls him her only consolation, the sole joy that she has in the world.

And she has not wanted to be alone in rejoicing. Oh no! Of all those who came every evening to say: "Is he coming back?" all those who repeated: "In a month, in a week, in a day, we'll see him again!" not one is lacking this evening. She is giving a ball, and it is necessary that Paul dance, in spite of his three nights spent in a carriage. His friends are so joyful: his friend, whom she enumerates with a child-like complaisance, and among whom she names Clarisse's husband, and Clarisse herself.

That overflowing of a mother's tenderness, that celebration of his return, those illuminated drawing rooms, the noise of carriages, the guests who are arriving, the sounds of the instruments tuning up, and then the waiting, the waiting with the palpitating heart, searching among the women coming in: all of that produces an intoxicating exaltation in him, a delightful anguish.

There she is! There she is!

He runs. She stops him with a cold smile, devoid of amour.

She has done well to stop him, for without that smile, his emotion might perhaps have compromised her.

She has done well; oh, yes—and yet, he is saddened by such a great prudence; a vague anxiety grips his heart.

What folly!

Finally, now, he can approach her without imprudence. A young man gets in ahead to him; he invites her to dance, and she smiles at him as he would have given anything in the world for her to smile at him on seeing him again.

How long he takes before going away... Finally, he goes.

Clarisse! Again that icy smile, and then indifferent words, a hand that no longer responds to his grip.

She no longer loves him; it is that young man she loves.

So much the better that she no longer loves him, so much the better that she has not deceived him any longer. After all, such an amour is not to be regretted; it will soon be consoled. To love a woman who does not comprehend your love would be horrible, it would depreciate it. It's necessary to take revenge for such inconstancy by a cold scorn; that will not be difficulty.

Ah! The young man isn't quitting her; she only has words for him, smiles for him.

They're only dancing with one another. Now he's leaning toward her ear; she's blushing, she's looking at him tenderly. Malediction! Malediction!

And his fists clench, and his teeth grind.

That fit of despair is succeeded by an even worse joy; an anxious malaise full of agitation and dejection; an excessive lassitude mingled with an imperious need for movement; his eyes are burning, his lungs are burning; his head is burning.

When two o'clock chimes, he has to leave the ball. It's stifling there.

He searches in vain for a chair in which to sit down. Not one can be found in the antechamber; it's in vain that he orders the domestics to bring him one. They don't obey him, because twenty new orders from the mistress of the house make them forget Paul's.

He remembers then that there is an old sofa at the end of a long corridor directly opposite the room where everyone is dancing, and he goes to sit down there.

Soon, he experienced strange sensations.

He could no longer hear the music; only the vague murmur of voices reached him at long intervals, and then came a great calm, to be interrupted again, a few moments later, by one of those instinct rumors.

An extreme fatigue, the warm and heavy atmosphere of the corridor, its obscurity, the murmurs of the drawing room, after so much stifling warmth, agitation and hubbub, the moving crowd talking soundlessly, the dancing devoid of music that were perceptible through the embrasure of a distant door as if through the undulations of a transparent gauze, plunged Paul into a sort of nightmare, the torpor of which blunted neither the anguish of the soul not the faculties of the senses, but which compressed everything with its iron hand and formed I know not what execrable assemblage thereof, with which a suffocation of the chest and an insipid aftertaste were combined.

He was suffering, in such a state, beyond what can be described, and yet he could not find the strength get out of it, and even found a sort of inexplicable charm in it. Someone walked around him, someone came to sit down beside him, without him paying any heed to it, without him making a movement that might have put an end to that cruel anguish.

That is what he was experiencing when a clear, guttural voice began to speak to Paul's left, and to proffer him confused words that he heard without understanding them, and which added further to the strangeness if his sensations.

It even seemed to him that the voice was one of the tricks of his dream, for there was a mockery in its bizarrely articulated words that associated itself with his memories and reawakened his pain in a cruel fashion.

"Ha ha!" said the voice. "How that young woman dressed in pink is abandoning herself softly in the arms of her waltzer. Do you know her? Excuse me, Monsieur, I don't live in Lille. What gazes they're exchanging! Either I don't know anything, or, upon my word, she's just reached the point of imprudence that precipitates into the abyss of dishonor."

As soon as the man spoke, Paul thought that he had glimpsed in the shadows the features of Clarisse's husband, and he understood the urgency of making the voice shut up that was revealing the young woman's fatal secret; but he experienced such a strange sort of enjoyment on hearing that denunciation, and had so little energy in his numb organs, that he could not find sufficient willpower to emerge from his horrible state, and he let the voice continue.

"Now she's passing in front of us again—how her breast is palpitating! How her hand is pressing her lover's! Now she's taking a piece of paper from her bosom; she's giving it to him."

And specters assembled around Paul; and they turned their icy gazes toward him; and there was a young woman there who was trying to lift up with her hands the brain matter that was spreading from her broken skull; and there was a young man who was covering his heart with his hand, and that hand was raised up by the force of the blood that was spurting from a large wound; and that woman was Clarisse, and the young man was her lover.

In the meantime, the voice continued: "How they're devouring one another with their gazes! How he's gripping her waist! Their disturbance is at its peak: they're doomed! They're doomed forever, I'm sure of it! Now their lips are meeting!"

A sudden, terrible noise woke Paul from his nightmare. A man, Clarisse's husband, ran with great strides and seized Paul's traveling pistols from the mantelpiece.

Two detonations, and the crowd rushed out of the drawing rooms.

And Clarisse hid her bloody forehead with her hands, and her lover pressed, with a dying hand, the wound that he had in his heart.

Théophile Gautier (1811-1872) was one of the stars of the Romantic Movement and began a memoir of his involvement with it that was unfinished at his death, published posthumously as Histoire du Romantisme *(1874). The preface to his classic novel* Mademoiselle de Maupin *(1835) expounded his doctrine as* l'art pour l'art; *the story was originally intended as a quasi-documentary account of the seventeenth-century cross-dressing opera star Julie d'Aubigny, who used the stage name Mademoiselle Maupin, but Gautier transfigured his central character into an archetype of his own. The novella* "Une nuit de Cléopâtre" *(1838), a similarly flamboyant transfiguration, launched a significant tradition of lush historical fiction. Gautier's introduction to the 1868 edition of Charles Baudelaire's* Les Fleurs du mal *crystallized and popularized the notion of "decadent style," for which the Decadent Movement of the fin-de-siècle was named.* "La Morte amoureuse" *was first published in* La Chronique de Paris, *23 & 26 juin 1836; "The Amorous Revenant" is original to the present collection; a previous translation by Lafacdio Hearn was entitled "Clarimonde."*[5]

Théophile Gautier: *The Amorous Revenant*

You ask me, Brother, whether I have ever loved; yes. It is a singular and terrible story, and although I am sixty-six years old, I scarcely dare to stir the ashes of that memory. I cannot refuse you anything, but I would not tell such a story to a less proven soul. The events are so strange that I can hardly believe that they happened to me.

For more than three years I was the victim of a singular and diabolical illusion. Every night, I, a poor country priest, led in dream—please God that it was a dream!—a life of a damned soul, a worldly life of a Sardanapalus. A single glance too full of complaisance cast at a woman nearly caused the loss of my soul, but finally, with the aid of God and my saintly patron, I succeeded in repelling the evil spirit that had taken possession of me.

My existence was complicated by an entirely different nocturnal existence. By day I was a priest of the Lord, chaste, occupied with prayer and holy things; by night, as soon as I had closed my eyes, I became a young lord, a fine connoisseur of women, dogs and horses, playing dice, drinking and blaspheming; and when I woke up at dawn it seemed to me, on the contrary, that I was asleep and dreaming that I was a priest. Memories of objects and words of that somnambulistic life have remained to me, which I cannot forbid myself, and alt-

---

[5] Available from Black Coat Press: "*One of Cleopatra's Nights*" in *The French Fantasy Treasury (Vol. 3)*, ISBN 978-1-61227-546-8; and "*Future Paris*" (1851) in *Investigations of the Future*, ISBN 978-1-61227-106-4.

hough I have never emerged from the walls of my presbytery, one might think, on hearing me, that I was a man returned from society worn away by everything, who has entered into religion and wants to end excessively agitated days in the bosom of the Lord, rather than a humble seminarian who has grown old in an unknown parish in the depth of woods, without any relationship with things of the present century.

Yes, I have loved, as no one else in the world has loved, an insensate and furious amour, so violent that I am astonished that that it did not cause my heart to burst. Oh, what nights! What nights!

Since my earliest childhood I felt a vocation for the condition of a priest, so all my studies were directed in that direction, and my life, until the age of twenty-four, was nothing but a long novitiate. Having finished my theology I passed successively through all the petty orders, and my superiors judged me worthy, in spite of my great youth, to take last redoubtable step. The day of my ordination was fixed for the week of Easter.

I had never gone into society; the world, for me, was the enclosure of the college of the seminary. I knew vaguely that there was something called "woman," but my thought did not pause thereon; I was perfectly innocent. I only saw my aged and infirm mother twice a year. That was the entirety of my relations with the outside world.

I did not regret anything; I did not feel the slightest hesitation before the irrevocable engagement; I was full of joy and impatience. No young fiancé had ever counted the hours with a more feverish ardor. I did not sleep without dreaming that I was saying mass; I could not imagine anything in the world finer than being a priest; I would have refused to be a king or a poet. My ambition could not conceive anything beyond.

What I am saying is to demonstrate to you the extent to which what happened to me should not have happened, and the inexplicable fascination of which I was the victim.

When the great day came I walked to the church with such a light step that it seemed to me that I was floating in the air, or that I had wings on my shoulders. I thought that I was an angel, and I was astonished by the somber and preoccupied physiognomy of my companions; for there were several of us. I had spent the night in prayer, and I was in a state almost akin to ecstasy. The bishop, a venerable old man, seemed to me to be God the Father inclined over his eternity, and I could see Heaven through the vault of the temple.

You know the details of the ceremony; the benediction, the communion under the two species, the anointing of the palms of the hands of the catechumens with oil, and finally, the holy sacrifice offered in concert with the bishop. I shall not dwell on that.

Oh, how right Job was, and how imprudent the man is who makes a pact with his eyes! I chanced to raise my head, which I had kept inclined until then, and I perceived in front of me, so close that I could have touched her, although she was in reality quite a long distance away and on the other side of the balustrade, a young woman of rare beauty, dressed with a regal magnificence.

t was as if scales fell from my eyes. I experienced the sensation of a blind man who suddenly recovers his sight. The bishop, so radiant a moment before, was suddenly extinguished; the candles paled in their golden candlesticks like the stars in the morning, and there was a complete obscurity throughout the church. The charming creature stood out against that background of shadow like an angelic revelation; she seemed self-illuminated, giving light rather than receiving it.

I lowered my eyelids, firmly resolved not to raise them again, in order to remove myself from the influence of external objects, for distraction was invading me increasingly, and I scarcely knew what I was doing.

A minute later, I opened my eyes again, for through my eyelashes I could see the colors of the prism sparkling, in a crimson penumbra, as when one gazes at the sun.

Oh, how beautiful she was! The greatest painters, when they pursued ideal beauty in Heaven and brought back to earth the divine portrait of the Madonna, did not even approach that fabulous reality. Neither the verses of the poet nor the palette of the painter could give an idea of it.

She was quite tall, with the figure and the deportment of a goddess. Her hair, of a soft blonde, was separated at the top of her head and flowed over her temples like two rivers of gold; one might have thought her a queen with her diadem. Her forehead, of a blue-tinted and transparent whiteness, extended broadly and serenely over two arcs of almost brown lashes, a singularity that added further to the effect of sea-green irises of an unsustainable vivacity and glare.

What eyes! In a flash, they decided the destiny of a man; they had a life, a limpidity, and an ardor and a brilliant humidity that I had never seen in a human eye; rays escaped from them like darts, which I distinctly saw terminating in my heart. I do not know whether the flame that illuminated them came from Heaven or Hell, but it surely came from one or the other. That woman was an angel or a demon, and perhaps both; she certainly did not emerge from the loins of Eve, the common mother.

Teeth of the most beautiful orient scintillated within her red smile, and little dimples were hollowed out with each inflexion of her mouth in the pink satin of her adorable cheeks. As for her nose, it had an entirely regal delicacy and pride, which revealed the noblest origin. Agate gleams played over the smooth and lustrous skin of her partly-uncovered shoulders, and rows of large blonde pearls, of a hue almost identical to the neck, descended over her breast. From time to time she straightened her head with an undulating movement of a snake or a strutting peacock and imprinted a slight frisson to the high frieze embroidered by daylight, which surrounded her like a silver trellis.

She was wearing a dress of nacarat velvet, and aristocratic hands of an infinite delicacy with long, plump fingers emerged from her broad ermine-lined sleeves, of such an ideal transparency that they let the daylight through, like Aurora's.

All those details are still as present to me as if they dated from yesterday, and although I was extremely troubled, nothing escaped me; I seized all the slightest nuances—the little black dot in the corner of the chin, the imperceptible down at the corners of the lips, the velvet of the forehead, the tremulous shadow of the eyelashes over the cheeks—with an astonishing lucidity.

As I gazed at her, I sensed doors opening within me that had been closed until then; obstructed ventilation shafts were cleared in all directions, allowing glimpses of unknown perspectives; life appeared to me in an entirely different aspect; I had just been born to a new order of ideas. A frightful anguish clawed my heart; every minute that went by seemed to be to be a second and a century.

The ceremony advanced, however, and I was carried far from the world whose entrance my nascent desires besieged furiously. Meanwhile, I said *yes* when I wanted to say *no*, while everything within me revolted and protested against the violence that my tongue was doing to my soul; an occult force wrenched the words from my throat involuntarily. That is perhaps what many young women do who march to the altar with the firm resolution to refuse in a striking manner the husband who is being imposed on them, not one of whom carries out her project. It is doubtless what many poor novices do when taking the veil, although they had decided to rip it into pieces at the moment of pronouncing their vows. One does not dare to cause a scandal before everyone or to deceive the expectations of so many people; all those wills and all those gazes seem to weigh upon you like a leaden cowl; and then, the measures have been so well taken, everything is so well regulated in advance, in a fashion so evidently irrevocable, that thought yields to the weight and collapses completely.

The gaze of the beautiful stranger changed expression in accordance with the progress of the ceremony. From the tender mildness that it had to begin with, it took on an air of disdain and discontentment, as if it had not been understood.

I made an effort sufficient to uproot a mountain, in order to shout that I did not want to be a priest, but I could not do it; my tongue remained nailed to my palate and it was impossible for me to translate my will by means of the slightest negative movement. While wide awake, I was in a state similar to that of a nightmare, in which one wants to cry out a word on which your life depends, without being able to do so.

She seemed to be aware of the martyrdom that I was experiencing, and as if to encourage me, she shot me a glance full of divine promises. Her eyes were a poem, every glance of which formed a song.

She said to me:

"If you want to be mine, I will make you happier than God himself in his paradise; the angels will be jealous of you. Tear apart the funereal shroud in which you are about to wrap yourself; I am Beauty, I am Youth, I am Life; come to me and we will be Amour. What could Jehovah offer you for compensation? Our existence will flow like a dream and will be nothing but an eternal kiss.

"Spill the wine in that chalice, and you are free. I will take you away to unknown isles; you will sleep on my breast, in a solid gold bed under a silver awning; for I love you, and I want to take you from your God, before whom so many noble hearts pour own floods of amour that never reach as far as him."

I seemed to hear those words to a rhythm of infinite softness, for her gaze almost had sonority, and the phrases that her eyes sent me resounded in the depths of my heart as if an invisible mouth had breathed them into my soul. I felt ready to renounce God, and yet my heart was accomplishing mechanically the formalities of the ceremony. The beauty darted a second glance at me so imploring and so desperate that sharp blades traversed by heart, and I felt more swords in my breast than the *mater dolorosa*.

It was done; I was a priest.

No human physiognomy had ever depicted an anguish so poignant. The young woman who sees her fiancé die suddenly beside her, the mother next to her child's empty cradle, Eve sitting on the doorstep of paradise, the miser who finds a stone in the place of his treasure, and the poet who has dropped the only manuscript of his most beautiful work into the fire do not have an expression more devastated and inconsolable.. The blood abandoned her charming face completely and she became as white as marble. Her beautiful arms fell alongside her body, as if their muscles had been disconnected, and she leaned against a pillar, for her legs buckled and gave way beneath her. As for me, livid, my forehead inundated by a sweat bloodier than that of Calvary, I steered unsteadily for the door of the church; I was choking, the vaults flattened upon my shoulders, and it seemed to me that my head supported the entire weight of the cupola on its own.

As I was about to cross the threshold a hand took possession abruptly of mine; the hand of a woman! I had never touched one. It was as cold as the skin of a snake, and the imprint of it remained, burning like the mark of a red hot iron. It was her. "Wretch" she said to me in a low voice. "Wretch, what have you done?" Then she disappeared into the crowd.

The aged bishop passed by; he looked at me with a severe expression. I had the strangest countenance in the world; I went pale; I blushed, I was dazzled. One of my comrades took pity on me. He took me and led me away; I would have been incapable of finding my way back to the seminary on my own.

At a street corner, while the young priest turned his head in another direction, a bizarrely-clad negro page approached me, and without pausing in his course, handed me a small portfolio with sculpted gold corners, making me a sign to hide it. I slid it into my sleeve and held it there until I was alone in my cell. I opened the clasp; it only contained two leaves with these words: *Clarimonde, at the Concini Palace.*

I was then so scantly acquainted with matters of life that I did not know Clarimonde, in spite of her celebrity, and I was completely ignorant of where the Concini Palace was situated. I made a thousand conjectures, each more extravagant than the last, but in truth, provided that I could see her again, I did not care in the least what she might be, great lady or courtesan.

That recently born amour had taken root indestructibly; I did not even think of trying to uproot it, so impossible did I sense it to be. That woman had taken possession of me completely; a single glance has sufficed to change me; she had breathed her will into me; I no longer lived within myself but in her and by means of her. I did a thousand extravagant things; I kissed the place on my hand where she had touched me, and I repeated her name for entire hours. I had only to close my eyes to see her as distinctly as if she were present in reality, and I repeated the words she had spoken to me under the portal of the church:

"Wretch, wretch, what have you done?"

I understood all the horror of my situation, and the funereal and terrible aspects of the condition I had just embraced were clearly revealed within me. To be a priest, which is to say, chaste, not to love, not to distinguish ether sex or age, to turn away from all beauty, to put out one's eyes, to crawl under the glacial shadow of a cloister or a church, only to see the dying, to keep vigil over unknown cadavers and to wear mourning oneself under a black soutane, with the consequence that a drape for your coffin can be made of your costume!

And I sensed life rising within me like an interior lake, swelling and overflowing; my blood was beating forcefully in my arteries; my youth, so long compressed, suddenly burst forth like the aloes that take a hundred years to flower and which bloom like a thunderclap.

What could I do to see Clarimonde again? I had no pretext to leave the seminary, not knowing anyone in the city; I would not even remain there, and was only waiting for the parish to be indicated to me that I was to occupy. I tried to loosen the bars on the window, but t was frightfully high, and, having no ladder, it was necessary not to think about it. And then, I could only climb down by night, and how would I find my way through the inextricable labyrinth of streets?

All those difficulties, which might have been trivial for others, were immense for me, a poor seminarian, amorous since yesterday, devoid of experience, money and clothing.

Oh, if I had not been a priest, I would have been able to see her every day; I could have been her lover or her husband, I said to myself in my blindness. Instead of being enveloped in my sad shroud, I could have had garments of silk and velvet, gold chains, a sword and plumes, like the handsome young cavaliers. Instead of being dishonored by a large tonsure, my hair could play around my neck in undulating curls. I could have a beautiful waxed moustache, I would be valiant. But an hour spent before an altar, a few words scarcely articulated, had removed me forever from the number of the living and I had sealed my own tombstone, pushed the bolt of my prison with my own hand.

I stationed myself at the window. The sky was admirably blue, the trees had donned their spring robe, nature was putting on a display of ironic joy. The square was full of people; some were coming, others going; young fops and young beauties, in couples, where heading for the garden and the arbors. Companions went by singing drinking songs; there was a movement, a life, an enthusiasm and a gaiety that made my mourning and my solitude stand out painfully. A young mother was playing with her child on the doorstep; she kissed his little pink mouth, still pearled by droplets of milk, and made him, while teasing him, a thousand of the divine puerilities that only mothers are able to discover. The father, who was standing a short distance away, was smiling softly at that charming group, and his folded arms were pressing his joy to his heart.

I could not bear that spectacle; I closed the window and threw myself on to my bed with a frightful hatred and jealousy in my heart, biting my fingers and my blanket like a tiger that had gone hungry for three days.

I do not know how many days I remained like that, but when I turned round in a furious spasmodic movement, I perceived Abbot Serapion, who was standing in the middle of the room and considering me attentively. I was ashamed of myself, and, letting my head fall upon my breast, I veiled my eyes with my hands.

"Romuald, my friend, something extraordinary is happening within you," Serapion said to me after a few minutes of silence. "Your conduct is truly inexplicable! You, so pious, so calm and so mild, agitating in your cell like a wild beast! Be careful, Brother, and do not listen to the suggestions of the Devil; the Evil Spirit, irritated because you have consecrated yourself to the Lord forever, is prowling around you like an avid wolf making one last effort to draw you to him. Instead of allowing yourself to be defeated, my dear Romuald, make yourself an armor of prayers, a buckler of mortifications, and combat the enemy valiantly; you will vanquish him. Proof is necessary to virtue, and the gold emerges finer from the crucible. Do not be frightened or discouraged; the best protected and the firmest souls have these moments. Pray, fast and meditate, and the Evil Spirit will withdraw."

Abbot Serapion's speech caused me to renter into myself, and I became a little calmer.

"I have come to inform you of your appointment to the parish of C***; the priest who possessed it has just died, and the bishop has charged me to go to install you there; be ready for tomorrow."

I responded with a sign of the head, and the abbot withdrew. I opened my missal and I commenced reading the prayers, but the lines were soon confused before my eyes; the thread of ideas became entangled in my brain, and the volume slid from my hands without my noticing.

To depart tomorrow without having seen her again! To add yet another impossibility to all those that were already between us! To lose the hope of encountering her again forever, barring a miracle! Write to her? By what means
could I get my letter to her? Given the sacred character I had taken on, in whom
could I confide, and who could I trust? I experienced a terrible anxiety.

Then, what Abbot Serapion had said to me about the artifices of the Devil
returned to my memory. The strangeness of the adventure, the supernatural
beauty of Clarimonde, the phosphoric gleam of her eyes, the burning impression
of her hand, the disturbance into which she had cast me, the sudden change that
had taken place within me, and my piety, vanished in an instant, all proved
clearly the presence of the Devil, and that satin hand was perhaps only the glove
with which his claw was covered.

Those ideas threw me into a great fear; I picked up the missal that had fall-
en from my knees on to the floor and I resumed my prayers.

The next day, Serapion came to fetch me. Two mules were waiting for us
at the door, charged with our meager valises; he mounted one and I the other, as
best I could. While passing through the streets of the town I looked at all the
windows and all the balconies in case I could see Clarimonde, but it was too
early and the eyes of the town had not yet opened. My gaze tried to plunge behind the blinds and through the curtains of all the palaces we passed. Serapion
doubtless attributed that curiosity to the admiration caused by the beauty of the
architecture, and he slowed the pace of his mount in order to give me the time to
see.

Finally, we arrived at the gate of the town and began to climb the hill.
When I was at the top I turned round in order to gaze once more at the places
where Clarimonde lived. The shadow of a cloud covered the town entirely; the
blue and red roofs were confounded in a general demi-tint, in which the smoke
of the morning fires floated here and there like flecks of white foam. By virtue
of a singular optical effect, one edifice that surpassed in height the neighboring
constructions, completely drowned by the mist, stood out, blonde and gilded by
a unique ray of light; although it was more than a league away, it seemed very
close. The slightest details were distinguishable: the turrets, the platforms, the
casements, and even the swallow-tail weathervanes.

"What is that palace I see down there, illuminated by a ray of sunlight?" I
asked Serapion.

He put his hand above his eyes and, having looked, he replied: "It's the old
palace that Prince Concini gave to the courtesan Clarimonde; terrible things
happen there."

At that moment—I do not know whether it was a reality or an illusion—I
thought I saw a svelte white form glide over the terrace, which glinted for a second and was then extinguished. It was Clarimonde!

Oh, did she know that, at that moment, from the height of the harsh road
that was taking me away from her, which I would never descend again, ardent

and unquiet, I was gazing fondly at the palace she inhabited, which a derisory play of the light seemed to draw nearer to me, as if to invite me to enter it as the master? Undoubtedly she did know it, for her soul was too sympathetically linked to mine not to sense its slightest shocks, and it was that sentiment which had driven her to go up to the height of the terrace in the glacial morning dew.

The shadow reached the palace, and there was no longer anything but an ocean of roofs and eaves, in which nothing could be distinguished but a hilly undulation. Serapion touched his mule, whose stride mine immediately matched, and a bend in the road hid the town of S*** from me forever, to which I was never to return.

After three days of travel through rather sad fields, we saw through the trees the weathervane on the steeple of the church that I was to serve, and after following a few tortuous streets bordered by cottages and gardens we found ourselves before the façade, which was of no great magnificence. A porch ornamented by a few ribs and two or three grossly-hewn sandstone pillars, a tile roof and buttresses of the same stone as the pillars: that was all. To the left was the cemetery, full of long grass, with a large iron cross in the middle; to the right and in the shadow of the church, the presbytery. It was a house of extreme simplicity and arid neatness. We went in; a few chickens were pecking rare oat grains scattered on the ground; apparently accustomed to the black coats of ecclesiastics, they were not frightened by our presence and scarcely moved aside to let us pass. A hoarse barking was heard, and we saw an old dog come running.

It was my predecessor's dog; it had dull eyes, gray fur and all the symptoms of the extreme old age that a dog can attain. I stroked it gently with my hand, and it immediately started walking beside me with an air of inexpressible satisfaction. An old woman, who had been the previous incumbent's housekeeper, also came to meet us, and after having taken me into a low-ceilinged room, she asked me whether it was my intention to keep her. I replied that I would keep her and the dog, and also the chickens, and all the furniture that her master had left her at his death, which caused her to enter a transport of joy, Abbot Serapion having immediately given her the price that she asked for it.

My installation completed, Abbot Serapion returned to the seminary. I therefore remained alone, with no other support than myself. The thought of Clarimonde began to obsess me again, and whatever efforts that I made to chase it away, I still could not succeed in it.

One evening, while walking in the paths of my little garden, bordered with box-trees, it seemed to me that I saw the form of a woman through the hedge, which followed all my movements, and two sea-green eyes between the leaves; but that was only an illusion, and having passed to the other side of the hedge I found nothing but a footprint in the sand, so small that one might have thought it a child's foot. The garden was surrounded by high walls; I visited all its corners and nooks; there was no one there. I have never been able to explain that circumstance, which, however, was nothing compared with the strange things that were to happen to me subsequently.

I lived like that for a year, fulfilling with exactitude all the duties of my position, praying, fasting, exhorting and assisting the sick, giving alms to the point of only retaining the most indispensable necessities for myself. But I felt within myself an extreme aridity, and the wellsprings of grace were closed to me. I did not enjoy the happiness that the accomplishment of a holy mission gives; my ideas were elsewhere, and Clarimonde's words often returned to my lips like a kind of involuntary refrain. O Brother, meditate this well: for having lifted my gaze to a woman once, for such a seemingly slight sin, I experienced for several years the most miserable agitations; my life was troubled forever.

I shall not dwell any longer on those interior failures and the victories that were always followed by more profound falls, and I shall pass directly to a decisive circumstance. One night, someone rang violently at my door. The old housekeeper went to open it, and a man with a coppery complexion, richly dressed but in a foreign fashion, with a long poniard, was outlined by the rays of Barbara's lantern. Her first movement was fearful, but the man reassured her and told her that he needed me immediately for a matter concerning my ministry. Barbara showed him upstairs; I was about to go to bed.

The man told me that his mistress, a great lady, was on the point of death and desired a priest. I replied that I was ready to follow him; I took with me what was necessary to administer extreme unction, and descended in haste. At the door, two horses as black as night were whinnying impatiently and breathing long trails of vapor over their breasts. He held the stirrup of one of them for me and helped me to mount, and then he leapt on to the other, only supporting himself with one hand on the saddle-horn. He tightened his knees and released the bridle of his horse, which set off like an arrow. Mine, the bridle of which he was holding, also started galloping and matched its pace perfectly.

We devoured the road; the ground filed beneath us, gray and striped, and the black silhouettes of the trees fled like an army in rout. We traversed a forest of a darkness so opaque and so glacial that I felt a frisson of superstitious terror running over my skin. The showers of sparks that our horses' shoes struck from the stones left a kind of fiery trail in our wake, and if anyone, at that hour of the night, had seen my guide and me, he would have taken us for two specters riding the nightmare.

Fire follets traversed the road from time to time, and jackdaws chirped piteously in the thickness of the woods, where the phosphoric eyes of a few wild cats gleamed from time to time. The manes of the horses became increasingly tangled, sweat streamed over their flanks, and their breath emerged noisily and urgently from their nostrils. When he saw them weakening, however, in order to reanimate them, the groom uttered a guttural cry that had nothing human about it, and the course recommenced furiously.

Finally, the whirlwind ceased; a black mass pricked by a few bright dots suddenly loomed up ahead of us; the footfalls of our mounts rang more loudly on and iron-studded floor, and we entered beneath a vault that opened its somber maw between two enormous towers. A great agitation reigned within the château; domestics with torches in hand were traversing the courtyard in all directions, and lanterns were going up and down from floor to floor. I caught confused glimpses of immense architectures, columns, arcades, perrons and staircases, a luxury of construction entirely regal and magical.

A negro page—the same one who had given me Clarimonde's note, whom I recognized immediately—helped me to descend, and a majordomo clad in black velvet with a golden chain around his neck and an ivory cane in his hand advanced toward me. Large tears were flowing from his eyes and running down his cheeks over his white beard.

"Too late!" he said, shaking his head. "Too late, Seigneur Priest; but if you have not been able to save her soul, come to keep vigil over the poor body."

He took me by the arm and led me to the funereal chamber; I was weeping as forcefully as him, for I had understood that the dead woman was none other than Clarimonde, so much and so madly loved.

A prie-Dieu was disposed beside the bed; a blue-tinted flame fluttering on a bronze paten cast a feeble and dubious light throughout the room, and caused to flicker here and there in the gloom from the projecting edge of some item of furniture or cornice. On the table, in a sculpted urn, a faded white rose was steeped, the petals of which, with the exception of a single one that was still holding, had fallen at the foot of the vase like odorous ears. A broken black mask, a fan, and disguises of every species, were trailing over the armchairs, enabling the inference that death had arrived in that sumptuous dwelling unexpectedly and without being announced.

I knelt down without daring to cast my eyes upon the bed, and I started reciting the psalms with a great fervor, thanking God because he had put the tomb between the idea of that woman and me, in order that I might add her name, sanctified henceforth, to my prayers. Gradually, however, that fervor relented, and I fell into a reverie. That room had nothing of the mortuary chamber about it. Instead of the fetid and cadaverous air that I was accustomed to breathe in funereal vigils, a languorous smoke of Oriental essences and I know not what amorous feminine odor floated gently in the lukewarm atmosphere. The pale light gave the impression of a half-light contrived for voluptuousness rather than the yellow radiance that trembles near cadavers.

I thought about the singular hazard that had enabled me to rediscover Clarimonde at the moment when I was losing her forever, and a sigh of regret escaped my breast. It seemed to me that someone had also sighed behind me, and I turned round involuntarily. It was an echo.

In that movement my eyes fell upon the sumptuous bed that they had avoided until then. The red damask curtains with large flowers, lifted up by golden tassels, allowed the dead woman to be seen, lying full length, with her hands joined over her bosom. She was covered by a cotton veil of dazzling whiteness, which the dark crimson of the drapes brought out more emphatically, of such finesse that it hid nothing of the charming form of her body and permitted the beautiful undulating lines to be followed, like the neck of a swan that even death had not been able to stiffen. One might have thought it an alabaster statue made by some skillful sculptor in order to be placed on the tomb of a queen, or a sleeping young woman on whom snow had fallen.

I could not stand it any longer; the atmosphere of the alcove intoxicated me, the feverish scent of the faded rose went to my head and I strode back and forth in the room stopping at every circuit before the platform in order to consider the gracious corpse under the transparency of her shroud. Strange thoughts crossed my mind; I imagined that she was not really dead, and that it was only a feint that she had employed in order to attract me to her château and tell me about her amour. For an instant I thought I saw her foot stir under the whiteness of the veils and disturb the straight pleats of the shroud.

Then I said to myself: *Is this really Clarimonde? What proof do I have of that? Might that black page not have passed into the service of another woman? I'm truly mad to be so desolate and to agitate thus.*

But my heart replied to me with its beating: *It's really her; it's really her.*

I drew nearer to the bed and I gazed with increased attention at the object of my uncertainty. Shall I confess it to you? That perfection of forms, although purified and sanctified by the shadow of death, troubled me more voluptuously than it should have done, and that repose resembled sleep so closely that one might have been deceived by it. I forgot that I had come there for a funereal office, and I imagined that I was a young husband entering the chamber of his bride, who was hiding her face out of modesty and did not want to let it be seen. Distressed by grief, bewildered by joy, shivering with dread and pleasure, I leaned toward her and took hold of the corner of the sheet; I lifted it up slowly, holding my breath for fear of awakening her. My arteries were throbbing with such force that I felt them hissing in my temples, and my forehead was streaming with sweat, as if I had shifted a marble slab.

It was indeed Clarimonde, such as I had seen her in the church during my ordination; she was as charming, and in her, death seemed one more coquetry. The pallor of her cheeks, the less vivid rosiness of her lips, and her long lashes, lowered and cutting through that whiteness with their brown fringe, gave her an expression of melancholy chastity and pensive suffering, of an inexpressible power of seduction. Her long loose hair, with which a few little blue flowers were still mingled, made a pillow for her head and protected with its curls the nudity of her shoulders. Her beautiful hands, purer and more diaphanous than hosts, were crossed in an attitude of pious repose and tacit prayer, which corrected what might have been too seductive, even in death, in the exquisite roundness and ivory polish of her bare arms, from which the pearl bracelets had not been removed.

I remained absorbed in mute contemplation for a long time, and the more I looked at her, the less I was able to believe that life had abandoned that beautiful body forever. I do not know whether it was an illusion or a reflection of the lamplight, but one might have thought that the blood had begun to circulate again beneath that mat pallor. However, she still maintained the most perfect immobility. I touched her arm lightly; it was cold, but not as cold as her hand on the day when it had brushed mine under the portal of the church.

I resumed my position, inclining my face over hers, allowing the warm dew of my tears to rain down in her cheeks. Oh, what a bitter sentiment of despair and impotence! What agony that vigil was! I would have liked to be able to pick up my life in a heap in order to give it to her and blow over her icy remains the flame that was devouring me.

The night was advancing and, sensing the approach of the moment of eternal separation, I could not refuse myself the sad and supreme tenderness of depositing a kiss on the dead lips of the woman who had had all of my amour.

O prodigy! A light breath was mingled with my breath, and Clarimonde's mouth responded to the pressure of mine; her eyes opened and resumed a slight luster; she uttered a sigh, and, uncrossing her arms, she passed them around my neck with an expression of ineffable rapture.

"Ah, it's you, Romuald," she said, in a voice as languid and soft as the last vibrations of a harp. "What are you doing? I waited for you for such a long time that I died; but now we are betrothed, I shall be able to see you and come to your home. Adieu, Romuald, adieu! I love you; that is all that I wanted to tell you, and I render to you the life, a minute of which that you have recalled to me with your kiss; I shall see you soon."

Her head fell backwards, but she was still surrounding me with her arms, as if to retain me. A furious whirlwind smashed the window and entered into the room; the last petal of the white rose fluttered for some time at the end of its stem, like a wing; then it was detached and flew away through the open window, bearing Clarimonde's soul with it. The lamp went out and I fell in a faint on the breast of the beautiful dead woman.

When I came round I was lying on my bed in my little room in the presbytery, and the former curé's old dog was licking my hand, which was dangling outside the blanket. Barbara was agitating in the room with a senile tremor, opening and closing drawers and stirring powders into glasses. On seeing me open my eyes the old woman uttered a cry of joy, while the dog yapped and wagged its tail; but I was so weak that I could not pronounce a single word or make any movement.

I found out subsequently that I had remained thus for three days, giving no other sign of life than an almost insensible respiration. Those three days are not counted in my life and I do not know where my spirit had gone during all that time; I have not retained any memory of it. Barbara told me that the same man with the coppery complexion who had come to fetch me during the night had brought me back in the morning in a closed litter and had gone away again immediately.

As soon as I was able to recover my ideas, I reiterated internally all the circumstances of that fatal might. At first I thought that I had been the victim of a magical illusion, but real and palpable circumstances soon destroyed that supposition. I could not believe that I had been dreaming, since Barbara had seen the man with the two black horses, as I had, and she described their equipment and appearance exactly. However, no one in the surrounding area knew of a château fitting the description of the château where I had rediscovered Clarimonde.

One morning, I saw Abbot Serapion come in. Barbara had sent word to him that I was ill, and he had come in all haste. Although that urgency demonstrated his affection and interest in my person, his visit did not give me the pleasure that it should have done. Abbot Serapion had something penetrating and inquisitorial in his gaze that troubled me. I felt embarrassed and culpable in his presence. He had been the first to discover my interior turmoil, and I held his clear-sightedness against him.

While asking for news of my health in a hypocritically honeyed tone, he fixed his two yellow leonine eyes upon me and plunged his gaze like a sound into my soul. Then he asked a few questions about the way in which I directed my parish, where I was happy there, how I spent the free time that my ministry left me, whether I had made any acquaintances among the local inhabitants, what my favorite reading was, and a thousand similar details. I responded to all that as briefly as possible, and he passed on to something else without waiting for me to finish. That conversation evidently had no relation to what he wanted to say. Then, without any preparation, as if he had just remembered an item of news and feared that he might forget it subsequently, he said to me in a clear and vibrant voice that resonated in my ears like the trumpets of the Last Judgment:

"The great courtesan Clarimonde died recently, after an orgy that lasted eight days and eight nights. It was something infernally splendid. The abominations of the feasts of Belshazzar and Cleopatra were renewed there. In what century are we living, good God! The guests were served by bronzed slaves speaking an unknown language, and seemed to me to have the appearance of true demons; the livery of the least of them could have served for the gala costume of an emperor. Many strange stories regarding Clarimonde had been running around for some time, and all her lovers ended in a wretched or violent fashion. It was said that she was a ghoul, a female vampire, but I believe that she was Beelzebub in person."

He fell silent and observed me more attentively than ever, in order to see the effect that his words had produced in me. I had been unable to forbid myself a movement on hearing Clarimonde named, and that news of her death, in addition to the pain it caused me by virtue of the nocturnal scene I had witnessed, threw me into a disturbance and a fear that appeared in my face, although I did what I could to master it. Serapion darted an anxious and severe gaze at me, and then said to me: "My son, I must warn you that you have one foot raised above the abyss; be careful that you do not fall into it. Satan has long claws, and tombs are not always reliable. Clarimonde's stone ought to be sealed with a triple seal, for it is said that this is not the first time that she has died. May God watch over you, Romuald."

Having said those words, Serapion went back to the door at a slow pace, and I did not see him again, for he left for S*** almost immediately.

I had recovered completely and resumed my habitual functions. The memory of Clarimonde and the old abbot's words were still present in my mind; however, no extraordinary event had come to confirm the funereal anticipations of Serapion, and I began to believe that his apprehensions and my terrors were over-exaggerated; but one night. I had a dream.

I had scarcely savored the first draughts of slumber than I heard the curtains of my bed open and the rings slide over the rails with a loud noise. I raised myself up on my elbow abruptly, and I saw the shadow of a woman standing before me. I recognized Clarimonde instantly. In her hand she was carrying a little lamp of the form of those that are placed on tombs, the light of which gave her slender fingers a rosy transparency that was prolonged by an insensible gradation as far as the opaque and milky whiteness of her bare arm.

Her only garment was the linen shroud that had covered her on her sumptuous bed, the pleats of which she retained over her bosom, as if ashamed to be so scantily dressed, but her small hand was not sufficient for that; it was so white that the color of the drapery was confounded with that of her flesh under the pale radiance of the lamplight. Enveloped in that delicate fabric, which betrayed all the contours of her body, she resembled a marble statue of an antique bather rather than a woman endowed with life.

Dead or alive, statue or woman, shadow or body, her beauty was still the same, except that the green glow of her eyes was deadened slightly, and her mouth, once so vermilion, was only tinted any longer by a faint and pale pink, similar to that of her cheeks. The little blue flowers that I had noticed in her hair were entirely desiccated and had lost almost all their petals—which did not prevent her from being charming: so charming that, in spite of the singularity of the adventure and the inexplicable fashion in which she had entered the room, I was not frightened for an instant.

She placed the lamp on the table and sat down on the foot of my bed; then she leaned toward me and said, in the voice, silvery and velvety at the same time, that I had only known in her: "I have waited for some time, my dear Romuald, and you must have thought that I had forgotten you. But I have come from far away, from a place from which no one else has yet returned. There is neither moonlight nor sunlight in the place from which I have come; there is only space and shadow; no road nor path, no ground for the feet, no air for a wing; and yet, here I am, for love is stronger than death, and it will finish by vanquishing it. Oh, the bleak faces and the terrible things I have seen during my voyage! How much trouble my soul has had, having reentered this world by virtue of the power of the will, in rediscovering its body and reinstalling itself therein! How much effort it was necessary for me to make before raising the slab with which I was covered! Look—the palms of my hands are all bruised by it! Kiss them in order to heal them, dear amour."

She applied the cold palms of her hands, one after another, to my mouth; I did indeed kiss them several times, and she watched me do it with a smile of ineffable complaisance.

I confess, to my shame, that I had completely forgotten the opinion of Abbot Serapion and the character that I had taken on. I had fallen without resistance at the first assault. I had not even tried to repel the tempter; the freshness of Clarimonde's skin penetrated mine, and I felt voluptuous frissons running over my body. Poor child! In spite of all that I had seen, I could not believe that she was a demon; at least, she did not have the appearance of it, and Satan has never concealed his claws and his horns more effectively. She had folded her claws back beneath her and was crouched on the edge of the bed in a posture full of nonchalant coquetry. From time to time she passed her little hand through my hair, and rolled it into curls as if to try out a new hairstyle for my visage. I let her do it with the most culpable complaisance, and she accompanied all that with the most charming babble. One remarkable thing is that I did not experience any astonishment at such an extraordinary adventure, and with the facility that one has in a vision of admitting the most bizarre events as quite simple, I did not see anything in it that was not perfectly natural.

"I loved you for a long time before having seen you. my dear Romuald, and I searched for you everywhere. You were my dream, and I perceived you in the church at the fatal moment; I said immediately: 'It's him!' I darted a gaze at you into which I put all the amour that I had had, that I had and that I would have for you: a gaze to damn a cardinal, to make a king kneel at my feet before his entire court. You remained impassive, and you preferred your God to me. Oh, how jealous I am of God, whom you loved and still love more than me!

"Unfortunate woman that I am, I shall never have your heart entirely to myself, I whom you have resuscitated with a kiss, Clarimonde the revenant, who has forced the doors of the tomb because of you and who has come to consecrate to you a life that she has only resumed in order to render you happy!"

All those words were punctuated with deliriant caresses that stunned my senses and my reason, to the point that I did not hesitate to console her by proffering a frightful blasphemy and telling her that I loved her as much as God.

Her eyes became vivid again and shone like chrysoprases.

"Truly? Really and truly? As much as God!" she said, enlacing me with her beautiful arms. "Since it is thus, you'll come with me, you'll follow me wherever I wish. You'll leave behind your vile black coats. You'll be the proudest and most envied of cavaliers, you'll be my lover. To be the admitted lover of Clarimonde, who has refused a Pope, is a fine thing. Oh, the good, happy life, the beautiful gilded existence we shall lead! When shall we depart, my gentleman?"

"Tomorrow, tomorrow!" I cried in my delirium.

"Tomorrow, so be it," she said. "I shall have time to change costume, for this one is a trifle succinct, and worthless for the voyage. It's also necessary that I go to inform my people, who believe me to be seriously dead and are desolate, to the extent that they can be. Money, clothes, carriages, everything will be ready; I shall collect you at the same time as this. Adieu, dear heart."

And she brushed my forehead with the edges of her lips. The lamp went out, the curtains closed again, and I saw nothing more; a leaden slumber, a dreamless sleep, weighed upon me and held me in a torpor until the next morning.

I woke up later than usual, and the memory of the singular vision agitated me all day long; I ended up persuading myself that it was only a vapor of my heated imagination. However, the sensations had been so vivid that it was difficult to believe that they were not real, and it was not without some apprehension of what might happen that I went to bed, after having prayed to God to distance evil thoughts from me and to protect the chastity of my slumber.

I soon fell profoundly asleep, and my dream continued. The curtains parted, and I saw Clarimonde, not, as the first time, pale in her pale shroud with the violets of death on her cheeks, but cheerful, brisk and sprightly, with a superb traveling costume in green velvet, ornamented with golden braid and tucked up at the side to allow the sight of a satin skirt. Her blonde hair escaped in large waves from beneath a large black velvet hat charged with capriciously contorted white feathers. In her hand she was holding a small riding crop terminated by a golden whistle. She touched me with it lightly and said: "Well, handsome sleeper, is this how you make your preparations? I expected to find you on your feet. Get up quickly, we have no time to lose."

I leapt out of bed.

"Come on, get dressed and let's go," she said, pointing her finger at a little package she had brought. The horses are getting bored and chewing the bit at the door. We ought to be ten leagues away from here already."

I got dressed in haste, and she handed the garments to me herself, laughing in bursts at my awkwardness and indicating their usage to me when I made a mistake. She combed my hair, and when that was done she handed me a little pocket mirror in Venetian crystal bordered with silver filigree and said: "How do you like it? Would you like to take me into your service as a valet de chambre?"

I was no longer the same, and I did not recognize myself. I did not resemble myself any more than a finished statue resembles a block of stone. I had the impression that my old face had only been a crude sketch of the one reflected in the mirror. I was handsome, and my vanity was sensibly tickled by that meta-morphosis. Those elegant clothes, that rich embroidered jacket, made me an entirely different person, and I admired the power of a few ells of cloth tailored in a certain manner. The spirit of my costume penetrated my skin, and after ten minutes I was passably conceited.

I made a few tours of the room in order to put myself at ease. Clarimonde watched me with an air of maternal complaisance, and seemed very content with her work.

"That's enough childishness; let's go, my dear Romuald. We have a long way to go and we won't get there."

She took me by the hand and drew me away. All the doors opened before her as soon as she touched them, and we went past the dog without waking it.

At the door we found Margheritone; that was the groom that had conducted me before. He was holding the bridles of three horses as black as the others, one for me, one for him and one for Clarimonde. Those horses must have been Span-ish genets born of mares fecundated by the zephyr, for they went as fast as the wind, and the moon, which had risen at our departure to light our way, was roll-ing in the sky like a wheel detached from its cart; we saw it to our right leaping from tree to tree and getting out of breath in order to run after us.

We soon arrived in a plain where. next to a clump of trees, a carriage was waiting for us, harnessed to four vigorous beats; we climbed into it and the postillions made them take an insensate gallop. I had one arm around Clarimonde's waist and one of her hands folded in mine; she leaned her head on my shoulder and I felt her semi-naked cleavage brushing my arm. Never had I experienced such an intense happiness. I had forgotten everything at that mo-ment, and I did not remember having been a priest any more than what I had done in my mother's womb, so great was the fascination that the evil spirit exer-cised upon me.

From that night on my nature was, in a sense, duplicated, and there were two men in me, one of whom did not know the other. Sometimes I thought I was a priest who dreamed every evening that he was a gentleman, sometimes a gen-tleman who dreamed that he was a priest. I could no longer distinguish the dream of the previous day, and I did not know where reality commenced and illusion ended. The conceited and libertine young man mocked the priest, the priest detested the dissolution of the young lord. Two spirals, entangled with one another and confounded without ever touching, represent very well the bicephalous life that was mine.

In spite of the strangeness of that situation, I do not believe that I touched madness for an instant. I always conserved very clearly the perceptions of my two existences. However, there was one absurd fact that I could not explain, which was that the sentiment of the same self existed in two such different men. That was an anomaly of which I could not take account, whether I believed that

I was the curé of the little village of *** or *il signor Romualdo*, the lover in title of Clarimonde.

At any rate, I was—or at least believed that I was—in Venice; I have not yet been able fully to disentangle what was illusion and reality in that bizarre adventure. We lived in a grand marble palace on the Canaleio, full of frescos and statues, with two Titians of great days in Clarimonde's bedroom: a palace worthy of a king. We each had our gondola and our liveried singer of barcarolles, our music room and our poet. Clarimonde understood life in a grand manner, and there was a little of Cleopatra in her nature.

As for me, I led the life of a son of a prince and I kicked up dust as if I had been of the family of one of the twelve apostles or the four evangelists of the Most Serene Republic; I would not have turned aside from my route in order to let the doge pass, and I do not believe that, since Satan had fallen from Heaven, anyone had been prouder and more insolent than me. I went to the Rialto where I played an infernal game. I saw the best society in the world, the sons of ruined families, women of the theater, crooks, parasites and assassins for hire.

In spite of the dissipation of that life, however, I remained faithful to Clarimonde. I loved her madly. She would have reawakened satiety itself, and fixed inconstancy. To have Clarimonde was to have twenty mistresses, it was to have all women, so versatile was she, changing and dissimilar to herself: a true chameleon. She enabled you to commit with her the infidelity that you might have committed with others, by taking on completely the character, the manner and the genre of beauty of the woman who appeared to please you.

She rendered my amour a hundredfold, and it was in vain that young patricians and even the old men of the Council of Ten made her the most magnificent propositions. A Foscari went as far as proposing marriage to her; she refused everything. She had enough gold; she no longer wanted anything but amour, a young, pure amour awakened by her, which would be the first and the last.

I would have been perfectly happy but for an accursed nightmare that returned every night, in which I believed myself to be a village curé, mortifying myself and doing penance for my diurnal excesses. Reassured by the habitude of being with her, I hardly ever thought any longer about the strange fashion in which I had made Clarimonde's acquaintance. However, what Abbot Serapion had said about her sometimes returned to memory and did not leave without causing me anxiety.

For some time, Clarimonde's health had not been as good; her complexion deteriorated from day to day. The physicians who were summoned did not understand her malady and did not know what to do about it. They prescribed a few insignificant remedies and did not return. Meanwhile, she became visibly paler and gradual colder. She was almost as white and as dead as on the famous night in the unknown château. I was desolate to see her perishing slowly thus.

Touched by my dolor, she smiled at me tenderly and sadly, with the fatal smile of people who know that they are going to die.

One morning, I was sitting next to her bed, and having breakfast at a little table in order not to quit her for a minute. While slicing a fruit I chanced to inflict a rather deep cut on my finger. Blood immediately emerged in a crimson trickle, and a few drops fell upon Clarimonde.

Her eyes brightened, and her physiognomy took on an expression of ferocious and savage joy that I had never seen before. She leapt out of bed with an animal agility, the agility of a monkey or a cat, and pounced upon my wound, which she began sucking with an expression of unspeakable voluptuousness. She swallowed the blood in little sips, slowly and preciously, like a gourmet savoring a wine from Xeres or Syracuse; she half-closed her eyes, and the pupils of her green eyes became rectangular instead of round.

From time to time she interrupted herself in order to kiss my hand, and then she recommenced pressing her lips to the lips of the wound in order to make a few more red droplets emerge therefrom. When she saw that the blood was no longer coming, she raised her eyes again, humble and brilliant, rosier than a dawn in May, her face full, her hand warm and moist—in sum, more beautiful than ever and in a perfect state of health.

"I shan't die! I shan't die!" she said, half mad with joy, hanging from my neck. "I can love you for a long time yet. My life is in yours, and everything that I am comes from you. A few drops of your rich and noble blood, more precious and more efficacious than all the elixirs in the world, have rendered life to me."

That scene preoccupied me for a long time and inspired strange doubts in Clarimonde's regard; that very evening, when sleep returned me to my presbytery, I saw Abbot Serapion, graver and more careworn than ever. He looked at me attentively and said: "Not content with dooming your soul, you also want to lose your body. Unfortunate young man, into what trap have you fallen?"

The tone in which he pronounced those few words struck me vividly, but, in spite of its vivacity, the impression was soon dissipated, and a thousand cares effaced it from my mind.

One evening, however, I saw Clarimonde in my mirror, the perfidious position of which she had not calculated, pouring a powder into the cup of spiced wine that she had the custom of preparing after the meal. I took the cup, pretended to bear it to my lips, and I put it down on a table as if to finish it later at my leisure; then, taking advantage of a moment when the beauty's back was turned, I emptied its contents under the table—after which I returned to my room and went to bed, determined not to sleep and to see everything that happened.

I did not have long to wait. Clarimonde entered in a night-dress, and, having removed her veils, lay down in the bed beside me. When she was sure that I was asleep, she uncovered my arm and took a golden pin from her hair; then she started murmuring in a low voice:

"One drop, nothing but a little red drop, a ruby at the tip of my needle! Since you still love me, it's not necessary that I die. Oh, poor love, his beautiful blood, of such a bright crimson color, I shall drink it. Sleep, my only wealth; sleep, my god, my child; I shall not do you any harm, I shall only take as much of your life as is necessary for mine not to be extinguished. If I did not love you so much, I could resolve myself to having other lovers, whose veins I would drain, but since I have known you, I hold everyone else in horror... Oh, the beautiful arm! How round it is! How white it is! I would never dare to prick that pretty blue vein."

And while saying that, she wept, and I felt her tears dripping on to my arm, which she was holding in her hands. Finally, she made up her mind, made a little puncture with her needle, and started sucking the blood that flowed from it. Although she had only drunk a few drops, the dread of draining me gripped her; carefully, she surrounded my arm with a small bandage after having rubbed the wound with an unguent that caused it to scar immediately.

I could no longer have any doubt; Abbot Serapion was right. In spite of that certainty, however, I could not help loving Clarimonde, and I would gladly have given her all the blood she needed to sustain her artificial existence. In any case, I had no great fear; the woman answered to me for the vampire, and what I had heard and seen reassured me completely. I had lush veins then, which would not soon be exhausted, and I would not haggle over my life drop by drop. I would have opened my arm myself and said to her: "Drink! And may my amour infiltrate into your body with my blood!"

I avoided making the slightest allusion to the narcotic that she had poured for me and the scene of the needle, and we lived in the most perfect accord. My priestly scruples, however, tormented me more than ever, and I did not know what new infliction to invent in order to master and mortify my flesh. Although all those visions were involuntary and I did not have any participation in them, I dared not touch the Christ with hands so impure and a spirit soiled by such debaucheries, real or imaginary.

In order to avoid falling into those fatiguing hallucination, I tried to prevent myself from sleeping. I held my eyelids open with my fingers and I remained standing against the wall, struggling against slumber with all my might; but the sand of somnolence soon fell into my eyes, and, seeing that all struggle was futile, I let my arms fall in discouragement and lassitude, and the current drew me back toward perfidious shores.

Serapion made me the most vehement exhortations, and reproached me harshly for my slackness and my lack of fervor. One day, when I had been more agitated than usual he said to me: "In order to rid you of this obsession there is only one means, and, although it is extreme, it is necessary to employ it: great evils require great remedies. I know where Clarimonde has been buried; it is necessary for us to disinter her, and for you to see the pitiful state that the object of your amour is in; you will no longer be tempted to doom your soul for a filthy cadaver devoured by worms and ready to fall into dust; that will assuredly render you to yourself."

For myself, I was so fatigued by that double life that I accepted; wanting to know, once and for all, whether the priest or the gentleman was the dupe of an illusion, I had decided to kill, to the profit of one or the other, one of the two men who was within me, or to kill both of them, for such a life could not endure.

Abbot Serapion equipped himself with a pickax, a lever and a lantern, and at midnight we headed for the cemetery of ***, of which he knew the lie and the disposition perfectly. After having run the light of the muted lantern over several tombs, we eventually arrived at a stone half-hidden by long grass and devoured by moss and parasitic plants, on which we deciphered the commencement of an inscription:

Here lies Clarimonde
Who was when alive
The most beautiful woman in the world

"This is it," said Serapion; and, placing his lantern on the ground, he slid the lever into the interstice of the stone and began to lift it up. The stone yielded, and he set to work with the pickax. I watched him do it, blacker and more silent than the night itself. As for him, bent over his funereal work, he was streaming with sweat; he was breathing heavily, and his hasty breath gave the impression of a death-rattle.

It was a strange spectacle, and anyone who had seen us would have taken us for profaners and thieves of shrouds rather than priests of God. Serapion's zeal had something harsh and savage about it, which made him resemble a demon rather than an apostle or an angel, and his face, with great austere features, profoundly outlined by the reflections of the lamplight, had nothing reassuring about it.

I felt a glacial sweat pearling on my limbs, and my hair was standing up dolorously on my head. Deep down I regarded the action of the severe Serapion as an abominable sacrilege, and I would have liked a bolt of lightning to emerge from the somber clouds that were rolling heavily overhead and reduce him to dust. The owls perched in the cypresses, disturbed by the light of the lantern, came to whip the glass heavily with their dusty wings, uttering plaintive moans; foxes were yapping in the distance, and a thousand sinister sounds emerged from the silence.

Finally, Serapion's pick collided with the coffin, the planks of which resounded with a dull and sonorous noise, the terrible noise than annihilates when one touches it. He tipped back the lid, and I perceived Clarimonde, as pale as marble, her hands joined; her white shroud only made a single pleat from her head to her feet. A little red droplet glistened like a rose in the corner of her colorless mouth.

At that sight, Serapion entered into a fury. "Ah! There you are, demon, indecent courtesan, drinker of blood and gold!" And he sprinkled the corpse and the coffin with holy water, tracing the form of a cross with his aspergillum.

Poor Clarimonde had no sooner been touched by the holy dew than her beautiful body fell into dust; she was no longer anything but a frightful formless mass of ash and semi-calcined bones.

"Behold your mistress, Seigneur Romuald," said the inexorable priest, showing me those sad remains. "Will you still be tempted to walk at the Lido and at Fusine with your beauty?"

I lowered my head; a great ruination had just been effected inside me. I returned to my presbytery, and Seigneur Romuald, Clarimonde's lover, was separated from the poor priest with whom he had kept such strange company for such a long time—except that the following night, I saw Clarimonde; she spoke to me, as she had the first time under the portal of the church.

"Wretch! Wretch, what have you done? Why did you listen to that imbecile priest? Were you not happy? And what have I done to you, for my poor tomb to be violated and the misery of my annihilation laid bare? All communication between our souls and our bodies is broken henceforth. Adieu; you will regret my loss."

She dissipated in the air like smoke, and I never saw her again.

Alas, what she said was true. I regretted her loss more than once, and I regret it still. The peace of my soul has been dearly bought; the love of God was not enough to replace hers.

That, Brother, is the story of my youth. Never gaze at a woman, and always walk with your eyes fixed on the ground, for, chaste and calm as you are, it only requires a minute for you to lose eternity.

Xavier Forneret (1809-1884) lived in Paris from 1837-40, and was enthusiastic to participate in Théophile Gautier's petit cénacle, *but Gautier and Gérard de Nerval never accepted him as one of them, deeming him to be an eccentric bourgeois devoid of talent; he allegedly became a recluse living in a Gothic folly. He could afford to publish his own work, and did, but it remained obscure until it was rediscovered by André Breton, and hailed as a significant precursor of Surrealism. Had the Symbolists ever noticed him, he might also have been hailed as an important precursor of their own Movement. "La Diamante de l'herbe" first appeared in 1840 in the collection* Pièce de pieces, Temps perdu, *published by the author.* "The Diamond in the Grass" *was first published in* Decadence and Symbolism: A Showcase Anthology *(Snuggly Books, 2019).*

Xavier Forneret: *The Diamond in the Grass*

According to what is said, I believe, the glow-worm announces its appearance, more or less renewed, more or less adjacent to a particular place, more or less multiplied, because, still according to what is said, it moves under the influence of what is going to happen, the glow-worm presaging either a tempest at sea or a revolution on land, in which case it is somber, reilluminates and is extinguished; or a miracle, in which case one scarcely sees it; if a murder, it is ruddy; if it is going to snow, its feet turn black; for cold, it is incessantly bright; rain, it change location; public festivals, it quivers in the grass and pours out innumerable little jets of light; hail, it moves jerkily; wind, it seems to sink into the ground; fine weather for the following day, it is blue; a fine night, it stars the grass almost as for public festivals, except that it does not quiver. For the birth of a child the worm is white; finally, at the moment when a strange destiny is accomplished, the glow-worm is yellow.

I do not know to what extent these sayings ought to be believed; but here goes: I shall tell a story.

One evening when all the breath of the angels was blowing over human faces—one of those evening when one would like to have a thousand lungs in order to give them to that air, which seems to come from the gardens of heaven—under enormous and old trees planted in the blades of grass, a detached house displayed to the moon its oblong and dilapidated wings.

There was water there, which wept in passing over a bed of thorns. There were also: many green-tinted stones, in which the fingers of time had made big holes; a great deal of moss round the stones; a great many dried leaves perhaps accumulated over three or four years; a great deal of mystery, a great deal of silence; a great deal of distance from anything that was human life. There, a man might have believed himself to be the first man or the last, at the creation or the judgment of God. Oh, how the moon appeared to offer to every leaf of the old trees, to every stone of the detached house, to the water that went away, to the branches that stayed, her grave melancholy and hers white tears! But soon she wearied of gazing at the earth, covered herself momentarily with an almost-black veil, and then there was no longer anything to illuminate the things of the abandoned place except a slight fire in the grass. It was a little glow-worm springing from all sides in stars; it was predicting a fine day, after the night that was passing.

Honeysuckle came over the roof of the house, sliding through the windows, twisting and letting itself collapse of old age; and when the moon reappeared, the house resembled a white head, having at its summit long tresses of green hair that came to caress the stone with eyes full of tears.

On the pavement, sprinkled with dust and old plaster detached from the ceilings and walls of the ruined dwelling, were the freshly imprints of a man's feet, and fine light marks that announced that a woman's feet had also brushed that place of profound solitude.

A bronze lamp, retained by a cord of pink silk, was vacillating imperceptibly in the heart of the building. Its wicks were in a state to give light, and it was easily recognized that they had been burning the previous night.

Over that lamp there was a shade, like that of a hooded lantern, and from that shade a brown-colored ribbon was attached to the only remaining arm of an armchair, the other doubtless having lost the battle of years.

One the very broad armchair, clad in a fabric that had once been amaranth velvet two places were marked; the interstice allowed it to be observed that the two people who had been sitting there had clung to one another very closely. Many places on the armchair were covered in dust, while elsewhere, everything was shiny, rubbed, waxed, and almost worn away by the bodies that seemed to have taken possession of one another frequently.

The armchair was facing the lamp, which was hanging a short distance from the ground and from it.

In addition to the water that was flowing outside, something could be heard inside the house that was quivering in all its corners; and when the gaze of the moon illuminated some of them, the eye distinguished objects similar to large patches of exceedingly black ink, to which hazard gave paws, against the whiteness of a piece of paper: objects moving and stopping, then moving again, and marking out beneath them trials of reflections like those launched by the wings of joyful cicadas or soap bubbles in the sunlight, or he scales of fish seen at a certain time of day; a clan of spiders, gathered together, with trousseau of webs, the despair of flies and the rescue of cut fingers.

The spider was displaying her independence proudly there, having nothing to fear, neither the screams of the child or the woman who might detect hers presence, not the duster of the valet the might stun her, nor the soles of shoes or slippers that might crush her, nor even the tongue of a candle that might burn her. The spider lived there in complete security in her dusty domain. The glow-worm would not have to put on for her its hue of strange destiny, its yellow hue. The spider spun herself a silken good fortune, soft and uniform, any day, at any hour, any minute, any second or any fraction of a second.

Flowers had shed their petals on the armchair and throughout the house. A little bench, covered by a cushion, touched the front feet of the set of repose, and only served the right-hand place; at least, one could suppose so; the remaining arm was also on the right.

Under the support of the little bench, disposed in the form of a drawer, there was an ussassi box that had often been disturbed and replaced in its case; its corners were softened, splintered and rounded out by dint of being touched and retouched repeatedly.

Nine o'clock chimed at the moment when the moon was giving her gaze, when the spider was spinning, when the glow-worm was shining.

The water, like the time, was still passing.

Soon, a young woman appeared in the line of earth and sand of a path. Her dress was white, and flying under the mouth of the wind. Her hair was agitating like gilded waves over her bosom, as pale as her dress and as breathless as her hair. Her mouth, oh, her mouth! You might have thought that she was posed on her lips, so much was she quivering, so much was the voluptuous agitation applied there that only exists when lips are on lips, when hearts are upon hearts. In all her features there was all hope; in the most covert of her gazes there was the death that a happiness often gives: you know, the death that arrives by means of a frisson that overtakes you, by means of a tightness that binds your veins, by virtue of the ecstasy that halts your life and leaves you the warmth of your blood; you know?

That is because, you see, the woman was going to an amorous rendezvous. She believed in God, of course: in God, the saints, the angels, in everything. Oh yes she believed. If you had been able to see her heart leaping in her breast in the midst of her holy beliefs you would have said to yourself: "What's the matter with that woman? Oh, what's the matter with that woman?"

And no matter how strong and well-armed you might have been, if she had been able to read your thoughts through your face, she would have replied to you: "Get back! Get back! Let me pass! I'm going to my amorous rendezvous, and even if, in passing, I have to leave you a part of my body on your sword, and several of my broken bones molded to that part of my body, provided that I still have enough to carry my heart to my lover's, provided that I have enough to give a breath to his kiss, a smile to his mouth, a gaze to his eyes, a tear to his soul, well, let my blood flow afterwards under the point of your weapon, let my flesh separate and spread under its blade, it's doesn't matter to me, you see, it doesn't matter! But please, my God, my God, let me go to my amorous rendezvous, let me go to the paradise of Heaven!"

And she went, she went, the young woman, caressing the earth with her feet, as if she had kissed it, perfuming, by her passage, the flowers and the air; leaving everywhere a little of her gaze, a little of her breath, a little of her soul.

She said: "So I'm going to look at him, to speak to him, to hear him, to touch him! Oh, yes, I shall have all that. My voice will mingle with his; but his is a thousand times softer. Oh, if you heard him, truly he makes me die with the words of his heart, truly. You can't imagine how he says: 'I love you!' No, for he never says it, and I hear it incessantly. The sun warms the veins of the earth; he burns mine. My God, how can I tell you what I feel? I'm very embarrassed. There's something, when he's there, utterly transparent, utterly illuminated, utterly suave, which rejoices, which astonishes, which overwhelms. I hear sounds, which bite the ear at first, and then caress it afterwards, and then envelop it with melody. I hear kisses, that silver of the lips, which ring all around me, then cries that begin, continue, sell, undulate and go away, fading out. Is that what I feel, what I hear, what I see? No, perhaps that's still not it. Sometimes images, thin leaves of gold, seem to pass over my head; whirlwinds of spirits, with wings that make no shadow anywhere come to brush my face; ribbons in shades infinite in number unroll. Spread out, crumple, shine and fall who knows where; a Genius, which God alone knows and sends, surrounds me with an impulsion that sometimes bumps me, retains me, chills me, reanimates me, melts me. It's as if I were receiving life three or four times, and death three or four times."

The young woman looked at the stones, the bushes, the grass, and murmurs to them what is agitating in her.

Soon, the path was lost in the location of the detached house and took the young woman away. She listened to its water, feels something very soft, very soft, and smiled at its little worm, which has just hidden the moon.

She went in.

The little worm turned yellow.

Immediately, she fell to her knees, made the sign of the cross and appeared open-mouthed before one of the places of the armchair. Her fingers mingled softly with bunches of violets and jasmine, separating their white and blue flowers from their stems; then she threw them on the armchair like a petty priest sprinkling incense at Corpus Christi. A barrier weighed upon he breath, and a veil of tears was over her eyes.

That adoration lasted almost as long it takes to say five *Pater nosters* and four *Ave Marias*...

After which the young woman got up, sat down, and did not light the lamp, because she was no longer occupied with anything; already, she resembled nothing more than a machine still moving slightly. She was anxious breathless, surrounded by frissons, for she was waiting, and no one came. She only brought the ussassi box out of its hiding place in order to kiss all its faces, all its sections, all its corners.

We shall not attempt to say what she felt during an hour, not seeing anyone enter the house. It would be as difficult to describe as the world is to remake. We only believe that a heavy smoke stifled her, that teeth gnawed her, that ropes of fire bound her heart, that she struggled, languished and died under something frightful.

Suddenly fear seized her when she saw, a little above the obscure lamp, eyes that were gazing at her.

For some time she remained fixed to the armchair by those two moving nails, but a sudden effort grabbed her by her dress and made her flee, sowing with her hips: "Oh, what if he were dead! Oh, what if he were about to die!" And she ran, she ran, and fell over her lover, who had just been murdered.

On the lamp in the detached house, there was an owl that was swaying gravely, and which, at the moment when the young woman went out, was mirrored by the glow-worm.

The next day, at the same hour, that glow-worm, which had turned yellow for the man, turned yellow for the woman; she poisoned herself where she had fallen.

Jules Janin (1804-1874) worked alongside S. Henry Berthoud as an editor of and contributor to periodicals launched by Émile Girardin, which lent considerable impetus to the Romantic Movement in the late 1820s and 1830s. His L'Âne mort et la femme guillotinée *(1829; tr. as The Dead Donkey and the Guillotined Woman) was one of the classic novels of the Movement.* "Le Mort magnetisé" *first appeared in the* Revue pittoresque *in 1845 (some months before the first publication in America of the Edgar Poe story usually known as "The Fact in the Case of M. Valdemar," which has a similar theme);* "The Magnetized Corpse," *first appeared in* The Magnetized Corpse and Other Paradoxical Tales *(2014).*[6]

Jules Janin: *The Magnetized Corpse*

With regard to good stories, here is one that was told to me by a trustworthy man, who claimed to be the friend of a friend of an eye-witness who played a significant role in the drama that I am about to relate to you briefly, not without making the ardent wish that the story in question might be honored before long by an adaptation for the theater—which is, as everyone knows, the greatest honor that can be desired nowadays.

Not six weeks ago, a young Englishman named Belfort was dying, quite simply, from a bad chest and a few crazy years recklessly spent. The young man, although he was nearing the end, did not regret losing his life too much, for he had had his fair share of amours, duels, bad debts, picnics, and even fine sermons—in short, his fair share of all the Parisian joys.

One of his friends, a man of science but a good enough fellow regardless, seeing that Charles Belfort would soon render his last breath, came to say to him, in his softest voice: "If it wouldn't displease you too much, my dear invalid, I'll use my abilities to magnetize you, and I'll choose the moment when you render up your soul; it seems to me that it will be a fine experiment, and that there's nothing about it likely to displease you. What do you say?"

"Not only doesn't your experiment displease me," the other replied, "but it seems to me to be very amusing and interesting, and I thank you for having thought of me for the proof, which will be decisive. Count on me, my dear doctor; you'll be content with my patience, I hope, and I'll be sure to let you know when the moment comes."

With those words, the two friends shook hands and separated, saying that they would see one another again soon. They were both full of hope, and it

---

[6] Black Coat Press, ISBN 978-1-61227-248-1.

would have been difficult to decide which of the two was the more content, the moribund or the magnetizer.

Two days went by—two centuries—while the magnetizer waited impatiently for the final agony, which did not seem to want to arrive for good and all. The dying man, for his part, lost patience, and he said to his friend: "Damn it, my dear chap, it's not my fault if death is treating me with such ill-will, but what consoles me is that you won't lose anything by waiting, and I'll be a magnificent subject."

On the night following this conversation, the sick man had a final crisis and fell into a comatose ecstasy; he started sketching fantastic spider-webs with his finger, and yet, in the midst of the most abominable grimaces, he still had the presence of mind to say to his comrade: "You have to lift my head, to hide the light that is hurting my eyes."

The other obeyed. He propped his moribund up in a sitting position, took away every importunate light and set about the operation; which is to say that never, absolutely never, had such beautiful passes and counter-passes—the whole customary apparatus, in short—been performed. The magnetizer was in the swim; but in the end, when he had enveloped the moribund—who lent himself to it with exemplary willingness—with his all-powerful fluid, and saw that his subject had arrived at magnetic perfection, the magnetizer started to interrogate him.

"How are you doing, Belfort? Where are you?"

"My dear friend," the other said, "I'm just dying; you've caught me just at the moment when the breath was leaving my body, and now it depends entirely on you to let me finish the job or to keep me here, suspended between being and non-being, which doesn't seem to me to be a disagreeable state, so far."

"Let's wait," said the magnetizer. "There's no hurry, Belfort, my friend." And with that, the magnetizer went to dinner, without taking the trouble to demagnetize his friend.

The next day the maker of magnetism reappeared in the mortuary chamber; everything was in its place, including the cadaver.

"Belfort," said the scientist, after a few preliminary passes, "what have you been doing since you died?"

"In truth, my dear chap," the dead man replied, "I've been obliged to follow you everywhere you went."

And with that, the dead man told the living one everything that the latter had done the day before: he had dined in a cheap eatery, and from there he had gone to stand on the steps of the Café de Paris; he had been given a ticket to the Vaudeville and he had seen some young women who were pretty enough, but some of whom sang out of tune; finally he had gone back home, and read a little of a novel that he had picked up on the way.

"And if you'll permit me to make an observation," the dead man said, "so long as I'm attached to you by a thread that only you can break, eat better, I beg you, remembering that I'm sharing the experience. You know that I like music, so don't expose me to hearing quavering voices that would spoil the most beautiful faces. All alone here, I'm getting bored, and I wouldn't be sorry if you were to read a good novel from time to time, but at least, for pity's sake, read it all the way through. Finally, if you please, don't go to bed so late; I become irritated not sleeping, because for twenty-four hours, I ought to have been sleeping eternally."

With these words, the man slumped back, and the magnetizer left the room, slightly discomfited by the strange spy that was dogging his heels.

The next day, the living man came back, and found his dead man a trifle numb. He warmed him up with a further dose of magnetic fluid, rendering him, if not life, at least a little color and the ability to speak.

"Ah!" said the dead man, raising himself up. "You're not showing me any charity. What! You go to see such hideous sick people, and I have to hear them coughing, spitting, howling, moaning and all the rest! In the street you follow a horrible woman reeking of musk, a woman in old shoes and a dirty skirt, and I have to keep you company counting the holes and the stains of the filthy creature! Then you go to meet up with some young people, and you tell them about your good luck! You make the streetwalker into a duchess, and a cotton apron into a silk skirt! When you're dead, you know, lying makes you feel ill. And what makes you feel even worse, when you're dead, is stupidity—some quip that would have made me laugh when I was of this world appears to me to be utter nonsense now that I can hear your mind with the ears of my own. So try to talk better my dear chap, and, if it's all the same to you, I'd be obliged if you didn't get drunk on adulterated wine; my throat's been torn apart by the alcohol you've swallowed."

Who do you think pulled a face? It was the living man, who was beginning to think that his dead man was damnable hard to please—because, after all, the previous evening's indulgence hadn't been deserving of such scorn. As for the lady with the worn-out shoes, the living man hadn't noticed the shoe, but only the foot and a little bit of the leg. However, he was fond of his dead man, and he resolved to keep a better eye on himself, in order not to give poor Belfort further reason for discontentment.

When he came back two days later, he found the deceased in a state of incredible excitement. The dead man was sweating copiously, with indignation legible on his distressed face.

First of all, the magnetizer set about trying to calm that anger; he blew his most soothing breath upon those irritated nerves, and appeased that motionless and frozen heart as best he could, which beat in memory.

"What is it, Master Belfort? Who's upset you? And for God's sake, what's the matter with you?"

"What's the matter with me?" replied the cadaver, after a long pause. "What's the matter with me, imbecile that you are? A curse upon the brazen threads that attach me to a fool like you! What's the matter with me! But my dear chap, for two days you've been going from one stupidity to another. The day before yesterday, it's true, you were well-groomed and well-dressed, but you'd fastened your belt too tight and I nearly choked. Your boots—or, rather, our boots—were well-polished, but they were too small, and if I could still walk, I'm sure that I'd be limping with my right foot.

"I've nothing to say about the lovely salon to which you took me; it was pleasant and it was calm; the clothes weren't at all garish; the mature ladies kept to their place, leaving the foreground to the young women; no one played the slightest sonata or read the slightest sonnet; people only spoke in even voices, neither too loud not too quiet, and said the nicest things—trivial but light, benevolent and sonorous. In brief, had it not been for your belt and your footwear, I would have blessed you for having taken me to such a beautiful place. But good heavens! Could you have been any more gauche, maladroit and absurd?

"In a corner of the little room to the left, a more beautiful woman than I ever saw with my mortal eyes was sitting; by dint of attention and will-power, via your terrestrial intermediation, I had attracted the benevolent interest of that amiable lady; already she was looking at me with a certain tenderness, and she was about to smile at me; our two souls were no longer any but one, and we were about to fall in love, when you turned your head like an idiot to greet I don't know what starchy spirit. Then the image of my beautiful lady fled, and if you live for a hundred years you won't find either another face as beautiful or another heart as noble.

"Idiot that you are, having done that, what do you do next? You know that I've left some glaring debts, and that I don't even have a tomb. You haven't a sou yourself; you live from hand to mouth; your rent hasn't been paid and never will be; in brief, you're as poor as a poet and an actor rolled into one—which is to say, abominably poor! Well, you sit down at a card-table, tremulously risk a wretched pistole, and, having won the hand, you pocket the money and run away like a thief!

"Now, do you know what you did there, Monsieur Idiot? You renounced getting your hands on a round sum of four lovely thousand louis d'or, for you'd have won the next thirteen hands, my son! With your four thousand louis you'd have had a carriage and I'd have had a first-class funeral. You'd have had a new suit and I'd have had an embroidered shroud. You'd have gone to seek your supper in the chorus of the Opéra, and I'd have gone to look for Monsieur Gannal.[7]

---

[7] Jean-Nicolas Gannal (1791-1852) was the pharmacist and inventor who founded and developed the modern techniques of embalming in the early 1830s, winning the Prix Montyon three times by virtue of the benefits thus provided to human society. In 1837 he obtained a patent for his embalming fluid and set up a commercial laboratory in the Rue Saint-Hippolyte.

"Damn your feeble intelligence—you can't make use of what little sense you have, but you amuse yourself dragging another man's intelligence around with you. Go away—you make me sick, wretched living individual that you are!"

When our magnetizer finally understood that whatever he did would surely attract criticism or sarcasm, he fell silent. Now that he felt that he was being followed and observed at close range by some invisible entity that he had retained on the boundary between the two worlds, the scientist dared not take a step in the street; he scarcely dared answer yes or no to the simplest questions that were addressed to him; if was as if he were deaf and dumb. At times he wondered whether he might be the magnetized man and the magnetizer that great motionless—but not speechless—cadaver, the mere sight of which had ended up making him shiver.

An idea, a thought, is such a powerful thing, even independent of life! An idea pursues you, obsesses you, more tenacious than a shadow, as eloquent as remorse or hope, full of starts, excitations and perils!

However, our man went back to his friend Belfort three days later. This time, once again, a great change was evident in his inanimate face; pure and simple scorn had replaced indignation and anger. The half-closed eyes seemed to be saying: "Away with you!" The tight lips were expressing an indescribable disdain. Every muscle, taut from top to bottom, held a contempt suspended from every thread connecting it to the soul.

"What's the matter now, my friend?" cried the living man, "You seem dazed. You can't say this time that I've done or said anything stupid, because I've stayed at home, alone, entirely given over to my thoughts."

"Oh, my dear fellow," the dead man said, "it's the contemplation of your thoughts that's giving me nausea. Motionless as you were, I was forced to look into the depths of that chaos you call your soul. But what kind of animal are you to occupy yourself with so many ignoble, frivolous and shameful things? When I was alive and I called you my friend, everyone said that you were a gallant fellow; you had a reputation for keen, even eloquent wit; you were credited with philosophy, probity and tact.

"For three days, unable to help it, I've been watching you very attentively—but my dear fellow, you're a complete mess! What you know, you know poorly; what you don't know, you replace with words as empty as your head. Your generosity is a certain organic weakness that ends up making your eyes red, and that's all. Your intelligence is represented by a few mechanical cog-wheels that rotate of their own accord like the wheel of a water-mill incessantly repeating the same tick-tock. Your courage—I've seen all the way its depths, your courage!—is a cardboard mask that frightens children. Your probity—let's talk about your probity!—is written in the margins of the commercial Code and the penal Code.

"Shame upon your vices, those of a badly brought-up child! I wouldn't give four sous for your vices; they make me sick, your wicked shameful vices: they're like a kind of boasting! As for your virtues, they're so worthless I wouldn't even give them to my lackeys; there's something limp and vain about your virtue, which bears some resemblance to a badly-cooked broth. Oh, I advise you not to lay bare the inside of your brain and your heart—it's not a pretty sight, although, on the other hand, it's very sad.

"And what ideas you have about other men! What thwarted ambitions! And I don't envy your work at all, my poor sir! What! You aren't ashamed, even of your castles in Spain, when you amuse yourself rambling on for entire hours in petty daydreams?

"Anyway, Monsieur, let's leave it at that—but I'm damnably sorry that I ever called you my friend!"

It would not have taken much on this occasion for the magnetizer to destroy his work and liberate himself from the unwelcome thought that was obsessing him. He left the mortuary chamber in a very bad mood, and on the way home he said to himself that it was, after all, quite an accomplishment to have stopped Belfort's discontented soul half-way.

Then again, the living man said to himself, sadly, *what good has it done me to have retained that dead man in the edge of his grave? To have myself told such rude home-truths, to hear the story of my everyday life told in such a cruel and grotesque fashion, no longer to be alone with my conscience, my thoughts, my ambitions, my self? If the clairvoyant that sees everything were, at least, to indicate some unknown science to me—a remedy for the gout or some hidden treasure easy to extract—I'd be rewarded for my troubles, but no! For having carried out the most difficult task, the most excellent miracle that magnetism has ever accomplished, here I am dragging behind me a bilious inquisitor who isn't content with anything, and who'll end up making me disgusted with myself.*

Thus the clever man reasoned; he was very annoyed, and firmly resolved to put an end to his dealings with such a miscreant, no matter what it cost.

As he was unable to sleep, the magnetizer went back to Belfort's house that same evening, at midnight.

Belfort watched him come in, and without waiting to be interrogated—for the magnetic fluid becomes, it seems, a habit, and replaces life as a well-lit candle replaces with winter sun—the dead man cried: "I'll tell you what you've just done, amiable doctor! You've quite simply decided to murder me! Yes, you're jealous of this artificial life, you're furious at my revelations, and you've decided to extract me abruptly from magnetic sleep in order to return me to dust and silence!

"That's handsome of you, Monsieur, it's glorious, what you're doing, coming to murder...a dead man! Coming to trouble a cadaver in his coffin! Attacking the thought of a man because the man, having become, thanks to you, a part of eternal life, is no longer able and no longer wants to flatter you!

"Well, get on with it, then, and turn me to dust—but that dust, when you've cast it to the wind, will summon to its aid another, bolder thought, to follow in your tracks, another gaze, even more clairvoyant, to read the depths of your soul, another avenger, even more implacable: remorse!"

At these threats the magnetizer fled, but, in his distress, he left the door ajar.

The neighbors of both sexes, who had initially kept their distance, took the chance, one after another, and finally all together, of coming to greet and interrogate the dead man, and picked up, here and there, some of those fine verities—I mean a few of those eternal, ever-living truths—that only the dead know how to voice appropriately. Husbands, wives, children, tenants, owners, masters and servants, the rich and the poor, all the way to the porter, each obtained a parcel of justice addressed to them.

The dead man spoke true words and expressed true notions, and what he said was, admittedly, cruel. If you asked him where fortune lay, he would point out a wart on the end of your nose; if you mentioned ambition to him, he would talk to you about modesty, economy and bonhomie. The female neighbors found him so ungallant that they slammed the door violently.

That was all that the late Monsieur Belfort wanted.

A week went by without the magnetized and the magnetizer seeing one another again; they were sulking, but it was obviously not up to the dead man to make the first move. The scientist finally understood that, and came back to his subject's bedside.

"I've thought about everything that has happened," Belfort said to him, "and I'd be glad if you were to carry through the plan you made the other day. You're right: wake me up, so that I can finish dying quietly. It had made such a good beginning, when you came along to disrupt it, that I'd already be devoured by worms and returned via the thousand pores of universal decomposition into the ocean of life and light. Wake me up, then, and I'll die entirely—and joyfully, for, this time, I'll amuse myself by gazing, not at your soul, which isn't beautiful, but at your body, which is very ugly.

"Only the other day—I caught you in that agreeable occupation—you were telling yourself how fortunate you were before, but please, where are these women who can look lovingly at an ape like you? You're badly-formed; you always have one shoulder higher than the other, this one over that one or that one over this one. Your hair started falling out a long time ago, and what's left is hanging on to rotten roots, like last year's thatch after the winter. Your eyes can still see, but I can see some sort of pellicle extending over your line of sight that doesn't augur anything good.

"Oh, if you could see those layers of yellow chalk encrusted in the joints of your fingers, which are corrupting your bones and are going to break them bit by bit, like the boot of torture, but more slowly, more insidiously and with a more obstinate verve!

"Your heart is swollen, my dear chap, and the point is being torn by some viscera or other that is wounded in its turn. Your left lung isn't much better than my right lung. Gradually infiltrating between your skin and your softened tendons I can see layers of thick fat which makes you resemble some sort of seacow. Your teeth are already turning yellow; they're loose in their bloody cavities. In your brain I can see veins swollen with apoplectic blood, ready to burst. You're doomed, you see, and—give me your hand—you're dead!"

On hearing those lugubrious words, the magnetizer begs the magnetized for mercy, pity and forgiveness. And, in order to free himself from the vision that is obsessing him, to expel from his mind that voice, which is pursuing him with such bruising stubbornness, in order not to remain exposed to that mockery and those prophecies of misfortune, the magnetizer sets about countermanding the magnetic fluid and destroying that artificial life.

The dead man resists, but in vain; it is necessary that a corpse, which is dead, should yield to a man who is still alive.

Gradually, the voice fades away. It utters one last gasp, and then Belfort, so eloquent a little while before, is no longer more than I don't know what, that which I don't know how to name in any language...

It was, in fact, for three weeks already that death had had possession of the cadaver, and now the magnetic breath had ceased, corruption and the worm took hold of their prey again and did not let go.

One shivers at the mere idea that the magnetizer might have died before having demagnetized his friend Belfort. How long eternity would have seemed to the latter then—unless his thought, obedient all the way to the abyss, or to Heaven, had followed the soul of magnetizer.

That would be another trial to attempt!

*"Erckmann-Chatrian" was the collective pseudonym used by Émile Erckmann (1822-1899) and Alexandre Chatrian (1826-1890), ardent Republicans and Romantics who serialized their earliest stories, including "*Vin rouge et vin blanc*" in the newspaper they edited in Strasbourg,* Le Démocrate du Rhin *in the aftermath of the 1848 Revolution, before reprinting them in* Histoires et contes fantastiques *(Strasbourg 1849; tr. as* A Malediction, Snuggly Books, 2019). *Their activity was severely restricted for some years after the coup d'état of 1851 but they eventually built the foundations of a successful literary career in the latter years of the Second Empire, reprinting "*Vin rouge et vin blanc*" as* "Le Bourgmestre en bouteille*" [The Bottled Burgomaster]. "Red Wine and White Wine" first appeared in* A Malediction.

Erckmann-Chatrian: *Red Wine and White Wine*

I have always professed a high esteem, and even a sort of veneration, for the noble wine of the Rhine; it sparkles like Champagne, it warms like Burgundy; it soothes the throat like Bordeaux; it fires the imagination like Spanish liqueurs; it renders us as tender as Lacrima Cristi; in sum, above all, it enables dreaming, unfurling before our eyes the vast field of fantasy.

Toward the end of autumn in 1846 I decided to make a pilgrimage to Johannisberg. Mounted on a poor nag with hollow flanks I had disposed two tin-plate pitchers in its vast intercostal cavities and I traveled in short daily stages.

What an admirable spectacle was that of the vineyards! They were the most beautiful days of my life. One of my pitchers was always empty, the other always full; when I quit one hillside there was always another in view. My sole regret was being unable to partake of that pleasure with a veritable appreciation.

One evening, as night was falling, the sun had just disappeared at the horizon but it was still launching a few stray rays between the large vine-leaves. I heard the trot of a horse behind me. I veered slightly to the left in order to let it pass, and to my great surprise I recognized by friend Hippel, who uttered a joyful exclamation as soon as he perceived me.

You know Hippel, his fleshy nose, his mouth adapted for wine-tasting and his triple-stage belly. He resembled the good Silenus, the follower of the god Bacchus. We embraced enthusiastically.

Hippel was traveling with the same objective as me; he traced out itinerary through the vineyards of the Rhingau. Sometimes we called a halt in order to give the accolade to our pitchers and to listen to the silence that reigned in the distance.

The night was considerably advanced when we arrived before a little inn nestling on the slope of the ill. We dismounted. Hippel darted a glance through a

63

little window almost at ground level. A light was shining on a table, and beside the lamp an old woman was asleep.

"Hey!" cried my comrade. "Open up, Mother."

The old woman shuddered, got to her feet and came to the window, where she stuck her wrinkled face against one of the panes. One might have thought it one of those old Flemish portraits in which ocher and bistre dispute priority.

When the old Sibyl had distinguished us, she grimaced a smile and opened the door.

"Come in, Messieurs, come in," she said in a quavering voice. "I'll go and wake my son; be welcome."

"A peck of oats for our horses, and a good supper for us!" cried Hippel.

"Good, good," said the old woman, hastily. She went out and we heard her climbing a staircase more rapidly than Jacob's ladder.

We stayed for a few minutes in a low and smoky room. Hippel ran to the kitchen and came to tell me that he had observed the presence of several quarters of bacon.

"We'll have supper," he said, caressing his belly. "Yes, we'll have supper."

Floorboard creaked overhead, and almost immediately, a robust fellow dressed in simple trousers, bare-chested and his hair unkempt, opened the door, took four steps and went out without saying a word to us.

The old woman lit the fire and butter started to sizzle on the stove.

The supper was served. A ham was placed on the table flanked by two bottles, one of red wine and the other of white wine.

"Which would you prefer?" asked the hostess.

"It's necessary to see," replied Hippel, presenting his glass to the old woman, who poured him the red wine. She also filled mine. We tasted it; it was a bitter, strong wine. It had a particular taste that I did not know, a perfume of vervain and cypress! I drank a few drops, and a profound sadness took possession of my soul. Hippel, on the contrary, clicked his tongue in a satisfied manner.

"Famous," he said, "famous! Where do you get it from, good Mother?"

"From a nearby hill," said the old woman, with a strange smile.

"A famous hill," said Hippel, pouring a new draught. It seemed to me that he was drinking blood.

"What the Devil to you think you're doing, Ludwig," he said to me. "Is something the matter with you?"

"No," I replied, "but I don't like red wine."

"It's necessary not to argue about tastes," observed Hippel, emptying the bottle and thumping the table.

"Same again!" he cried. "Always the same, and above all no mixing, lovely hostess! I know better than that. Damn, this wine is reanimating me; it's a generous wine."

Hippel leaned back on the back of his chair. His face appeared to me to decompose. In a single draught I emptied the bottle of white wine; then joy returned to my heart. My friend's preference for the red wine appeared to me to be ridiculous, but excusable.

We continued drinking until one o'clock in the morning, he drinking the red, me the white.

One o'clock in the morning! It is Madame Fantasia's hour of audience. The caprices of the imagination display their diaphanous robes embroidered with crystal and azure, like those of the bluebottle, the beetle and the damsel-fly of dormant waters.

One o'clock! It is then that the celestial music tickles the ear of the dreamer and blows the harmony of invisible spheres into his soul. Then the mouse trots; then the owl deploys its downy wings as passes silently above our heads; then, to, the vampire extends its pointed muzzle over the artery of its victim and pumps a trickle of blood as thin as the hair of an angel. Its crouching body inflates like a blister and its great wings fall back by its sides, quivering, like those of nocturnal moths.

"One o'clock," I said to my comrade. "It's necessary to get some sleep if we want to leave tomorrow."

Hippel stood up, tottering.

The old woman conducted us to a room with two beds and wished us a pleasant slumber.

We got undressed; I stayed on my feet longer in order to put out the light. I had scarcely lain down when Hippel was profoundly asleep; his respiration resembled the breath of the tempest. I could not close my eyes; a thousand bizarre figures were fluttering around me: gnomes, imps, and the witches of Walpürgisnacht were executing their cabalistic dance on the ceiling. A singular effect of the white wine!

I got up, I lit my lamp and I approached Hippel's bed, drawn by an invincible curiosity. His face was red, his mouth open; blood was making his temples throb. His helps were moving as if he were trying to speak. For a long time I stayed motionless beside him; I would have liked to plunge my daze into the depths of his soul, but slumber is an impenetrable mystery; like death, it keeps its secrets.

Sometimes Hippel's features expressed terror, sometimes sorrow, sometimes melancholy; sometimes they contracted, and one might have thought that he was about to weep.

That fine face, made for bursting into laughter, had a strange character under the impression of dolor.

What was happening in the depths of that abyss? I could see a few waves rising to the surface, but whence did those profound commotions come?

Suddenly, the sleeper sat up, his eyelids opened, and I saw that his eyes were white. All the muscles of his face quivered; his mouth seemed to want to utter a cry of horror…then he fell back and uttered a sob.

"Hippel! Hippel!" I cried, pouring the contents of a jug of water over his head.

He woke up.

"Ah!" he said. "God be praised, it was a dream! My dear Ludwig, I thank you for having woken me up."

"That's all right, but you're going to tell me what you were dreaming."

"Yes…tomorrow…let me sleep; I'm tired."

"You're an ingrate Hippel! Tomorrow you'll have forgotten everything."

"Damn it," he said, "I'm tired…I can't do any more! Let me be…let me be."

I did not want to let go. "Hippel, you'll fall back into your dream, and this time, I'll abandon you without mercy."

Those words produced an admirable effect.

"Fall back into my dream!" he cried, leaping out of bed. "Quickly, my clothes! My horse! I'm leaving! This house is accursed. You're right, Ludwig, the Devil lives within these four walls. Let's get out of here!"

He got dressed precipitately. When he had finished I stopped him.

"Hippel," I said, "Why run away? It's only three o'clock in the morning; let's repose."

I opened a window; the fresh nocturnal air penetrating into the room dissipated all our dread.

Leaning on the window sill, he recounted the following:

"We were talking yesterday about the famous vineyards of the Rhingau. Although I've never traveled in this country, my mind is doubtless preoccupied by it, and the strong wine we drank gave a somber color to my ideas. The most astonishing thing is that I imagined in my dream that I was the burgomeister of Welche[8]—a nearby hamlet—and I identified so completely with that person that I could make a description of him as of myself. That burgomeister was a man of medium height, almost as fat as me. He wore a coat with long tails and brass buttons; along his legs he had another row of little buttons like the heads of nails. A tricorn hat coiffed his bald head. In sum, he was a man of stupid gravity, only drinking water, only esteeming money, and only thinking about extending his property.

"As I had taken on the burgomeister's coat, I had also taken n his character. I. Hippel, would have been scornful of myself if I had been able to know myself…animal of a burgomeister that I was! Isn't it better to live cheerfully

---

[8] *Welche* or *Velche* is a pejorative term used by German for foreigners in general, but particularly the French.

and not to care about the future than to pile up coins and distill bile? But there it is…I'm a burgomeister.

"I get out of bed and the first thing that worries me is knowing whether the workmen are laboring on the vines. I have a crust of bread for breakfast. A crust of bread! He must be a skinflint, a miser! Me, who breakfasts every day with a good cutlet and an excellent bottle! Anyway, it's all right. I take—which is to say the burgomeister takes—a crust of bread and puts it in his pocket. He orders his old housekeeper to seep the room and prepare dinner for eleven o'clock. Broth and potatoes, I think. A poor dinner! No matter…he goes out.

"I could make you a description of the house, the road, and the mountain," Hippel told me. "I have them before my eyes.

"Is it possible that a man, in his dreams, can imagine a landscape like that? I saw fields, gardens, meadows, vineyards. I thought: *that one's Pierre's, that other one's Jacques, that one's Henri's*, and I stopped in front of some of those parcels, saying to myself: *Damn, Jacob's clover is superb*, and further on: *Damn, that arpent of vines would suit me very well.* But in the meantime, I felt a sort of numbness, an indefinable headache. I hastened my pace. As it was morning, the sun rose suddenly and the heat became excessive. I followed a little path that climbed through the vines on the slope f the hill. The path petered out behind the ruins of an old castle, and I could see my four arpents further on. I was in a hurry to arrive there. I was out of breath as I penetrated in the midst of the ruins. I stopped in order to get my breath back, but the blood was buzzing in my ears and my heart was thumping in my breast like a hammer on an anvil. The sun was on fire. I tried to resume my route, but I was suddenly struck as if by a sledgehammer; I fell down behind a section of wall, and I understood that I had just been struck by apoplexy.

"Then a somber despair took possession of me. *I'm dead*, I said to myself; *the money I've amassed with so much difficulty, the trees I've cultivated with so much care, the house I've built—all is lost, all will pass to my heirs. Those wretches, to whom I didn't want to give a kreutzer, will enrich themselves at my expense. Oh, traitors, you'll be gladdened by my misfortune…you'll take the keys from my pocket, you'll share out my wealth, you'll spend my old. And I…I'll witness that pillage! What a frightful torture!*

"I sensed my soul being detached from the cadaver, but it remained standing beside it.

"That burgomeister's soul saw that its cadaver had a blue face and yellow hands.

"As it was very warm and a sweat of death was trickling over the forehead, large flies came to settle on the face. One of them entered into the nose…the cadaver didn't budge! Soon the entire face was covered, and the desolate soul couldn't chase them away!

"It was there…there, for minutes that it counted like centuries. Its Hell was commencing!

"An hour went by; the heat was still increasing; not a breath of wind in the air, not a cloud in the sky!

A goat appeared alongside the ruins; it was browsing the ivy and the wild herbs that grew in the midst of that rubble. As it passed close to my poor corpse it bounded sideways, and then came back, opened its large eyes anxiously, sniffed the surroundings and continued its capricious route along the ledge of a tower. A young pastor who perceived it then ran to pick it up, but on seeing the cadaver he uttered a loud scream and started running as fast as he could toward the village.

"Another hour, as slow as eternity, went by. Finally, whispers and foot-steps are heard behind the enclosure and I see climbing, slowly...slowly... the justice of the peace, followed by his clerk and several other people. I recognize all of them. They make exclamations at the sight of me. 'It's our burgomeister!'

"The physician approaches my body and chases away the flies, which flut-tered and swirl like a swarm. He looks, lifts up an arm that is already stiff. Then he says, indifferently: 'Our burgomeister has died of a devastating apoplectic fit; he must have been there since this morning. You can take him away, and have him buried as quickly as possible, for this heat hastens decomposition."

"'In truth,' said the clerk, 'it's no great loss to the commune. He was a mi-ser, an imbecile who didn't understand anything about anything.'

"'Yes,' added the judge, 'and he had a very critical expression.'

"'That's not astonishing,' someone else said. 'Fools always believe them-selves to be intelligent.'

"'It will be necessary to send for porters,' said the physician. 'Their burden will be heavy; the man had more belly than brain.'

"'I'll draw up the death certificate. What time shall we put on it?' said the clerk.

"'Put that he died at three o'clock.'

"'The miser!' said a peasant. 'He was going to spy on his workers to have a pretext for docking their pay at the end of the week.' Then he folded his arms and looked down at the cadaver. 'Well, burgomeister,' he said, 'what good does it do you know to have pressured the poor people so much? Death has scythed you down just the same.'

"'What's that in his pocket?' said another. He fetched out my crust of bread. 'This is his breakfast!'

"They all burst out laughing.

"Chatting in that fashion, the fellows headed for the exit from the ruins. My poor soul heard them for a few more seconds, and then the sound gradually ceased. I remained in solitude and silence.

"The flies came back in thousands.

"I don't know how much time passed," Hippel went on, "for in my dream, the minutes were endless. However, the porters arrived; they cursed the burgomeister as they lifted my cadaver. The poor man's soul followed them, plunged in an inexpressible dolor. I went back down the same path that I had climbed, but this time I saw my body carried before me on a litter.

"When we arrived at my house I found a crowd of people waiting for me; I recognized my cousins of both sexes, unto the fourth generation!

"The stretched was set down. They all passed me in review.

"'It's really him.' said one.

"'He's really dead,' said another.

My housekeeper also arrived, and put her hands together sympathetically. 'Who could have foreseen this misfortune?' she exclaimed. "A big, fat man, so healthy! How little we are!'

"That was my entire funeral oration.

I was taken inside and laid down on a bed of straw.

"When one of my cousins took the keys from my pocket I tried to utter a cry of rage. Unfortunately, souls have no voice. In sum, my dear Ludwig, I saw my writing-desk opened, my money counted, my credits calculated; I saw the seals put on, I saw my housekeeper stealing my best clothes covertly; and although death had freed me from all needs, I couldn't help regretting the thousandth part of the money that I saw stolen.

"I was undressed and a chemise was put on me; I was nailed between four planks and I witnessed my own funeral.

"When I was lowered into the grave, despair took possession of my soul. All was lost…!

"It was then that you woke me up, Ludwig; and I think I can still hear the earth falling over my coffin."

Hippel fell silent and I saw a frisson run through his entire body.

We remained meditative for some time, without exchanging a word. The song of a cock informed us that night was nearing its end; the stars appeared to be fading as daylight approached. Two more cocks launched their piercing voices into space, and responded to one another from farm to farm. A guard dog came out of its niche in order to make its morning round, and then a skylark, doubtless drunk on dew, twittered a few notes of its joyful dong.

"Hippel," I said to my comrade, "it's time to go if we want to take advantage of the cool air."

"That's true," he said, "But before anything else, it's necessary to have a bite to eat."

We went downstairs. The innkeeper was in the process of getting dressed. When he had put on his smock he served us the debris of our meal. He filled one of my pitchers with white wine, the other with red wine, saddled our two nags, and wished us bon voyage.

We were not yet half a league from the inn when my friend Hippel, always devoured by thirst, took a mouthful of red wine.

"Brr!" he said, as if struck by vertigo. "My dream, my night's dream!" He urged his horse to a trot in order to escape that vision, which was painted in strange characters in his physiognomy; I followed at a distance, my poor Rocinante, demanding to be spared...

Soon the sun rose; a pale rosy tint invaded the somber azure of the sky. The starts were lost in the midst of a dazzling light, like a pearly gravel in the depths of the sea.

With the first rays of the morning, Hippel stopped his horse and waited for me.

"I don't know," he said, "what somber ideas have taken possession of me. That red wine must have some singular virtue; it flatters my throat but attacks my brain."

"Hippel," I responded, "It's necessary not to dissimulate that certain liquors contain the principle of fantasy, and even of phantasmagoria. I've seen cheerful men become sad, sad men become cheerful, intelligent men become stupid and reciprocally with a few glasses of wine in the stomach. It's a profound mystery; what insensate being would dare to doubt that magical power of the bottle? Is it not the scepter of a superior, incomprehensible power, before which we must bow our heads, since everything within us is sometimes submissive to the divine or infernal influence?"

Hippel recognized the force of my arguments, and remained silent, as if lost in an immense reverie.

We were following a narrow path that snaked along the banks of the Quiech. The birds were making their songs heard; grouse were uttering their guttural cries and hiding beneath the broad vine leaves. The landscape was magnificent, the river murmuring as it flowed through little ravines. To the right and the left hills unfurled charged with superb harvests.

Our route formed a bend as it climbed the hillside. Suddenly, my friend Hippel stopped dead, his mouth open, his hands extended in an attitude of stupor; then, as swift as an arrow, he turned to flee, but I grabbed the bridle of his horse.

"What's the matter Hippel?" I exclaimed. "Is Satan lying in ambush before you? Has Balaam's angel made his sword shine in your eyes?"

"Let me be!" he said, struggling. "My dream! It's my dream!"

"Come on, calm down, Hippel. The red wine undoubtedly has harmful properties; take a mouthful of this one, it's a generous juice that drives away somber imaginations from the human brain."

He drank avidly; the beneficent liquor reestablished equilibrium between his faculties.

We poured the red wine, which had become as black as ink, on to the path; it formed large bubbles as it seeped into the ground, and it seemed to me that I heard dull groans, confused voices and sighs, but very faint—so faint that one might have thought that they were escaping from a distant country, and that our ears of flesh could not grasp them, but only the most intimate fibers of the heart.

It was the last sigh of Abel when his brother felled him in the grass and the earth drank his blood.

Hippel was too emotional to pay attention to that phenomenon, but I was profoundly struck by it. At the same time I saw a black bird as big as a fist emerge from a bush and fly away, uttering a little cry of terror.

"I sense," Hippel said to me then, "that two contrary principles are struggling in my being, the black and the white, the principles of good and evil—let's go!"

We continued our route. "Ludwig," my comrade soon said, "things happen in this world that are so strange that the mind ought to be humiliated and tremulous. You know that I have never traveled in this country. Well, yesterday, I dreamed, and today I see with my eyes the fantasy of the dream looming up before me. Look at this landscape; it's the same one that I saw yesterday in my slumber. Here are the ruins of the old castle where I was struck by apoplexy. Here is the path that I traveled, and over there are my four arpents of vines. There isn't a tree, a stream or a bush that I don't recognize, as if I had seen them a hundred times. When we've gone round this bend in the path, we'll see the hamlet of Welche in the depths of the valley. The second house on the right is the burgomeister's. It has five windows on the upper part of the façade, four and the door on the lower part. To the left of my house—which is to say, the burgomeister's house—you'll see a barn and a stable. It's there that I enclose my livestock. Behind it, in a small yard under a vast stall, are my two-horse press. Finally, my dear Ludwig, such as I am, I'm resuscitated. The poor burgomeister is looking at you through my eyes, speaking to you through my mouth, and if I didn't remember that before I was a burgomeister, a skinflint, a miser and a rich landowner, I was Hippel, the bon vivant, I'd hesitate to say whom I am, for what I see reminds me of another existence, other habits and other ideas."

Everything happened as Hippel had predicted; we saw the village in the distance, in the depths of a superb valley between two rich hills, the houses scattered along the banks of the river. The second on the right was the burgomeister's.

All the individuals we encountered, Hippel had a vague memory of having known; several of them appeared so familiar to him that he was on the point of calling them by name, but the word remained on his tongue; he could not disengage it from his other memories. In any case, on seeing the indifferent curiosity with which people were looking at us, Hippel sensed clearly that he was unknown and that his face masked the defunct soul of the burgomeister entirely.

We dismounted in front of an inn that my friend identified to me as the best in the village; he had known it for a long time.

A new surprise: the mistress of the inn was a stout woman, widowed for several years, whom the burgomeister had once coveted in a second marriage. Hippel was tempted to throw his arms around her; all his old sympathies awoke simultaneously. However, he was able to moderate himself. The true Hippel

71

combated the matrimonial tendencies of the burgomeister within him. He therefore limited himself to asking, with his most amiable expression, for a good breakfast and the best wine in the place.

When we were at table, a very natural curiosity led Hippel to ask what had happened in the village since his death. "Madame,' he said to our hostess with a flattering smile, "you doubtless knew the former burgomeister of Welche?"

"Do you mean the one who died three years ago of an apoplectic fit?" she asked.

"Precisely," replied my comrade, fixing a furious gaze upon the woman.

"Oh, did I know him!" cried the woman. "That eccentric, that old skinflint who wanted to marry me! If I'd known that he'd die so soon, I'd have accepted. He proposed to me a mutual donation to the last survivor."

That response disconcerted my dear Hippel somewhat...the burgomeister's self-esteem was horribly offended within him. However, he contained himself.

"So you didn't love him, Madame?" he said.

"How is it possible to love an ugly, dirty, repulsive, miserly skinflint?"

Hippel stood up in order to look at himself in the mirror. On seeing his cheeks full and plump, he smiled at his face, and came back to take his place before a pullet, which he stated to tear apart.

"In fact," he said, "the burgomeister might have been ugly and dirty; that doesn't prove anything against me."

"Are you one of his relatives?' asked the hostess, very surprised.

"Me! I never knew him. I'm only saying that some people are ugly, and others handsome; because one has a nose placed in the middle of the face, like your burgomeister, it doesn't prove that one resembles him."

"Oh no," said the woman, "you don't have any of his family's features."

'Besides which,' said my comrade, 'I'm not a miser, myself, which demonstrates that I'm not your burgomeister. Bring us another two bottles of your best wine."

The lady went out, and I seized the opportunity to warn Hippel not to launch into conversations that might betray his incognito.

"What do you take me for, Ludwig?" he cried, furiously. "Know that I'm no more a burgomeister than you are, and the proof is that my papers are in order."

He took out his passport. The hostess came back.

"Madame," he said. did your burgomeister resemble this description?" Je read: "Medium forehead, large nose, thick lips, gray eyes, tall stature, brown hair."

"Very nearly," said the lady, "except that he was bald."

Hippel passed his hand through his hair, crying: "The burgomeister was bald, and no one would dare to sustain that I'm bald."

The hostess thought that my friend was mad, but as he stood up while paying the bill, she said nothing.

When we arrived on the threshold, Hippel turned to me and said in a brusque tone: "Let's go."

"One moment, my dear friend," I replied. "First you're going to take me to the cemetery where the burgomeister is at rest."

At that proposition, his face fell. "No!" he cried. "No, never! You want to precipitate me into the claws of Satan, then? Me, stand on my own grave! That would be contrary to all the laws of nature...you can't think so, Ludwig!"

"Calm down, Hippel," I said. "At this moment you're under the empire of invisible powers...they're extending their nets over you, so delicate and so transparent that no one can perceive them. It requires an effort to dissolve them; it's necessary to restore the burgomeister's soul, and that's only possible at his tomb. Do you want to be the thief of that poor soul? It would be a manifest theft, and I know your delicacy too well to suppose you capable of such an infamy."

Those invincible arguments convinced him.

"Oh well," he said, "yes, I'll have the courage to trample underfoot those remains, of which I've taken away the heavier half. Please God, let such a theft not be imputed to me. Follow me, Ludwig; I'll take you.

He walked at a rapid, precipitate pace. holding his hat in his hand, his hair scattered, waving his arms, stretching his legs like an unfortunate accomplishing the final act of despair, and stimulating himself in order not to weaken.

Firstly we traversed several small streets, and then the bridge of a mill, the heavy wheel of which was stirring up a white sheet of foam; then we followed a path that crossed a meadow, and we finally arrived, behind the village, at a rather high wall covered in moss and clematis. It was the cemetery.

In one of the corners the ossuary stood, in the other a neat house surrounded by a small garden.

Hippel launched himself into the room. The gravedigger was there; along the walls there were wreaths of immortelles. The gravedigger was sculpting a cross; this work absorbed him to such an extent that he stood up, frightened, when Hippel appeared. My comrade fixed him with a stare that must have frightened him, because he remained utterly nonplussed for several seconds.

"My worthy man," I said to him, "Take us to the grave of the burgomeister."

"There's no need," cried Hippel. "I know it." Without waiting for a response, he opened the door that led to the cemetery and started to run like an insensate, leaping over the graves and shouting: "It's there! There! We have it!" Evidently, the spirit of Evil had possessed him, for as he passed he knocked over a white cross crowned with roses—the cross of a little child!

The gravedigger and I followed him at a distance.

The cemetery was vast. Thick, lush dark green grass rose to three feet above ground. The cypresses dragged their long tresses on the ground, but what struck me immediately was a trellis backed up against the wall and covered with a magnificent vine so laden with grapes that the clusters were falling on top of one another.

While walking I said to the gravedigger: "You have a vine there that must bring you a good deal."

"Oh, Monsieur," he said, in a plaintive tone, "that vine doesn't bring me anything much. No one wants my grapes; what comes from death returns to death."

I stared at the man.. He had a false gaze; a diabolical smile contracted his lips and his cheeks. I didn't believe what he was saying to me.

We arrived at the burgomeister's tomb. It was near the wall. Opposite, there was a, enormous vine cep, swollen with juice, which seemed stuffed with it, like a boa constrictor. Its roots doubtless penetrated all the way to the depth of the coffins and disputed their prey with the worms. Furthermore, its grapes were a violet red, while those of the other ceps were a slightly vermilion blue.

Hippel, leaning on the vine, seemed a little calmer.

"You don't eat these grapes," I said to the gravedigger, "but you sell them."

He went pale and made a negative gesture.

"You sell them to the village of Welche, and I can name you the inn at which people drink your wine," I exclaimed. "It's the Fleur-de-lis inn."

The gravedigger trembled in every limb. Hippel wanted to hurl himself at the wretch's throat; it required my intervention to prevent him from tearing the man to pieces.

"Scoundrel," he said, "you've made me drink the essence of your burgomeister. I've lost my personality!"

Suddenly, however, a luminous idea crossed his mind. He turned to the wall and adopted a certain favorite attitude of Flemish painters.

"God be praised!" he said, turning back to me. "I've returned the burgomeister's soul to the earth. I'm relieved of an enormous weight."

The next day we continued on our way; my friend Hippel had recovered his natural gaiety.

Gérard de Nerval was the name employed in later life by Gérard de Labrunie (1808-1855), who began his literary career as a translator of German Romantic texts, before becoming a poet and fiction writer of considerable repute, most notably with the novellas Sylvie *(1853) and the posthumously-published* Aurélia *(1855), signaled by André Breton as one of the key precursors of Symbolism. Prone to nervous breakdowns and always fearful of going mad, he was eventually found hanged in circumstances sufficiently strange to lead some of his friends, including X. B. Saintine, to deny that it was a case of suicide. "Le monstre vert" originally appeared as "Le Diable vert, légende parisienne" in* La Silhouette, *7 octobre 1849 before being reprinted under the more familiar title in* Contes et facéties *(1852). "The Green Monster" is original to the present volume.*[9]

Gérard de Nerval: *The Green Monster*

I. The Devil's Château

I am going to talk about one of the oldest inhabitants of Paris; it was once known as "the devil Vauvert"—from which results the popular sayings "it's the devil Vauvert!" and "Go to the devil Vauvert!" which is to say: "Go take a walk in the Elysian Fields."

Porters generally say "It's the "It's the *diable aux vers*" to refer to a very different place.[10] That signifies that it is necessary to pay dearly for the commissions with which they are charged. But that is, of course, a vicious and corrupt locution, like several others familiar to the Parisian people.

The devil Vauvert is essentially an inhabitant of Paris, where it has resided for many centuries, if historian can be believed. Sauval, Félicien, Sainte-Foix and Dulaure have recounted its escapades at length.

It seems to have initially inhabited the Château de Vauvert, which was situated in the location occupied today by the joyful Bal de la Chartreuse, at the extremity of the Luxembourg Gardens, opposite the grounds of the Observatoire, in the Rue d'Enfer.

That château, of sad renown, the ruins of which became attached to a convent of Chartreux, in which Jean de la Lune, the nephew of the Antipope Benoît

---

[9] Available from Black Coat Press: *The Prince of Fools*, ISBN 978-1-61227-872-8.

[10] The wordplay linking *"le diable aux vers"* [the devil of the worms, or the devil of poetry] to "the diable Vauvert" does not translate, the phonetic similarity between vert [green] and vers [worms, or poetry, depending on context] being non-existent in their English equivalents.

XII died in 1414. Jean de la Lune had been suspected of having relations with a certain devil, who might have been the familiar spirit of the former Château de Vauvert, each of those feudal edifies having its own, as everyone knows.

Historians have not left us anything precise regarding that interesting phase.

The devil Vauvert occasioned further mention in the epoch of Louis XIII. For a long time, every evening, loud noises had been heard in a house constructed from the debris of the dormer convent, the owners of which had been absent for several years. That frightened the neighbors considerably. They went to inform the lieutenant of police, who sent a few archers.

Those soldiers were astonished to hear the clinking of glasses mingled with strident laughter. It was thought at first the forgers were having an orgy, and, judging their number from the intensity of the sound, they went to fetch reinforcements. It was judged once again, however, that the squad was insufficient; so sergeant wanted to take his men into that lair, where it seemed that the noise of an entire army could be heart.

Finally, in the morning, a sufficient body of troops arrived; they penetrated into the house, but they found nothing there. The sunlight dissipated the shades.

They searched all day long; then they conjectured that the noise was coming from the catacombs, which are situated, as everyone knows, beneath that quarter. They got ready to penetrate thereto, but while the police were making their preparations dusk fell again, and the noise recommenced, louder than ever.

This time, no one any longer dared go down, because it was evident that there was nothing in the cellar but bottles, and that it must be the Devil that was making them dance. They therefore contented themselves with occupying the street and asking the clergy to say prayers.

The clergy supplied an abundance of orisons, and they even sent holy water through the cellars' ventilation shafts by means of syringes.

The noise persisted.

II. The Sergeant

For a whole week a crowd of Parisians obstructed the vicinity incessantly, frightening themselves and demanding news.

Finally, one of the provost's sergeants, bolder than the others, offered to penetrate into the accursed cellar, in return for a pension that would revert, in the case of his decease, to a dressmaker named Margot. He was a brave man, more amorous than credulous. He adored that dressmaker, who as a very well-dressed and economical individual—one might even say a trifle miserly—who had not wanted to marry a simple sergeant devoid of any fortune. By gaining the pension, the sergeant became a different man.

Encouraged by that prospect, he exclaimed that he did not believe in God or the Devil, and that he would reckon with the noise.

"What do you believe in, then?" asked one of his companions.

"I believe," he replied, "in the criminal lieutenant and the Provost of Paris."

That was saying too much in very few words.

He took his saber in his teeth, a pistol in each hand, and ventured into the stairway.

The most extraordinary spectacle awaited him when he reached the floor of the cellar.

All the bottles were delivering themselves to a hectic saraband, performing the most graceful steps. The green labels represented men and the red labels represented women.

There was even an orchestra there, established on the wine-racks. The empty bottles were resonating like wind instruments, broken bottles like cymbals and triangles, and cracked bottles rendering something like the penetrating harmony of violins.

The sergeant, who had drunk a few glasses before undertaking the expedition, seeing nothing there but bottles, felt greatly reassured, and started dancing himself in imitation.

Then, increasingly encouraged by the gaiety and charm of the spectacle, he picked up an amiable bottle with a long neck, a pale Bordeaux, it appeared, carefully labeled in red, and pressed it amorously to his heart.

Frenetic laughter burst forth on all sides. The sergeant, intrigued, dropped the bottle, which shattered into a thousand pieces.

The dance stopped; cries of fright were heard from every corner of the cellar, and the sergeant sensed his hair stand on end on seeing that the spilled wine appeared to be forming a pool of blood.

The body of a naked woman, whose blonde hair spread out on the floor, soaked by damp, was extended at his feet.

The sergeant would not have been frightened by the Devil in person, but that sight filled him with horror; thinking that, after all, he had to make a report of his mission, he seized a green label that seemed to be sniggering in front of him, and cried: "At least I'll have one!"

An immense snigger replied to him.

Meanwhile, he had reached the staircase, and, showing the bottle to his comrades, he shouted: "Here's the evil spirit. You're chicken" (he used a stronger expression) "not to have dared to go down there!"

His irony was bitter. The archers ran into the cellar, where nothing was found but a broken bottle of Bordeaux. The rest were in place.

The archers deplored the fate of the broken bottle, but, brave henceforth, they all came back, each with a bottle in his hand.

They were given permission to drink them.

The provost's sergeant said: "For myself, I'll keep mine for the day of my wedding."

He could not be refused the promised pension; he married the dressmaker, and..."

Do you suppose they had lots of children?

They only had one.

III. What Followed

On the day of the sergeant's wedding, which took place at the Râpée, he put the famous bottle with the green label between himself and his wife, and affected only to pour the wine for her and for him.

The bottle was as green as nausea, the wine as red as blood.

Nine months later, the dressmaker gave birth to a little monster, entirely green, with red horns on the forehead.

Now go, young women, go and dance at the Chartreuse, on the site of the Château Vauvert!

However, the child grew, if not in virtue, at least in size. Two things troubled his parents: his green color and a caudal appendage that seemed art first only to be a prolongation of the coccyx, but gradually took on the appearance of a veritable tail.

Scholars were consulted, who declared that it was impossible to perform an amputation without compromising the life of the child. They added that it was a very rare case, but examples of which could be found in Herodotus and Pliny the Younger. No one in those days could foresee the theory of Fourier.[11]

As for the color, that was attributed to a predominance of the bilious system. Several caustic substances were tried, however, in order to attenuate the excessively pronounced hue of the epidermis, and after numerous lotions and frictions, they soon succeeded in rendering it bottle-green, then sea-green, and finally apple-green. For a moment, the skin seemed to white completely, but nightfall brought back the tint.

The sergeant and the dressmaker could not be consoled for the chagrins that the little monster caused them, who became increasingly headstrong, bad-tempered and malicious. The melancholy they experienced led them to a vice all too common among people of their sort; they took to drink.

But the sergeant never wanted to drink any but wine labeled in red, and his wife wine labeled in green.

Every time the sergeant was dead drunk, he saw in his sleep the bloody woman whose apparition had frightened him in the caller after they had broken the bottle.

That woman said to him: "Why did you press me to your heart and then immolate me...me, who loved you so much?"

---

[11] The utopian philosopher Charles Fourier suggested in one of his futurological essays that one day the human race might develop useful prehensile tails.

Every time the sergeant's wife had indulged too much in the green label, she saw a large devil of frightful aspect appear in her sleep, who said to her: "Why are you astonished to see me, since you drank from the bottle? Am I not the father of your child?"

O mystery!

When he reached the age of thirteen, the child disappeared.

His parents, inconsolable, continued drinking, but they no longer saw a renewal of the terrible apparitions that had haunted their slumber.

IV. Moral

It was thus that the sergeant was punished for his impiety, and the dressmaker for her avarice.

V. What Became of the Green monster.

Nobody was ever able to find out.

Paul Féval (1816-1877) became a feuilletoniste *during the first wave of commercial success of newspaper serials, in the mid-1840s, and survived the difficult aftermath of the 1848 Revolution to become one of the most prolific and successful* feuilletonistes *of the Second Empire, most famous for historical adventures stories such as* Le Bossu *(1857), many of them set in his native Bretagne. He played a significant pioneering role in the development of generic crime fiction in* Jean Diable *(1862) and the* Habits Noirs *series (1863-1875). His supernatural fiction tends to the grotesque, often developing a species of slapstick horror-comedy highly original at the time. His eldest son, who signed himself Paul Féval* fils, *also became a prolific writer of popular fiction. "Le Chevalier Ténèbre" first appeared in* Le Musée des Familles *in avril-mai 1860.*[12]

Paul Féval: *Knightshade*

I. One of Archbishop de Quélen's Soirées

Dinner had been taken at the Château de Conflans, the home of His Grace the Archbishop of Paris. It was not merely a priests' banquet; there were women present. Along the river bank on the road to Charenton white dresses could be seen among the green lawns.

I do not know why that part of the Parisian countryside seems so sad. Are they not charming, those meadows where the Marne arrives to marry its waters with those of the Seine? Wine is gaiety, it is said; how is it that the ocean of wine that floods the town of Bercy does not enliven those heart-rending pastures in the slightest? Bacchus, whose praises are sung by our drunken poets, is there; can he not brighten up those mournful horizons? The Seine cannot contrive a smile while passing between them; the very trees seem sad. Ivry is sullen and

---

[12] Available from Black Coat Press: *Anne of the Isles*, ISBN 978-1-932983-92-0; *Bel Demonio*, ISBN 978-1-61227-708-0; *The Cadet Gang*, ISBN 978-1-935558-45-3; *The Companions of the Silence*, ISBN 978-1-61227-706-6; *The Companions of the Treasure*, ISBN 978-1-934543-26-9; *Heart of Steel*, ISBN 978-1-935558-05-7; *The Invisible Weapon*, ISBN 978-1-932983-80-7; *John Devil*, ISBN 978-1-932983-15-9; *Knightshade*, ISBN 978-0-9740711-4-5; *The Parisian Jungle*, ISBN 978-1-934543-03-0; *Revenants* ISBN 978-1-932983-70-8; *'Salem Street*, ISBN 978-1-932983-46-3; *The Sword Swallower*, ISBN 978-1-61227-024-1; *Vampire City*, ISBN 978-0-9740711-6-9; *The Vampire Countess*, ISBN 978-0-9740711-5-2; *The Wandering Jew's Daughter*, ISBN 978-1-932983-30-2; *The White Wolf*, ISBN 978-1-61227-832-2; *Gentlemen of the Night & Captain Phantom* (stage plays), ISBN 978-1-932983-81-4.

sulky on one bank; on the other the park—which is so beautiful, in spite of the dismal pleasure-gardens on its edge, that its lawns should extend gloriously in the sunlight—is sulky and sullen behind its grey walls, at the gate of which two sickly lions devoid of spirit or courage wrestle two boars, which yawn as they defend themselves.

It is an exit. Parisian storytellers and chroniclers find the melancholy zone which starts at Charenton and extends as far as Bicêtre an ideal setting for their werewolves, brigands and phantoms. That flat country was a little less ugly in the past than it is today but it had a worse reputation in those days. As your aged uncles will tell you, nights thereabouts were full of horrors. Sabbats were held—big ones—not far from the present site of Ivry railway station; the cemetery of the same name did not have a single grave whose stone could keep it sealed, whether it was made of modern plaster or ancient cement. All the marble tombstones would raise themselves up at midnight, and whenever the darkness was briefly penetrated by the faint rays of the veiled moon, a long procession of the emergent dead could be seen to move slowly and silently upriver towards the monasteries of Vitry.

Archbishop de Quélen,[13] as everyone knows, was not only a very eminent prelate but a perfect gentleman. His generosity towards the poor, an established historical fact, restrained his taste for luxurious and grandiose display, but his aristocratic heritage would not permit him to shut himself off from society. His receptions were carefully planned, especially those involving his closest friends. All shades of Royalist opinion would find an open and level field there, providing a lively opposition to the Restoration government in the very bosom of the House of Lords.

The events of our story took place in 1825; the Archbishop was then in his late forties, at the very height of his power as a primate of the Church of France and as a politician. In order that the glory surrounding him should lack for nothing, the Academy had also opened its doors to him.

This prelate—whose home some miserable wretches, who insulted the genuine people in taking the name of "the people", came to burn the day after the Revolution of July 1830—followed a well-known custom. He had made it a rule that after each of his receptions he would distribute to the poor a sum equal to the cost of his feast. I have heard it said by men who have never given anything to anyone that he would have done better to give twice as much and not receive visitors at all—well, perhaps. It would be necessary, in order to put together a jury capable of judging these good souls, to take immediate exception to all incapacity, all envy and all hatred. That would be hard work, and the pre-

---

[13] Hyacinthe-Louis de Quélen (1778-1839) was a peer of the realm as well as Archbishop of Paris, a post to which he was appointed in 1821. Relatively liberal by the standards of the time and place, he attempted unsuccessfully to obtain an amnesty for the Revolutionaries who were still in exile.

liminary hearing for the selection of the jury could take a long time. I said "perhaps" because although it is good to give, to *do* good is often better, because the eventual result is greater. The Lord Bishop de Quélen's feasts were productive, from the viewpoint of his benevolence. They rarely ended without misfortune having deducted its tithe from their serious and noble pleasures.

That was not all, however; Archbishop de Quélen also had another custom of which the Faubourg Saint-Germain and the court sometimes complained bitterly. He was a committed patron, always surrounded by an army of protégés, and he fought for these protégés with a courage that was as meritorious as it was redoubtable. His banquets were the peaceful tournaments where he broke lances on behalf of youth ardent to succeed, or old age eager to return after injury to the battle of life. I could name men in the highest places who would have good cause to remember the feasts of the Lord Bishop de Quélen.

It was an evening in September, in the same year that had seen the coronation of Charles X and the prodigious enthusiasm of Paris for the prince that Paris would, so soon afterwards, condemn to death in his absence. The weather was stormy and oppressively warm. Although night had begun to fall—dinner had been served at three o'clock, as was the fashion of the time—no one thought of going back indoors. The park was a welcome refuge from the torrid heat. The shade of the tall trees was fairly cool, and a light breeze blew fitfully from the low and ponderous river, trying to stir their leaves.

The majority of the guests had come together again in the vast hall of verdure that was then the pride of the district, although the railway line to Lyon has since destroyed it. The Archbishop, who was by birth the Comte de Quélen, was originally of Breton descent; he belonged to the family that descended from the ducal houses of Aiguillon, Chaulnes and La Vauguyon; he was related to the Chateaubriants, the Rohans, The Dreuxes, the Guébriants, the La Bourdonnayes, the Coislins and the Goulaines. The gathering of all these names at the château, that evening, might have been a reunion of the general staff of François de Bretagne, or the court of Duchess Anne.[14]

Such is the mysterious power of certain places that within that brilliant circle, in the glades where important theological questions had been debated from the days of François de Harlay, founder of the Château de Conflans, to those of the His Lordship de Talleyrand-Périgord, the predecessor of the present archbishop, the talk was all of brigands, werewolves and phantoms. To the great amusement of the women—and of the men too—marvelous tales of revenants were told, in the spirit of pure theater. On the stage where the audience had reassembled, the narrators "did their turns," as actors say, pointing their fingers this

---

[14] François II was the last Duc de Bretagne when that region was still independent from France; his daughter Anne de Beaujeu became one of the most powerful women in Europe served as regent for the French king Charles VII.

way and that at the very fields that had served as scenery for their supernatural dramas.

The crowd, as always, included both believers and skeptics. Under the Restoration, the Faubourg Saint-Germain had its little philosophical corner, and we know of more than one marquis of that era whose life was spent in imitation of Monsieur de Voltaire. In the matter of werewolves, incredulity is understandable, as it is with regard to phantoms, but brigands! That requires explanation. The skeptics on the subject of brigandage took refuge in a question of chronology. According to them, the day of the authentic brigand—the romantic, picturesque, dramatic brigand—was done. The present era only had mere thieves; by way of recompense, however, the same skeptics contended that it did have a truly remarkable quantity of them.

Now, I defy you to take a ring of secular trees, about two or three hundred meters from an old château, and to place thereabouts, on a dark and stormy night, an assembly of thirty people discussing horrific or mystical subjects, without a kind of vague fear leaching into the conversational mix. I shall make a significant concession, granting you two levels of incredulity—indeed, I will go even further, if you wish and grant you unanimity of skepticism, including the narrator himself, provided that he is skilful, and I will still bet against you, so certain am I of what I say: the frisson of fear will arrive.

The frisson always arrives. It is not necessary, in the final analysis, for anyone in a circle affected by such a spirit to be a believer or victim of superstition. The frisson requires nothing but a powerful imagination. At the appointed moment, while the ordinarily timid restrain a tremor, the strongly imaginative suffer nervous attacks and become faint. The "strongly imaginative" are typified by the brave boy who sings at the top of his voice in the darkness in order to allay his fears.

Among the more strongly imaginative members of the party on that evening at the Château de Conflans was a beautiful woman, very spiritual and very eloquent, whom we shall call the Princess de Montfort (because the actual names and titles of the persons in question must be protected; the princess, having a leading role in our play, must be given the benefit of appearing incognito). She was there with her younger son, the Marquis de Lorgàres, a tall, pale and handsome adolescent, who had been destined for the Church but had hesitated over his vocation. The Princess, who adored her younger son, affected a certain severity in her treatment of him, concealing her approval of the new route that he wished to take: the young marquis was ambitious to become a diplomat. The Princess was a slightly eccentric woman, but she was blessed with great intelligence and a good heart.

His Grace the Archbishop expressed no opinion on the matter of the supernatural or the persistence of brigandage, and seemed preoccupied with other matters. There were fors and againsts. His Lordship the Bishop Frayssinous of

Hermopolis,[15] who was then the Minister of Ecclesiastical Affairs, was an enthusiastic believer in the supernatural and had already recounted some fine tales. He was just beginning another when the Princess interrupted:

"It's getting cold. Shouldn't we go back indoors?"

It would be inaccurate to speak of laughter bursting out. Laughter, especially of a mocking kind, does not "burst out" above a certain social level—but the Devil is everywhere and he never loses an opportunity. There was, in response to the words "it's getting cold", a gentle murmur which tickled the ears of the Princess sufficiently to compel her to cry out: "Don't think that I'm afraid! Let's go!" The young and beautiful Comtesse de Maillé got up and came to drape a summer cloak over her aunt's shoulders.

"Auntie," she said, "let's tremble for a little longer—it's so nice!"

And everyone, in unison, cried: "Yes! Your story, My Lord Bishop!"

Instead of answering the general plea, the Bishop of Hermopolis remained silent for a moment. Then, in a restrained voice whose altered tone caused more than one heart to beat faster, he asked abruptly: "Are you not here, Monsieur von Altenheimer?"

There was another moment of silence. The moon displayed half her face between two storm-clouds that were as solid and heavy as slugs of lead. The Princess called her son to her side.

"Indeed I am," a deep baritone voice replied, profound and full of metallic vibrations. "I am here, My Lord."

The person who had spoken was unseen. His voice seemed to come from the trunk of a huge dead elm whose leafless branches took fantastic form in the sudden moonlight.

"Come closer Baron, I beg you," the Bishop replied, "and relate to us, in accordance with the Galland formula, one of those tales that you tell so well."

A man of tall and slender stature immediately moved into the middle of the circle. It seemed to the Princess, in the grip of her powerful imagination, that he had sprung from the earth, so sudden was his appearance. Nothing in the world could have renewed her determination to retreat to the château.

The light of the moon fell directly upon the newcomer, and it is a fact that everyone saw something extraordinary in him. That may also have been a result of the general predisposition. No one knew him; no one had seen him at dinner. He was doubtless one of those who had been invited purely for the after-dinner discussion; several other members of the audience were in the same situation. His costume, which was black from top to toe, was very formal, resembling that of the other layman present. Why, then, use the word *extraordinary?* It was a mystery, quite inexplicable. Save for the pallor of his long Teutonic features, he

---

[15] Denis-Luc, Comte de Frayssinous (1765-1841) was Louis XVIII's court preacher; we was appointed as Bishop of Hermopolis and elected as a member of the Académie Française soon after the succession of Charles X.

was like all those who surrounded him, and yet the word was appropriate. The company was dumbstruck, as if a trapdoor had opened to allow the passage of a fantastic individual. The moon scarcely had time to illuminate him before it was hidden by a large cloud and obscurity enveloped him again.

"I am at His Lordship's disposal," said the baritone voice.

"That is most kind," replied the Bishop of Hermopolis, adding as he took the newcomer's hand: "Ladies, I have the honor of presenting to you the privy councilor Baron von Altenheimer, director general of the police of His Majesty the King of Wurtemburg..."

The privy councilor must have bowed, I suppose, but no one saw it.

"...And elder brother," the illustrious Bishop continued, "of Monsignor von Altenheimer, prelate of Rome, Chamberlain to Our Holy Father..."

"Here present," put in a tenor voice, as soft as a note from a flute. That tenor voice reassured the beautiful women a little.

"What kind of story does My Lord Bishop desire?" the baritone voice asked. "Phantoms or brigands? We have both of them in the Black Forest."

"Phantoms!" half the circle voted.

"Brigands!" opined the Princess, under the influence of her strong imagination.

The fearful, on the other hand, eager for a fine time of mortification by terror, demanded: "Vampires!"

Whereupon His Grace the Archbishop de Quélen, with a mildness in which a light note of irony was perceptible, said: "One could make an agreeable mixture out of all these good things."

"That's it! That's it!" cried the Bishop of Hermopolis, in the voice of a man who is certain of the virtue of what he has produced. "Baron, these ladies desire a tale to make their hair stand on end, in which there is a phantom, a brigand and a vampire all at the same time!"

"Hilarious," said the soft tenor voice, "The tale of the brothers Ténèbre is precisely that."

"Yes," the baritone replied, at the utmost depth of its range, "you're right, Benedict: the tale of the Ténèbre brothers!"

"The name is well-chosen!" murmured the Princess, suppressing a giggle while her hand closed convulsively upon the arm of her son, the Marquis de Lorgàres.

"The name is not chosen at all!" replied the Monsignor, his tone a trifle piqued. "Everyone in Germany has heard of the Ténèbre brothers."

"And everyone in Paris will have heard of them soon," said the privy councilor quietly, as if he were speaking in spite of himself.

Even if the name had not been chosen for effect, one could nevertheless say that it was as appropriate as any that might have been invented. The circle drew closer. This was not included in the program of the soirée, which would culminate in a benefit concert, but it was worth ten times as much as the entire banquet. Chance gave to His Lordship's guests an unexpected performance, a delightful surprise--and, although no one could explain exactly why, it is certain that the hearts of our beautiful ladies were considerably stirred by emotion and alarm.

Baron von Altenheimer resumed an oratorical tone that served to emphasize his German accent. "Your excellencies, and most illustrious persons, my brother and I are strangers in the capital of France, and we are both charged with a difficult mission. We desire to be worthy of the generous welcome that has been extended to us, and of the protection that we have been promised. My brother Benedict will sing some traditional Westphalian songs for you this evening, and a few original Christmas ballads. I have a voice that is good enough for the chorus but not for solo performance, so I am glad to have found an opportunity to make myself equally agreeable.

"Historical legends and other traditional tales featuring the supernatural are so very abundant in our homeland that I would have had a thousand to choose from in attempting to satisfy your curiosity. I prefer, however, to set aside our popular tales and tell you a true story of the same kind, based in my personal experience and that of my brother. Here, a little while ago, I heard some very powerful people of both sexes discussing age-old controversies say: *There are no more specters.* A very illustrious lady exclaimed: *There are no more authentic brigands; the times of Rob Roy, Schinderhannes, Zawn, Schubry, Mandrin and even Cartouche are gone. We no longer have anything but thieves!* I admit that we have an enormous number of thieves, but I am compelled to affirm that we also have brigands. Leaving aside the successors of Fra Diavolo in southern Italy, Hungary, Bohemia and the southern provinces of Austria still produce bandits fully worthy of that name. On the other hand, specters continue to lift up the stones of their graves just as they did in the past: nothing changes in that sphere. I have seen vampires in the region of Belgrade and phantoms in our own cemetery at Tübingen."

We are relying here upon our memory, and we have made every effort to reproduce Baron von Altenheimer's preamble word for word. The manner of his delivery was remarkably well-suited to his style. To begin with, there was in both a depth of naivety, which imparted an emphasis to certain expressions. On the surface, there were unequivocal signs of knowledge: a literary mixture of the philosophical and the scientific; the overall impression, however, was one of oratory pretension, with a distinct whiff of charlatanry, as serious as the black robe of a professor.

His Lordship the Bishop de Quélen leant towards the ear of his neighbor and said to him: "That's Germany."

The judgment is not without profundity. That is Germany, indeed: that old wives' wisdom; that bourgeois philosophy; that naive predisposition to make a discourse of what Pagliacci called *patter*; all of it accompanied, supported and perhaps saved by a sort of nobility, which may deserve the name of truth. The ladies would not have made any such analysis, but the Baron's preface pleased them regardless. The session turned into a public lecture in the German manner, concerning phantoms and brigands—the two most frightful and interesting things in the world.

The propitious moon, as if to join the party, emerged in full from behind its cloud to muffle the dread that might have prevented us from paying full attention. The illuminated glade gained a sort of gaiety without losing its poetry.

The tall, black-clad German could be seen distinctly now, his two wide eyes shining in his long pale face. His younger brother, the monsignor, stood beside him; he was shorter and plumper, wearing a garment that was not quite a frock-coat and not quite a cassock, after the fashion of the priests of Rome.

The elder brother wore a badge of office as florid as that of any privy councilor in the tales of Hoffmann. The younger wore no decoration at all, save for a long chain of polished steel, which passed around his neck above the dark collar of his coat and dangled by his right side. On the end of the chain was a rectangular object, also of polished steel, which seemed to contain a breviary or a missal.

All around them, the circle of listeners emerged from the shadows: heads handsome or venerable, foreheads furrowed, blonde tresses, avid eyes, mouths agape...

"Most illustrious friends," Baron von Altenheimer continued...

II. Chandor Castle

"In 1821 there was a magyar family living in the ancient Chandor Castle near the banks of the river Tisza, not far from the city of Szeged—which is some seven leagues around and has eighty thousand inhabitants. All magyars are aristocrats, but these were princes of the house of Baszin, whose founder had befriended Matthias Corvinus, the Charlemagne of the Danube nations.

"Chrétien Baszin, Prince Jacobyi, possessed an immense fortune, evidence of which was met throughout the land; he had thousands of peasant serfs, including Serbs, Czechs, Croats and Walachians. His estate was as big as a province and extended as far as that isle of vineyards surrounded by a sea of maize where Turkeve harvests the amber liquid of its royal vintages.

"The massive walls of Chandor Castle, situated on the edge of an oak-forest, overlooked the Tisza. Its four large thickset towers bulged at the top like the turbans of the Turks who had constructed them in olden times. From the tops of the towers one could see the minarets of Szeged in the distance, beyond the vast cornfields. Its pasturelands fed eight hundred horses and twice as many cattle: proud Hungarian beasts with pearly hides and widespread white horns. The prince was as generous as he was magnificent: fifty places were always set at the enormous square table that was placed every day when the bell sounded noon on a silver dais in a cedarwood-paved courtyard beneath the open sky.

"You, ladies and gentleman, are the happy citizens of the most civilized nation on the globe, but you probably do not have an accurate idea of the aristocratic life in certain other countries that you call barbarian. There, we did not have—I say *we* because I have spent many years with the prince in Chandor Castle—all the refinements of your spotless, white and dainty French dinner services, and perhaps we lacked the fine delicacies of the portable luxury, if I may call it that, that you carry in your luggage on your tours of Europe, but we lived in a grand and luxurious style nevertheless, among all the proud display of absolute power.

"It is for such as them, the last high barons, that the purest juice of your Bordeaux grapes in carefully extracted; it is for them that the most piquant spirit of your champagnes is trapped. The American Indians, it is said, sell their gold for small quantities of whisky; you sell your nectars for small quantities of gold, and it is, alas, only rarely that a French gullet is permitted a taste of those astonishing ambrosias. To taste your wines you must go to Russia or the far shore of the Danube. Chevet sends his fresh vegetables and preserves, Lesage his pastries; we have everything that you have—and we have, in addition, the noble game of wild boars and your champagne whisked in the crushed pulp of our water-melons.

"Thus far, there is no hint of menace in my tale; but the sky is blue above our heads and the moon is bright; nevertheless, the storm is there, and it will break soon enough. Prince Jacobyi did not know the extent of his fortune. Once a month his stewards brought him their accounts, which he accumulated, unread, in his library. Vast as it was, his library gradually became cluttered, its tiled floor hidden beneath untidy heaps of paper. Each month he signed, unread, a warrant addressed to his banker in Pest, in order to obtain money by means of a mortgage.

"'Such as they would have to rob me prodigiously,' he would say, 'if they were ever to get to the bottom of my inheritance!' And when he looked at his daughter Lenore, a sweet-natured golden-haired angel, he would exclaim: 'I defy anyone to prevent this one from being the richest heiress for a hundred leagues around!'

"That was what he said, and truer words were never spoken by any man alive; but he had two stewards in his house and a banker in the city of Pest. As the proverb says, one steward is enough to devour an estate.

"Lenore was fourteen years old. It was already obvious that she was as beautiful as her mother, whose smiling portrait illuminated the house. Her life was solely devoted to learning; in those barbarian lands young women are highly and extensively educated. She had only one friend in the entire world: a girl of her own age—also a Magyar and an aristocrat, but poor—with whom she had been raised. Lenore had recently experienced the first tragedy of her life: Efflam, her companion, had left her to visit her father and mother, who lived near the border, not far from Belgrade.

"One evening, two Walachian gypsies arrived at the castle. They belonged to a wandering tribe that had camped in the banate of Timisoara on the other side of the Tisza. They had rowed across the river, which flows as fast as the Rhone and is three times as wide as the Seine, although it is only a tributary of the royal Danube. The night was just like this one, and I remember that the setting moon was continually appearing and disappearing behind black clouds so thick that its gleam could not tint their fringes with silver. The tortuous mirror of the waters of the Tisza were soon to be plunged into the profoundest obscurity. The storm was in the south-east, the direction from which the menacing clouds were moving. The two wretches asked for hospitality.

"Lenore had been sad since the departure of Efflam, and the prince—who adored her—said to her: 'These people know how to juggle and do conjuring tricks. Would you like them to come in to entertain you?'

"Lenore shook her head languidly to signal her refusal, but when a servant said that the tribe had come from Belgrade her eyes lit up.

"'Bring them in,' she instructed.

"They were two brothers, the older still young, the younger very young indeed. They gave their names as Mikhael and Solim. Mikhael was the taller, and his features gave every evidence of his origin among those lost children of a forgotten civilization who are strangers in every nation of the world, having nether law nor God: the Egyptians of Scotland, the bohemians of France, the gitanos of Spain, the zingari of Italy. Solim, by contrast, had a pale fresh face, blue eyes and blond hair.

"The prince ordered them to entertain Lenore. Solim sang the strange melodies of the Moldavian lands, accompanying himself on his rounded guitar with two steel strings. Mikhael performed the dances of Yataghan, and both of them juggled with wine-glasses, bottles and knives.

"Lenore only yawned, and the prince made a gesture of dismissal.

"'Hospodar,' said Mikhael, instead of obeying, 'wouldn't your daughter like to hear a good story?'

"His impudent eyes were fixed upon Lenore, who blushed and seemed ill-at-ease. The prince knitted his brows and opened his mouth to call for his servants, but the gentle voice of Lenore stopped him.

"'Father,' she said, 'I would like to know...'

"Mikhael immediately took a step towards the girl, threw his cap upon the floor and knelt upon it, while Solim remained standing in the middle of the room, his eyes lowered and his arms crossed upon his breast. Mikhael reached out, demanding Lenore's hand, which she offered to him in spite of herself. He examined it minutely for a long time, speaking periodically in an unknown language. These words were addressed to Solim, who still stood motionless in the middle of the room; they seemed to make an extraordinary impression on him. His limbs trembled, the veins in his forehead swelled up, and the hair on his head shook. It was as if the pythoness of old were on her tripod.

"Mikhael had examined the hand, but it was Solim who played the oracle, saying: 'Hospodar! Woe is mine, who must cry woe! I see through the night, in the distance, the vampire Ange whose eyes are upon your daughter...'

"The prince burst out laughing, while Lenore grew pale.

"'Are there still vampires?' cried the prince, who was still amused.

"Mikhael returned to stand beside his brother and put his hand over Solim's mouth. The prince's face clouded over. Thumping the table with his hand, he said: 'For my part, I want to know! And remember that the Chief Magistrate of Szeged would not trouble himself at all about a couple of miscreants suspended from the trees in my park!'

"'Lord,' Mikhael relied, slowly, 'you have enough servants to guard your daughter, and you owe us some recompense for having warned you.'

"'Who is this vampire Ange?' asked Lenore, all a-tremble.

"Solim replied, while wiping the sweat from his brow: 'It is the younger of the Ténèbre brothers.'

"'And who are the Ténèbre brothers, knave?' cried the prince.

"'You have the right to abuse me, Lord,' Mikhael replied, drawing himself up to his full height. 'You are strong and I am weak. You also have the right to chase me out into the gathering storm and to have me beaten by your Slovaks, but I have no desire to tell you anything but the truth: the Ténèbre brothers are two of the dead.'

"Lenore huddled close to her father, while Solim repeated, as if he were an echo: 'Two of the dead!'

"The prince took his daughter in his arms and said: 'Explain yourselves.'

"'Hospodar,' Mikhael began, 'are they not dead, and thoroughly dead, who have swayed in the wind for three days and three nights on the gallows? We wander ceaselessly, as you know, in search of the bread that never satisfies our accursed hunger. Between Itàbe and Semlin the gallows of Magnate Karolyi, the High Lieutenant of the Banate of Timisoara, is to be found. We passed close by it on the twenty-seventh of October of last year, three days before the feast of All Hallows. There were two men hanging there, one large and one small. We stripped them bare, and went on our way.

"'On the first of November, as we returned towards Itàbe, heading for Belgrade, we found the two executed men again, still stripped bare, surrounded by a flock of crows. We made camp on the flat area between the gibbet and the Danube.

"'At midnight, we were awakened by the sound of the crows, which were cawing plaintively. There was no moon, but there was another light, brighter and more vivid than moonlight. Where was it coming from? By means of that illumination we saw a huge cloud of fleeing crows. We saw, too, the gibbet, silhouetted in black against the strange aurora, with its two corpses slowly swinging.

"'Two white horses with flowing manes ran right past us, bearing neither bridle nor saddle; they glided like arrows, but we heard not the slightest sound of their hoofbeats. They both halted beneath the gallows, one beneath the taller hanged man, the other beneath the shorter. We saw the four limbs of the executed men move, separating one from another.

"'A sudden glare ripped through the cold November clouds like summer lightning; the two gallows-ropes broke at exactly the same moment and the two cadavers fell as one, legs apart, on to the two horses, which galloped away to the sound of a thunderclap...'

"'See how feverishly my poor, dear Lenore is shivering,' said the prince. 'Take your tall stories to hell with you!'

"Solim lowered his arms, murmuring: 'My brother Mikhael has told the truth.'

"And Lenore, whose pretty white teeth were chattering, said: 'They are amusing me, Father; let them go on.'

"'At Itàbe,' Mikhael continued, 'we asked the names of the two criminals, and were told that they were the Ténèbre brothers: Ténèbre the bandit and Ténèbre the vampire. Now, in the middle of the Great Hungarian Plain there are two graves that you can see for yourselves, one large and one small. Each is covered by a black stone, both of which carry inscriptions in the French language: on the larger one. *Jean Ténèbre, Chevalier*; on the smaller, *Ange Ténèbre, Prêtre*. Educated men say that they are the tombs of two French noblemen who came with many others to help the voivode John Hunyadi defend Christendom against the Turks four hundred years ago. Men who are not educated affirm that for four centuries there has lain beneath these marble slabs an oupire and a vampire: one an eater of human flesh, the other a drinker of human blood.

"'Hospodar, one thing is certain! On many occasions, during the four hundred years, those graves have opened, to the terror and the horror of the surrounding country. Sometimes, two corpses were found beneath the stones, one tall and one short, which gave every indication of recent death: eyes open and shining, blood liquid in the veins, tongues moist and lips red. At other times, the open graves displayed nothing but their emptiness: two black cavities from which the odor of death emerged. It is certain, moreover, that many attempts have been made to destroy these graves: the marble slabs have been broken, the rubble dispersed, the ground leveled—and invariably, when some time has passed, the two black stones resurface beneath the grass or the corn, intact once again, bearing the same funerary inscriptions.

"'Lastly, it is certain—as the registers of the courts testify—that within the last twenty years alone, the brothers Ténèbre have been hanged in a dozen different places in Hungary, and seven times impaled in Turkish territory.

"'But supernatural occurrences make little impact, unless they happened in the recent past. It is a story of the recent past that I want to tell you now. After having wandered for six months in the Turkish lands and traversed part of Serbia, our tribe returned towards Belgrade and camped once again on the banks of the Danube, below Semendria.

"'At midnight, Those of our kin who were keeping watch perceived two lights moving slowly downstream on the surface of the river. They went to investigate, and found two leather bags, one large and one small, drifting in the current, each one bearing a lamp and a placard headed *The Pasha's Justice*. The placard attached to the larger bag also bore the name *Jean Ténèbre*; that of the smaller, the name *Ange Ténèbre*.

"'These two cadavers had been set afloat because the treasury of Belgrade had been looted three days previously and the daughter of the learned treasurer had been found dead in her bed, as white as an alabaster statue. We heard of the theft and the murder later—but when our sentinel came to wake us we saw a long black boat that drifted by itself in the current with no one to steer it. The black boat came abreast of the two dying lights and, a moment later, had turned against the current as swiftly as a bird in flight, and was steered upriver by two men, one tall and one short.

"'We arrived on the following day--the day beginning this very week--at the gates of the town of Petrovaradin in Slavonia...'

"'Where my dear Efflam is, father,' murmured Lenore, offering her face to her father's kiss.

"It was morning,' Mikhael continued. "We pitched our tents in the place reserved for our tribes, under the ramparts of the town between the cemetery and the black ditch watered by the river Drave, into which the bodies of dead animals and executed criminals are carelessly thrown. We thought that there must be a festival in the town, because a great throng of peasants was pressing at the gates. When we were allowed to enter we found that the festival was a public execution by the sword. On the scaffold, we saw two condemned men, one tall and one short. And two names were on everyone's lips: the brothers Ténèbre! Hospodar, the heads fell: I saw it with my own eyes...'

"'The heads fell,' Solim repeated, 'and they rolled across the planks of the scaffold.'

"'And we returned to the camp,' continued Mikhael, 'behind the cart which carried the executioner's work. The two heads and the two bodies were thrown into the ditch in front of us while, on the far side of our tents, a poor child of fifteen years was carried to the cemetery.'

"'Her name! The name of the dead girl!' cried Lenore, as if she had been seized by a heart-rending presentiment.

"'Efflam,' replied Mikhael.

"'Efflam!' repeated Solim, with lowered eyes and flared nostrils.

"Lenore put both hands to her breast and collapsed, deprived of her senses, into her father's arms..."

Baron von Altenheimer paused at this point, and Monsignor Benedict took the opportunity to say, in a very soft voice: "I admire the memory of my dear brother the privy councilor. While he was speaking, it seemed to me that he could still hear that rogue the Chevalier Ténèbre—for no one here can have failed to divine that Mikhael, the pretended gypsy, Mikhael the Romany, was none other than the elder of the brothers Ténèbre."

III. A Wedding in Venice

The Princess much preferred that tale to others, which might have featured French brigands or indigenous phantoms. The overall impression produced on us by a tale will, it must be admitted, depend on the involuntary response of the listeners themselves. This remark is particularly true with respect to fictions calculated to produce fear. No legend or fantastic tale will ever produce in a Parisian drawing-room the shivers that will find you out by a huge log fire, gathered around the enormous fireplace of an ancient château. Specters no longer come into Paris, as everyone knows. Listeners can be amused, but not frightened—but in cases like the present one, amusement can only be truly or fully obtained in being frightened.

Baron von Altenheimer's tale seemed curious, and that was all. All that it had contrived in its audience was that level of emotion that is so easily produced in the theatre, as soon as the curtain rises half-way and some unknown person crosses the darkened stage with his hat tilted over his eyes. Fear no longer exists. Parisians cannot be frightened—not top-drawer Parisians, at any rate—by the vampires of the Drave and French cavaliers interred for four hundred years in the Great Hungarian Plain!

The Princess was so completely cured of her terror that she looked at her son the marquis and laughed. She found that he was very pale, and was on the point of asking him whether he could take such solemn nonsense seriously, but everyone seems pale by moonlight. The Princess let go of the Marquis; she had no further need of his bodily protection.

"Monsieur le Baron," said the benevolent and courteous Archbishop of Paris, "we did not expect such good fortune. Permit me to thank the Bishop of Hermopolis for all the pleasure that you have given us this evening."

The audience chorused its approval. In high society, as our readers well know, the bravos are always polite, and triumphs are a thousand times sweeter.

But the Bishop of Hermopolis was not content. He had hoped for more than this. One expects a great deal from the virtuosos one has produced. Several signs of impatience had escaped His Lordship. "It must be admitted," he said, in his rich southern accent, "that Monsignor von Altenheimer has favored us with an unfortunate revelation! How can you expect us to be interested in the story, now that we know how it ends?"

"Does Your Excellency really know how it will end?" asked the hollow voice of the Baron.

That single sentence was sufficient to make everyone pay attention. The Bishop, already modifying his tone, said: "Seeing that we know that the two bohemians are none other than Jean and Ange Ténèbre in person, young Lenore will surely be devoured..."

"By no means!" cried the Princess, all her courage evaporating. "I certainly hope that we shall be able to save her...isn't that so, Monsieur le Baron?"

The privy councilor to His Majesty the king of Wurtemburg offered a respectful bow to the whole audience, and directed more specific ones at the Minister and the Princess. By the rays of the moon, one could see a satisfied expression upon his long face. He took from his pocket a big golden box, embellished with large sparkling diamonds, which sent scintillating reflections in all directions.

"Noble ladies and gentlemen," he replied soberly, playing with his royal snuff-box—which looked for all the world like a handful of pure light—"my brother Benedict has done no wrong. Nor has he, as His Excellency appears to believe, given away the punch-line of the joke—God grant that it were, in fact, a joke! Unhappily, in telling tales like these one can disdain such cleverness. There is no need to manage with due care the petty effects and little surprises that storytellers usually employ. I will give you further proof of this by telling you straight away that the Ténèbre brothers are now in Paris, and that I have come here in pursuit of them, at my own risk and peril."

This time, the majority of the audience-members started violently, while the remainder pricked up their ears. The Bishop of Hermopolis, who stubbornly insisted on seeing the matter from an artistic viewpoint, clapped his hands and cried *bravo*. The Princess recalled her son, the Marquis de Lorgàres, to her side.

"That's some joke," she murmured.

Baron von Altenheimer slowly inhaled a pinch of snuff, then—just as slowly—he wiped the back of his hand on his black coat. It must be admitted that such a gesture is more effective at the Comedie-Française; it really requires a frill. Even so, it wasn't bad, for a Westphalian.

"Now!" the Baron continued, in a deliberate tone. "I shall proceed as swiftly as I can to the matter of the crown jewels of Wurtemburg. Consider, noble ladies, the fact that in the nineteenth century, we live our lives surrounded by prodigious events that, for some reason, we neither see nor deny. Personally, I am a believer, because I have learned the truth to my cost. I believe in the Chevalier Ténèbre, the most audacious, the most improbable, the most authentically diabolical brigand who ever lived; I believe in Ange Ténèbre, the vampire. I have seen the pale remains of his victims, from which not a drop of blood could be recovered.

"What is the exact nature of beings like these, and where do they fit into the known categories of God's Creation? I don't know. A theory that could accommodate such monstrosities would have to extend much further than ordinary moral failings or deviations from the common mould. There must be prodigies within the order of created beings that are immediately superior to mankind and, in consequence, unknown to mankind. Seeing that the fraction of the work of God that is visible and tangible to us presents anomalies—since we encounter in our streets hunchbacks, hare-lips and idiots—it may be that death itself, or the mechanical organization of life, if you prefer, is similarly subject to deviations and derangements. It may be that the clay of which we are formed is occasionally treated with other and more powerful reagents..."

"Monsieur Privy Councilor...brother," Monsignor Benedict interrupted at this point, "I beg you to drop this subject, lest you become enmeshed in the toils of sinful materialism."

This was said with gentle severity. Baron von Altenheimer extended his hand to his younger sibling and said: "I beg your pardon, brother."

"It could be explained, up to a point," Monsignor Frayssinous put in, "without any recourse to materialistic philosophy..."

"Of course, Excellency, of course," the Baron interrupted respectfully, "but it's entirely my concern. I have my reasons for believing, so I believe; that's quite sufficient. An objection of a different order has been put forward, which appears to me more serious, because it challenges my conduct. The question needs to be put to me: if you are a believer, as you affirm, how is it possible that you would compromise your good character by such vain speculations? You accept the reality of these two creatures of popular superstition, and you commit yourself to their pursuit! Why? To kill them, even though they are immortal? Ladies and gentlemen, in our German universities we call this a disputation. I believe that these creatures have existed for four centuries and more...

At this point, the Baron was interrupted by a murmur mingled with a certain amount of politely-muffled laughter.

"He is superb," the Bishop of Hermopolis said, in a low voice. "He sets out these follies with such magnificent *sang-froid*."

"...For four centuries and more," repeated Baron von Altenheimer. "That is my utterly firm and very well-established opinion—but I do not believe that they are immortal. Tradition is definite upon this point. No oupire or vampire can resist combustion. As it will probably fall to me to defend France, I propose to put this theory--advocated by all ancient authors--to the test by taking the miscreants to Stuttgart, where they will be carefully burned, after which their ashes will be divided into small portions and transported in several different directions before they are scattered on the ground. If they rise again, after that, then will be the time to say that the privy councilor, Baron von Altenheimer, is nothing but a poor head without a brain!"

There were some in the audience who thought that the tall German gentleman with the *basso-profundo* voice was simply and deplorably mad. Others supposed that he was joking. The remainder, among whose ranks was the Princess, were inclined to concede that his was a rather ingenious method of exterminating oupires, vampires and the like.

"You will not be surprised to know," Baron von Altenheimer continued, "that misfortune was not long arriving in the house of Prince Jacobyi. His daughter was carried off that very same night. How vast the sums were that the brothers Ténèbre had appropriated by theft is unknown—but it is certain that they loved money. Some said that they had buried fabulous treasures in various different places in southern Germany.

"Prince Jacobyi was advised that his daughter Lenore would be returned safe and sound on payment of a ransom of half a million florins, but he was warned that if he made the slightest effort to recover her by force, or by recourse to the law, the child would be lost to him forever.

"He did not hesitate. Forty-eight hours later he had the twelve hundred thousand francs—and Lenore, safe and sound, as promised, slept in her own bed that night. But it happened that the Chevalier Ténèbre and his brother Ange, the vampire, were not the only bandits who had dealings with the Magnate: his two stewards and his banker in Pest were also vampires, after their own fashion. They had been mining his fortune for a long time, and the loan of five hundred thousand florins caused an explosion.

"All his creditors demanded settlement of their mortgages at the same time, and in the full amount. The Chandor domain was put up for public auction. It was not so much an estate as a country; even in the depths of Hungary it was worth more than two million louis. The prince, once the sale was made, had only just enough to pay off his debts—but the two stewards and the banker in Pest were now as rich as lords.

"The prince became an expatriate. He may be in England, or Italy, or perhaps in France. He lives, it is said, on what his daughter earns...

"My lords, the night would be entirely gone and the new day born before I could complete a detailed account of the horrors with which the voice of the public has charged the brothers Ténèbre. Their name, if spoken aloud in the regions through which the Danube flows, will not only put women and children to flight but strong men. Captain, or Chevalier Ténèbre, as he is variously known, has fought pitched battles against entire troops of Austrians and Turks; he has plundered tax-collectors and routed their protective escorts ten times over. Ange, his brother, is no soldier, but don't think him any less dangerous for that. He is a master of disguise, well able to play any role; the captain and he are on an absolutely equal footing. They amass their fortune ceaselessly, and I have often heard it said in Hungary, not only by the common people but in the reception-rooms of the Archduke in the Imperial Palace at Ofen, that if there were a kingdom for sale, the brothers Ténèbre would be kings.

"Last year in Venice, at the beginning of spring, the entire city was celebrating the marriage of the young Comtesse Barberini, the god-daughter of Her Royal and Imperial Majesty, to the scion of the Policeni family: it was the reunion of two of the greatest Lombardo-Venetian fortunes and from the dawn of the day the city wore the face of public celebration. The poor people of Venice

96

knew Pia Barberini as an angel of charity. It was said that Andrea Policeni—formerly a spirited young man, a king of patrician pleasures, the last of those mysterious Romans who slid under the Rialto in former times, behind the curtains of so many gondolas, when moonlight blanched the palace of the marble Venus risen from the crest of the wave—had divested himself of the dark mantle of the adventurer, cast it away and become a saint at her behest.

"I was in Venice, my lords, not on any political mission on this occasion, but merely to embrace my beloved brother, who was enrolled in the army of God, stationed in Rome with the Holy Father. Venice is half-way between Stuttgart and the Eternal City..."

As if each of the two brothers had yielded to an irresistible impulse of tenderness, their hands sought and clasped one another. The audience approved; the gesture was greeted with softened expressions, as a demonstration of the beautiful love that flourishes in families.

"We each made a journey, to meet one another at the half-way point," Baron von Altenheimer continued, in a slightly emotional voice. "At the wedding, in which we assisted, there were representatives of all the aristocracies in the world, but there were two strangers, in particular, who excited the curiosity of the entire city: John Stuart, Earl of Glasgow, the son of the pretender Charles Edward Stuart—and, in consequence, the legitimate heir to the English throne—and his younger brother Charles, the Duke of Richmond.

"The common opinion, to tell the truth, holds that the last Stuart died in Rome without issue; but even in Rome, as my brother Benedict can assure you, many eminent persons reserve doubts in that regard. The pretender, who had lived in fear of the combined intrigues of the House of Brunswick and his own brother, Henry Stuart, Cardinal Duke of York, had contracted a secret marriage and concealed the birth of his son, the supreme hope of a dynasty threatened on all sides. The Earl of Glasgow was in possession of papers of the utmost importance. Certain titles, emanating from sources so respectable that to persist in doubting them is almost sacrilege, become unbelievable. The majority of the noblemen of Venice addressed the Earl of Glasgow as 'Majesty'.

"There was, moreover, the evidence of two particularly handsome faces—and, one might almost say, *historic* heads. John Stuart, who was a tall man, had a long and bilious face as similar to his father's as two drops of water on his coat of arms. His younger brother, by virtue of his curly blond hair and the delicate cut of his features, might easily have been mistaken for the subject of Van Dyck's portrait of Charles I—especially given his stature, for Charles was as short as his namesake.

"In the ancestral hall of the Barberini Palace there was a table of blue porphyry, supported by four massive silver feet. All the gems to be worn at the wedding had been assembled there; it was a jewel-case that a queen would have envied.

"There were the diamonds to be worn by the present Comtesse Policeni, who was a Howard, like the fifth wife of King Bluebeard, Henry VIII of England; those of the grandmother, Rose Gritti, and the great-grandmother, Ann Gradenigo; the ruby necklace in which Phébus of Lusignan had married Catherine Pépoli; the diadem of Catherine Cornaro, her mother, the queen of Cyprus; and the sapphire rivière of Tranquille Paléologue, the wife of the last doge but one—and all of that on the bridegroom's side.

"On the bride's side could be seen the solitaire known as the Montserrat, the rose-cut diamond that the Dukes of Austria had carried in their crown; the seven brilliants of Pallas Comnàne—the Pleiades; the bracelets of Antonia Doria of Genoa, who became the wife of Nicolas Barberini in the denouement of that eternal drama whose principal roles are Romeo and Juliet; the ring of Cardinal Frégose--and outshining all that marvelous finery—the wedding-present sent to his god-daughter by His Majesty the Emperor of Austria.

One touching incident occurred that can be told in a few words: the king without a crown, that heir to such misfortune and such grandeur, the Earl of Glasgow, advanced towards the porphyry table, laden with all these treasures, and asked for permission to throw upon it a simple string of pearls that had been worn by the unfortunate Mary, Queen of Scots. I can still see his venerable figure and the nobly ingenuous air of his young brother, as the affianced couple offered their thanks to him.

"And I swear, on my honor, that I did not begin to recognize in them the two sordid gypsies of Chandor Castle...!"

There arose in the circle of listeners such a murmur of astonishment that the Baron's words were literally cut off.

"Bravo! bravo! bravissimo!" cried the Bishop of Hermopolis. "That's what I call, for the sake of delicacy, a sudden reversal of fortune!"

"What?" said His Grace the Archbishop de Quélen. "That's too bad...!"

"I've guessed it," murmured the Princess. "In placing the false pearls on the porphyry table, the King of England slipped some beautiful diamond up his sleeve..."

Baron von Altenheimer offered her a dignified bow, and replied: "Beautiful lady, nothing escapes the perspicacity of the French. Except that the Chevalier Ténèbre did not perform his conjuring trick with all the world looking on, nor were the pearls false—for, that very night, he took them back, along with everything else that was on the porphyry table.

"What?" the cry went up. "All of them?"

"All of them," confirmed the soft voice of the monsignor, "including the silver legs of the table."

IV. Baron von Altenheimer

The windows of the château, visible between the trees, were illuminated one by one. The final preparations were being made for the archbishop's charitable distribution.

"We shall soon be interrupted, Baron," said the Bishop of Hermopolis, "but in the meantime, the ladies would dearly like to hear the end of your story."

"In other words, Your Lordship, you want me to cut it short," replied the King of Wurtemburg's privy councilor. "Well, in the first place, I am at the disposal of Your Excellency, and that of His Grace and all the other eminent persons who have done me the honor of listening to me—and in the second, I really do have only a little left to tell.

"I have not yet told you that the family of King Wilhelm, my master, is the most numerous surrounding any throne in Europe.[16] His Majesty has four children by his two marriages; his very illustrious son, likewise has four children; his five very respectable uncles have an even greater wealth of descendants, and such an assortment of children, grandchildren, sons-in-law and daughters-in-law, that the five collateral branches boast no less than fifty princely heads. God, the protector of France, also seems to concern himself a little with the dynasty of Wurtemburg.

"Now, all this notwithstanding, until 1823 King Wilhelm did not have a direct heir of the male sex. There was, in consequence, great joy in Wurtemburg when, on the sixth of March, the birth of a prince royal was announced, who was privately baptized, according to the rites of the Lutheran church, Charles Frederick Alexander. The king wanted to postpone the definitive baptism ceremony, in order to express the full extent of his gladness, and so that all the friends of the court might gather for a feast that would be both a public and a family celebration.

"There is no time to contrive any petty surprises, and in any case, after everything that had gone before everyone will be able to guess that the Ténèbre brothers came to the feast—but under what pretext, and in what form?

"I beg you, my dear lords and ladies, not to gauge these two truly prodigious beings according to the measure of your timid impostors, your bird-brained brigands or those phantoms whose puerile roles are restricted to the gratuitous terrorization of female feebleness and the poltroonery of little children. My judgment, which I have not sought to hide from you, is that we are faced here with the supernatural, employing means which are beyond our comprehension to satisfy two purely human passions: Avarice and Lust. Interred beneath those two black stones, covering the two graves on the Great Hungarian Plain,

---

[16] Wilhelm I of Wurtemburg (1781-1864) was notorious for his several marriages and numerous mistresses.

99

are not two corpses but two deadly sins, incarnate since the beginning of the world...in other places, there must be other marble slabs covering those other vampires which are always dead and yet always alive: Ambition, Wrath, Hatred, Dishonesty and Pride.

"You, who are amazed by the petty comedy played out by your Comte Pontis de Sainte-Helène,[17] should not be tempted to make comparisons. Don't say that there are difficulties, or impossibilities, in my story, or anything else that might be masked by that loose term, *implausibility*, which is the protestation of minds that are too narrow against truths that are too broad.

"Yes, certainly, there were difficulties involved in entering that court, in order to mingle with the princes and princesses whose alliances embraced all Europe like a familial net. Yes, certainly, there were what the vulgar call impossibilities standing in the way of their presentation, under some royal name—and how else could they present themselves?—in that palace teeming with the guests and friends of all the real kings. Anyway, the brothers Ténèbre, as you would expect, chose their disguises and their roles with great care.

"This was not an occasion of the ingenuous phantasmagoria of Venice. Wurtemburg does not treat fallen royalty with such religious chivalry; it is a new and pragmatic realm, which has no fear of alloying its dynastic blood with that man who became your emperor, and who, a mere four years ago, paid with his death on a desert island for the magical splendor of his victories. What was required here was, if you will permit me to express it thus, a solid emanation of an extant power. The occasion required someone living, not dead; it required, in a word, a personage that all the princes and all the princesses could call 'cousin,' without creating a diplomatic incident or starting a war: a representative of a peaceful and relatively weak state.

"Where could that state be found? Not Russia, from which had come the late queen, the daughter of Paul I, and whose armies were commanded by Prince Alexander, the king's uncle; nor Prussia, where Prince Auguste, the nephew of the king, served in the guards; nor Austria, where princess Marie, the cousin of the king, bore the title of Archduchess; nor any part of Germany, where Nassau, Saxe-Altemburg, Bade, Stolberg, Waldeck, Hohenloe, Tour-et-Taxis were all sons-in-law or fathers-in-law; nor the Netherlands, where a betrothal had already been secured between the heir to the throne and Princess Sophie, who was still in her cradle; nor England, where Duke Louis, the father of the actual queen, lived; nor even France, the adopted fatherland of Duke Frederick Philip. Where, then?

---

[17] Pierre de Pontis, Comte de Sainte-Hélène was the pseudonym adopted by the fraudster Pierre Coignard (1774-1834), who ingratiated himself with Louis XVIII after being released from a prison camp, falsely claiming to have been a political prisoner condemned for royalist sympathies. After being exposed be was condemned again in 1819.

"There is a troubled land, one of the greatest in history, but which seems in our modern epoch to be hiding behind its mountainous wall, ashamed of its decadence. Germany no longer knows Spain, now that the house of Austria has ended its reign in Madrid. The noise of your last war, the heroism of your princes and your soldiers at the Trocadero, reached us as a muffled echo, too distant to be heard. Spain is a China in the middle of Europe—but you know what effect that the ambassadors of India had on the court of Louis XIV; a literal Chinese ambassador would have caused a stir throughout Europe. At the baptism of our prince royal, no one paid any attention to the son of the Spanish infanta.

"Were there, then, no official diplomatic links between Spain and Wurtemburg? Yes, there were; there was still a Spanish *chargé d'affaires* in Stuttgart, but he was tricked into becoming an accessory. Notes were exchanged between Madrid and Stuttgart; it was my responsibility to look at them, and I looked at them. I am not particularly intimate with most of that which surrounds me but I am, after all, a learned man; in my own country I am an accredited savant. I hold doctoral diplomas from four universities. My sight is good, my health has not deteriorated under the strain of mental labor, I am perfectly sane, and yet those documents seemed authentic to me!

"I am not afraid to say it: it was a veritable miracle! Anyone who has been admitted into a chancellery, whether by the humble door that I use or by the one that opens to the knocking of Your Excellencies, knows what a mountain of impossibilities—I will use the word, this time—must be climbed in order to create false diplomatic correspondence. Each such dispatch passes through a hundred hands that must be corrupted, and before a hundred eyes that must be blinded; but the correspondence was manufactured. I have in my files here in Paris a letter signed by King Ferdinand, but written by the Chevalier Ténèbre or by Ange Ténèbre the vampire!

"That's not all, however. The court at Wurtemburg had issued real and authentic notes; the court of Spain had responded, that much is certain. Add the suppression of the real documents to the creation of the false ones and your minds may boggle at their leisure—for that, I repeat, is a miracle.

"What remains to be told re-enters the category of ordinary prestidigitation. Once the two creatures had been able to trick me, acting and speaking as they did before me—who has paid so dearly for their acquaintance—it was merely a question of artfulness. It must be admitted that they had had all the time in the world to become accomplished impostors and admirable comedians. But those papers...!"

Baron von Altenheimer fell silent, as if his retrospective astonishment had choked him, and Monsignor Benedict sighed as he shook his blond head. "Ah! Don't you see...the papers! The papers! There is the miracle!"

Archbishop de Quélen leaned over to whisper into the ear of the Bishop of Hermopolis. "Well, it's stunning, I must admit...but it's only an audacious phantasmagoria, isn't it?"

"It's the truth," Bishop Frayssinous replied. "The pure truth! I have seen the Baron's own letters of credit, in the company of the prefect of police. He is highly respected at court. Besides, there's his brother, the Chamberlain to His Holiness..."

"But how is it," murmured the Archbishop, "that we have never heard talk of any of this?"

"It only happened a few days ago, Your Grace! The baptism of the prince royal of Wurtemburg took place at the end of August, and September has just begun."

"It was exactly a fortnight ago," said the Baron, who appeared to have fully recovered his composure. "All Stuttgart took part in the celebration, whose like had never been seen in our homeland. Fifty princes and princesses of the German and Northern courts were received at the castle—who, together with the army of princes and princesses related by blood, formed a veritable royal crowd. His majesty said, joyfully: 'I have waited two and a half years, but it is a complete success. There is not a single fay missing from my son's cradle!'

"He certainly appreciated how much he owed to the courtesy of the states of Germany and the North, but that which flattered him even more was the unexpected tribute from the South; what made his success complete was the presence of Don François de Paule, Infante of Spain, and his august companion, Louise-Charlotte de Bourbon, daughter of François I, king of Sicily.

"The Infante was a man of twenty-three years, dark-skinned but seeming not a day older than his ostensible age. It would have taken a sorcerer to detect any trace of resemblance between that bold and taciturn young man and the pretended heir to the royal privilege of the Stuarts, a stiff and desiccated old man whose ravaged features were already crowned with white hair. As for the infanta Louise-Charlotte, we all knew that she was born in 1804, and was in consequence twenty-one years of age—and noble, gracious and charming! The Chevalier Ténèbre could pass for the king of actors, but there is no greater comedian than brother Ange: that is a magician who could make you see the sun at midnight!

"It was the brothers Ténèbre, and their brilliant retinue was probably the same gypsy band that camped on the far bank of the Tisza in full view of Chandor Castle. And that royal farce—which, it must be said, was probably unique in the annals of the world—was paraded for three full days before the assembled houses of Europe!

"It was the brothers Ténèbre! The denouement you already know, in part: the crown jewels of Wurtemburg disappeared during the second day. On the third day an angelic child died, the daughter of Chancellor Reinhardt, who had been placed with the infanta in the capacity of maid-of-honor. That same day there was a general clear-out so audacious that the astonishment which seemed exhausted was reborn. Everything had gone: the jeweled ornaments of the princes and princesses alike.

"The Infante and the Infanta had done a great deal of dancing that evening. As midnight approached, Monsieur Metternich, whose sister is the king's aunt, asked the Archduchess Marie, the older sister of the queen, what had become of the eagle modeled in diamonds that she normally wore at her throat. The archduchess searched and, while searching, said to Monsieur Metternich in her turn: 'Prince, where is your Golden Fleece necklace? Where is your Annunciation string? Where is your Danish brooch?' An immediate outcry went up, everyone perceiving at the same time that they had been robbed. The king—the king himself!—had been stripped of the emblems of his identity! The doors of the palace were shut, but it was too late. The Infante, the Infanta and their retinue had already gone, carrying booty whose worth could not be estimated at less than a million gold crowns."

"At the very least," Monsignor Benedict added, equably.

A noise of carriage-wheels on the roadway, coming towards Conflans, was heard. The wind, which had begun to blow in gusts, carried vague sounds along the brilliantly-illuminated side of the château: fugitive instrumental notes groping in search of harmony. The Archbishop of Paris gave the signal to return, saying: "We can't be late arriving at our little concert!"

Everyone immediately stood up. The sensation of terror was utterly dispelled, for the very simple reason that the most recent episodes narrated by the baron had no trace of the diverse emotions that had previously agitated the assembly. The Venetian tale had been set in broad daylight; the adventure in Stuttgart had taken place by the bright light of a thousand candles; there had been no further return to the kind of dark and mysteriously moonlit night that surrounded the archbishop's guests. Baron von Altenheimer's vampires and brigands had taken on the character of a comic opera.

The Princess took the arm of her son and bodyguard, the young Marquis de Lorgàres. Pleased with herself because she was no longer trembling, she had just opened her mouth to reproach Baron von Altenheimer because she had not been sufficiently frightened, when she saw two eyes fixed upon her. They had that particular gleam that the eyes of animals of the feline genus take on in the darkness.

Madame de Montfort was an intelligent person, who knew perfectly well that vampires rarely interest themselves in princesses of a certain age; nevertheless, the gaze startled her. It belonged to Monsignor Benedict, who pointed a white and delicate finger, on which a magnificent solitaire sparkled, at the wide lawn in front of the château and said in a honeyed voice: "I would like to point out to Madame the Princess how easily even the simplest things can be reinvested with genuinely fantastic aspects by darkness."

In the middle of the lawn, a white object could be seen, which was moving slowly, cutting across the dark expanse of grass. It was a woman, but the way in which the diffuse rays of the moon fell upon her billowing dress really did give her the appearance of a ghost. She glided through the dark obscurity of the park like a hazy apparition. The arm of the young marquis trembled beneath his mother's.

"Gaston! What is it?" she cried. "Are you trying to frighten me as well?"

"The wind is chilly," Gaston mumbled.

At that moment the Archbishop said; "Do you see that phantom? It is my charming and angelic protégée Mademoiselle d'Arnheim, who will perform some beautiful classic masterpieces by the German masters for us. Ladies, I recommend her to you with all my heart, for she is a Christian Antigone who supports her father in his old age. The Opéra is richer than we are, and has offered to pay two thousand louis a year for her unparalleled voice and admirable delivery. Mademoiselle d'Arnheim, who comes from a good family and is as pious as a prayer, would rather remain poor than risk her soul for gold; she is content to give lessons. I have promised to help her and would be very grateful to anyone who would like to second me in that good work."

The white form had disappeared behind the trees lining the avenue.

"Gaston," said the princess, "you must go to see Monsieur Récamier[18] about the beating of your heart. I can feel it against my arm; it's a veritable palpitation."

Baron von Altenheimer had drawn nearer to the archbishop. "My Lord," he said, after a respectful hesitation, "perhaps I do not understand the French language well enough to express things very delicately. I am rich. Would it be possible for me do something, via Your Lordship, for the young lady who has the honor to be your protégée?" As he spoke he took a pocket-book from inside his coat. The archbishop looked at him and reached out a hand; it was only to clasp his, for he murmured: "Monsieur le Baron, you are a good-hearted man!" The Baron, however, pretending to have misunderstood him, deposited the wallet in the archbishop's hand, bowed in an exaggerated fashion and disappeared into the crowd of guests.

The princess came to a sudden halt at the foot of the steps and said to her son: "Gaston, I think I have left Madame de Maillé's cloak on the grass...

The marquis immediately retraced his steps, and had no difficulty in finding the cloak. As he turned to leave the lawn again he saw a brilliant rectangular object at his feet, glittering in the grass at the spot formerly occupied by Monsignor Benedict. He picked it up, in order to return it to its owner; it only required a single glance for him to recognize the roman prelate's velvet-bound steel-boxed missal.

By the time the marquis got back to the château, everyone else had gone in. While crossing the entrance-hall he shifted the missal in his hand and the box opened of its own accord between his fingers. He tried to close it again, but

---

[18] Joseph Récamier (1774-1852), chief physician at the Hôtel-Dieu and a professor at the Collège de France. He is remember primarily for his contribution to gynecology.

could not; it had a secret spring, whose mechanism had doubtless been released when it fell upon the ground.

While Gaston tried to readjust the catch, the pages of the missal opened, and he glanced down at the two exposed pages.

He stopped dead, as if thunderstruck, stifling the cry of amazement that rose unbidden from his breast...

V. Conversational Trifles

The great hall of the Château de Conflans was arranged for the concert. The orchestra was set on a stage, before which a Nuremberg organ-chest had been placed. Five or six rows of chairs faced the stage, most of them occupied by women and children, in "the costume of the archdiocese", as it was known in the district at the time. These were not ball-gowns—most definitely not; there were chaste sleeveless jackets and decorous wimples everywhere—but nor was it everyday clothing. The dresses were smart and ornaments were worn. The male members of the assembly—priests, aristocrats and civil servants—were standing around the perimeter.

Immediately after entering, Princess de Montfort had sought out Doctor Récamier and laid hold of him, in order to talk to him about the palpitations suffered by her son the marquis.

"He's a good boy, doctor," she said, "and so different from his brother, Monsieur le Duc! That one will be the death of me, my nerves are so bad. Whereas Gaston, you know, is exactly the opposite. I don't know why he lost his religious vocation; to me, the boy certainly seems to be cut from clerical cloth. I can't see him in any other garb, and he'd suit a tonsure. The diplomatic corps! I ask you, does he look like a diplomat? But we lost you, doctor; you weren't with us in the garden. We have been listening to a most original German storyteller, who immediately put us in mind of the Devil...wherever did you get to?"

Her gaze scanned the room and picked out Baron von Altenheimer, who was standing near to the entrance door. In the candlelight, the fantastic aspects of his person seemed quite lost. He was probably thirty years of age, but his plainness made him seem older. He had, appropriately enough, one of those faces with which all our readers are familiar, which lasts from the twentieth year until old age and which common parlance calls ageless. He had long, pronounced features, rather pale and drawn, with bushy eyebrows over his sad eyes. His thick hair was brushed down over his forehead, with two thin and lobeless ears projecting from it. His unusually wide mouth wore an expression of naive placidity. His entire physiognomy, in sum, was emphatically bourgeois and common. His carriage was stiffly erect, and his black coat was as distressingly ill-fashioned as his trousers, which were cut several fingerbreadths too short, exposing silk socks of an extreme thinness. His shoes were robust, with pearly buckles. The princess noticed that his ankles looked like two knots on a stick.

"There, nevertheless, is the romantic unknown who made us feel an immediate shiver," she continued, laughing. "The moon and darkness are all that is required to play those kinds of tricks! After ten o'clock at night, my niece Madame de Maillé mistakes all the oak-stumps beside the highway for African lions escaped from menageries, and every post for the brigand Rinaldo Rinaldini, about whom she has read in tales of Italy. The gallant German has spoken a great deal about the Danube, but I'm sure that the Danube peasantry has less deplorable tailors. His brother is nice. There's the costume I'd like to see on Gaston!"

Doctor Récamier responded with an assortment of eloquent smiles, as appropriate. Women in general found him extraordinarily attentive. His awesome medical reputation was founded on the most basic of principles: he healed all maladies by prescribing no remedies.

The brother was, indeed, "nice," although the word seemed a trifle familiar in the mouth of a princess as a description of a Roman prelate in the hall of the Archbishop of Paris. He carried his clerical coat with a proper and perfect grace. His blond hair, smooth and fine, was pierced at the centre by a microscopic tonsure; it fell upon his cheeks—which were slightly too rosy—in soft curls, giving him the appearance of a cherub. The Princess was not the cause of that blush; she had used the right word in spite of herself; Monsignor Benedict was "nice."

"Hold on!" the princess went on, touching the doctor on the arm. "Look over there, at my mirror image!" Her smile, impregnated with that maternal mockery whose falsity always demands contradiction, indicated a tall young man, too slender but very handsome, who was leaning on a window-ledge. His eyes were lowered, perhaps because they had just encountered his mother's."

"Well!" said the doctor, "I would never have recognized the Marquis de Lorgàres. He's grown up into a remarkable cavalier!"

The Princess blushed with pleasure. "Don't you think he's rather too pale?"

"A nervous temperament...an affusion of cold water in a warm bath...a tonic regime without too much excitement...lots of healthy exercise...distraction...I would be honored to pay him a visit..." The doctor bowed and tactfully withdrew, delicately disengaging his arm from hers.

The princess fluttered her eyelashes at Gaston, and turned around.

As soon as the Princess had turned her back Gaston lifted his own eyes again. His gaze, which certainly seemed a trifle feverish, fixed itself on a closed door half-hidden by the orchestra. The Marquis de Lorgàres was evidently waiting for someone, and that someone would soon be coming through the door. But was it only anticipation that made his eyes seem hollow and put sweat upon his brow?

At the other end of the room, the Archbishop of Paris approached the Bishop of Hermopolis.

"Is the Baron von Altenheimer a personal acquaintance of yours, My Lord," he asked.

"Not at all," replied Bishop Frayssinous. "He was presented to me by his brother, who brought me letters of introduction from Cardinals Pacca, Gaysruk and Riario Sforza, as well as a note signed by the prefect of the Congregation of Rites. I know that he has the ear of my colleague at the Ministry of the Interior and of the prefect of police..." He broke off and said: "But here comes the very man! We shall have more information now!"

The prefect of police had indeed come in, and the two prelates could see him exchanging a handshake with Baron von Altenheimer, who was still standing by the door.

"Many of the things he said to us," the Archbishop said, "suggested a mental state which was, to say the least, bizarre..."

"He's a German," Bishop Frayssinous put in, "and a storyteller—two halves of madness!"

"A generous madness—prodigal even," the Archbishop of Paris persisted. "Did you notice that he gave me his pocket-book for Mademoiselle d'Arnheim?"

I thought I saw that—what was in the pocket-book?"

"A sum so large that I don't know whether it was a mistake on his part. Ten banknotes, a thousand francs each."

"Ten banknotes of a thousand francs!" repeated the astonished Bishop of Hermopolis, before adding, in a lower voice: "But we in France are poor, while these Teutons spend money like water."

The orchestra began playing a motet by Lesueur. Baron von Altenheimer maintained his stiff and awkward posture through the first few bars, but as the French master's majestic and grandiose endeavor was further extended it seemed that the Baron's own stature matured in parallel. His pose altered as he drew himself up to his full height and his breast swelled, filling out the folds of his black coat. Little by little, his eyes lit up for all to see, and his nostrils dilated as if thrust aside by ardent breath. Once again he became the centre of attention, instantly acquiring the reputation of an enthusiastic music-lover.

"I fear, your Lordship," the prefect of police replied, in the meantime, to the questions of the archbishop, "that Wurtemburg has no *chargé d'affaires* in Paris at the moment; Austria is representing its interests for the time being. I will consult the ambassador tomorrow. Messieurs von Altenheimer seem to me to be eminent men and quite dependable. The Baron is a close friend of Prince Metternich—Prince Talleyrand has told me as much...as far as the authenticity of their mission is concerned, it is not my place to comment upon it, alas. The brothers Ténèbre are evildoers of the most dangerous kind, and we have the dubious honor of their presence in Paris. A bold, extraordinary and highly improbable theft was committed yesterday at the home of His Lordship the Duc de Bourbon—who is, in fact, one of Baron von Altenheimer's patrons. Antiques and jewelry worth more than fifty thousand crowns have been abstracted from his gallery, including three Isabey miniatures, five of Madame de Mirbel, two enamels by Petitot and three rapier-guards that the late prince brought back from Florence. Her Majesty sent for me today; she desires to see Baron von Altenheimer."

"And is there any trace of your men?"

"My Lord, Baron von Altenheimer has a brigade of highly-skilled legal practitioners in his company--including, it is said, two detectives from Scotland Yard...yes, if you're not familiar with the English police, two sleuths chosen from the finest that London has to offer...The king seems to desire that the Baron has a certain freedom of action...I can only stand aside..."

The prefect of police made no attempt to conceal his bad humor; he was obviously a little jealous of the Baron, and thought it outrageous that anyone could dismiss his proven troops in favor of the militia of some petty country no bigger on the map than his thumb.

Whether something happens in the halls of a noble house or on the footpath of a muddy street, rumor spreads with a magical rapidity. Within five minutes, the occupants of the best seats and the remotest recesses were equally acquainted with the circumstances of the audacious theft committed by the brothers Ténèbre. No one had the least doubt that it was the work of the brothers Ténèbre.

The awful celebrity of the brothers Ténèbre, however well its groundwork had been laid by the German's story, had been no more than a light hidden beneath a bushel while the self-interest of the crowd had not been involved. There is a world of difference between a scourge that is only in the mind and a scourge that is alive, menacing and present. Do you remember the immense shock that ran through the social scale from one end of the Seine to the other, in consequence of the sudden fame of that other demon, cholera? Baron von Altenheimer had certainly said that "the brothers Ténèbre are in Paris," but words are worth far less than facts and a fire does not bring forth cries of terror when all one can see is smoke. The brothers Ténèbre had confirmed their presence by what the prefect of police himself had called a "highly improbable" theft. What timing! The German Baron went up sharply in everyone's estimation. An immediate link was established between him and the superb bandits, whose Homer he had become. Henceforth, many of the ladies would find something interesting, and strange, in that pale and elongated face, unfortunately attached to those ungraceful shoulders.

The interest was soon further extended. While a circle formed around the two prelates chatting to the prefect of police, a servant came in and handed a letter to the Baron. The servant's livery was unfamiliar. The Baron discreetly acquainted himself with the contents of the letter, shaking his head in a concerned manner and exchanging a few words with his brother; then he crossed the room, his steps determined and ponderous, to stand before the Archbishop of Paris.

"Your Grace," he said, "I had no need, in order to desire an introduction to Your Eminence, of any other motive than the admiration that I have expressed for your person; nevertheless, I did have another motive. I knew that the brothers Ténèbre would come to your episcopal château this evening."

There was a profound silence around the Archbishop, who paled visibly.

"They won't find the Condé gallery here," he murmured, with a smile.

"They will find someone that it is in their interest to approach," replied the Baron, "and they know, moreover, that His Lordship the Bishop of Hermopolis will deliver a sermon and raise a collection on behalf of the Christians of the Holy Land."

"That could be postponed," said Bishop Frayssinous.

"I humbly beseech Your Excellencies to do no such thing!" von Altenheimer exclaimed. "To begin with, I give you my word of honor that neither the illustrious master of this house, nor his guests, have anything at all to fear. I have my men all around the château, and twenty-five gendarmes from the Bercy precinct are awaiting His Grace's permission to enter its grounds..."

"It's news to me!" cried the prefect of police.

"They are operating according to the written orders of the Ministry of the Interior," said the Baron, half-withdrawing a large ministerial document from the side pocket of his jacket.

The prefect interrupted the gesture and said, not without a certain resentment: "That's fine...so much the better! They can do without me, for now."

"Illustrious colleague," von Altenheimer replied in a sincere voice, extending both hands towards him, "if I may employ that term with respect to a man such as you, we are joined in a desperate battle here, and I beg you not to withdraw your aid. If the brothers Ténèbre slip through our hands now they will lose themselves in that Black Forest called London, and the pursuit will have to be handed over to another authority. Have I committed some offence against etiquette or neglected some formality of rank? Forgive me, dear sir—I am a foreigner; my king has charged me with a very difficult task; I am doing my best..."

The honest privy councilor's voice was almost tearful. The two prelates thought that it was their duty to address a few conciliatory words to the prefect. The audience, deeply moved by the idea of the drama that might well reach its climax before their very eyes, and beset by diverse sensations mingling fear, curiosity, expectation, whispered its opinions. That good and noble congregation discovered that it had been conscripted in its entirety—unknowingly, but not against its wishes—to serve as the bait in a rat-trap. That function has a name in the language of thieves which has also lent its color to the speech of honest men: a vile and detestable name which we need not write down because everyone knows it. But what pleasure children take in playing the brigand beneath the great chestnut-trees of the Tuileries!

We all have a little of the child ingrained in us: witness the success, in recent years, of the revival of the innocent pleasures of farcical comedy. We know that everyone loves to dress up and that everyone loves to see others dressed up, the donkey always in the lion's skin and the lion sometimes in the donkey's skin...and then, there is the joy of becoming something else for a little while: the joy of quitting, if only for a moment, the abhorrent role of mere spectator! Think on it! There have been conspiracies—serious and terrible conspiracies—that have no other origin. We can credit to the same account that pure gladness that takes possession of the human being at the thought of a prank, and which grows in direct proportion to the social standing of those who plan the escapade. Does a king not derive a thousand times as much pleasure from playing truant than a schoolboy?

It would not be overly reckless to declare that everyone at the château of His Lordship the Archbishop of Paris that evening was something of a policeman--everyone, that is, with the exception of the prefect of police, who was thinking of handing in his resignation. Dukes and princesses, lovely wives and charming daughters, ordained priests, peers of the realm and cross-bred sons alike surprised themselves by throwing themselves wholeheartedly into a game of cops and robbers. The concert had a new twist, by courtesy of a different kind of music. What disguise would the two bold villains have adopted to gain entry to the home of the archbishop? Through what keyhole had they come? There were imaginative marquises who could already see the Chevalier Ténèbre in a cardinal, and brother Ange the vampire in a young German canoness...

Baron von Altenheimer was certainly a clever man, for he sensed the common sentiment and immediately exploited it. "Illustrious people," he said, as if he were addressing a prayer to the whole gathering, "I can say that my fate is in our hands. I have let you in on my secret without being forced to do so. Join with me in an endeavor that is both important and noble, given that our victory could save the fortunes of many families and the lives of a great many Christians. Be on your guard! I can guarantee that the brothers Ténèbre will be here within the hour. Take account, therefore, of any unfamiliar face among those of your friends and acquaintances. Remember that the range of their disguises is limited by the nature of their physiques: one tall, one short, rather like the figurative relationship that exists between my beloved brother and myself. They could present themselves as an old man and a young one, a husband and his wife, or a father and his daughter..."

As he pronounced these last words, the sliding doors behind the orchestra opened. A young woman dressed in white, escorted by an old man of considerable stature, appeared on the stage.

The sight of them caused a shiver to run through the assembled audience...

VI. O Fount of Love!

The young woman was Mademoiselle d'Arnheim, the archbishop's protégée, who had no wish to earn forty thousand francs in the theatre; the old man
was her father. If the Princess had glanced at that moment towards the window-
bay in which her son Gaston was standing she would certainly have been astonished by the change wrought in his features.

Gaston de Lorgàres was, as we have said, a handsome young man, of an
excessively timid and slightly faint appearance. His mother, who loved him
madly, nevertheless entertained some doubts as to the scope of his intelligence.
She still saw him as a child, and wondered why the spark of virility had not
sprung forth within the peaceful adolescence which seemed to have lasted far
beyond his twentieth year.

Many a noble husband, it is said, does not know the first thing about the
heart of his wife; one might add that many a noble mother struggles in vain to
fathom the mind of her son, even though the book lies open before her eyes.
Noble mothers often have not the least gift for intellectual rapport; a working-
class mother always knows her Charles or Jean-Marie, but Madame la Duchesse
is often totally ignorant of Monsieur le Comte or Monsieur le Marquis.

What would have astonished the Princess de Montfort, at that moment, was
that the spark in question was springing forth in a newly-conceived passion. He
was still pale and his large black eyes had lost none of their timidity, but beneath
his half-closed eyelids there was a gleam of brightness. He was a statue of flesh
and bone, for the moment, but there was a soul within that marble. I doubt that
even the affusions of cold water in a warm bath prescribed by Doctor Récamier
could have calmed the beating of that heart. Although it is impossible to put the
judgment to the test, I fear that palpitations of that sort require a different kind of
remedy.

The flame that burned between Gaston's long eyelashes was directed towards a particular target. His gaze was riveted to the young girl in the white
dress who had stepped forward on to the stage. The Archbishop of Paris had
said, in speaking of her, "my angelic protégée". He had not exaggerated. The
wonderful oval of her face, framed by shining blonde hair, did indeed resemble
the delicate profiles which the imagination of great art has lent to celestial en-
voys. She seemed to be about eighteen years old at the very most. It was as if
her clear and soft expression were veiled by melancholy. She was as beautiful as
a dream of Raphael...

Now then! Fantasy has its limits, has it not? Could it really be the case that
this seemingly seraphic head belonged to brother Ange Ténèbre, the vampire?
We raise the issue because that thought had taken feverish possession of three-
quarters of the assembly. Everyone had measured with a single glance the proportional relationship of the Baron von Altenheimer and his young brother,
Monsignor Benedict. It was certainly very close to that pertaining to the adora-

111

ble young girl and the old man who accompanied her. The last words of the Baron, listing the possible disguises of the brothers Ténèbre, had been a father and his daughter and here, coming on the scene as if on cue, were a young girl and her father!

You must take due note of the fact that the brothers Ténèbre were capable of anything. Had not the vampire played the role of the Spanish infanta in Stuttgart? Fifty gazes avidly interrogated Baron von Altenheimer, who had taken up his position beside the entrance door once again, and Monsignor Benedict, who was standing beside him—but the Baron remained impassive, and Monsignor Benedict maintained a honeyed smile upon his lips. Bear in mind, if you will, that this proved nothing: they were two artful men, and it was necessary that the brothers Ténèbre had no clue that their presence was suspected.

She was certainly beautiful, that young girl, but there were many among the assembled women who found, on due consideration, something intimidating about her. What was it? What caused those vague feelings of unease? It was neither the clear blue of her eyes, nor the delicate tint of her complexion, nor the virginal purity of her bearing, nor the halo of her blonde hair. No, it was nothing in particular, but rather the whole ensemble. That was it! She was simply *too beautiful!*

As regards the old man, the Chevalier Ténèbre had hidden his satanic brow well beneath that venerable mass of snowy hair. That had not happened overnight. What deep wrinkles! What a ravaged complexion! What strength of character! But what mortal sadness! One could go to the Great Hungarian Plain and search beneath the crop-fields for the black graves; one could lift up the stones which carried the mysterious inscriptions. There would be nothing there! One would have to look elsewhere for the Chevalier Ténèbre and the vampire priest.

The orchestra played two long chords, followed by a battery of arpeggios, to which accompaniment Mademoiselle d'Arnheim sang Haydn's *Fons amoris*. She had a mezzo-soprano voice of magnificent integrity and incomparable worth. The women had expected a contralto, but they were no longer held back by the objections of rationality. What use is reason when it runs up against things that are irrational, mad, impossible, supernatural? In any other circumstances, they would have admired, perhaps passionately, the almost pious manner—expressive of asceticism, even of divine candor—in which Mademoiselle d'Arnheim interpreted the work of the Viennese master. They were connoisseurs; the tender majesty of style could not have escaped them, not the splendor of the voice—but, I ask you, what did all that signify when it was a matter of diabolical illusion? Were they even listening? I don't know. If they were listening to anything, it was the insistent and confused poetry of their fevered brains...

In his window-bay, Gaston drank deliriously from that enchanted cup; by the door, Monsignor Benedict put his open hand over his eyes, doubtless to hide his inquisitive expression. The latter was playing the dilettante, but the Princess, who was on the lookout, thought she saw a piercing gleam between the fingers. It was the monsignor's eyes, fixed upon Mademoiselle d'Arnheim.

When the last note died within the throat of the virtuosa, and while the orchestra played its final chords, Baron von Altenheimer—who had remained until now as stiff as a bronze statue—gave a noisy lead to the applause. The women immediately followed his lead, thinking that they were playing their part. The two prelates—and, for the most part, the male half of the assembly—were entirely sincere in their long-drawn-out applause. It was a veritable triumph; the unanimity of the acclamation was broken by a single protestation. Gaston alone did not applaud, because his two hands were tightly clasped upon his heart.

It was not the custom in His Grace's salons to bestow noisy ovations upon the artistes, but everyone concurred in this instance in prolonging the tribute; feigned enthusiasm came to the aid of genuine enthusiasm, and one would have to look to the pits of theatres to obtain some idea of the din that lasted for several minutes in the Archbishop's hall.

There was one singular circumstance. At the first bravos, the tall figure of the old man, who had taken a seat to the left of the orchestra and slightly of the rear, came erect again. Painful surprise could be read in his eyes, like an expression of wounded pride; then his white head fell upon his breast again, and two large tears ran down his cheeks.

Mademoiselle d'Arnheim, blushing from her shoulders to her forehead, bowed deeply, took hold of her father's arms, and disappeared.

Archbishop de Quélen made a tour of the room, collecting opinions with paternal pleasure. Everywhere one heard the same things. *How charming! Perfectly charming! An admirable voice! What spirit! Marvelous style!* Those whose ears had played them false or rendered them deaf—the majority of those in the concert-hall—spoke more loudly than the sensitive, and those women who were putting their hearts and souls into their new profession made the warmest bids of all.

Baron von Altenheimer had become a statue once more. His expression, as mysterious as a closed book, made no response whatsoever to all the beautiful eyes that were fixed upon it. The moment had not yet arrived; it was necessary to be prudent.

There was, however, one curiosity that was closer to the boil and stronger than all the other impatiences. The Princess could not take it any longer. She turned towards her son, who was dreaming—God only knows of what—in his window-bay, and she beckoned to him urgently.

The Marquis de Lorgàres roused himself, and obeyed.

"Gaston," the Princess said to him in a low and very mysterious voice, "do you understand what is happening here?"

"What is happening, Madame?" Gaston replied. "Yes, of course."

"Would you do me a favor?"

"With pleasure."

"Go strike up a conversation...discreetly, you understand...with Baron von Altenheimer, and..." She interrupted herself, somewhat discouraged. "But you're so timid, my poor boy." Then she added, presumably to herself: "And so simple!"

"What?" Gaston demanded, in a manner that his mother thought distinctly unappreciative.

"And ask him to tell you, in confidence," she went on, with a smile of renewed hopefulness, "whether those were *the ones for whom we are looking out.*"

"The ones...?" Gaston repeated. "Which ones do you mean, Madame, if you please?"

The Princess tapped her foot and replied: "In God's name! The brothers Ténèbre!"

Gaston stared at her, utterly stupefied. The Princess saw immediately that hope had misled her. Gaston's hauteur had evaporated. "Go," she said, regardless, "and do what you can."

Gaston did not hesitate. He went immediately towards Baron von Altenheimer. His mother followed him with her eyes and said to herself: "His brother, the Duc, has matured perfectly well. Poor Gaston is obviously retarded. One must accept whatever one gets."

At that moment Gaston resolutely set himself beside the Baron, who greeted him with the same fulsome gestures that he extended to everyone. Gaston did not seem disconcerted. A conversation was quickly established between himself and Monsieur von Altenheimer. Gaston spoke, in truth, very freely and made himself heard.

How happy his mother was! Doubly delighted—for she was witness to the progress of her son and her son was the bearer of her news—the happy mother triumphed in her heart and in her mind. *Whatever one gets*: the dictum of all mothers!

This, however, was how Gaston, Marquis of Lorgàres, accomplished the highly confidential mission entrusted to him by the Princess.

"Monsieur le Baron," he said, "I have listened to you this evening with a good deal of pleasure and interest."

"I am grateful to Monsieur le Marquis..." the German began.

"And you will understand better," Gaston continued, "when you know that the remarkable subject of your tale is conjoined, for me, with a series of family considerations. We are, Monsieur le Baron, first cousins once removed of Field-Marshal Victor de Rohan, Prince de Guémenée, Duc de Rohan, de Bouillon and de Monbazon, who presently resides in Hungary..."

Altenheimer bowed.

"And as the heads of the family of the late duchess," the young marquis continued, "who died childless, as you must know, we possess several properties there, near Debrecen, which are not let but are quite considerable..."

The Princess, meanwhile, was saying to herself: *What's this? What's he saying now? Monsieur le Baron seems to be paying very close attention to him!*

This was nothing less than the truth: Monsieur von Altenheimer was all ears. Gaston continued: "After certain digressions which added much, from my point of view, to the piquancy of your tale, I saw that you were pleased to conceal beneath the frivolous spirit of the storyteller a considerable depth of actual knowledge..."

"Ah, Monsieur de Marquis..."

"If you will permit me...This is not a compliment, but a matter of preparing the way to ask you a great favor."

"I am entirely at your disposal," the Baron said.

"A thousand thanks...it concerns our properties in Hungary...my brother, the Duc, was the victim of a certain youthful recklessness, and when he came into a part of his inheritance he was able to mortgage the estate of Niszar. It is seven hundred leagues from Paris to Debrecen. Without making any accusation against German or Hungarian lawyers, I merely state the facts: the Niszar estate has been sold at public auction to pay the mortgagees..."

"How long ago was this?" the Baron asked, sharply.

"Three years ago, perhaps four..."

"You are sure that five years have not passed?"

"Perfectly sure. My brother, Monsieur le Duc, was only seventeen then."

"And he must have had time to squander the estate. That's right...I'm with you, Monsieur le Marquis."

"I have heard some report," Gaston continued, earnestly, "of the Hungarian laws regulating the right of repurchase after a forced sale, but no Magyar authors have been translated into French and their use of Latin idiom does not always seem clear to me...Mayreuth fixed at four years the period of facultative redemption and the full right..."

"Mayreuth," said the Baron, correcting the spelling of the name, "is an obstinate pedant who is no longer read...the Austrian court, in giving Hungary the benefit of its ancient legislation, has codified the matter. The legal period of redemption and the automatic right of repurchase is five years and a day from the date of the public auction...and it is not without precedent for the period to be extended on the basis of a request submitted to the Chancellery, with supporting documents..."

Gaston bowed ceremoniously in his turn.

"Monsieur le Baron," he said, taking his leave, "I beg you to accept all my thanks."

"Now then, Marquis," his mother said to herself as he came back towards her, "do me the favor of giving me the three essential points of that sermon you preached to him?"

"Madame," Gaston replied, with a smile that the Princess had never seen before, "I have begun my diplomatic career. These privy councilors, it seems to me, are very difficult to get around."

"He did not want to answer your question?"

"Indeed he did."

"Tell me, then," the Princess said, petulantly. "Tell me immediately."

"Mother, Monsieur le Baron told me that the two men in question are here..."

"Oh! I was sure of it!"

"But no one," the young marquis finished, calmly, "has recognized them: neither you, nor anyone here, has identified them as yet."

"Oh!" repeated the Princess, in a very different manner. "He's just making fun of you."

Gaston kissed her hand with a grace that made her think again. "Madame," he replied, with a slight hint of mockery that completed her discomfiture, "would you like me to do you a second and even better favor?"

"What, Gaston?"

"Would you like me to go into the next room, to talk to Monsieur d'Arnheim himself?"

"And ask him if he is the Chevalier Ténèbre?" The Princess laughed.

"To find out without asking him, Madame," Gaston corrected.

The Princess took him by the hand and put her mouth very close to his ear. "If you can do that, Gaston," she said, "I will give you a Tilbury carriage like the one your brother has."

"I would prefer something else, Madame," the young marquis replied, gravely.

"What then? Tell me."

Only promise," Gaston replied, "not to talk about me to my cousin Emerance for six weeks."

The Princess burst out laughing, showing her teeth, which were still quite beautiful.

"Monsieur le Marquis," she said, "I forbid you to fall in love! Someone must have waved a magic wand over you." She pointed a finger at him tenderly and added: "Go! And find out whether this Mademoiselle d'Arnheim is really an old priest dead for four hundred years!"

The young marquis negotiated a passage towards Archbishop de Quélen and said to him: "My Lord, my mother has asked me to speak to Monsieur d'Arnheim about the possibility of taking lessons."

"Excellent!" murmured the Archbishop, who took Gaston the hand, led him to the door situated behind the orchestra, and opened it. "My good Monsieur d'Arnheim," he said, raising his voice, "I bring you an ambassador. This is the beginning. If it please God, our dear child will soon be obliged to refuse lessons!" He closed the door behind Gaston.

There was no one in the room but the old man and the girl. Mademoiselle d'Arnheim, at the sight of the young marquis, changed color two or three times. Her father lowered his eyes while the vivid blush showed on her cheeks.

Gaston, so eloquent a moment ago, stood before them with a pale face and silent lips.

VII. A Proposal of Marriage

On the other side of the door the concert continued. The Nuremberg organ warbled beneath the fingers of Monsignor Benedict, who was playing a charming ditty, the famous Bolognese Christmas carol *Jesu bambino*.

As for our three individuals, the silence had not yet been broken and the unease was growing. Monsieur d'Arnheim finally made an effort to overcome the awkwardness, and began: "You came, Monsieur, to discuss with me the possibility of lessons to be given by my daughter...?"

He stopped. No word are adequate to describe the humiliated pride, the crushed nobility, the bitter regret, mingled with resignation, melancholy and love, with which the old man pronounced those few words.

Gaston took a step towards him.

"Prince," he said, in a low voice, "you are mistaken. That is not why I am here."

"Prince!" echoed Monsieur d'Arnheim, whose limbs had begun to tremble, while his daughter hid her tearful face between her hands. "Prince...!" Then, placing his tremulous wrists on the arms of his chair as he made ready to rise to his feet, he said: "To whom do you think you are talking, Monsieur?"

"I know," Gaston replied, his voice having hardened again, "that I am talking to Chrétien Baszin, Prince Jacobyi."

The old man slumped back in his seat. "Who told you that?" he demanded, darkly.

"Lenore, your daughter."

"Lenore! My daughter!" He turned towards Mademoiselle d'Arnheim, whose hands were clasped together as if in prayer, perhaps to implore Gaston to be quiet.

Monsieur d'Arnheim stood up. "Who are you?" he demanded.

"Gaston de Montfort, Marquis de Lorgàres, second son of the Prince de Montfort."

"Ah!" said Monsieur d'Arnheim, his gaze moving back and forth between the young man and the girl. Then he asked one more time: "What do you want from me, Monsieur le Marquis de Lorgàres?"

"I want to ask for the hand of your daughter. I love her, and she loves me." This was said in a distinct voice, with head held high and a steady gaze.

Mademoiselle d'Arnheim had closed her eyes and had let herself fall into a chair.

In the next room, the sweet voice of the monsignor embellished another carol, harvesting at the end of every verse a rich crop of merited applause.

The old man looked once again at his daughter. It was not anger that was in his eyes; it was bleak despair. "You've deceived me!" he murmured.

Mademoiselle d'Arnheim threw herself towards him. He thrust her back, but not rudely, while he added, addressing himself to Gaston: "Monsieur de Marquis, to take the last possession of a ruined man is to steal from the altar!"

"Father!" cried the girl. "Good and noble father! I will never leave you, and I swear to you that I have never done anything deserving of reproach."

"In that case," said the old man, directing a scornful glance at Gaston, "this is a madman, who should go away!"

"Not before I have your answer, Prince," the young marquis replied. "I have told the truth: I love your daughter; she loves me; and I ask for her hand."

"You have spoken to this man, Lenore?" Monsieur d'Arnheim demanded.

"Never, Father," she replied, in a faint voice.

"How, then, does he dare to boast...?"

"Father," the young girl interrupted, sliding to her knees., "he is not boasting...but if he knows it, his heart must have told him, for we have never exchanged a word."

"There is a mystery here...." began the old man, whose stern face had gone as white as snow.

His daughter interrupted again: "There is nothing, Father," she said, "but my love for you and our destiny. While you were ill, and after having sold everything that you possessed in the world, it fell to me one day to go in search of medicines without having the money to pay for them. I was refused credit. I sat down on the step of the shop, exhausted and discouraged.

"And you begged for alms, child!" cried Monsieur d'Arnheim, his eyes lighting up.

"I would have done, Father, if I had thought of it. But I was utterly lost, and I thought of nothing but coming back to you, and of dying with you. Monsieur le Marquis was passing by; he stopped before me; I did not see him. Mina had followed me; Mina went towards him..."

As the name Mina was spoken, a little black spaniel bitch came out from beneath Monsieur d'Arnheim's armchair, in order to jump on to a chair and from there to the table next to which Gaston was standing. She began to lick Gaston's hand. The old man averted his eyes.

"I remember that in the depths of my distress I prayed fervently to God," Mademoiselle d'Arnheim continued. "I implored him to work a miracle and to send to my father the manna that the celestial birds had carried to those lost in the desert. When Mina returned, Monsieur le Marquis was no longer there, but Mina put her muzzle between my knees, and in the folds of my dress I saw the glitter of a gold piece..."

Monsieur d'Arnheim let out a groan. Mina leapt with one bound to the carpet and went to comfort him; he pushed her aside as gently and as sadly as he had pushed his daughter away.

"We are Baszins!" he murmured. Then he asked, his voice taking on a different tone: "How was the acquaintance renewed?"

"You have been ill for three months," the young woman replied. "That grand and luxurious residence which you are in the habit of admiring is the town house of the Princess de Montfort; I don't know how Mina knew the way. Whenever the gold piece was spent, Mina went out again, and always returned with manna."

"And you knew whence this manna came, did you not?"

"From God, whose help I had implored, Father."

"And you let Mina out! Had you no shame?"

The old man's lip quivered; his eyelids fluttered like those of a woman fighting to hold back tears

"Father," said Mademoiselle d'Arnheim in a low voice, "I let Mina out because she brought the breath back to your lungs and the blood to your veins... and I had no shame because I already loved the hand of that God who sent us his manna."

"Thank you," murmured Gaston, his eyes moist.

"But what did you expect? What did you expect?" cried the old man, in anguish.

Mademoiselle d'Arnheim lifted her angelic gaze towards the heavens, and replied: "Father, I put my trust in God."

There was a momentary silence. Monsignor Benedict was still chanting his mild Italian devotions. Monsieur d'Arnheim looked Gaston in the face, then he offered his hand

"Chrétien Baszin, Prince Jacobyi, as you have called him, and as I called him myself in former times, is indebted to you, Monsieur le Marquis," he said, slowly. "He sees that you are a noble and generous young man. Perhaps he would even have been flattered by your quest in happier times--but he cannot ignore the fact that the house of de Montfort is one of the richest in France. Chrétien Baszin could never permit his daughter to enter such a family as that unless the gate were opened wide; he possesses nothing but his pride. If the Princess de Montfort herself came in search of the Princess Jacobyi, then it might indeed be God's wish to contrive the union of two great houses."

"If that is what is required, that is what will be done," Gaston replied, without hesitation. "I give you my word."

But what, you may ask, of that cousin Emerance to whom the Princess had said too much about Gaston? Was not Monsieur le Marquis being much too forward, for a timid young man? We do not know, to tell the truth, whether his mother would have been delighted or desolated by his words. The chick, it seems, had broken his shell with one blow of his beak and come out in his full plumage.

Gaston shook Monsieur d'Arnheim's hand and respectfully kissed the young woman's; it was a sort of conditional betrothal. Then, raising himself up again, he went on in a brisk tone: "Prince, would you recognize, if chance were to bring you face to face with them, the two gypsies who received hospitality at Chandor Castle, on the night when your daughter was kidnapped?"

Mademoiselle d'Arnheim started in surprise, and became as pale as an alabaster statue.

"How do you know...?" the old man stammered.

"There are many things I need to explain to you, Prince," the young marquis interrupted, "but this is neither the time nor the place. I beg you to be content with answering my question."

"I would recognize them," said Monsieur d'Arnheim, through gritted teeth, "ten years from now!"

Gaston cocked an ear. Monsignor Benedict had finished singing.

"Prince," he went on, "you are destined to find yourself, perhaps this very evening, face to face with those who have accomplished your ruination..."

"Rubbish!" cried the old man.

"We have mentioned God more than once in this interview," said Gaston gravely. "He moves in mysterious ways. A person who seems to me to know what he is talking about has predicted that the brothers Ténèbre will put in an appearance, this evening, in the Archbishop's house. When Mademoiselle d'Arnheim goes to perform again, you will doubtless accompany her. Look around, but be sure to hide your legitimate anger and rightful resentment. It is vitally important to you, to your daughter, and also to me, your future son-in-law, that no one except me penetrates your secret. We shall draw apart from one another, but there must be a signal. If you recognize the two evildoers, promise me two things: make this gesture openly, and no other; and abstain absolutely from taking any action." He touched his right hand to his brow, with all five fingers extended.

Monsieur d'Arnheim hesitated for a moment, then he said: "I trust you, young man, and I will do as you ask."

As soon as he had received that promise, the Marquis de Lorgàres bowed twice, putting into the smile that he addressed to Lenore everything that he could not express in words. Then he moved rapidly towards the door opposite to that which had admitted him.

He crossed the hallway, descended the staircase, and went out into the gardens. It was not to calm his simmering blood, nor to refresh his bare head, that the Marquis de Lorgàres made this nocturnal expedition. He looked around him attentively as he went, and paused from time to time in order to listen.

The night was black, but Paris was not asleep, and the noise of the city could still be heard in the distance. Above that muted din other sounds, closer and more distinct, were discernible: footsteps, whispers, muffled laughs. All around the château, the darkness was populated.

Gaston reached the park and found a wooded place. He pushed his way into the heart of a thicket, looked around once more, listened more carefully, and finished by secreting beneath the thickest foliage an object which he took from his bosom.

Then he retraced his steps to the château and went back into the salon by the main door...

Baron von Altenheimer, who seemed to have appointed himself as a concierge, so faithfully had he stuck to his post, gave a slight start of surprise at Gaston's appearance. It was only momentary; afterwards, his face resumed its placid expression.

"Monsieur le Marquis has not heard my brother Benedict, then?" he said.

"Yes indeed," Gaston replied. "Heard, and applauded."

The monsignor thanked him, and the Baron added: "I did not see you go out, Marquis."

"A little fresh air," Gaston replied, as he went on into the room. "It's stifling in here."

"Monsieur le Marquis," the Princess said to him, in a tone intended to be most severe, "you have been gone thirty-five minutes, by the hands of the clock. Your conduct is extremely improper." But she added, pointing her finger at him: "I shall give you a penance, if you have not brought me a generous armful of news."

"Has nothing happened here?" Gaston asked.

"I have a stiff neck from looking this way and that," the Princess replied. "The doctor pretends that it is all a huge practical joke. But these devotees of the profound wisdom know nothing, you know...now, Gaston, we are losing our heads. You are interrogating me and I have been good enough to reply—everything is upside-down!"

Gaston remained silent.

"How pale you are," his mother said, uneasily. "You should have brought some color back with you. You owe me an explanation, Gaston my boy. We have begun our first romance, have we not? Be honest! Poor Emerance! Speak, Gaston, I insist. What have you been doing since you left the room?"

"Madame," replied the young marquis, forced to make the effort to save his dream, "I do not believe that this is a romance, but it is a strange story nevertheless. Tomorrow, if you will permit, I will submit to your levy: I have the greatest need to talk to you."

There is no word to express the passion for knowledge that mothers have. It would be unjust to give the name "curiosity" to such a profound desire. The Princess's astonishment was magnified. She no longer recognized in her son the child of old of whom she had said: "When will the man awaken in him?" The man had awakened, with a definite start! The princess, completely overtaken, was still searching for the child and no longer understood.

Gaston would not have got away so lightly if there had not been a great stir in the salon. The Bishop of Hermopolis moved towards the stage, and an emotion that had no direct relationship to the sermon that he intended to give took hold of the audience. The appearance of the brothers Ténèbre had been anxiously anticipated since the quest for them had begun. The Archbishop's salon was beset by curious maladies, fears, desires and fevers—none of which, most assuredly, had anything to do with the unfortunate Christians of the Holy Land.

As the Bishop of Hermopolis took his position on the stage the Princess only had time to say: "Will you tell me, at least, who these people are—the d'Arnheims?"

"You shall know tomorrow, Mother," Gaston replied, as he moved away. "It is for precisely that reason that I need to see you."

Bishop Frayssinous began to speak, commanding silence.

There are still many people alive who were personally acquainted with the illustrious author of the *Défense de la religion*. All of them agree in saying that the public eloquence of the Bishop of Hermopolis was distinguished above all by measured argument, moderation and an abundance of proofs deduced with calm authority and certitude; but they add that his private eloquence was another thing entirely. He had a southern ardor in his blood and a lively impulse to charity in his heart. When he went into battle against the selfishness of worldly men for the purpose of extracting alms he was not a regular soldier in the apostolic army but a lightly-armed sharpshooter: a zouave, if such an anachronism is permissible. He never retreated; he was prepared to make arrows from any kind of wood. One recalls what Monsieur de Talleyrand said of the sermon preached at the home of the Duchesse d'Angoulême on behalf of the widows and orphans of the war in Greece: "He had our charity by the throat!"

In this instance, his theme was just as real and even more urgent; it concerned those unhappy Christian families scattered throughout Palestine and groaning under Turkish domination. In more recent times, the Eastern war has educated us on that subject, and no one is ignorant of the lamentable barbarities which formerly cast a shadow on the light of the guiding stars of our century, but there was at that time an almost impassable barrier between Europe and those cries of agony. Their first harrowing echo was, however, heard that evening in the hall of the Château de Conflans.

Bishop Frayssinous had, moreover, to contend with a general inattention, for the fever that had gripped the crowd was a rude rival to his speech. After several minutes had passed, though, that inattention had been tamed, and every face took on an expression of intense concentration, directed towards a common focus: the orator.

All those previously-stifled moans; all those previously-unheard cries, all those groans extracted by long and intolerable torture, were reunited in one single voice to burst forth like a thousand simultaneous death-rattles in the bosom of that rich, brilliant and happy assembly. The discourse did not last long, but when it ended, there was sweat on every brow and a tear in every eye.

The Bishop of Hermopolis came down from the stage then, and the Archbishop of Paris embraced him effusively before handing him the huge red velvet purse in which the collection was to be taken.

As soon as he took his first step, the prelate began to accumulate an abundant harvest of gold pieces and banknotes. The force of good example mingled with that desire to emulate which peevish philosophers call vanity. The Marsh apparatus extracts arsenic from the same soil that gives us wheat for outer bread; in the moral order, as in the physical order, is there anything on earth that is entirely pure? Having rendered the eternal negative in answer to that question, the point of great and good works is to ameliorate intoxication, to tame passion, and to direct impetuousness towards a noble end. The Princess donated her bracelet. From that moment on, jewelry rained into the increasingly-heavy and swollen purse. Ear-rings, brooches and strings of pearls hastened to join the Princess's bracelet. Charity also has its auctions.

"Monsieur le Baron," said the Bishop of Hermopolis, as he arrived at the entrance-door, "I know that you have already despoiled yourself on behalf of another unfortunate; I shall take care to ask nothing of you."

Baron von Altenheimer was in the process of making a little paper trumpet out of an envelope. He was doing his best, but his large clumsy hands were making rather a mess of it.

"Give, my dear brother Benedict," he said, after an interval when he paid no attention to His Excellency.

Monsignor Benedict removed from his finger the exceedingly beautiful solitaire which had excited the admiration of the assembly, and dropped it into the purse. It was a gift fit for a king. The Bishop of Hermopolis bowed and was about to pass on, when the Baron said to him: "If you would graciously permit it, Your Lordship, I would like to keep a little snuff—it is a distinctly tyrannical habit..."

The bishop turned back. Into the little trumpet he had fabricated, rather awkwardly, Baron von Altenheimer was busy emptying the contents of his splendid gold snuff-box encrusted with diamonds the size of peas. Having achieved the transfer, he slipped the box into the purse, adding with perfect simplicity: "A thousand thanks, Your Lordship."

The box was worth three or four times as much as the ring. The gesture had a tremendous effect, especially the little trumpet and the thousand thanks. More than one person wondered whether the kingdom of Wurtemburg, which had the honor of harboring the Black Forest within its narrow bounds, might actually be Eldorado.

The brothers von Altenheimer had resumed their peaceful and modest attitudes, and the Bishop of Hermopolis continued his collection, which had already produced a fortune.

"Mademoiselle d'Arnheim, for the finale," said Archbishop de Quélen, signaling to the orchestra. One of the musicians went in search of the virtuosa.

Gaston had his offering in his hand at the moment when Monsieur d'Arnheim and his daughter reappeared on the stage. He saw the avid gaze of the old man make a rapid tour of the room and come to a halt, staring fixedly at the entrance-door, next to which the two brothers Altenheimer were standing in isolation.

The reaction experienced by Monsieur d'Arnheim was so violent that he staggered like a man about to fall backwards.

"Well, Marquis," said the Bishop, whose purse had been extended towards Gaston for several seconds.

"Well, Gaston," repeated the Princess, who was watching him. "He has given silver," she gasped, almost immediately afterwards, as she collapsed into an armchair. "Doctor, he has given silver! My son, to the collection of the Minister of Ecclesiastical Affairs! For the Christians of the Holy Land! Mademoiselle d'Arnheim must indeed be an ancient ecclesiastic! See! Gaston is mad! That's an enchantress in flesh and bone! He's twenty-three years old! Are there affusions of cold water administered in warm baths powerful enough to prevent young men from behaving like idiots? I have longed for him to assert himself a little, but not like this! Lord Above! The Duc has already tried to drive me mad. And can you imagine, to cap it all, that he does not want to hear talk of his cousin Emerance—a charming girl, in good standing at court?"

She aired her grievances as best she could, but we must admit to you, in confidence, that there was a smile beneath her anger.

The Bishop also laughed as he left the young marquis, whose hand had let three forty-sou pieces fall into his collection: the only ones! He realized well enough that a mistake had been made.

But Gaston was not laughing; his entire being was in his eyes. I do not know whether he had even noticed the look of timid tenderness that Mademoiselle d'Arnheim had darted towards him while entering. He had eyes for no one but her father: her father, whose white hair quivered on his forehead.

Slowly, so very slowly, Monsieur d'Arnheim lifted his right hand to his forehead, on which the five trembling fingers rested for a moment, fully outstretched.

Gaston let out a deep sigh, and lost himself in the crowd.

VIII. The End of the Soirée

The brothers Ténèbre had not yet put in an appearance. The two prelates, the prefect of police and a few other important people were counting up the collection in a small room just off the hall, whose door stood open, while Mademoiselle d'Arnheim sang Mozart's *Ave verum*, accompanied by the orchestra.

The admirable artiste surpassed herself in rendering the admirable work. The quietened crowd was all ears, when everyone was suddenly subjected to a violent shock. Baron von Altenheimer half-opened the entrance-door and shouted at the top of his voice: "Look out!"

At the same time, he threw himself into the neighboring room where their Lordships were.

From the other side of the half-open main door, several voices replied: "Yes!"

The monsignor was already at a window, rapidly turning the handle that would release its lock. "Look out, everyone!" he cried, cupping his hands like a megaphone.

From all sides, distant voices replied from the park: "Yes! Yes! Yes!"

There is no need to add that the orchestra and the singer immediately fell silent.

There was a moment of indescribable tumult. The first woman's scream gave birth to a hundred, as is always the case. The men in the great hall launched themselves towards the small room, those in the little room raced back into the larger one.

Not one of them saw anything, search as he might, but everyone believed that others had seen something. By the time three minutes had gone by, two dozen women had fainted.

"Here! In the garden!" cried a voice from outside.

There was a sudden surge towards the window.

"Here, on the stairs!" shouted another voice.

The door was shut.

Gunshots were heard in the distance.

Baron von Altenheimer reappeared then, with his big black coat buttoned up. His head was held high and his eyes shone.

"I must beg your pardon," he said, calmly. "Come, brother Benedict...I will have them, or die trying!"

The monsignor also had the bearing of a little hero. They hurled themselves through the door together and disappeared, amid the myriad pleas of women begging them not to expose themselves to any risk.

Once they had made their exit, the hue and cry faded into the distance, then died away.

When three more minutes had passed, a profound silence reigned in the hall of the Château de Conflans. No one said a word, save for two men half-hidden behind the orchestra, one of whom was struggling as hard as he could against the other.

"Why did you stop me?" Monsieur d'Arnheim demanded, exhausted by his efforts.

"Prince," replied Gaston, Marquis de Lorgàres, "I give you my word of honor that they shall not escape!"

Others were coming out of their trance. Each one took hold of himself and looked at his neighbors. So little trace of the tempest remained all around them that it might all have been a dream. Besides which, the von Altenheimers were gone. Everyone listened; no one felt obliged to speak. Everyone felt a vague apprehension growing in himself: an uneasy impression of having been duped.

There was no longer any noise of footsteps outside, nor of shouting, not of gunshots.

The Archbishop was the first to speak. "There is something inexplicable in this business."

"These conflicts of interest between the Minister of the Interior and the Prefecture are an outrage!" the prefect of police added, peevishly.

"Did you see something, Madame la Marquise?" the Princess asked her neighbor,

"Something, Madame? No, I cannot tell you what I have seen. I closed my eyes, as one does when gunshots ring out in the theatre...but I sensed...oh, I am sure that I smelled something burning..."

"Aunt," cried Madame de Maillé. "Leonie saw a man in black."

"I saw it too," said the doctor. "A huge hairy body..."

There was some laughter. Perhaps it only required a frank and well-chosen word to turn the whole thing into a joke, but the word was not forthcoming.

The Bishop of Hermopolis said: "Let's finish counting the collection." But he had hardly put a foot into the little room when he made an exclamation of amazement.

The jumpy nerves of the audience had settled a little; there was no renewal of the panic. But as His Excellency, rather than stepping back, hurled himself towards the table which occupied the centre of the little room, he was followed across the threshold by several other men and a few women.

His Excellency, who stood before the table with his head lowered and all strength gone from his arms, was soon surrounded.

"Mercy!" cried Archbishop de Quélen, wringing his hands. "Our collection!" That was all that was said. The noble assembly fell into that particular species of silence which follows utter mystification.

The table was bare. Not one of the objects lately contained by the red velvet purse was to be seen.

"See!" said the prefect of police, eventually. "If the Minister of the Interior had only consulted my people..."

"Monsieur!" interrupted the Archbishop, with a wrath whose wellspring was the frustration of his charity. "There was not only the Ministry of the Interior in this, but the Court of Rome and the Chancellery of the Kingdom of Wurtemburg! We have lost the wealth of the poor, and someone is making a mockery of us!"

"One tall, and one short," murmured the Princess, repeating the words that Baron von Altenheimer had spoken for the first time in the verdant arena.

"It was them! It was them!" twenty voices cried at the same time.

"The Baron is the Chevalier Ténèbre..."

"And the Monsignor is brother Ange, the vampire!"

IX. An Essay on the Philosophy of Theft

All men whose trade is deception, or the foiling of deception—which is to say, all game and all hunters; for example, the admirable thieves of London, who learn their profession at a university, and the equally admirable detectives of Scotland Yard who are trained to follow their tracks across the pavements of that great Babylon—will tell you that there are two principal methods of rendering oneself invisible, not including Aladdin's lamp. One is to hide, the other to display oneself while covering one's face with a mask; to lurk in the shades of night, or to confront the light of the sun valiantly.

In two words: cunning and audacity.

Cunning is primarily associated with the old school; audacity is the forté of the modern movement. The majority of the gentlemen savants whose field of study is the art of thievery recommend audacity very highly, and do not scruple to say that wiliness has had its day. The honorable Josuah J. Marshall, the pride of the London criminal fraternity, who was sentenced to hang at the Old Bailey as the reign of King George neared its end, put it thus: "Tell the constable that you are Jack Sheppard and he will not believe you; prove to him, by means of your birth-certificate, that you are Jack Sheppard; steal his watch, his purse, his shirt and his truncheon, and he will laugh, saying: Get away! Jack Sheppard!"

In all good things, you can be certain, the spirit of the English will find the extreme; but there is a great deal of truth in the opinion of the honorable Josuah J. Marshall, and the fact that he was hanged does not disprove his theory. A true gentleman of the criminal fraternity accepts the inevitability of the noose philosophically, as the rest of us are forced to accept the inevitability of death. It is, in either case, a mere matter of time; that is a fact of life. The issue at hand is to live as well as one can, or to put off being hanged as long as possible. Josuah J. Marshall attained the ripe old age of eighty-three years before being hanged. He bequeathed his methods and is philosophy to his children and his children's children.

Now go into the prisons and ask the governors by what means their boarders most frequently escape. Their response will be unanimous: *however they can*. Do not be content with that overly vague reply; get to the bottom of the question. Establish the categories. It will not put the jailer in a good mood, of that you can be sure, because you will put your finger on some remembered wound, ancient or modern, but in the end you will know this: there are more escapes at noon than midnight, more by the main gate than by underground tunnels. The majority escape with heads held high, faces bare and a smile upon their lips, bowing politely to the concierge's wife and saying "Good-day, my friend" to the guard.

The human mind is made that way; it has a passion for contradiction. Precautions can, in the final analysis, only be excited or intensified by the affirmation: "I am not a thief." That is sufficient in itself to provide a constable or a gendarme with a motive to put you to the test in case you are a liar. But say to him "I am a thief," and he will feel a perfectly natural temptation to try and prove the opposite.

This is a serious matter. There was recently to be found in London, behind Drury Lane, a very respectable place where practitioners of the art demonstrated various ways of picking a lock without spoiling it. The course was open to the public, and we had the honor of being present—Rule Britannia! Whereas the preceding considerations were matters of university education, this was a primary school.

If Baron von Altenheimer and Monsignor Benedict really were the brothers Ténèbre, they had obviously employed the Marshall procedure. Except that, as the German bandits were still studying their Plutarch, they had been obliged to build up their own reputation in the Archbishop's salon and sing their own epic. Then they had cried out, after the fashion of the honorable Josuah J. Marshall: "We are the brothers Ténèbre!"

And no one had believed them.

They had, to be sure, not said it in so many words, but they had arranged matters in such a way that the thought had occurred to everyone—and that thought had, indeed, occurred to everyone at the given moment; but everyone had said, like the constable to Josuah J. Marshall: "The brothers Ténèbre! Get away!"

Once a thought has come to knock at the door of the imagination, and has been refused its hospitality, everything is set: the blindfold is covering your eyes, tied in a triple knot. That is the real import of the calculation.

Now, gentlemen of the second rank have been seen to operate in this jolly manner by taking the name of Jack Sheppard. Had the von Altenheimers, then, stolen the identities of the brothers Ténèbre? Where did the falsehood end within their tale? Did the brothers Ténèbre actually exist, or was there not even an atom of truth at the bottom of their shameless lies?

The prefect of police climbed into the first available carriage and returned to Paris at full speed. The ability of that eminent magistrate is proverbial; undoubtedly, he must have put the battalions of his secret army into the field without delay. He found not the least trace, however, in the archives of the Prefecture, of the Chevalier Ténèbre or of brother Ange the vampire, nor the least trace of Baron von Altenheimer or Monsignor Benedict. It appeared that mounting a hunt for an oupire and a vampire was no trivial enterprise!

The remainder of His Lordship's guests withdraw sadly. The good Archbishop, on going to his room, kept one secret consolation in the depths of his heart. There remained to him, to lighten the burden of his misfortune very slightly, the certainty that the pocket-book destined for Mademoiselle d'Arnheim had never left his person. He wanted to count the banknotes again.

Alas, the pocket-book had vanished, along with His Lordship's magnificent pastoral cross!

X. The Missal

That evening the Princess de Montfort did not have the hand of her usual cavalier to help her down from her carriage. For the first time, the Marquis had left his mother in the lurch.

The princess was a strong-minded woman, as we have observed, and the opinion of all strong minds is that the doors should be thrown wide open once youth has reached its end. But among women, especially strong-minded women, there is a world of difference between theory and practice. One paltry ghost story had brought the Princess's entire body out in gooseflesh, even though she did not believe in ghosts. Youth must come to an end, but the Princess was decidedly heartsick when she took the hand of Doctor Récamier as she mounted the steps of her town-house.

"You have a touch of fever, my lady," the doctor said to her, "and I'm not surprised, after everything that has happened. Take my advice: have a nice warm bath tomorrow morning, with a simple affusion of cold water."

"When I think, doctor," the Princess sighed, "that I took that demoiselle d'Arnheim for...oh, the shameless villains! Leonie felt a hairy hand...she's a little mad, poor thing...but look at Gaston, with the bit between his teeth! Oh, I hope he's done the right thing, leaving the seminary! She's pretty, at least. There's nothing to be said. And poor Emerance has a slight squint...but not unbecoming, eh? What a party! It was too terrible, doctor!"

The doctor took his leave, saying: "In a nice warm bath, my lady, a simple affusion."

If anyone had asked the Princess where her son was at that moment, she would have replied without hesitation and with perfect confidence: "My son Gaston is prowling around Mademoiselle d'Arnheim." She might perhaps have added, in her capacity as a strong-minded woman: "At least the Duc never chases after angels!"

In spite of her long experience and ample powers of deduction, the Princess would have been in error in this case. Gaston was not prowling around Mademoiselle d'Arnheim; Gaston was all alone, making his way on foot across the three leagues that separated the Château de Conflans from the Rue de l'Université.

Gaston had indeed escorted Monsieur d'Arnheim and his daughter as far as the humble carriage that awaited them at the gate of the château, but there he had left them, saying to the old man: "Whatever time it may be when I call on you tonight, you must see me; you will understand the reasons for my actions then." He had then gone back towards the château, but instead of going in to find his mother, who would have pestered him for news, he had circled the building and then gone back into the park.

The moon was hidden; the sky was still full of huge, heavy and slow-moving clouds, through which its light occasionally showed for brief intervals. Gaston retraced the route that he had followed during the soirée; he seemed very agitated. When he reached the patch of woodland the darkness was so deep that he hesitated, unsure of his path.

The mysterious noises that he had heard earlier within the park and its environs had ceased now. All was silent save for the distant murmur of the great city, whose presence also revealed itself by the red tint reflected from the low clouds that lay over it.

Such fears are childish! thought the Marquis de Lorgàres. *Even so, I have heard it said that the whole world is vulnerable to such effects, including the king...I am no exception.*

He had passed into an elm-wood, whose undergrowth was composed of thorn-bushes and privet, entwined with serpentine honeysuckle. It was here that he had come during the soirée; he remembered it well—but the elm-grove extended for more than an acre. How could he locate one particular spot in the midst of that profound obscurity?

He took advantage of one shaft of moonlight to move out of the wood, and then he set himself to follow the edge of the stand of trees, looking for the little footpath that he had already missed once. A second glimmer of light showed him a dozen petty paths winding into the undergrowth, all very similar. At the same time, he heard the sound of carriage-wheels on the driveway; the guests were going home and the doors would soon be closed. He had to make haste.

Gaston picked one of the footpaths at random and followed it for a hundred paces; it led him straight to an enormous stump surrounded by heaps of dead wood. He retraced his steps at a run and took another route, then another: they both took him deeper into the wood. The lights were being extinguished in the château. It would no longer be possible to leave by the gate.

An entire hour went by while he searched in vain, and Gaston had quite lost heart, when a shaft of moonlight lit a spark at his feet. Something flat and metallic glittered in the brushwood. He bent down, picked up the object that he had previously hidden there, buttoned his coat over his precious find, and made for the wall that enclosed the park.

A stone wall is a small obstacle to a twenty-year-old in good health. He climbed over it easily, without injury to anything but the knees of his trousers and the cuffs of his black coat. I dare say that His Grace's guard-dogs howled a little, but Gaston was already on his way along the highway.

There was an official on duty at the toll-gate, sleeping in that extraordinary fashion which does not prevent officials from seeing confusedly and moving slowly. There are barriers on every road into Paris, whose presence is vital to the taxation of wines and spirits. The somnambulist, seeing a bare-headed man whose trousers were ripped at the knees and whose coat was torn at the cuffs, leapt to the conclusion that he must be a smuggler intent on the fraudulent intro-duction of a vast quantity of wine, and sounded the alarm in order to rouse his five companions from the same magical sleep. The six functionaries, moved by the best of intentions, demanded that Gaston should either show them his import license or pay his duty.

When Gaston demanded to be allowed through, he was seized and searched, but released again because the officials had found nothing on him but a little missal bound in velvet and enclosed in polished steel, at the end of a length of chain, also made of steel. Gaston, when he saw the missal in the hands of these good men, fell into a chair and almost lost consciousness—but the unanimous opinion of the officials was that even if the object were hollow and full of proof spirit, its capacity was too small for any tax to be payable.

Gaston accepted the return of the missal as if he were taking possession of a treasure and hurried on his way, without bidding farewell to the men in green who had persecuted him while they were lost in a dream.

The missal was, as we have already established, bound in velvet and her-metically encased in steel, sealed by an antique lock; its solidity seemed proven. A large number of ecclesiastics possess breviaries of that sort, but we have no intention of laying a trap for the perspicacity of the reader. The little book was most certainly the one which had formerly hung, attached to a steel chain, around the neck of Monsignor Benedict. Gaston had found it on the ground and picked it up when the archbishop's guests had left the lawn after the story-telling. But why had he not returned it to Monsignor Benedict? Why, instead, had he hidden it as if he were concealing a treasure? The young and handsome Marquis de Lorgàres certainly did not look like a thief.

To tell the truth, it could hardly have been an object of very great im-portance, since Monsignor Benedict had not even noticed that it was missing during the three hours that the concert had lasted.

Or could it?

It was about two o'clock in the morning when the Marquis arrived at the end of the Rue de l'Université, in front of his mother's town house. The de Montfort residence was situated not far from the Bourbon palace, close to the corner of the Rue de Courty. Gaston did not pause at the impressive gateway; he turned the corner of the Rue de Courty, still running, and rang the doorbell of a modest house which backed on to the rear garden of the mansion.

This simple topographical detail will perhaps explain to the reader the innocent and mute mystery of the sentiments of Gaston and Lenore. Lenore's bedroom window looked out upon the vast garden where Gaston had—for an entire month—been taking endless walks.

The door opened. Gaston went up to the second floor and was introduced by Monsieur d'Arnheim himself into a rather squalid apartment. The little spaniel, Mina, came to welcome her friend.

The silent and somber Monsieur d'Arnheim opened the door of his study and closed it behind them.

The clock on the Bourbon palace was sounding five o'clock when Monsieur d'Arnheim's study-door opened again to let Gaston out. Some agreement must have been reached between them, because they shook hands before parting.

X. The Statement of Account

There was a large bowl of punch steaming on the table. It was already half-empty. They were both there: the tall one and the short one.

Baron von Altenheimer was pacing back and forth across the room, with an enormous Prussian pipe clenched in his teeth. His thatch of black hair was gone; this was a tall young man, nearly bald, and what hair he had was reddish-brown. His black coat had been replaced by a Turkish jacket criss-crossed and edged with gold embroidery.

Monsignor Benedict, wearing a crimson satin dressing-gown, was stretched out on an old sofa with a Havana cigar between his lips. Under the dressing-gown the black collar of his clerical garb was visible, the sluggard not having taken the trouble to get out of it. The room was large and high-ceilinged, but it was untidy and ill-furnished. It had two beds. A distinct odor of low-life was in the air.

They both gave every impression of being in a good mood, and there was a brotherly intimacy in their chatter.

There'll be a big noise in the corridors of power in the morning," the tall one said, laughing.

"Better there than here," replied the short one. "I love the Rue de Richelieu. If I ever settle in Paris for good, I'll treat myself to a house on the corner of the Rue de Richelieu and the boulevard."

"Personally, I prefer that nice house that looks out on the Rue de la Paix," the Baron replied. "I think it's the Osmond house. I must pay my respects there some day...but think of the row we kicked up last night!" He went on laughing.

"You were superb," said the younger brother, insincerely.

"And you were very pretty," the older riposted, "but I must admit that when it comes to dupes, these Parisians are the cream."

"The most intelligent people in the world," Benedict murmured, yawning.

The Baron resumed his pacing. "There were a lot of trinkets in that collection," he went on, disdainfully. "Except for your ring and my snuff-box, I didn't see much apart from the Princess's bracelet..."

"You're telling me," Benedict replied. "Parisians have jewels specially made for collection days."

The Baron smiled and downed a glass of punch in a single draught. He filled up the monsignor's glass, which had also been drained, albeit in smaller gulps. "We won't get as much as a thousand louis for the lot," he said. "Paris is a dump, I tell you."

"For work, certainly...but when one retires from the business..."

"All right then," the elder interrupted, depositing his immense porcelain pipe on the table. "You said it. Let's talk business. It's already one o'clock in the morning and it's scarcely worth going to bed—we have to be on the road to Boulogne by four."

"I'm tired," said the monsignor, yawning for the second time and stretching lazily on his sofa.

"We have to, for safety's sake..."

"Leave off! Who the devil do you expect to winkle us out of here?"

"Stranger things have happened," the tall man said.

"There are two places made for hiding in," the shorter man replied. "Paris and the Black Forest—and Paris is ten times as good as the Black Forest!"

"But you agreed..." said the Baron reproachfully.

"I've changed my mind," Benedict said, drily.

"You no longer want to leave?"

"Of course...but not tonight."

"Why not?"

"I have my reasons."

"It's foolishness," complained the elder, testily.

"Possibly," the younger replied, "but I'm my own master, and am at liberty to be foolish."

The Baron made an effort to contain the anger that was rumbling within him. "Look here," he said, abruptly but without losing his temper. "What mischief has Satan put into your head? Tell me!"

"Very well, Old William," Monsignor replied. "I don't want us to fall out over this; there's probably a nice stroke or two to be pulled in London these days. I'll tell you my reasons, just as if you had the right to call me to account. To begin with, we have nothing to fear here; not one of our hirelings knows where we are. No one even knows that English is our mother tongue, since you had the honor of being raised within sight of the Tower of London and I was born in the parish of Saint Giles, not two steps from Oxford street, where I did my earliest jobs. So, tomorrow morning, we get out of this slum; we go to Vincennes, clean ourselves up in the woods and we come back, arm in arm, to the toll-gate: William Staunton, bookseller of Ave Maria Lane and Mrs. Olivia

Staunton, his young companion, both on their first trip to Paris, their pockets full of guineas and determined to have a jolly good time. We come down somewhere in the vicinity of the Palais-Royal—and who'll see what has become of the privy councilor to the King of Wurtemburg and the Pope's chamberlain?"

"It's absurd," said the older, coldly. "Is that all?"

"No. If you're absolutely determined to be gone, I'll go too—but not until tomorrow evening, and not without Mademoiselle d'Arnheim."

The Baron's pallor gave way to redness. "Do you know who that d'Arnheim girl is?" he murmured, through clenched teeth.

"Of course!" the younger man replied. "It's Lenore...I gave her up for twelve hundred thousand francs when we were poor, but today I'd pay two millions for her...I love her!"

"Imbecile!" said the elder, harshly. "you've risked your life ten times for a few louis..."

"I love her, do you hear?" cried the blond man, raising himself up on his elbow. "I want to carry her off, and I shall! Don't shrug your shoulders like that! It's a long while since you were in command here, Old William. I'm no longer a child; my word counts for just as much as yours."

Old William—since another name has been given to Baron von Altenheimer, we might as well use it—crossed his long arms over his breast and said: "You don't suppose, Bobby, that I'd help you to play that sort of game?"

Bobby—which was perhaps the monsignor's true name—replied: "Didn't you help me with the blond girl in Itàbe? And pretty Efflam in Petrovaradin? And the girl in Venice? And the one in Stuttgart? And the rest? Me, I've always helped you, like the minor player who feeds the cue to Kemble or Talma. I'm as good an actor as you are, William, and you need me more than I need you."

Smiling scornfully, the tall man turned his back and went to refill his glass.

"Just listen," the short man went on, "and you'll see that we both know how to put together a plan of attack. When you donated your pocket-book with the thousand-franc notes—which wasn't bad, I admit—I thought of something better. I went to His Lordship in my turn and said to him: 'Your Highness, could you tell me where this respectable Monsieur d'Arnheim lives?' What could His Highness think but that the fortune of his protégés would be made if we were to go there? I have the address: in the Rue de Courty, at the corner of the Rue de l'Université. Tomorrow, I'll spend half an hour making up my face in the image of a very respectable marquise, fifty or sixty years old. There was just such a one at the Archbishop's; I'll copy her perfectly. I shan't bother to mention the costume, which is a mere bagatelle. Thus transformed into a dowager, I arrive at the Baron d'Arnheim's house at the hour when society ladies are wont to circulate, in mid-afternoon. Madame la Comtesse de Chastellux...or de Noailles...or de Mortemart...some irresistible name, at any rate...on behalf of the Archbishop of Paris. I go in; I explain that I heard the young and interesting virtuosa yesterday at the Château of Conflans. I have a niece...or the daughter of my poor eldest son, who is dead. I have found that she has a natural bent for music, which is not surprising, since her father had such a lovely voice! 'Would you like to get into my carriage, my dear child? I want to introduce you to my daughter-in-law...' In spite of all your skepticism, you can't pretend that there's anything in the least difficult about it. The little one gets in..."

"And you take her all the way to London in one go?" the erstwhile Baron von Altenheimer interrupted, sarcastically.

"You'll allow me to suppose," Monsignor Bobby replied, acidly, "that a boy like me, transformed from a dowager into a great lord, could easily succeed in pleasing a young girl..."

"You'll allow me to suppose," the tall man interrupted again. "that a stupid act is the greatest stupidity of all! Even if it were supposed that a boy like you, a little less highly-born than my boot, is exactly what is required to play the role of Don Juan, I'd still say that it's absurd. Firstly, the Prince might recognize you. Secondly, I don't want to be inconvenienced on our travels by a woman."

The smaller man lay back on his pillow and sent a long plume of smoke spiraling towards the ceiling. "Ripe fruits that one hesitates to pick go bad," he muttered, clenching his teeth. "Between the two of us, I believe the pear is ripe; if we stay together, William, it will go so bad that we'll get it into our heads to cut one another's throats before long."

"I've a mind to..." William began, his voice tremulous and menacing.

"There, you see!" Bobby said, coldly. "the pear's ripe—we must go our separate ways."

The tall man made a determined effort to contain his anger. He drank two glasses of punch in rapid succession, and then he said: "All right, then—let's split up!"

"The share-out won't be difficult," said Bobby, who seemed much less emotional than his elder partner. "It won't take long. The banknotes are in two lots in the missal. I anticipated that our association wouldn't last forever and I've always taken care to divide them up into wads of equal value."

"Oh, you anticipated that, did you?" William said. "When I found you so poor, and so ragged."

"Were you rich?" Bobby demanded, before adding: "Go on, Old William, we have nothing for which to reproach one another. If you've earned your share, I've deserved twice as much."

"Ungrateful spawn," murmured the tall man. "But you're right—it's time to part...where's the missal?"

Bobby put his cigar between his lips and patted his side beneath the dressing-gown. "Good accounts make good friends," he said. "You should have a statement listing the exact contents of the missal in your pocket-book."

"I have the pocket-book."

"Get it out, so that we can settle up." He was still rummaging among the ample folds of satin. He was showing no obvious signs of anxiety.

"Right!" said the tall man.

"Right," Bobby echoed. "I must have put it under my pillow when I came in, as I usually do. Go see."

William crossed the room and snatched the pillow from one of the beds. "There's nothing here," he said. "You have it on you."

Bobby got up. His expression was seized by a vague dread. Instead of continuing to pat the satin of his dressing-gown he tore it from his body, to gain better access to the costume which he had worn at the archbishop's soirée. Both hands groped about his left side. He became very pale and his cigar fell from his lips. William, who was following him with a determined stare, was red in the face but he said not a word.

They moved towards one another, each now clutching an open blade produced from who knows where. They came face to face in the middle of the room, looking deep into one another's eyes as if to read the minds behind them, and they said with one voice, through gritted teeth: "You've stolen the missal!"

Bobby tried to duck under William's thrust, while William swayed backwards in the attempt to avoid Bobby's. Then they set themselves on guard again, standing toe to toe, the long face of the taller looming over the blond head of the smaller. Bobby's neck was bleeding and there was a red stain in William's armpit; both thrusts had struck home.

They paused for a moment thus, their left hands splayed before their breasts, ready to parry, while their right hands trembled as they gripped their daggers tightly. Both men obviously knew enough about the art of fencing to concentrate on protecting the head and the heart, leaving the limbs to take their chances—it doesn't matter much if one is wounded there, provided that one kills one's opponent. Each of them knew that he would have to sacrifice a little blood of his own to purchase a full measure of the other's.

Their eyes shone like four red-hot coals. Perhaps William seemed stronger, but Bobby was the more terrible. On seeing them both inflamed by rage and intent on murder, one would have bet on the knife of Ange the vampire against the dagger of the Chevalier Ténèbre.

William was the first to drop his weapon, having first taken a step back. Bobby lowered his arms, saying: "You're scared, and you're going to give back the missal!"

"I'm not scared," the tall man replied, "but I can see that the chain is still around your neck. You haven't stolen it—you've lost it!"

"Lost it!" cried Bobby. "The chain is pure steel. It would carry a hundred books."

"Yes," the other interrupted, while seizing a loose end of the chain. "It's broken!"

Bobby dropped his knife in his turn.

"Right by the rivet," he murmured. "But how was it that I didn't feel the absence of the weight? I know! I remember! On the lawn, I pulled on the chain and it resisted...." He jerked violently at the other end of the chain, which detached itself from the material of his vestment.

"A flaw," he stammered. "And the broken link was caught up in the fold of my costume."

William took the chain, while Bobby, who had froth at the corners of his mouth, closed his fist and said: "I bought that chain in Frankfurt, at number three the Zeil. I'll make an express trip to Frankfurt to tear that shopkeeper's heart out."

They knew only too well that they had both made a mistake. Neither could maintain their suspicions in the face of that mute witness, the broken chain. They were now entirely given over to consternation.

William took one end of the chain in each hand and pulled them apart with all his strength; the chain remained solid.

"It only had the one flaw," he murmured.

His pocket-book was on the table, ready to verify the count. He opened it and began to read in a faint voice: "Two banknotes of fifty thousand pounds...number one...two million five hundred thousand francs!"

"The Bank of England only took five impressions from the plate," Bobby sighed, "and we had two of them."

"Number two," the tall man went on, "two banknotes of a thousand pounds...Number three, two banknotes of a thousand pounds... Number four, two banknotes of a thousand pounds..."

"There were a hundred of them" Bobby interrupted him.

"Another two million five hundred thousand francs! Number one hundred and two, two banknotes of five thousand pounds...that was after the Venice job... Number one hundred and three, from the same job, two banknotes of four thousand pounds... Number one hundred and four..."

Bobby threw himself on the pocket-book, tearing it from William's grasp, and pressed it tightly between his hands.

"We had millions!" said the tall man, collapsing in a fit of tears. "Millions and millions and millions..."

"Millions and millions and millions!" echoed the small man, grinding his teeth like a tiger.

They were still looking at one another.

"Shall we kill one another?" Bobby said, coldly.

William picked up the punch-bowl in both hands and drank down its remaining contents in one draught. Then he drew himself proudly up to his full height and he too said; "Shall we kill one another?"

But Bobby had already put his blade away. He began to pace back and forth across the room. William let himself fall into a chair. There was a long silence.

"Brother," said the short man, in the end, "you said it a little while ago: we've often risked our lives for a few louis."

"Do you have a plan?" William asked, his eyes calm and clear now.

"There are two possibilities, brother. Either the missal is still on the lawn, in the place where it fell, or one of the archbishop's guests picked it up."

"That's true."

"We mustn't forget that in either case the missal is secured by a secret catch that would defy the most skilful of locksmiths."

"I believe so."

"We have two more parts to play: one on the grassy stage, the other in the bedroom of the man—whoever it might be—who had the misfortune to find the missal."

They took one another by the hand and said in unison, in a low voice: "He's a dead man!"

XII. The Princess Gets Up

Shortly before dawn the dogs guarding the Château de Conflans began to howl. It is a matter of record that the archbishop's guests got little sleep that night. At four o'clock in the morning, or thereabouts, two men—one tall and one short—climbed over the wall and went into the woods. They wore the costumes of working men, but they were both well-armed beneath their shirts.

Dawn, when it broke, found them in the clearing where the friends of the Archbishop of Paris had gathered as night fell on the previous evening. They were both crawling on the grass, searching the shadows with their eyes.

"We won't find it," said the tall one, abruptly rising to his feet.

"Why's that?" the shorter one demanded.

"Because someone got here before us."

"What makes you think...?"

"Get your bearings, now that it's not as dark," William replied. "I'm on the exact spot where you were standing as I finished my story, and my foot is where the missal fell."

"Should have fallen."

"*Did* fall," the tall man insisted. He pointed a finger at the grass between his feet.

The smaller man approached, got down on his knees and leaned over the designated spot. He could clearly see the bruised grass, and beneath it, the imprint cut into the soil by the sudden arrest of a rectangular object. He immediately got to his feet.

The two brothers, without saying a word, redirected their steps towards the wall of the park. The first part had been played, and the game lost; the second had yet to begin.

As they approached the wall, William suddenly stopped, saying: "Someone else came this way last night."

Bobby's educated eyes were already examining a section of the wall whose tapestry of ivy had been disturbed. The broken shoots had not had time to go yellow, and the detached foliage was still fresh.

"A scrap of cloth!" he cried.

"Fine cloth," said William. "That never belonged to the clothing of some night-prowler. Look at these tracks!"

The footprints left by the marquis were, indeed, visible on the dewy ground.

"Dancing-shoes," William went on. "A foot like a woman's!"

Bobby climbed in car-like fashion to the top of the wall, where something white was lodged.

"G. L. and the crown of a marquis!" he cried, throwing a handkerchief to William.

"Gaston de Lorgàres!" murmured William. "Why didn't he leave the château by the main gate?" He climbed the wall in his turn.

The two of them took the road to Paris, pensively.

"Anything under your shirts?" asked the guard at the toll-gate.

William stopped, as an idea came into his head. Striking the pose, innocent and astute at the same time, of a concerned citizen, he said instead of answering the question: "Are you also responsible for arresting thieves?"

"Why do you ask?" the official countered, while patting the tall man's shirt in a tokenistic fashion.

"Because it's my opinion that our thief must have come this way."

The official, three-quarters awakened by curiosity, said: "What thief?"

"The sharp dresser who was carrying Monsieur le curé's brand-new breviary, that's who!"

"Well, I never!" exclaimed the man at the toll-gate. "There's a turn up!"

He said that in such a manner that sweat immediately sprang up on William's and Bobby's foreheads. Their hearts beat faster. They said, as one: "You got him!"

"He had no duty to pay," the official retorted, stoutly, "and I'm no gendarme."

"What time was it when he came through?" William asked, sadly.

"An hour after midnight...he'll be a long way off by now, if he's still running."

Later that morning, an impoverished old woman took up a position in the Rue de Courty, not far from the house where Monsieur d'Arnheim lived, while an unfamiliar beggar established himself on a step facing the house occupied by the Princess de Montfort.

This occurred some considerable time before the Princess, whose sleep was prolonged by the emotions and exertions of the previous night, was ready to face the new day. Her first words, after waking up. were an enquiry as to Gaston's whereabouts.

"Monsieur le Marquis," her chambermaid replied, "has already presented himself three times asking to speak to Madame la Princesse."

"It couldn't be helped, Justine. I feel weak, and I haven't the strength to get up to receive him. Tell him to come in."

An instant later, Gaston was introduced into his mother's bedroom.

"My dear child," the Princess said to him at once, "You know me, and you know that I don't like to scold. Today, when even I might be inclined to reprimand you, I shall abstain, because I want you to trust me, to trust me absolutely. Something extraordinary has happened to you; I know that. Would you like to make your confession to me?"

"With all my heart, mother," the young marquis replied, kissing her hand tenderly. "It is precisely for the purpose of telling you what is happening to me that I have taken the liberty of demanding an interview with you this morning."

"Then I shall listen, Gaston, asking only one thing of you: that you are perfectly frank with the mother who loves you."

The Marquis blushed slightly, but he replied without hesitation: "You might well complain about me, Madame, but not of any lack of frankness. I want to marry."

The princess reeled from the blow, taking cover beneath her bedclothes. The timid Gaston had gone for good, it seemed.

"I must point out," the lady replied, her eyebrows furrowing in spite of herself, "that you are a child, in love for the first time, and that you have gone mad."

It seemed that Gaston was prepared for that kind of reaction, for he lifted his mother's hand to his lips again.

"To marry a singer...!" the Princess began, angrily.

"Permit me, Madame, Gaston interrupted her, very softly. "I hope to furnish proof in the course of this conversation...I am in love, as you have done me the honor of observing, in the second place. I admit that much. As for having gone mad, it's said that such is the lot of lively minds illuminated by superabundant imagination; in my mind and my conscience I feel that I am out of reach of that danger; I am not at all well-endowed for going mad. If my cool, practical and prosaic character has no other advantage, it protects me from that..."

"Oh, get on with it!" the Princess cried, impatiently.

"Which brings us to the singer, Madame, and since you have asked me to be frank, I will admit, frankly, that I am astonished and wounded by that insinuation. I have long attained the age when such pranks are played, and I have noticed that the stubborn regularity of my conduct has occasioned a certain mockery among my friends. I believe I can even affirm that it has sometimes put a smile on my mother's lips..."

"Oh, Gaston...!"

"My God, Madame, youth which does not pass, as it is said, is entitled to raise a smile...I have been living like a little saint. On the other hand, no crisis or malady, chivalrous or romantic, has ever troubled my existence, which has been as peaceful as the lovely little stream that winds through your park at Chelles—which you yourself have bitterly reproached for having neither a waterfall nor a whirlpool... Were I not a de Montfort, I would say that I had good bourgeois blood in my veins, retaining from the first of January to Saint Sylvester's day the moderate and calm temperature of mediocrity..."

"What case are you pleading now?" the Princess interrupted him, raising her eyes. "You're like a Norman lawyer this morning. Are you starting your diplomatic career with me?"

"I have renounced diplomacy, Madame," Gaston replied, calmly. "My vocation is to make a rich marriage and to live on my estates."

"A rich marriage!" echoed the stupefied Princess. "Your cousin Emerance has fifty thousand francs a year."

"My mother might perhaps have been able to deduce," Gaston replied, lifting the Princess's hand to his lips for the third time, "that if I have not shown overmuch eagerness in the matter of that union, it is because I have another, more important, party in mind."

Madame de Montfort rubbed her eyes with her knuckles. She suspected that she was not yet fully awake.

"More important!" she repeated, perhaps more shocked by the manner of the expression than the idea itself. "Are you really there, my boy?"

"I believe that I have been unkindly judged thus far, Mother," Gaston replied, "and my preamble, which may have seemed overlong to you, can hardly have modified your opinion on that score. I can only do myself justice by telling you that I am a respectful son, obedient and loving—but marriage, Madame, is one's entire future!"

"I have never tried to force you..." the Princess began.

"Of course, Mother, of course—but do you imagine that you had not made it clear what path your maternal affection wished me to take? My cousin Emerance..."

"Say no more, I beg you, about your cousin Emerance, Gaston! Your cousin Emerance was not an accessory to the building of my beautiful castles in Spain. I don't even know if we would have been able to obtain her hand."

"I don't know either, Madame, and I don't care. It is in Hungary, not in Spain, that I have built my own imaginary castles." He stopped, as if a vision had suddenly taken hold of him.

The Princess looked at him, open-mouthed. "And what connection have you ever had with Hungary?" she asked, after a pause.

"You have forgotten, Madame," Gaston replied, "that you commissioned me, some time ago, to take steps to withdraw your interest from the property at Debrecen owned by my brother the Duc.

"And you met the daughter of some local magnate in the lawyer's office?"

"I implore you, Madame, not to make fun," the young marquis said, seriously. "there was never a subject less suitable for joking... Do you remember the story told last night by the Baron von Altenheimer?"

The Princess clapped her hand together. "I knew that there was some extravagance under all this!" she cried. "I suppose it concerns the lovely Lenore, daughter of Prince Jacobyi."

You are right, Madame," said Gaston, unblinkingly.

"What an evening!" the Princess went on. "I dreamed of those cunning scoundrels all night. I refused to believe their silly story as a matter of principle... Look, Gaston, all joking aside, I want to talk to you seriously..."

"Does the party not seem suitable to you, Mother? " asked the young marquis, his calmness put to the test.

"What party? Are we going back to the vampires of yesteryear and that stupid phantasmagoria? Don't talk to me about marrying the Sleeping Beauty or some other fairy tale. Stop now, Monsieur le Marquis, or you'll have me convinced that your mind is definitely unhinged."

"Madame," said Gaston, unhurriedly, "Hungary is not Faerie. Our cousin Camille, Prince of Guéménée and de Rochefort, was married only last year to the Princess of Wertheim-Rosenberg, and we ourselves are descended from the ancient kings of Hungary through Charlotte de Croy d'Havré, my great-grandmother on my father's side.

The Princess took her flask, opened it, closed it again, then opened it again so that she could close it again. In every country where there are flasks, such gestures indicate the exhaustion of patience.

"I suppose," the Marquis continued, redoubling his persuasive efforts, "that any teller of fantastic tales, whether honest man or bandit, might take the name de Montfort—which you wear so well, Mother dear—and introduce it into his tale like the one we heard yesterday. Would that prevent you from being at the head of a noble French family? Madame, I beseech you to believe that the information I have does not come from Baron von Altenheimer—if that really is his name. I am speaking seriously of serious matters, and I have come to ask you whether you are willing to approach Prince Jacobyi on my behalf to ask for the hand of his daughter in marriage."

If the Princess had been standing up she would have fallen down.

"This is too much, Monsieur le Marquis!" she said, sitting up straight again. Then she added, in a sarcastic tone: "And to what part of the world would it be necessary to address the letter to this Oedipus, soliciting the hand of his Antigone?"

"I would not have dared to compare the one that I love to the saintly figure bequeathed to us by antique poetry," Gaston replied, still perfectly placid. "The letter must be addressed to Chrétien Baszin, Prince Jacobyi, at Chandor Castle, near Szeged, Hungary."

The Princess opened her eyes wide. Gaston," she murmured, "is there really something at the bottom of all this?"

"I don't know how to convince you of that elementary truth," the Marquis replied, "except to assure you that there is a young lady who will be your daughter-in-law and who will bring me a dowry of five or six hundred thousand francs a year."

"This is so extraordinary!" murmured the Princess. "You have said not a word to me before today!"

"I confess, Madame, that I have only been a man for twenty-four hours."

"You cannot hope, however," said Madame de Montfort, in a tone which was already much changed, "that I will embark upon an enterprise of this sort without explanations and proofs."

"Mother," replied Gaston, solemnly and sincerely, "I will give you clear and precise explanations—but as for proofs, it will be necessary to content yourself with the word of honor of a man who has never told a lie."

"Is it your own word of honor?"

"It is my own word of honor, Madame."

"I will listen, my son. Remember the name that you bear, and what indignity and cowardice there would be in deceiving your mother."

Gaston set out, briefly and clearly, the provisions of Hungarian legislation regarding matters of litigation.

All princesses have some understanding of the language of business. Let us not be deceived; only those possessed of considerable fortunes are elevated to such a condition, and that prose is the very soil in which the poetry of grandeur flourishes. The Princess de Montfort understood readily enough the mechanism by which feudal rights could be repurchased: a powerful instrument, which is not as insolently injurious to the idea of progress as the principle of inalienability or the right of primogeniture, but which works usefully and ceaselessly to consolidate great territorial domains.

"Chrétien Baszin, Prince Jacobyi," Gaston continued, "having been dispossessed at the end of 1821, has until the end of 1826 to buy back his estates, at the same price at which they were sold, without any regard to any further or partial sales which have taken place since then. That is the law. So much the worse for those who have taken advantage of the same law! Prince Jacobyi, profiting from the benevolence of the law, has bought back his castle and his lands, which are as vast as a province."

"*Has* bought back?" the Princess repeated. "The deal is done, and completed, is it not? You can assure me of that, under oath?"

"I assure you, under oath, Mother," the young marquis replied, firmly, "that the magnate Jacobyi will receive your request at Chandor Castle, of which he will be the sole and sovereign master. I assure you, under oath, that if I introduce Lenore into your house, it will be as Princess Jacobyi, sole heir to her father's immense fortune."

143

Everything had now been said. The Princess remained silent and Gaston allowed her time to reflect. We shall take advantage of the pause to admit to the reader that, given the character of Madame de Montfort—who was otherwise a most excellent and charming princess—Gaston had chosen, with devastating tact, the only route which could possibly have won her consent. He had played the part of the money-lover so admirably that the first words his mother spoke were: "I fear, in truth—yes, my child, I fear—that the idea of a fortune...in marriage, believe me, a fortune is not everything!"

"I like a fortune, Madame."

"Undoubtedly, but the wife herself..."

"But I adore the wife, who is an angel!"

"Very well, Gaston. Ring for my chambermaid. I want to get up. We shall see...we shall think on it..."

Instead of ringing the bell, Gaston went to the sideboard to pick up one of those ornamental rosewood boxes called *papeteries*. He placed the charming object on the coverlet in front of his mother. It contained blue ink (which princesses and Doctor Récamier love, although I hate it myself), Surrey paper as glossy as satin, a steel pen—the first one, invented by Perry—and Spanish wax that exhaled a light and temperate perfume. Gaston opened the dainty desk, arranged the pad of paper and dipped the Perry pen into the blue ink.

"I have rivals," he murmured, "and time is pressing."

If he had done as others do; if he had put his head upon his mother's bosom, saying only: "I love..." Who knows? Perhaps it would have worked as well. We are describing what actually happened.

The Princess, who was a woman of style, wrote a dignified and concise letter, perfectly polite but getting straight to the point. She was paid in full, for Gaston hugged her as if she were some poor woman of the suburbs and as if he, the Marquis, were wearing the shirt of some Parisian urchin. Such extravagant gestures of affection, proscribed by etiquette, are nevertheless well worth having.

Gaston fled with his prey. We cannot say for sure whether he noticed the beggar sitting on the step facing the main gate of the de Montfort house, or the poor old lady stationed across from the the house where Monsieur and Mademoiselle d'Arnheim were living. He could have seen both of them, for he went directly from the grand gate to the humble door on the Rue de Courty. What cannot be doubted is that the beggar and the poor old lady saw him; they abandoned their posts instantly, meeting at the corner of the two streets and exchanging several words in a low tone.

Gaston did not stay more than a quarter of an hour in Monsieur d'Arnheim's house. He came out, his face radiant, and went on foot towards the Rue de Lille. The beggar walked behind him, while the poor woman went back to her sentry-duty. The beggar returned an hour later and said to the old woman: "He's ordered a carriage."

"When for?"

"I don't know...let's wait for nightfall."

At five o'clock, Gaston returned to the town-house in a cab. As he passed the threshold of the gateway the beggar went towards the old woman and said: "He's going in to dinner. We have an hour to do likewise."

They went off together. They were gone for no more than five minutes, but it was too much.

Every sentinel knows that he must have a very good reason to abandon his post. The Marquis had not, in fact, gone in to dinner. He could have been seen coming out again a few moments later, on horseback, and turning once again into the Rue de Courty. A carriage and horses drew up before Monsieur d'Arnheim's house, and Monsieur d'Arnheim came out in his travelling clothes to take his place in the carriage. The driver whipped his horses into motion and Gaston galloped alongside.

The carriage went right through Paris and made its exit through the toll-gate at La Villette, then took the Strasbourg Road. Gaston maintained his escort over a considerable distance; darkness had fallen when he turned back.

In the meantime, the beggar and the old woman had taken up their posts again and continue their vigil. At about six o'clock, the old woman went to find the beggar. "The Devil with this!" she said.

"Wait," the other replied. patiently, in a deep baritone voice. "The time will come and the place suits our purpose. There's not so much as a stray cat in the Rue de l'Université. We can sit down now on either side of the door."

Scarcely had they taken their places on benches of the kind which are set at the entrances of a great many town houses in the Faubourg Saint-Germain than the hoofbeats of a horse were heard in the distance. The ragged couple paid no attention to the noise; it was not a horseman that they were waiting for.

The horseman approached and stopped directly in front of the closed gate. The beggar and the old woman stayed in their corners until the moment when the horseman cried out, in an imperious voice: "The gate!" Then they started, both as one.

They leapt to their feet, and a second bound carried each of them to one side of the horse. Gaston was seized by both legs, dragged to the ground, stabbed and searched from head to toe within the blink of an eye.

"Nothing!" said the beggar.

"Nothing," echoed the old woman, with a curse.

The gate opened. The old woman and the beggar took to their heels and, while still in full flight, threw off their rags. One could then have seen, under the next street-lamp, two men running with equal rapidity: one tall, one short.

As for Gaston, the servants who came to open the gate found him bathed in his own blood beside his motionless horse. His breast had been pierced by two thrusts of a dagger.

XIII. The Black Graves

The Marquis de Lorgàres was confined to his bed for four months by his wounds. The thrusts had been masterly; either might have been fatal, and Dupuytren[19] was able to boast for many years afterwards of that particular cure. In the meantime, Prince Jacobyi's reply arrived in Paris—bearing the address of Chandor Castle—and was favorable.

As one would expect, the Princess, although she trusted the Marquis's word completely, had not been deterred from obtaining information from her cousins the de Rohans, who were established in Hungary. It was, after all, part of her duty as a mother. The information thus transmitted was, like the Prince's reply, favorable.

The Prince had bought back his lands. The Prince was, as before, one of the greatest lords of the Austrian Empire.

The marriage of the Marquis de Lorgàres to Princess Lenore took place in Szeged, at the beginning of March 1826.

Early in April that same year, a little old man with a pleasant face and an easy-going manner was trudging along the high road from Pest to Szeged, pulling a hand-cart containing a poor creature who looked like a living corpse and who had, moreover, lost his reason. Not far from Szeged, upstream of Morzau, there is a spring whose water is clear, protected by a little minaret from the dust of the road. The water of that spring was blessed by Saint Miklos, and has the power to cure madness. The little old man was a good father who had come from the region of Ofen, dragging his unfortunate son every step of the way.

Since that era our French engineers have laid four parallel iron bars all the way from Pest to Belgrade, via Szeged. It only requires a few hours to cross that vast plain. The last time I saw Szeged, that strange town which contains as many bells as the entire district of Beauce, it had an old pupil of our École Polytechnique for its king. He was in the process of building a thousand-meter bridge across the Tisza: a magnificent bridge to carry the railway. Austrian engineers came to study the work, carried out by a human ant-hive in which one could identify twenty races and whose members spoke fifteen languages.

I realized then that the confusion of languages had counted for nothing in preventing the erection of the Tower of Babel. The bridge marched upon the waters, so to speak, supported by great tubular columns, and I saw a daguerreotype machine with the round eye of its black chamber already focused on its arches. This is our future civilization—but on that same voyage I saw accused and condemned men, stretched out entirely naked on the damp earth in the cellars of Turkish forts: forts whose walls, flanked by corpulent towers, looked over that same Parisian bridge. We have, however, already raised the possibility

---

[19] The military surgeon Guillaume Dupuytren (1777-1835).

that men might break out of prisons, even those whose stones have been set permanently in place.

In 1826, the high road entered the city via a lake of mud in winter, a sea of dust in summer. The dust of Szeged is famous in Hungary, and the mud too. Ingenious Magyars set planks end to end in order that these precipices may be crossed, but the regulations require carriages to pass alongside them lest they be rendered useless, and the trusting pedestrian who dares to set foot upon them is almost certain to fall off.

The pious father, the hand-cart and the son arrived two hours before sunset at the horribly churned-up plain called the Place Joseph II, in the shadow of the beautiful Byzantine Church of Saint Job. The hand-cart stopped in front of a sort of caravanserai, bearing a sign depicting a saint clad in red, whose interior courtyard, as large as one of our public squares, was bordered by worm-eaten wooden arcades. The little old man asked politely for the least expensive room in the inn, deposited his son there and went out to get his papers stamped by a government official. His passport bore the name Petroz Aszuth, leather-merchant of Kaiserbad.

The servants in Hungarian inns are usually Slavs and, in consequence, almost as garrulous as the staff of French taverns. Before dinner was served everyone knew the whole story of little Petroz Aszuth, who was taking his idiot son to the spring of Saint Miklos. The poor lumpen boy was certainly in great need of the spring. The innkeeper's daughter who took him his food was kind enough to strike up a conversation with him to relieve his boredom slightly, but she returned saying: "One might as well talk to Schwartz, the guard-dog!"

The night was already well-advanced when the little old man came back. He did not want any supper and immediately went up to his room. As soon as he was inside he locked the door and drew the curtains over the window.

The idiot leapt from his bed and put on a blond wig. You would have immediately recognized the long lean figure of Baron von Altenheimer. "Do you know something, Bobby?" he asked, animatedly.

Bobby removed his dirty beard, which was making his rosy cheeks itch, and plunged his face into a basin of fresh water, displaying the pretty face of Monsignor Benedict.

"Well," he says, "this place hasn't changed—they still chatter like magpies. I know the story from beginning to end."

Tall William sat down on the foot of his bed and to smoke his porcelain pipe. "Go on," he said.

"It was the marquis all right," Bobby replied, lighting his cigar. "He's given the missal to old Jacobyi, who's bought his hovel back..."

"Then they're thieves like us!" William cried. "The missal only had five hundred thousand florins of his, from Lenore's ransom, and he'd have needed six times that to buy his estates back!"

Bobby shrugged his shoulders. "If they'd kept the lot," he replied, "I could almost have forgiven them—after all, it's every man for himself, isn't it? But since old Baszin got back his castle, his forests, his lakes and his fields, he's taken out all his mortgages again and borrowed exactly the same sum as the excess he took from the missal. Even before he celebrated the marriage of his daughter he had delivered our cash into the hands of the Primate of Hungary, the Archbishop of Graz. The fact has been advertised in Vienna, Venice, Stuttgart, Paris and everywhere else, and all the sheep that we have fleeced have turned up, demanding their wool! Pillaged, all of it! Not a single florin of our little hoard remains—and if there were anything left, the rogues would still be queuing up!"

"Wretches!" William groaned.

"Let me tell you," Bobby went on, "everyone is talking about us here. Since we've done what we came to do, we'd best be on our way. They know everything! The story of our Paris venture has become legendary. The tale of the Archbishop's collection is all the rage. And the missal itself...but it's the story of the missal that I want to tell you. The Marquis was running an errand for his mother when he picked up the missal. His intention was to return it to me, but the missal had fallen so unluckily that the secret catch had been sprung. Nothing was broken, but the steel casement could be opened as easily as one might open a book. The marquis did exactly that, perhaps by chance, and the two fifty-thousand-pound banknotes leapt to his eyes. He understands English, and you had taken care to acquaint him, a few minutes earlier, with the story of the father of Lenore, with whom he was already in love even though he had never spoken to her..."

"I remember!" murmured William. "He had the nerve to ask me for information about rights of repurchase, on the pretext that his brother had property in Debrecen..."

"When he asked you for that information, his plan was conceived," Bobby went on. "He's a smart fellow and I won't regret the bullet that smashes his head."

William took a flat square bottle from his overcoat, which contained brandy. He took a big gulp. "Ever since that business," he said, "we've been unable to get back on our feet. All our capers have gone wrong, in London, in Berlin, in Vienna--he's the cause of all our misfortune!" He passed the bottle to Bobby, who drank before repeating: "He's the cause of all our misfortune!"

"When we've bled him dry, he must die!"

"He must die!" Bobby echoed, again. "I have all the necessary information. They talk of little else in Szeged, because of the story of the missal, which has been on everyone's lips. He's spending his honeymoon at Chandor. He hunts and he fishes. A big hunt is planned for tomorrow.

"We'll be there!" snarled William.

We'll be there. We must be up early—let's get some sleep, Old William."

The next morning, before daybreak, the little old man from Kaiserbad hitched himself up to his vehicle and carted his maniac son off towards the welcoming spring. The servants of the inn were most impressed by the conduct of the little old man; they pointed him in the right direction and wished him good luck.

The way to the spring was the road to Chandor Castle. After an hour's march, at the moment when dawn silvered the horizon, the hand-cart reached the vast forests of the Baszin domain.

The old man left the main road and pushed the hand-cart into a dense wood. The invalid son, suddenly recovering the agility appropriate to one of his age, leapt on to the moss and opened the false bottom of the cart, from which he extracted two double-barreled shotguns and two costumes of the kind worn by Czech peasants. The change of clothes was affected in no time, and the cart hidden under a bush.

It was not a moment too soon. In the distance, the sound of horns could already be heard.

That day, the Marquis de Lorgàres heard several gunshots fired from cover while he was chasing a wild boar. One shot hissed past his ear, and so that he might be certain that he had not been the victim of an illusion, another bullet lodged itself in the material of his hunting-jacket.

But William and Bobby had said it: fortune was against them.

They were found and recognized, and had to show their pursuers a clean pair of heels. When they came to recover their hand-cart and their disguises they found that the cache had been looted. The road of retreat was closed to them; they could not resume their roles in Szeged.

The spent the night in the woods, resolved to flee; their enterprise had failed. They knew that by the following day the news of their presence would spread throughout the land with lightning rapidity. As soon as they could, they had to put the Tisza between themselves and the crusade that their old misdeeds had launched against them.

"We'll come back later!" William said.

"There'll be a time when Lenore is alone in the castle," Bobby added.

Arriving at the edge of the forest, they saw shadows moving along the river-bank. They had presumed too much in thinking that they had a night to spare; the crusade had already taken up its arms.

They were two determined and tireless individuals, a small army in their own right. They were both fit and they knew the territory well. They conferred for a few minutes and decided to take on the hunt while darkness could provide cover for their flight. The choice of direction was vital; now that the Tisza crossing was closed to them, they could either retrace their steps towards Szeged, then push on towards Kolocza and the Danube, or go upstream to Czongrad, where there was a pontoon bridge.

They decided on the latter course and dived straight into the forest. The night was very dark, which was in their favor.

At two o'clock in the morning they arrived at the Czongrad bridge, at the moment when the moon—which was in its last quarter—showed its pale and narrow crescent above the horizon.

While they were crossing the bridge unhindered, already congratulating themselves at this first success, they saw boats coming swiftly up the water-course; at the same time, they heard the muffled sound of hoofbeats made by horses coming along the bank they had just quit.

Was it the Devil himself who had put their enemies on their track?

The moon illuminated them, and their path was discovered.

"Fire!" cried a voice, which came from the nearest boat. They realized immediately that it was old Baszin in person.

They ducked down just in time to avoid a volley of shots which passed over their heads.

The horses on the bank took to the gallop and their hooves were soon drumming on the planks of the bridge.

William and Bobby, desperately accelerating their pace, had reached the other bank. They threw themselves into the cornfields which covered the whole plain between the Tisza and Turkeve. There, they cowered like two partridges in a furrow, getting their breath back.

The cavalcade was already in the field and the cornstalks rattled, shaken by the passage of the horses. There was one moment when the two fugitives had pursuers to the right and left of them, in front of them and behind—but then the hunt passed by.

The foot of the rearmost horse touched William's head, but he stifled a gasp and kept silent. Its rider was Chrétien Baszin, Prince Jacobyi, who had disembarked on the bank and rejoined his galloping horsemen. "Form up in fours!" he cried to those who were ahead of him. "The wretches have made two attempts to assassinate my son-in-law! They shall not escape! Close ranks and beat thoroughly!"

The sounds gradually retreated into the north-east, in the direction of Turkeve. William and Bobby recovered and took a new course, this time heading towards Timisoara, whose wild landscape was almost certain to provide them with adequate shelter. But the horsemen were beating the fields in a zigzag fashion and from time to time our fugitives were obliged to turn aside from their path. Day broke when they were crossing a second river at a ford, bellow the town of Ghila, which was situated on an island. There was no further shelter thereafter but the tall cornfields of the Great Hungarian Plain.

They were tortured by fatigue, and it was necessary for them to cross a large open space, but chance had put some distance between themselves and the hunt for the time being.

"We must make the most of the last few minutes of darkness," William said. "One last effort!"

They hurled themselves forward, running in a straight line towards the cornfields. On attaining the edge of that ocean of verdure, they looked back in order to scan the ground they had covered. No one was in sight: the hunters had lost their trail. They ran on into the young cornstalks like stags plunging into a forest. After taking a few paces more they threw themselves on the ground, utterly exhausted, pressing their burning faces to the fresh earth.

"I couldn't have taken another step to save my life!" said Bobby, in a choked voice.

William consulted his watch. "We've been on the run for eleven hours," he said, "and we've covered more than twenty leagues."

"Do we have time to rest?"

"The sun's coming up. In broad daylight they'll soon pick up our trail."

"You're very calm," murmured Bobby.

"Because I'm certain that I can still save myself," William replied.

"How's that?"

"In ten minutes, we can be back in the graves!"

"The graves!" cried Bobby, leaping triumphantly to his feet, no longer feeling fatigued.

The day brightened and the hunters found their trail again. They followed the fresh tracks which cut across the fields of the Great Hungarian Plain at the gallop. They were certain now of their quarry. For the Chevalier Ténèbre and brother Ange, the vampire, to escape it would be necessary for the earth to open beneath them and swallow them!

The hunters went on and on, guided by their master, Prince Jacobyi. At a certain place, though, the tracks became confused, tangled like a ball of string-- and then there was nothing.

The earth had indeed opened up and swallowed them. There was no doubt about it.

XIV. The Tall One and the Short One

September came again. One stormy day, the sun shone on the flat country to the east of Paris, near the confluence of the Marne and the Seine, where two or three more factory-chimneys were smoking.

A train of bundled wooden logs and barges laden with barrels drifted sadly down the river, bound for Bercy, as gloomy as a wine-cellar—but one which contained, in its casks and bottles, novels, sword-thrusts and vaudevilles, Regency rendezvous and songs in honor of the God of good souls, the poetry of the boudoir and the barrier, spirits of every quality, the laughter and smiles of old age for the young and of youth for the old, extravagances for everyone; in sum, all the joy--true and false, sincere and adulterated--which maintains for three hundred and sixty days of every year the chronic folly of the Parisian Carnival! Jean Raisin, elder son of Suresnes, licensed inhabitant of Courtille, has dethroned Bacchus, who is too gentlemanly a god.

I once had a nightmare in which I saw Homer revived, with scarlet pimples on the end of his nose. I asked him for news of Achilles, Hector and Agamemnon; he replied that Bordeaux, Mâcon, Epernay, Beaune, Lunel, Cognac and Montpellier had disputed one day the honor of having shown him the light, and that he had written, between two barrelfuls, the twenty-four songs of the *Berciad*.

That is the repulsive underside of our century: this insulting odor of bad wine, mingled with the noxious fumes of poetic tobacco-smoke, which is all the rage.

When evening came, white dresses were again to be seen here and there on the lawns of the Conflans park beside the Seine, grouped as if in flower-beds. As on the day on which our story began, Archbishop de Quélen was holding a charitable soirée, and the exact parity of circumstance spares us the necessity of elaborate description. The scenery was the same and the guest-list was almost identical. The Bishop of Hermopolis, now as before, was to deliver a short speech, and the same singer—yes, the very same, although she had changed her name to Madame la Marquise Lenore de Lorgàres—had been engaged to perform at the concert. She was there, as lovely as youth and happiness, under the wing of the Princess de Montfort, her mother-in-law.

You must certainly have seen, at some time in your life, some pretty little girl, excited by her love for some brand new doll. There is nothing offensive in the comparison; that is exactly how the Princess was in respect of her charming daughter-in-law—quite mad, in effect, with all the liveliness and joyousness that kind of madness brings. She was ten years old again; she had a constant need to smile and caress. The pretty Madame de Maillé let slip at one point: "If that were not my aunt, who has the authority of a princess, I would say that her wheedling ways were in very bad taste." But that was unjust; it is always necessary that good taste should permit good humor.

At dusk, a few drops of rain put all the dresses, white or not, to flight. They took refuge in the hall, where the chairs were already set out for the concert.

It would have been impossible, given the place, the people and the similitude of the setting, to prevent memories resurfacing.

"I hope," said the doctor, who was still enthusiastically prescribing affusions of cold water taken in warm baths, "that His Lordship the Bishop of Hermopolis will put the produce of his collection in a safe place this time."

"Oh!" the cry went up. "The brothers Ténèbre are not here this evening!"

I cannot deny that a slight shiver of apprehension was manifest here and there in the audience. More than one gaze turned involuntarily towards the entrance-door, beside which Baron von Altenheimer, with his long pale face, and

Monsignor Benedict—one tall and one short, the oupire and the vampire—had installed themselves on that eventful night so long ago.

"I wonder what became of those two bold adventurers?" said the Bishop of Hermopolis.

Marquise Lenore turned pale.

"She had one of her migraines yesterday!" exclaimed the princess. "Ask Gaston about that, when he comes, Your Lordship."

"Is the story so very terrible?" asked the Archbishop.

"Yes, it is very terrible...let it be... you'll make me ill!"

It was like throwing a cup of water on a raging fire. A hundred voices were raised, among which, to tell the truth, those of the two prelates were included.

"There's a story here!"

"Oh, Madame la Marquise, please! Do tell!"

Lenore smiled sadly. "Mother," she said to the Princess, "I can't refuse these women the finale of a drama in which they have played a role, but the denouement is horrible; I ask your permission to cut the story short."

"Not too short!" they implored. "The word *horrible* isn't nearly as intimidating as it is believed to be.

The charming Marquise de Lorgàres collected herself for a moment, then began: "Did the person who took the name of Baron von Altenheimer, in relating the incident that caused the ruination of my father, happen to mention a young girl named Efflam, who was my friend and companion?"

"Yes indeed," came the reply from all side. "Efflam, the young Magyar girl, whose parents lived at the Turkish border: one of the vampire's victims!"

"A poor angel who has her rightful place in Heaven," Lenore replied, in a melancholy tone. "Efflam's father left Petrovaradin after his daughter's death; his wife did not survive her grief. He went to live in an isolated cabin in the middle of the Great Hungarian Plain. He was in great distress.

"He had heard tell of the two black graves that were sometimes occupied by the bodies of the Chevalier Ténèbre and his brother Ange, the vampire, who were forced to return at least once a year to their mortuary domicile. He had heard, too, that if it were possible to take them by surprise and burn their hearts with a red-hot iron, the world would be freed forever from those two monsters.

"He waited for his opportunity. He went out every morning to lift up the black marble slabs which covered the two graves..."

"So these two graves actually exist?" Archbishop de Quélen asked.

"Certainly," the Princess replied. "I saw them myself while I was there for the wedding...one great and one small, with the inscriptions you know."

One day last April," Lenore went on, "during a hunting-party in the Chandor forest, two assassination attempts were made against the person of the Marquis de Lorgàres, and that same evening my father was told that the brothers Ténèbre were in the vicinity. It is necessary to tell you, at the risk of diminishing the interest of the story somewhat, that the Chevalier Ténèbre is an old employee of the London police, and that his brother Ange, the vampire, came straight from Botany Bay, whence he had been transported as a common thief. The chevalier was named William Moore and the vampire Bob, or Bobby, Bobson. A few weeks after the adventure I want to relate to you Szeged was full of police officers from London, following the trail of our two phantoms.

"My father put the whole household on horseback, arming the entire force, in order to search the area. The chase began as night was falling. At two o'clock in the morning, the fugitives were recognized, but they slipped out of sight until morning, when their tracks were found and followed. The trail led my father and his troop into the middle of the the Great Hungarian Plain, more than twenty leagues from Chandor. There, it ended. One might have thought that the two fugitives had vanished into thin air. My father and his men returned to the castle on the following day, after a day of futile searching.

"That night, however, when our men had gone, David Kuntz, the father of my poor Efflam, went, as was his custom, to lift the marble tombstones.

Under the first he saw a sleeping man; under the second, another in the same state. He sharpened a ploughshare in order that he might heat it up and plunge it, as was their due, into the hearts of the oupire and the vampire, but his courage failed him. Instead, he went to find huge and heavy rocks, which he deposited on the slabs of black marble in such a fashion that no human force would be able to disturb them again. Afterwards, he spent several days collecting bits of wood, dry vegetation and straw, an enormous quantity of which he piled up above and around the two graves.

"Each time that he returned, he heard voices coming from the ground, asking him for mercy, but he paid them no heed.

"The voices gradually became fainter. The one which came from the larger grave fell silent first, and then the other faded in its turn. They had pleaded for twenty-eight hours each.

"The pile of combustible material was now as high as a two-storey house. David Kuntz set it alight. It burned, and continued smoldering for three days. It took a further three days for the tombstones and the surrounding earth to cool down again. It was, in consequence, not until the seventh day after the fire that David Kuntz was able to take the rocks away and lift the marble tombstones. He found beneath them two human corpses—one tall and one short—which had kept their shape, but were now the color of charcoal. When he put out his hands to touch them, the two corpses fell into dust..."

"And since that moment," added the Princess, "you will understand that nothing more has been heard of the brothers Ténèbre."

As she finished, the prefect of police came in, followed by Gaston and his father-in-law, Prince Jacobyi. The Prince seemed anxious; Gaston's face had a mortal pallor.

"My Ladies," asked the prefect of police, "do you remember those two audacious bandits who robbed our protégés in the Holy Land, at this very same event last year?"

The question sounded so strange, after the tale told by Lenore, that it was met by a profound silence.

"Their exploits are following the same course," the prefect continued, in a light tone. "Here is a newspaper from The Hague, which tells of their latest *tour de force*. Anna Paulowna, the Princess Royal and Princess of Orange, was robbed of her diamonds in broad daylight, and in their place in the jewel-case was a visiting card: an old Flemish woodcut depicting two men, one tall and one short, the tall one wearing armor and the short one costumed as a priest. Under the former were the words *Le Chevalier Ténèbre*; under the latter *Brother Ange, the Vampire...*"

There was a protracted murmur in the hall, which covered the voice of Prince Jacobyi asking of his son-in-law: "Will you let me see that letter?"

Gaston, without replying, unfolded a piece of paper that he had crumpled in his hand. The prince took it and read:

See you soon!

And by way of signature:

The tall one and the short one.

Jules Lermina (1839-1915) was an active Anarchist who became a prolific feuilletoniste *in order to support his family after the fall of the Second Empire, having avoided involvement in the Commune because he was drafted into the National Guard as the price of his release from prison and sent away from Paris to fight the advancing Prussians. Much of his early fiction, explicitly inspired by the example of Edgar Poe, was collected in* Histoires incroyables *(1885) and* Nouvelles histoires incroyables *(1888). When his eldest daughter married the* bouquiniste *Henri Chacornac, who specialized in Occult texts, Lermina enabled the household to move into a shop that was frequented by all the leading members of the French Occult Revival, with which Lermina became involved, albeit somewhat skeptically.* "La Vengeance d'une araignée*" was first published in* Le Diogene *on 25 août 1861. "A Spider's Revenge" was first published in* The Secret of Zippelius and Other Stories *(2011).*[20]

Jules Lermina: *A Spider's Revenge*

"Tell us a story!"

"Not tonight."

"But you promised, earlier."

In the end, they insisted so strongly that I was persuaded.

We were in the Brasserie des Martyrs, in one of the first floor booths; we had already consumed a dozen *moos* and our heads were beginning to weigh heavy.

I began:

"You remember Damien Vernier; he was a worthy and honest fellow, lively and witty, who wore, as they say, his heart on his sleeve. It wasn't necessary to ask him for a favor; he divined your need before you could express it.

"In spite of his insouciance, though, he could not resist the unexpected blows that struck him: ruination, poverty, the death of a mistress…everything, in sum, seemed to be in league against him. From then on his complexion became leaden, his eyes hollowed out; his previous cheerfulness changed into a sort of funereal irony. When someone spoke to him, he hardly seemed to hear, and conversed in a low voice with people who were no more.

---

[20] Available from Black Coat Press: *The Battle of Strasbourg*, ISBN 978-1-61227-324-2; *Mysteryville*, ISBN 978-1-935558-27-9; *Panic in Paris*, ISBN 978-1-934543-83-2; *The Secret of Zippelius*, ISBN 978-1-935558-88-0; *To-Ho and the Gold Destroyers*, ISBN 978-1-935558-34-7; and *"Quiet House"* in *The Germans on Venus*, ISBN 978-1-934543-56-6.

"Stripped of his fortune, the dandy became an employee, and to receive every day the meager pittance that he needed, Damien consented to imprison himself in one of the other cages invented by Cardinal la Balue, which is called Bureaucracy.[21] He spent his days, therefore, scratching away with an irritated and feverish pen on paper that was given to him white and which he was obliged to blacken.

"I remember his office; it was a small dark room. It had one big window, but it looked out into a courtyard so narrow that one could touch the opposite wall by reaching out a hand. He could scarcely see with sufficient clarity on sunny days, and in winter, a lamp was indispensable.

"Beside the window and along the wall about which I want to talk to you, ran a domestic water-pipe. Between the pipe and the window-frame there was a gap of about twenty-five centimeters.

"One day when I went to call on him, Damien seemed sadder and more agitated than usual. When I asked him the cause of his distress, he pointed to the window and said: 'Look.'

"I couldn't see anything at first, but by following the direction of his finger attentively I perceived a spider's web in the gap between the pipe and the window, thick, grey and heavy. The animal must have worked on it for a long time; it was one of the seven wonders of the Arachnid realm.

"In sum, though, I saw nothing there but something perfectly natural, and I turned an interrogative gaze to Damien. 'Oh,' he went on, 'you don't understand? Well, listen. *She*'s not there—she's gone back into her hole, but if you could see her...*she*'s horrible, with her body as big as a hazelnut, hairy and long-legged... Look! Look!'

"Indeed, as if responding to the summons of the voice that was talking about her, the Spider emerged from the corner in which it had been huddled: a monster; something dark and formless, which strode rapidly over the web, then suddenly stopped, to flee a moment afterwards into its lair.

"Damien was horrible pale! He squeezed my hand convulsively and murmured: 'I'm afraid of her!'

"We must kill it," I said then, advancing toward the window.

"'No, no!' Damien almost screeched, with a shiver of terror. 'Don't do her any harm—she avenge herself!'

"He slumped into his armchair; I could not say anything to reassure him; I divined an obsession.

---

[21] Jean de Balue (1421-1491) held several posts in the government of Louis XI; when he was eventually convicted of treason, he was imprisoned in a large wooden cage, which was still exhibited to tourists in Loches many years later. He did not actually invent the cage in question, but the clergyman who did was subsequently imprisoned therein himself; hence the confusion.

"Suddenly, Damien seemed to be gripped by a sudden idea; he had just lit a cigarette, and was still holding the lighted match in his hand. He stood up and threw the match at the web. Then he waited, anxiously.

"The thick web did not catch fire immediately, but a few seconds later it was in flames from end to end, and a kind of spray shone upon the length of the wall.

"Blood rose to Damien's cheeks; his eyes shone; a sigh of relief emerged from his breast.

"'If *she* were dead!'

"I left him considerably calmer.

"I came back two days later. When I went in, he was bent double in front of the window, and seemed to be studying something attentively.

"The Spider was there, working with its feet to reconstruct its web; it was active, vivacious.

"I coughed. Damien stood up abruptly. Drops of sweat were pearling on his brow. 'There she is!' And he laughed like a lunatic.

"I tried to take him out for coffee. 'Oh no,' he said. 'I prefer to watch her work...she's not afraid of me, you see...look, she's laughing...'

"He seemed to be seized by an inexpressible fury, snatched the match with which I was lighting the cigarette in my lips, and let it fall upon the web.

"The Spider fled and the match went out, having made a large hole in the torn web.

"A moment later, the animal attempted to take account of what had happened...it ran forward, but when it arrived at the discontinuity caused by the fire it lost its footing and fell.

"It hung on by one leg and its other antennae, and tried to climb back up. Damien pointed his finger at it. The horrible animal contorted itself, writhing gymnastically, extending its jaundiced underbelly; the eyes ornamenting its head were clearly visible...

"It was horrible.

"It succeeded in regaining its web and its corner.

"Damien fainted.

"A week later, Damien came to my home, slammed the door behind him and bolted it.

"'Safe!' he murmured. 'I've escaped her...oh, how she's pursued me!'

" Who? Pull yourself together.'

"'Her! The SPIDER!'

"I made him take a drop of brandy; he recovered a measure of calm. 'That beast wants me dead—she'll avenge herself, you'll see!'

"He plunged his head into his hands. 'I told myself that it was necessary to finish it—that one of us had to kill the other. I destroyed her web; she wove it more solidly. She spread herself out over the threads that stopped the matches...then I became cowardly...I spied on her, watched out for her, and whenever

I saw her somber back standing out against the grey of the fabric, I would have liked to burn her with my gaze…then, this morning…oh!' He let himself slump backwards. 'This morning, when I saw her, I picked up the tongs and crept forward…I stretched out my arms…I was an inch away from my enemy…I reached further forward and I brought together the two iron stems. I took hold of her…I squeezed…horror! I'd gripped one of her legs. With a violent effort, she tore off the limb, which remained in the tongs. I shouted, and tried to flee…no, it was impossible…the animal became furious…I saw her grow larger, swell up…with her remaining legs she braced herself against her web and leapt on to the window-sill. I saw her black legs reach out like arms of bronze…I closed my eyes…then she touched me…I felt her arrive on my face…her arms were suspended over my neck…and she kissed me!

"'I ran out of my office…she pursued me…there was something like the gallop of a furious horse behind me…I sensed her presence, I saw her…I fled without knowing where I was going. And I arrived here, at your house…but…everything is firmly closed…

"'Look! Look! Her arm…there…under the door…she's going to catch me!'

"Damien fell backwards on to the floor; he was foaming at the mouth.

"I put him in my bed and went in search of a doctor.

"Everything that was done proved futile. He was doomed.

"He was bled. 'There, you see,' he whispered to me. 'She's here! She's drinking my blood!'

"Gradually, his pulse weakened; his eyes became dull and glassy. He seemed to be trying to push something away with his arms—and when he died, I saw a supreme expression of disgust on his lips. 'Oh!' he cried. 'How cold her lips are!'"

We were overwhelmed.

"Waiter," one of us shouted. "another *moos*!"

X. B. Saintine (1798-1865) was one of the pioneers of Romantic prose, with a story series launched in 1823 in Le Mercure du dix-neuvième siècle, *allegedly narrated by the immortal* "Jonathan le visionnaire" *(translated in* Jonathan the Visionary*) who was subsequently credited as the hypothetical author of* "Histoire d'une civilisation antédiluvienne" *(1832), a striking dramatization of the theory of cultural decadence. Best known as a prolific writer of vaudevilles, Saintine also achieved success as a novelist with the classic* Picciola *(1836; tr. as* Picciola; or, The Prison Flower*), one of the core works of the Romantic Movement, in which the life-enhancing symbolism of a flower growing in an exercise yard enables the psychological survival of a desperate political prisoner. His last collection of short stories,* La Seconde Vie *(1864) consists entirely of accounts of dreams and visions and is a significant precursor of Symbolist prose;* "Psylla, le mangeur d'or" *first appeared in* The Second Life.[22]

X. B. Saintine: *Psylla, The Gold-Eater*

A little grass snake, with faded colors, almost effaced, had introduced herself into my home—in order to warm herself by the fire, I suppose, for the north wind was obscuring outside, and frost was obscuring the panes of the casement.

In France, one generally mistrusts all sorts of snakes, inoffensive grass snakes as well as vipers with a mortal bite. Perhaps that mistrust is wisdom, but I once traveled in the Orient and I was imbued there with the idea that a snake brings good luck to a house.

Furthermore, in Sardinia I had seen the ladies of Cagliari lifting up with care and tenderness a gracious little necklace snake,[23] their favorite plaything and their principal ornament, which, one might say, belongs both to their family and their jewel-box. It seemed to me that my newcomer, in spite of her paltry and miserable appearance, must belong to the same species.

I granted her hospitality, therefore, leaving her free to choose whatever refuge seemed good to her. From time to time, in the epoch of intense cold, she came back to warm herself by my hearth. Her coat, duller than ever, came away

---

[22] Available from Black Coat Press: *Jonathan the Visionary*, ISBN 978-1-61227-751-6; *The Second Life*, ISBN 978-1-61227-750-9; "*Astronomical Journeys*" (1864) in *The Germans on Venus*, ISBN 978-1-934543-56-6; "*The Paradise of Flowers*" and "*The Great Discovery of Animules*" (both 1864) in *The Supreme Progress*, ISBN 978-1-935558-82-8.

[23] The common French term for *Natrix natrix*, known in England as a grass snake, is *couleuvre*, often expanded to *couleuvre à collier* [necklace snake].

in patches, and then tatters; that inspired me with a sentiment akin to repugnance, but my pity pleaded in her favor.

When spring returned, one beautiful morning, I saw her again; she had made a new skin. What a metamorphosis! Her supple body scintillated in a marvelous network of ocher and dark pink. My boarder was charming thus. Doubtless flattered by the quietly astonished attention I paid to her, in order to enable me also to appreciate her *savoir faire*, she began by slowly unwinding her coils, in which the daylight was reflected by the tiny prismatic facets of her scales, and, with a measured movement full of grace, she went to the threshold of the garden, turning her head occasionally to see whether I was following her.

In fact, I had followed her. Then she wound itself like convolvulus around a slender tree-trunk, reached the higher branches and suspended herself there, swaying; then, allowing herself to slide along the tree, with a rapidity that made me shiver with dread that she might fall and injure itself, she swiftly attained a small stone basin, where she started to swim, her head out of the water, holding her neck curved in the manner of a swan.

The next day we were friends; I had already found a name for her: Psylla.[24]

In the following days, alerted by a slight hissing, I perceived her, sometimes emerging from one of my bookshelves, sometimes from one of the leaves of my parquet. When the weather was favorable we went into the garden together, where she resumed hers customary exercises in suspension and natation; if not, I replaced the flowering ash-tree in which she loved to perch; having become familiar, it was around me that she wound, enlacing my neck in one of her coils and allowing her extremities to hang down over my breast.

Oh, she really was a necklace snake! But never, in Cagliari, where I had seen so many of them, had one appeared to me so richly rutilant. Her contact caused me an impression that I could not define, and if, raising her pretty head to the level of my face, she looked at me with her little black eyes, illuminated by a spark, I sensed that I was under a strange, fascinating charm, which seemed to be attacking reason itself.

Many other things in her regard astonished me. We had already been living in the same abode for several months, but I could not divine to which corner of the house she retired for the night; I also did not know how and on what she nourished herself. In vain I offered her the tastiest fruits and treats impregnated with honey or sugar; she scarcely brushed them with hers little forked tongue, seemingly only touching them to be obliging and to respond to my good intentions.

Commonly, reptiles—or at least, so I had heard it said—make their meals of heifers' milk. I put at Psylla's disposal a bowl of the purest milk, which only

---

[24] *Psylla* is the Greek word for flea, but the French word *psylle* also means snake-charmer, the word apparently being borrowed in that context from that of a Libyan tribe..

inspired a profound sentiment of repulsion. Hazard soon enabled me to discover, however, that she did not feel the same repugnance for all liquids.

I invited a few friends to dinner; as I was drinking to their health with an excellent red wine from Alicante, Psylla, who had take refuge behind a tapestry when they came in, suddenly emerged from her hiding place, launched herself toward me with an abrupt and rapid movement, coiled round my extended arm and drank avidly from my glass.

Another surprise awaited me.

One morning, I opened the secret drawer where I had carefully deposited a roll of gold coins a long time before, in case of emergency. I did not find my gold in the drawer; I found my necklace snake there, semi-torpid.

At the movement I imparted to the item of furniture, she woke up, uttered a shrill hiss, and fed into the depths of the writing-desk, where a hole communicated with a crack in the wall.

Now I knew the route by which she had introduced herself into the drawer, but I did not know how my gold had departed therefrom.

I thought it was a domestic theft; I kept watch, on the alert. Soon, I acquired the certainty that Psylla ate gold, making her nourishment thereof.

A tradition returned to my memory. In certain countries, it is said, snakes are skillful in discovering treasures. Did they discover them, then, to their own benefit?

Not being rich enough to allow my boarder to persevere in such a diet, I resolved to part from her. But how? The habit of seeing her every day had already projected roots into the depths of my heart. I was obstinate nevertheless in weaning her from all nourishment of that sort, hoping that she would come of her own accord to a more convenient aliment.

A hope deceived twenty times over! Fruits and milk were decidedly antipathetic to her. From day to day I saw her beautiful colors fade; Psylla became languid and paltry again, as in the epoch of misery when she had introduced herself into my dwelling. She no longer even had the strength to raise herself up toward me in order to resume her customary station.

Gradually, my rigor relaxed. My Alicante wine, she was able to drink at her discretion, and under its revivifying influence, her crimson shades reappeared, but her beautiful diamond-shaped yellow patches, discolored and withered, hollowed out and became ulcerated.

I could not see Psylla perish thus before my eyes. The gold that remained to me passed to her; that was the affair of a few weeks.

Then I sold my least useful furniture, and my rarest books. I borrowed. Once filled in, the abyss opened again. Even exhausting my strength in incessant labor, I would not have sufficed for the task quickly enough, nor with sufficiently considerable results. I became a gambler: a determined gambler.

My house became a gambling den. I only lived from then on in the midst of companions equally avid for gain. Some had to satisfy the demands of a deceptive luxury, others to steep hearts numbed by the abuse of pleasures in violent emotions. I had to content the appetites of Psylla, for whom I now seemed to feel nothing but indifference, and even hatred. But did she not keep me riveted beneath her magnetic gaze?

After a few strokes of luck, the game turned against me; it ended up exhausting my last resources. For a month, not a single gold coin shone under my gaze; I only gambled any longer on my word. It was necessary that she do without gold, even if she died of it; what did it matter to me?

Psylla did not perish, however; every day even seemed to add to her splendor and beauty.

It did not take me long to perceive that my companions in gaming were secretly subsidizing her avidity. I felt humiliated; I felt jealous; and my amity for her revived on contact with evil passions.

For her I endured shame; for her I fought.

A rare friend, a true friend, had tried to enlighten me as to my situation; I replied to him with a denial; he reiterated what he said; I spat in his face. We only saw one another again with épées in hand. In the duel, only I was wounded, thank God.

Laid on my bed, with my arm bandaged, I became drowsy. After an hour, on awakening, I felt bitter frissons running through my body; a cold sweat was streaming on my brow. Painfully, I turned my semi-extinct gaze in the direction of my wound. The bandage had been lifted up; a little oval head, oblong and flattened, slid underneath it, was drinking the blood that flowed from it.

I made an effort to stand up, but fell back, breathlessly, on to my bed. And I saw Psylla withdraw herself slowly, weighed down as she was by all the blood that she had just drunk.

What I also saw, which I remarked above all, was that she was then more beautiful than ever. Her plaques of bright crimson had turned to scarlet, and gave her body marvelous reflections.

Were blood and gold indispensable, then, to the blossoming of her complete beauty?

Like a coward. I strove—would you believe it?—to give a favorable meaning to that infamous, abominable crime. In spite of my mental disturbance, I remembered the tale of the ancients that attributed to snakes an innate science of medicine; at Epidaurus, in the temple of Aesculapius, the oracle was rendered by a snake. Is not a snake still the emblem of the healing art today?

Perhaps Psylla had just saved my life.

Should I think about avenging myself on her, of expelling her from my home?

It seemed to me that if I sent her away she would take my happiness with her...

My happiness! Where was it? Poverty was crushing me, and by her fault; repose, study and amity had deserted my abode, and by her fault. Everything in me ought to have revolted against her, speaking to me of ruination, abasement, degradation...

Well, nothing came of it; I was blind; I was mad, or I was going mad, when, one morning, Lalagé came into my home and put her foot on the head of my gold-eater, my blood-drinker.

Today, I wonder whether my adventures with the necklace snake were really only a dream.

Auguste Villiers de L'Isle-Adam (1838-1889), whose father spent much of his life trying to prove that he was a hereditary Comte—a delusion he inherited—idolized Baudelaire and threw himself into the Bohemian lifestyle he thought befitting a poet, which did not prove helpful to his actual production, several of his projects remaining incomplete. He found it easier to finish short stories, his first collection being Contes cruels *(1883; tr. as* Sardonic Tales*), which certainly did not invent the genre in question—S. Henry Berthoud and Petrus Borel had pioneered it more than half a century earlier—but provided it with its definitive label and offered an important exemplar to Decadent prose writers. He followed it with his much-rewritten novel* L'Ève future *(1886; tr. as* Tomorrow's Eve*), but died as soon as the Decadent Movement began according him a belated heroic status. "Claire Lenoir" was first serialized in the* Revue des lettres et des arts, *13 octobre-1 décembre 1867; the translation was first published in a slightly different version in* The Vampire Soul and Other Sardonic Tales.[25]

Auguste Villiers de L'Isle-Adam : *Claire Lenoir*

Memorandum of Doctor Tribulat Bonhomet, honorary Member of Several Academies, Associate Professor of Physiology, regarding the Mysterious Case of the Discreet and Scientific Individual, the Widowed Lady, Claire Lenoir

"Non moechaberis."[26]
Moses

To My Illustrious Contemporaries
T.B.

I. Precautions and Confidences

Touched with Pensiveness...
Thomas De Quincey[27]

---

[25] Available from Black Coat Press: *The Scaffold*, ISBN 978-1-932983-01-2; *The Vampire Soul*, ISBN 978-1-932983-02-9.

[26] The seventh commandment: "Thou shalt not commit adultery.

[27] De Quincey, in reflections on his childhood in the *Confessions of an Opium-Eater*, asserts: "WE, the children, were all constitutionally touched with pensiveness...." The phrase was singled out by Baudelaire in his essay on De Quincey.

The chain of dark events that I have taken it upon myself to record (in spite of my white hair and my disdain for vainglory) appears to me to comprise a sum of horror capable of troubling the minds of experienced lawyers. I must confess, at the outset, that I am only delivering these pages to a publisher as a concession to sustained pressure from devoted and proven friends. I dread the prospect of immersing myself for a second time in the sad necessity of attenuating—by means of the efflorescences of my style and the resources of a rich fluency— their unusual and suffocating hideousness.

I do not think that Fear is a universally profitable sensation. Would it not be the act of a madman to spread it recklessly in the minds of others, motivated by vague hope of profiting from the scandal? A profound discovery is not to be hastily thrown under the trampling feet of the procession of human thought. It requires appropriate seasoning in advance of mental digestion. Any great news, carelessly announced, can alarm—often to the point of madness—a large number of pious souls, overexcite the caustic faculties of wastrels, and reawaken the antiquated neurosis of "demonic possession" in timorous minds.

It is certainly true, however, that to make people think is a duty that takes precedence over an abundance of scruples. Having weighed it all up, I shall speak out. Everyone must answer to his own conscience. Besides, my century reassures me; for every feeble mind that I might overstrain, there are many strong minds that I might enlighten. When I say "strong minds," I am not speaking lightly. As for the veracity of my story, no one, I wager, will recklessly poke fun at it; for, even admitting the possibility that the following account is rooted in a falsehood, the mere idea of their possibility is just as terrible as a conclusive and accepted demonstration of their authenticity. When one thinks about it, are not all things possible in our mysterious universe?

When I say "mysterious" rather than "problematic" I am not (if I may be permitted to repeat myself) speaking lightly.

Any digression on this subject, sketched in haste and without being properly tested, would be idle.

Now, my readers may certainly be assured that I am not scheming to obtain any purely "literary" honors. In truth, if there is any objective beyond the personal that I despise even more than the conventional expressions of high-flown language, it is that of the "litterateurs" and their henchmen. I don't give a fig for all that!

Having been reduced to introducing myself to the public, the first thing I ought to do, to get it out of the way, is to describe myself.

I have often asked myself why people sometimes burst out laughing or seem disconcerted when they see me for the first time, but I cannot figure it out no matter how hard I think about it. It seems to me, without being boastful, that my appearance ought rather to inspire thoughts along the following lines: "How pleasing it is to belong to a species that has produced an individual like that!"

Physically, I am what might be described in scientific terms as a "second epoch Saturnian"[28] I have a tall and bony figure, and a slight stoop brought on by thinking to excess. The tormented oval of my face advertises my wisdom and forethought. Under my bushy eyebrows grey eyes shine forth penetratingly from their cavities, like Saturn and Mercury. My forehead is high, the barrenness of my temples announcing that they no longer sup the convictions of others because their nourishment is complete. My head is slightly hollowed out at the sides, like those of mathematicians. Hollow temples are crucibles![29] They distil ideas so that my nose can judge their quality and offer its verdict.

My nose is considerable in dimension—large, even. It is an invasive nose, an atomizing nose, hooked in the middle like the arch of a foot—which, in anyone but myself, would indicate a tendency to dark obsession. The nose, you see, is the expression of the human capacity for reason; it is the organ that goes before, which enlightens, which proclaims one's presence, which scents trouble and which points the way. The visible nose corresponds to the impalpable "nose" which everyone carries within himself from birth. If, therefore, as a nose develops, one part grows imprudently to the detriment of the others, it corresponds to some lacuna of judgment, to one particular thought nourished to the detriment of others. The corners of my pale, pinched mouth are the folds of a shroud; it is set so close to the nose so that it may take advice before speaking lightly—like a crow picking nuts, as the saying goes.

Without my chin, which gives me away, I might be taken for a man of action; but a senile Saturn, skeptical and lunatic, has chopped it off with a stroke of his scythe. The color and texture of my skin is as durable as that of my peers in its symbolic contemporaneity. My ears, delicately lobed and extended, like those of the Chinese, advertise the scrupulousness of my mind.

My hand is sterile: the Moon and Mercury dispute the lines in its palm. The gnarled and spatulate middle finger has scars on the second joint, which do not affect its operation. The edges of my hand are vague and wan; clouds formed by Venus and Apollo have rarely confused that sky; my willful thumb rests upon the hazardous hill where Venus indicates her tendencies. The palm, however, is definitely that of a manipulator; the fingers can fold upon it like a woman's, with a certain coquettishness, touching the various arenas of their perfect education. I am, at any rate, the only son of the petty doctor Amour Bonhomet, well-known for his dismal adventures in the Mines.

Ever since I first became aware of who I was I have worn the same kind of clothes, appropriate to my personality and gait, to wit: a wide-brimmed felt hat, like those worn by Quakers and the Lake Poets; a large double-breasted over-

---

[28] The "Saturnian Epoch," in contemporary occultist thought, was the era preceding the Deluge.

[29] The French *Tempes creuses, creusets!* has a much better ring to it than its English translation.

167

coat, always buttoned, like the grandiose phrases in which my thoughts are habitually couched; an old walking-stick with a red knob; a large diamond solitaire—a family heirloom—on my Saturnian finger. I am a match for the ancient Romans in the precious quality and delicate whiteness of my linen; I have the honor of possessing the same feet as King Charles the Great in my Souwaroff boots, with which I trample down the soil very well: I nearly always have my suitcase in my hand, for I travel abroad more than Ahasuerus. I am proud to believe that I wear the face of my century, that I am, in fact, its *archetype*.

In brief, I am a doctor, a philanthropist and a man of the world.

My voice is sometimes shrill and sometimes (especially when I speak to women) rich and profound—and it can go from one to the other seamlessly, as I please. I have neither wife nor parents, thus having no attachments to society of any kind—so I must hope, at least. I live on an annuity, provided by the little wealth left to me. My visiting card is formulated thus:

DOCTOR
TRIBULAT BONHOMET
EUROPE

These are my particular moral principles:

The mysteries of positivist science have had exclusive command of my attentive faculties since the sacred moment when I first came into the world, often to the exclusion of every other human preoccupation. Infinitely tiny things, like those my beloved master Spallanzani named *Infusoria* have been the ultimate object of my research from a tender age. To provide for the needs of my profound studies I have eaten through the enormous legacy of my ancestors. Yes, I have dedicated the mature fruits of their centuries of sweat to the purchase of lenses and other apparatus requisite to denude the arcana of the temporarily-invisible world!

I have compiled the names of all my predecessors. *Non est hic locus*[30] to dwell too long on the enlightenment that I believe I have added to theirs; posterity will deliver its verdict on that subject, if I ever publish. What it is important to establish is that the analytical, magnificatory minuteness of my mind is so essential to my nature that the entire joy of life is, for me, concentrated in the precise classification of the most wretched Tenebrio beetles, according to the bizarre entanglements—like some very ancient handwriting—formed by the nerves of such insects, narrowing phenomenal horizons which still remain immense in the retinas which reflect them! Reality thus becomes visionary; and I feel that I am entering a new level of the Domain of Dreams, microscope in hand!

But I am jealous of my discoveries, all of which I keep concealed. I have a mortal hatred of vulgar people, squalid as they are. When anyone questions me

---

[30] This is not the place.

on this subject, I play dumb. I try to pass for a mere fleck. And I take great delight in thinking that I could disconcert those faces if I were to tell them what surprising and previously-unknown things my instruments have allowed me to glimpse!

Let's leave it at that; perhaps I've already said too much...

My religious ideas are restricted to the absurd idea that God created man, and *vice versa*.

We do not know where we come from; Reason remains in doubt. I should add, to be frank, that Death astonishes even more than her sad Sister; one can't make head nor tail of it. All enquiry into its mysteries results, inevitably, in a kind of analysis that inverts the logic according to which we satisfy ourselves, grudgingly, with a "course of life" which is obviously provisional and local.

As for ghosts, I'm not at all superstitious. I give no credence to insignificant twaddle about "signs", which is so much ballyhoo, and I don't believe that the dead monkey about with us. Just between ourselves, though, I don't like cemeteries or other overly dark places--or people who exaggerate! I'm only a poor old man, but if Pluto set me on the steps of a throne at birth, and if it only required a word from me, now, to wreak havoc among all these fanatics, I'd say that word—just "like peeling an apple", as the poet says.

Nevertheless, I have to confess that I'm subject to a hereditary ailment which has long made a mockery of my reason and will-power! It consists of an apprehension: an anxiety, without any precise source; an anguish, in a word, which seizes me like a panic attack, making me savor all the bitterness of an abrupt infernal disquiet—frequently on account of derisory futilities! Doesn't it make one grind one's teeth to feel one's soul poisoned as mortally as that? Just thinking about it makes me sick.

Having a cultured mind, I have the most enlightened views on everything, but—and this is odd—although I know how to explain, for example, the noise of the wind, both acoustically and physically, by reference to sudden extremes of heat and cold, when I actually hear the wind, I'm afraid. Amid the thousand shudders of Silence—produced by the simplest causes—I become pale. Whenever the shadow of a bird crosses my path, I stop and, putting my suitcase down, I mop my brow—a disconcerted traveler! Then, I am oppressed by the weight of a nervous dread of heaven and earth, the living and the dead. It's pitiful! And I surprise myself by saying, in spite of myself: "Oh! Oh! What can it mean—this caravanserai of apparitions, queuing up to disappear incontinently? Is the Universe meaningless? Is the all-devouring Universe—an infinite chain in which everyone's feet are consumed by the jaws of the next—destined to fall victim to the voracity of some Aeon? What will be its earthworm? Tell me, noise of the wind, bird which passes by...and you who know the answer, O Silence?"

Such are the inconceivable, fervent, poetic and—in consequence—grotesque whims that haunt me and trouble the lucidity of my ideas. It's merely an illness; I'm an *anguisher*. I've treated myself with douches, quinine, purgatives, astringents and hydrotherapy—I'm better now, much better. I have begun to reassure myself and to recognize that Progress is not a dream—that it is spreading throughout the world, illuminating it and, ultimately, elevating us towards spheres of choice which are uniquely worthy of the leaps of our most disciplined imaginations. That is no longer questionable, today, among men of good taste.

I still have fits, though...

In the world, I conceal this emotion as a matter of politeness. If I happen, at some party, to spend too long chatting to a woman she never knows—fortunately, I can see it in her eyes—that at a given moment, at the very instant when I am letting some innocent bonbon melt in my mouth, smiling, with a soft and syrupy voice, droning on about "fanatics"...she never knows, I tell you, that at that very moment, the rusty, profound and lugubrious knell of midnight is reverberating within me—or that the Midnight in question sounds more than a dozen strokes!

Now, I have an inveterate habit, adopted years ago as a veil for my chosen endeavors. It allows me to go into any society, to chat with men, women and children and to be well received. I hardly dare to name it, so fearful am I of misplaced mockery. I am talking about the habit of matchmaking. The brochette of my decorations has no other source.

As to why I adopted this habit, it's extremely simple.

To begin with, let's mention my weakness for Voltaire, the author of the immortal "Micromégas", where a fair number of my countless discoveries are, so to speak, prefigured. Even so, my admiration for that invaluable writer is by no means servile; everyone must strive, in fact, to develop in himself a profound contempt for his teachers and all those who, having raised him, have sought to inculcate their own ideas in him. What I admire in Voltaire is that ability lauded in Pozzo di Borgo[31] and Machiavelli—my favorite teachers—which consists in trampling underfoot all respect for his peers while maintaining an exterior appearance of obsequious humility: a perfect disguise to which the term "supreme" would be wholly appropriate! I recommend, in passing, that kind of charity. It is the only one worthy of being taken seriously; it serves to hide one's real objectives. Now, I am not anxious, on my own account, to make known my devotion, body and soul, to the _Infusoria_. Visits, questions, consultations and compliments have prevented me from bringing the desirable concentration to my vertiginous studies. On the other hand, as it is necessary that I talk, when I happen to find myself in company, I am eager to talk to everyone about that which most interests him, in order to avoid any questions about the nature of my scientific

---

[31] The Italian diplomat Charles-André Pozzo di Borgo (1764-1842) was a privy councilor of Tsar Alexander I and was blamed by some Frenchmen by having supplied advice that helped to occasion the disastrous culmination of Napoléon's Russian campaign.

researches, and isn't it nearly always _marriage_--his own or other people's--that preoccupies the most risible sons of Woman? Everyone knows that.

And that's how, without overtaxing my imagination, I have slid into the intimacy of so many people, and how—miraculously aided by Chance—I've made numerous marriages!

Most of the unions accomplished under my auspices have been favored by Heaven, even though, many a time, in my haste, I have brought couples together with their feet off the ground, as they say. Well, it always comes out right in the end. Except once—and it is the astonishing couple I riveted together in that union that I now intend to bring to everyone's attention.

Ought I to say, all things considered, that it was not happy, that marriage whose definitive and unnamable crisis gave way to my most deadly discovery? I would be an ingrate, *vis-à-vis* Destiny, if I had the impudence to think so for a second! Science—true Science—is inaccessible to pity; where would we be without it? In addition, even though the affair was the source of ample damnation for me—of a nameless terror which turns over in my brain to the point at which I am scarcely able to write, so that I, Tribulat Bonhomet, professor of diagnostics, have come to doubt my own existence and that of other things much more clearly evident—I maintain my Voltairean opinion. I do not repent what I did! I wash my hands of the responsibility of having completed that catastrophe! And I take pride in still being one of the finest minds to have escaped the hands of the Most High. All truly modern men, all the minds who sense that they are "in the movement" will understand what I mean.

I shall limit myself to a succinct statement of the facts, as they presented and represented themselves. Let whoever desires to do so attempt to explain the story; I shall not overburden it with any scientific theory. The general impression it creates will thus depend on the intellectual capacity furnished by the Reader.

II. Sir Henry Clifton (1)

> To me, the city, blurred by fog and soft
> lights represented the earth, with its
> sorrows and its graves—left far behind,
> but not wholly forgotten.
> Thomas De Quincey, *Confessions*[32]

In the last days of July 1866 a gala dinner was given in honor of Captain Brick of the British merchant vessel *Wonderful*, then making sail for the coast of Brittany. When coffee was served at the end of the meal I was embroiled in con-

---

[32] The quotation is not exact, having been taken from Baudelaire's essay rather than the original.

171

versation with the person seated next to me, Lieutenant Henry Clifton. He was about thirty years old, with regular features and the tanned complexion of a seaman. His expression was friendly and I found his reserved manner congenial.

That night was our first real conversation, the casual chat which takes place between a ship's officer and a mere passenger having been succinct in our case. We had set out from Ireland and, plunged into the study of my dear infusoria, I had remained below decks most of the time, experimenting with pickling brine.

We had exchanged a few words regarding our arrival at Saint-Malo, scheduled for the next day; then—the effects of the wine and the bright lights having given us a headache—we went up on deck to get some fresh air and light our cigars.

I had refrained, during the banquet, from getting mixed up in the discussion of politics which had inevitably broken out over dessert. Such arguments always become animated on occasions of that sort, and only interested me when they involved women. Well, who could be insensible, under such circumstances, of their delicate smiles, their gracious and ill-timed exclamations, their sensible manner, of the laudable efforts of their eyes to appear penetrating, troubled, surprised, and so on? I say again: discussing politics with women is a captivating business, which makes one think. In order to be worthy of their esteem and confidence, my face always becomes more benevolent on such occasions, more paternal, and softer than usual. I deliver my lines gravely, lowering my eyes as I spout the most outrageous absurdities—to which my white hair lends dignity— with the result that the entire sex hangs on my every word, as if I were a magician.

Anyway, political conversation would be just as amusing with the virile sex, if one could only bring the necessary grace and entertainment into it, although I've never heard anyone say anything worth taking seriously about the future course of events.

Sir Henry Clifton, like me, had never opened his mouth. This was why I had a high opinion of him. Nothing is more difficult, in my view, than keeping silent at his age. In politics, I presumed, he ought to share my ideas, which I can summarize thus:

In every country, every citizen worthy of the name has about three hours of leisure a day, between work and sleep. Ordinarily, he fills these moments of respite with petty chitchat, innocent and easily-digestible, about the affairs of his fatherland. Now, if nothing happens that is remarkable or "serious", what would he have to talk about? He would become bored, for want of a subject of conversation, and the boredom of citizens is nearly always fatal to Heads of State. The arms are ready to get busy when the tongue is idle, and when it is necessary to fill the aforementioned three hours, yesterday's conversationalist becomes today's rioter. That is the sad secret of revolutions.

It appears to me, therefore, that it is the duty of every good government to stir up, as often as possible, wars, epidemics, dreads, hopes—events of every

172

kind. It does not matter, in the ultimate analysis, whether they are fortunate or unfortunate, as long as they are capable of feeding the petty, innocent and easily-digestible chitchat of every citizen. After twenty, thirty or forty years of incessant *who goes there?* kings have diverted attention; their reign is tranquil. Adequately entertained, the whole world is content. This, in my view, is one of the best definitions of grand diplomacy: when the hand of God has bestowed on one the honor of being a leader of men, one must at all costs occupy the minds of one's citizens, so that all attention is deflected from oneself. Even my beloved master Machiavelli—I weep as I pronounce his name—never found a formula as neat as that! This explains my indifference to the events and the political disruptions and complications in which the governments of Europe are embroiled; I leave interest in the controversies they stir up to minds rotted by an innate thirst for killing time.

For this reason, I silently commended Sir Henry Clifton for his reserve and his quiet way of drinking. Actually, he was in a worst state than the drunken sailor in the song; he had more color in his cheeks and I saw that he was about to wax sentimental. I was perfectly sober myself, so I decided to watch over him as if he were my patient.

The night was full of stars. The north-west wind freshened and gently pushed us forward; the red lantern on the quarter-deck illuminated the foam and silver vapor of the waves breaking on the ship's hull. The hurrahs of the officers gathered around the punch-bowl reached us from time to time from below decks, mingling with the heavy sound of the waves.

Seeing the Englishman fall silent, I feared that he was about to ask me what I did for a living, perhaps even about my work so I launched into conversation according to my infallible method. "Hold on, my young friend," I said. "I know what you need! Shall I tell you? It occurred to me the first time I had the pleasure of shaking your hand." At this point I lowered my voice, staring vaguely into space like a man talking to himself. "Very well, I'll wager that what would suit a capable person like you is an adventurous yet experienced widow—a beautiful woman, second-hand, with a fortune--oh yes, a *Thousand-and-One-Nights* fortune! That's just it." I raised my eyebrows abruptly, fixing my dull eyes on his epaulette, and added: "Yes, that's exactly what you need."

After a stunned pause, as expected, Sir Henry Clifton steadied himself, using his little finger to shake the ash from the end of his cigar. "Ah!" he said. "What an excellent, shrewd doctor you are—sent by the Devil, if I understand you right."

With my eyes utterly lost in celestial space, I placed my hand gently on his arm and whispered in his ear: "An introduction can be arranged for Monday, if nothing gets in the way, at one or two o'clock, and you can be married in six weeks. If I'm wrong, I promise to cut off my head right here, on the stern-post!"

"He took my by the hands, astounded. The fish had bitten; I had avoided interrogation on scientific matters.

"I believe I understand, at last," he muttered, after a pause. You are offering me something like..."

He stopped, out of a modesty for which I was grateful.

"A legitimate wife, lieutenant."

"A wife!" he finished, in an uncertain voice that as even slightly tremulous.

"And why not, lieutenant?" I replied, scenting a mystery. "Your profession of mariner...considerable skill, aristocratic company, a good career..." I interjected, mechanically, "is not incompatible with a distant hearth. It is the softest nest for those...that you have the habit of casting off!" I added, smiling agreeably. "Nevertheless, if you're not interested, stay as you are. I won't say another word."

After a momentary pause, as if he had thought about it long enough, he withdrew slightly and said: "Monsieur!" Then, retreating into himself, probably thinking, *he's a harmless eccentric*, he said: "Thank you for the kind thought, doctor. I'll tell you something in return."

We were there. Constance had done its work on the impressionable child.[33] I pricked up my ears, solemnly.

"It's doubtful," he went on, "that we'll ever meet again. Oh well! I must refuse your generous offer because there is a woman whose face I shall never be able to forget so long as I live."

"Ah!" I said, smugly. "Very well—I understand." I added, under my breath: *I would have been surprised if it were not so, but let me say to you...*

I sat up straight and made an expansive gesture of desolation, and said: "What a pity! It really is a shame!"

If there was anything of the Devil in me, it was that I had not the slightest idea what woman I could offer to him. My principal preoccupation was merely to avoid any question concerning infusoria.

"And she is married!" murmured Sir Henry Clifton in a low voice, as if he were talking to himself.

I felt tears moistening my eyes.

"Can I do anything for you?" I asked him, at hazard, with profound tenderness. And I added, in a low voice: "It's just that I'm a slick operator in complicated negotiations."

There was a moment of the most peculiar silence, during which I felt the young man watching me as if he were undecided as to whether to slap my face or embrace me. I had known in advance that my words, correctly interpreted, would make a favorable impression on his mind.

"Thank you, my friend...my old friend," he finished up saying, in a voice whose violent emotion melted my heart, "but the poor woman must never see me again..."

---

[33] Constance is a kind of wine, but the word can also mean "perseverance."

His distraught eyes no longer seemed to register my presence. Bitterly, he went on: "I dare say that she's blind even now, as I speak. Yes! Yes, it's all because of her poor eyes...!" And he lowered his head, which was doubtless still aching, into his hands.

At those words, I slowly removed the cigar from my mouth, and shot a terrible glance at Sir Henry Clifton, in the darkness. Although I have no idea why, the young man had made me think of my strange and beautiful friend—or , to be more specific, of the unfortunate *eyes*—of my worthy friend Madame Claire Lenoir.

I silently took my watch out of my pocket and rose to my feet.

"I look forward to seeing you again, my young lieutenant," I said. "You have your secrets. "There are times when one ought to be left alone, and I respect such occasions..."

He shook my hand without raising his head. I buttoned my coat securely against the wind and I went down to my cabin, abandoning Sir Henry Clifton to his dreams, under the particular protection and inspiration of the night, the persistent wine and the sea.

III. Supererogatory Explanations

"That which *sees*, in our eyes, watches from hiding on
this side of the depths of our fleshly pupils."
Lysiane d'Aubelleyne.[34]

I went to bed in haste. My thoughts rocked along with my hammock, swaying with the movement of the boat. I supported myself on my elbows.

It was actually with the Lenoirs that I intended to stay for a fortnight after disembarking. A letter posted from Jersey had warned them of my coming; they would be expecting me.

Had I seen them since their wedding, three years ago? No, not once. I had an awful feeling, it seemed to me, of being somehow involved in their marriage. Indeed, during a rather long sojourn I had spent in the Pyrenees, at Luchon, for the sake of my health, I had become acquainted with Claire's family. An honest and respectable family of merchants, if ever there was one! Their only daughter was a very beautiful girl, about twenty years old, I think, when circumstance threw us together. Hers was a very educative kind of beauty. She had chestnut-brown hair, lovely features and a complexion like jade, which sometimes seemed almost luminously transparent.

---

[34] Lysiane d'Aubellyne was the heroine of a story that Villiers rewrote several times before publishing it as *"L'Amour suprême."* The quotation does not feature in the published version.

175

The frontal region of her skull was, unfortunately, rather large, disclosing a useless cerebral capacity which could only be reckoned detrimental in a woman.

Her eyes were pale green. Excursions among the mountain crags had exposed her eyes—such large eyes!—to the hot and dusty wind that blows from the south. Her sight, which was naturally weak to begin with, had become much worse, and the unanimous verdict of her physicians was that she would soon lose it altogether.

However, in musing one day on the similarity of the names Lenoir and Luchon,[35] and my old comrade Césaire Lenoir of Saint-Malo, the idea had come to me that Claire, instead of being called Mademoiselle, could became Madame Lenoir without overmuch difficulty.

Why not?

I wrote immediately to the excellent Césaire, who hastened to Luchon. That coincidence of names was easily exploited by me as the pretext of a formal introduction. Césaire was a man scarcely forty-two years old; the marriage was soon consummated. I rubbed my hands together in glorious satisfaction, having made the two of them happy.

Lenoir took his wife to Saint-Malo, installing her in his property at no. 18, Rue des Mauvais-Pâleurs, his usual place of residence. His occasional letters to me indicated that his happy home was untroubled by any anxieties, save for Claire's threatened loss of sight.

How could Sir Henry Clifton, the amiable and aristocratic child of the sea, have become acquainted with the young woman? Could I conclude—supposing that it was indeed Claire Lenoir about whom he had spoken—could I think it possible, that she had failed in her marital duty? No! Such a thought was hideous; I was imagining things.

Besides which, Claire—beautiful Claire—was a studious woman and a collector: a metaphysician, unless my memory was playing me false. A savant! An impossible creature! An ecstatic! A quibbler! A wordsmith! A dreamer. Go on! It could not be her that the lieutenant had intended to sully with an accusation of adultery.

At that point, I smiled to myself and pulled my blanket over my head. As far as the young Englishman was concerned, I shrugged my shoulders and went to sleep.

---

[35] The alleged similarity, invisible in English, probably relates *louchon* [cross-eyed] to *le noir* [as in the "bull's eye" of an archery target]. Villiers was very fond of tortured wordplay.

IV. The Mysterious Paragraph

Besides, in these lethargic times,
As devoid of gaiety as of remorse,
The only smile that still makes sense
Is that of a dead man's skull.
Paul Verlaine.[36]

The bell signaling our arrival woke me up. We were in the harbor at Saint-Malo. It was eleven o'clock, or a little later; the sun was shining brightly. I took my walking-stick and my suitcase, leapt on to the gangplank and joined the flow of travelers going down to the quay, my boots flecked with the spume of the sea.

The first thing I did after setting foot on the soil of my illustrious fatherland was to go into a cafe which looked out over the entire foreshore--and, in the distance, the tomb of the Vicomte de Chateaubriand, an old minister of Charles X whose ethnographic works on savage tribes are said to be remarkable.[37] I ordered my usual enormous dose of absinthe, then sank back into my seat and—distracted by nostalgia—took up the first newspaper that happened to come to hand.

It was a local paper someone had left behind on the seat—soiled, tattered and long out of date. Now that I think about it, it comes back to me, distinctly, that the waiter wanted to tear it out of my hand and give me a more recent one instead, and that I resisted him with the reflexive action of any man from whom someone tries to take something away.

In skimming through the paper my eyes were caught by a paragraph situated between a new case of encroachment on the part of the clergy--judiciously pointed out by the reporter—and an infallible recipe, recommended by some fly-by-night quack, for curing the most terrible earaches. This is what the paragraph said:

"The Academy of Sciences in Paris has determined the authenticity of a most surprising fact. It is henceforth established that animals destined for our nourishment, such as sheep, cattle, lambs, horses and cats, retain in their eyes, after the fatal stroke of the butcher's sledge-hammer, the imprint of the objects of their last gaze. It is a veritable photograph of paving-stones, stalls, gutters and vague figures, among whom can nearly always be distinguished that of the man

---

[36] This quatrain is reproduced in Verlaine's *Oeuvres completes*, on the assumption that Villiers might have obtained it from Verlaine rather than simply making it up.

[37] A joke, referring to Chateaubriand's "romance of the primeval forest, *Atala* (1801), intended as a satire of Rousseauesque notions of "noble savagery", but interpreted as an homage by many readers.

who strikes them down. The phenomenon lasts until decomposition sets in. As Ignorance diminishes, this discovery will obviously figure nobly among its companions in the already much-enriched catalogue of the achievements of our enlightened century."

I had known this fact before, with particular reference to its recent application by the North American police, as advertised in the same country—and that will, I hope, leave not a shadow of a doubt in the mind of the Reader. But what struck me was a personal phenomenon that reading the piece then produced in me: a certain kind of *appropriateness* which the fact seemed to me to possess at that moment, even though it was conveyed by some miserable provincial joker.

That sensory deprivation could have been nervous fatigue, moral and physical, induced by my voyage; I therefore proceeded to examine myself. Then, mechanically, I raised my eyes, and my gaze fell upon a man standing, arms crossed, against a foremast two hundred fathoms away. I recognized the noble lieutenant. Our eyes met as we turned spontaneously to look straight at one another, as if we had been discomfited. Why? Neither of us ever knew.

To cut short the dark thoughts that began to rise in my mind, I rose abruptly to my feet, downing the absinthe in a single gulp. Then, showing the place a clean pair of heels, I strode off rapidly along the road which led to the maritime district where the Lenoirs lived—a slightly out-of-the-way road which was deserted at that time of day.

The sun was hot; I stopped from time to time to wipe my forehead and to cast a troubled glance behind and to either side of me.

V. The Blue-Tinted Spectacles

> Lovely eyes of my child, adored arcana,
> You remind me of those magic grottoes
> Where, behind a crowd of lethargic shadows.
> Forgotten treasures dimly scintillate.
> Charles Baudelaire, *Spleen et Idéal*.[38]

Half an hour later I was in front of an isolated country house, the home of my best friend Césaire, the good doctor. I say "doctor" because that's the correct term, but Lenoir was, at bottom, something of a fool—a natural person, if ever there was such a thing under the Sun! I rang the bell; an old manservant came to open it for me, escorted by an enormous red-haired basset-hound, which served the household as both watchdog and rat-catcher.

The manservant took me to the dining-room, asked me to wait, and went out. It was an ordinary ground-floor room. Through the window, which opened

---

[38] Slightly misrendered from *"Les Yeux de Berthe,"* added to later editions of *Les Fleurs du mal.*

on to the garden, came the fresh odor of trees. An ancestral portrait hung on the wall; a shaded lamp sat on the cloth-covered table. A large oak-framed mirror over the mantelpiece reflected the old grandfather clock and the antique candelabras. The room was shot through with provincial quiet and the calm of isolation. I stood there with my hat and stick in one hand and my suitcase in the other, savoring the whole experience of that silent freshness, full of echoes.

Then, taking a brief tour, I thought: *One could be happy here!*

The movement left me standing in front of the mirror; in the glass I saw the door open soundlessly behind me, giving passage to a being whose appearance caused me to start in surprise. It was a woman wrapped in a green velvet dressing-gown with red tassels; two long ringlets of chestnut-colored hair fell, *à la Sévigné*, on to her bosom; her eyes were hidden by a pair of gold spectacles with enormous round blue lenses as big as six-livre coins, extending almost as far as her eyebrows and the high-set bones of her pale cheeks. She came in like a ghost, showing her teeth in a polite smile. I have said before and will ay again: the unexpected sight of her sent a thrill of surprise right through me.

"So it's you, Monsieur Traveler," Claire Lenoir said to me in a voice as mordant and vibrant as a silver bell. "We went to wait for you on the quay yesterday evening! Stay there, and have a quick glass of this old Madeira; Césaire will be down in a minute."

Once I had put my luggage in a corner, hastily, I took her by the hands. "Is it really you?" I murmured. "Is it possible?"

The young woman looked me up and down, somewhat taken aback.

"Of course," she said. "There's no doubt about it! Why so surprised, my dear Monsieur Bonhomet? I did not realize that I had changed so much...oh!" She suddenly burst out laughing. "I know what it is! It's my spectacles! That's right—you haven't seen me since the day...alas, my friend, I'm resigned to wearing them, at my age, in the hope of prolonging my sight. Look! Look!"

And, lifting the large spectacles up with both hands, she let me see her *Eyes*.

They had a brilliance so vitreous, so pure, that her gaze was as cold as a gemstone; they hurt me. They were two emeralds.

"Put them back," I said. "A sudden draught might be dangerous."

Her eyelashes closed over the pupils.

I don't know what it is about my eyes," she said, doing as she was told, "but I can tell, when I blink, that it is as much for the benefit of other people as for my own that I need to wear these thick glasses."

There was a silence. I understood that the moment had come for me to sing her praises; the situation certainly seemed to require it! But when I opened my mouth--to draw some comparison with the most gigantic stars in the vault of Heaven beloved of the nocturnal angels--another person appeared behind the glass-paneled door.

It was Lenoir.

179

As soon as he had recognized me his eyebrows shot up and drew apart; he came in like a cannonball and threw himself into my arms without a word, with such frank enthusiasm that he nearly bowled me over. He knocked the breath out of me.

"Here I am!" I said to him, "and it's a real pleasure to see, my dear Lenoir, that the years have treated you well." Smiling, and feeling myself to make sure that none of my ribs had been broken, I added: "As strong and vigorous as ever!"

He called the servants, getting quite out of breath, while his wife filled my glass with Madeira; he told them to take my things up to the room that had been made up for me. After which, we went into the drawing-room and set about chatting.

VI. I Kill Time Before Dinner

> You fall silent, O sinister voice of the living!
> Leconte de Lisle.[39]

The furnishings, curtains and wall-hangings of the little dining-room were dark red; there were alabaster vases on the mantelpiece. In the shadows was a painting in the style of the Rembrandt school; there were sickly violet dahlias in a vase on the piano. A model of a warship made by my friend in his spare time, complete with rigging and cannons, was suspended from the ceiling as if it were a chandelier. The window was open, looking out over the shore of the Atlantic.

Sinking into the sofa, between Césaire and his wife, I offered them a sketchy account of my journeys through the five continents, my explorations of mountain peaks and the bowels of the Earth—from the summit of the Illimani to the depths of the silver mines of Poullaouën. I talked about the geysers and volcanoes of Iceland; the pointed skulls of the Seminoles; the rites of the Juggernaut; the Chinese tortures whose mere nomenclature would fill a dictionary as capacious as Bottin; the cults of African sorcerers who dance naked with sulfurous torches aflame in their armpits; the passport tattooed on my back that had been given to me as a sign of affection by Zouézoué-Anandézoué-Rakartapakoué-Boué-Anazenopati-Abdoulrakam-Penanntogomo V, king of the isles of Honolulu and Moo-Loo-Loo; Indian trees under each of whose leaves Buddhist maxims are inscribed; the serpent cults of the cannibals of Tierra del Fuego, the serpents in question being those who can kill human beings by biting shadows cast on sand by the sun; the sap of the cruciferous hemlock of the south pole, whose infusion can still produce hallucinations containing visions of the antediluvian world; the Canadian religion based on the belief that the universe was created by a great hare; the niam-niams, men with the tails of chimpanzees,

---

[39] From "Dernière vision" in Poèmes barbares (1862).

which are classified above the gorilla and below the Kaffir negro in the apparent scale of living creatures, as I have established in my treatise entitled *On the Tadpole*; the Tibetan High Lama, whose regal visage is always veiled from the moment of birth to that of death; the Zealander tribal chief Ko-li-Ki (King of Kings) who lives exclusively on large chunks of flesh cut by machetes from the choice parts of the bodies of his subjects, in advance of his passage through their midst. I talked about huge trees, waves, rocks and distant adventures. I held the dice; I threw the ball back; I rang the bells of pleasantry; I narrated all these traveler's tales with great aplomb. I talked about this and that, right and left, without rhyme or reason—thinking that it was, after all, quite a treat for them.

In brief, I was charming.

They both seemed rather stunned, looking at me as if they hardly recognized me. I pity such provincial minds, which have to listen hard to know if it's raining.

Anyway, to tell the truth, I was rather annoyed with Lenoir, because he had squeezed me a little too tenderly between his muscular arms; I don't like expansive gestures.

Evening drew on; the rays of the setting sun lit the three of us with a rather sinister glow in the depths of the red room.

During a moment of profound recollection the old manservant discreetly pushed the door half-open, and intoned these words:

"Madame is served."

We got up. I stretched my legs and screwed up my mouth, bent my arm and offered it to Madame Lenoir—who deigned to support herself upon it.

Césaire followed us, pensively holding his nose with the tips of his thumb and index finger, having furtively taken a pinch of snuff. His contemplative attitude did not escape my notice, even though he was behind me—because, like all tactful people, I have eyes in the back of my head.

Illuminated candelabras were brought in; their glare was reflected by the glasses, the tablecloth and the crystal bowls.

We sat down and deployed our napkins with a certain silent solemnity, thanks to the atmosphere created by my conversation, but after the first glass of Bordeaux we all had smiles on our faces.

VII. Musical and Literary Chitchat

> A dinner with much clucking
> Madame de Sévigné.

At the table, Claire talked about music in an improbably scientific fashion that I did not expect to find in an unfortunate woman

She mentioned a certain German maestro whose name and epoch I have quite forgotten: a "miraculous genius" she said, "but only accessible to the intelligence of the initiated, to complete human beings." His works concerned Brabantine legends, a phantom ship), a virtuous warrior kidnapped by the goddess worshiped at Paphos, someone called Tout-Fou, a mythological hotchpotch in four parts, and so on. These last-named compositions seemed to fill Madame Lenoir with an inexplicable admiration. I remember quite clearly that she talked to us about a certain *crescendo in D* resplendent, -she said with childish enthusiasm, with "terrible hosannahs"[40]

She also specified some "Pilgrim's Song" or other, "whose profound lassitude has something of the eternal!" This song captivated her to the point of distraction. If it could be believed, "it was, at first, stifled by enlacements of the aphrodisiac laughter of mocking sirens who appeared among the reeds by the light of the moon". This took place "near to an enchanted mountain. This signified, simply, that the wheedling instigations of our passions sometimes obscure in us, earthly pilgrims all, the memory of the celestial fatherland—an idea that never occurred to any other note-cruncher, one must suppose, given that it is so puerile. "But," added Madame Lenoir, "the mystic fanfare bursts forth in the end, triumphantly dominant: a choice decisively made, after due reflection, in the twilight; a hymn of glory and martyrdom, putting the shadows to flight—an authentic mission of Hope!"

At his pronouncement I felt wild laughter rise into my throat. It was obvious that Madame Lenoir, abusing the privileges of her frivolous sex, desired to amuse herself at my expense. I deemed it advisable to take it all in good part, and her praise of this schemer enlivened the conversation during the first two courses.

After that, she ventured opinions on literature; there, I was on firmer ground. In the Chinchas, rightly esteemed for their famous fertilizer, while suffering from an illness that I do not need to name, I had read a few books in order to stave off nocturnal boredom. There were two or three works by a prodigious writer whose books had already made him a ton of money--which is, for me as for all people who are incapable of eating their fill of words, the best possible recommendation. His pen is the most fecund and forceful in our great country and the elite of both sexes throughout the five continents argue over his products, such as they are. I have forgotten his name, but his kind of talent—which all his contemporaries strive in vain to attain--consists of cleverly veiling the most scabrous situations in order to strike the imagination of the reader with a chain of harrowing, but logical, vicissitudes in which the main characters (usually taken from the lowest strata of society) lift the heart, nourish the spirit and calm needlessly scrupulous consciences. His heroes are mainly interesting in that they die on one page only to be brought back to life on another. In those

---

[40] Villiers was one of the most vocal of Richard Wagner's early advocates in France, and visited the composer in his homeland. "Tout-Fou," translatable as "Holy Fool" must be Parsifal. The "Pilgrims' Chorus" is in *Tannhaüser*.

pages, which the eye races feverishly through, are simultaneously projected the venerable shades of Orpheus, Homer, Virgil and Dante, if not Chapelain[41] himself. In sum, this man, this moralist, represents, here and now, the purest expression of modern Art in its Renaissance and its Maturity. And everyone loves his work. Personally, after that exile in the Chinchas I was desperate to plant my furtive and uncertain feet on French territory again so that I could commit myself entirely to reading his new collections and periodicals loaded down with his genius, but only found a few feeble scraps authored by his powerful pen strewn hither and thither.[42]

I forgot to say that I had also read two or three volumes of an old parliamentary deputy and former peer of France—if I can believe what I was told, inadvertently, by the captain—and the works of an American short story writer published in Richmond, South Carolina.[43]

I must confess that the prose of the peerless novelist, the Moralist of the Chinchas, had genuinely refreshed my heart. His characters, as solid as wood, had filled me with excitement, and oft-times with emotion—notably, one of them named, I think, Rocambole. The only fault I could find in him--and I say this in all humility--is that he was sometimes, perhaps, a little...metaphysical... a little--how shall I put it?--a little too abstract...in the end, as one might say, a little too _head-in-the-clouds_, as all poets are, alas.

Ah, when will a writer appear who talks to us of true things? Of things that happen! Of things that everyone in the world knows by heart, which run, have run and always will run through the streets—of *serious* things, in sum! Such a man would be worthy of public esteem because he would be the public's own Pen.

As for the old Deputy, his "verses", according to his own astonishing expression, warmed my bile. They were, as far as I can remember, a kind of potpourri of discontinuous legends without, as they say, rhyme nor reason. Mahomet, Adam and Eve, the Sultan, the regiments of the Swiss army and knights errant were all in there; it was, in its entirety, the most chaotic and extravagant lumber-room that ever came out of a fevered brain. A few nice words, here and there, some right-minded appreciations, only made them all the more dangerous, in my view, to feeble minds. I cannot understand that such an individual has

---

[41] The epic poet Jean Chapelain (1595-1674), a founding menbr of the Académie Française, was not considered to have had any great ability.

[42] The subsequent reference to Rocambole confirms that the writer to whom Bonhomet is referring is the popular but much-derided feuilletoniste Pierre-Alexis Ponson du Terrail.

[43] Viliers knew very well that the RFIchmond with which Edgar Poe waas asocated was in Virginia.

been appointed as a parliamentary deputy: that collection gave me a truly pitiful idea of our beautiful French language.[44]

Did I mention the American? That one appeared to me to be a hearty fellow with a nice line in colorful rhetoric. But one thing that struck me was the way he labeled his works. He called them, rather conceitedly, "unparalleled stories" or "extraordinary tales" or some such. I have read all these stories and have tried in vain to see anything extraordinary in what he relates. It is, in fact, the last word in banality—presented, it is true, in a bourgeois manner, but banal nevertheless. It sent me off to sleep many a time, in a delightful way. I can only conclude that the title was chosen by the editor to pique the curiosity of vulgar readers.

Claire Lenoir blushed deeply at the name of the Moralist of the Chinchas and confessed to me, in utter confusion, that this was the first time she had heard mention of him.

At this naive confession, unable to believe my ears, I naturally favored her with a sideways, almost snakelike, glance. It must be admitted that it was a sad reflection on a woman well-versed in the study of Literature and abstruse questions of philosophy. What had she read, then, I wondered? Of what did that little empty head dream?

Even so, her provincial candor warranted a certain indulgence, and I had no wish to abuse her charming hospitality by parading my superior knowledge, so I restricted myself to talking about the deputy and the American short story writer—whose names still, inexplicably, escape me. I described them, as I said, in the appreciative terms set out above.

Madame Lenoir appeared to listen to me most attentively for some time; she seemed to be entirely ignorant of what I wanted to say. But when I had specified the subjects—to which I returned forcefully—of some of the deputy's "legends" and the titles of some of the "unparalleled tales" of the gentleman from South Carolina, she shivered as if she had woken up with a start, and her face look on a most peculiar expression. I can vouch for that! Something demonic...indefinable, that's the word!

She immediately transfixed me with her emerald eyes, covered by her spectacles, and stared at me as if slightly stupefied. Then, taking hold of the carafe, she refilled her glass, drank a draught of pure water, replaced the glass in front of her plate and suddenly, without any reason, burst out into musical, half-stifled laughter. I looked back at her, pity mingling with suspicion, and wondered about her state of mind.

She soon recovered a more decorous appearance and—I have very good ears—I heard her murmur in a very low voice: "Why laugh? It is written: *the dead shall not praise you.*"[45]

---

[44] The work that Bonhomet is failing to appreciate is Victor Hugo's *La Légende des siècles.*

I literally did not know what to think. I looked at Césaire; he was devouring a saddle of hare with tomatoes, rolling his eyes as if drowning in ecstasy, and said not a word.

"Yes, it's the mysterious Law," the young woman continued, so quietly that I could hardly hear her. "There are beings so constituted that, even in the midst of cascades of light, they cannot help seeing shadow-beings. There are souls that have gained profane substance, haphazardly clad, which pass into the sepulcher of their mortal senses and are there immured."

I reprimanded her, silently, for this epigram, evidently addressed to her husband, but politeness demanded that I pretend not to have heard it.

"Ha ha!" I exclaimed. "You see, dear Madame Lenoir, I'm a straightforward man myself."

"There are other beings," she continued, softly, "who know the roads of life and are curious about the paths of death. Those, who must submit to the realm of the Spirit, disdain the years in order to possess Eternity. In the depths of their sacred eyes they are alert to a gleam more precious than a million tangible solar systems like ours, from our equator to that of Neptune. And the world, in its unconscious obedience to the Laws of God, only rendered justice to itself and dedicated itself to DEATH on the day when it was written: *Woe betide those who dream!*"

And she murmured the words—senselessly, in every respect—of Lactantius, in his *De morte persecutorum*, so very quietly, this time, that I divined rather than heard them: "*Pulcher hymnus Dei homo immortalis!*"[46]

She leaned on her elbows, her chin in the palm of her lovely hand, as if she had forgotten that we were there.

The compliment was undoubtedly exaggerated; I am far from being as beautiful a soul as she desired—so I poured myself an ample glass of Château Margaux brought back from the Indies and, to tell the truth, felt little compassion for that futile farrago.

"Dear Madame," I replied, courteously, "I have always partaken of those sentiments that you have broadcast, the inverse of those which seem to me to be worthy—and it is even in my nature to render service, almost unconsciously, as you say, to the good natures that I encounter on my way."

"Really, doctor?" she said.

"Yes, really," I replied. "And, to be sure, it happens, sometimes, that I make the acquaintance of young men who go through life full of enthusiasm, with laughter on their lips, joy and generosity in their hearts. Ah, these poets, these gentle children—what services I have done for them!"

---

[45] Presumably a paraphrase of a line in verse 17 of psalm 115, rendered in the A.V. as: "The dead praise not the Lord, neither any that go down into silence."

[46] "Immortal man is a beautiful hymn of God." Lactantius Firmianus was a Christian apologist of the early fourth century.

I stopped for a moment to savor my memories.

"Well?" Claire murmured, looking at me.

"Well," I added, in a paternal tone, "I don't know how it happens, but I've established that, in my experience, they gradually lose the habit of laughing, and even of smiling."

It seemed to me, as I completed that sentence, that Claire experience a thrill—the nervous thrill, a sign of health after a meal, that stupid people call "the little death".

Lenoir interrupted his work momentarily, lifted his head, and looked at me with a bizarre seriousness; then, without saying a word, he plunged back into his dinner.

"Finally, dear Madame Lenoir," I went on, "by way of conclusion, I've always liked good writers—and just as the daisy-chain of modern children is nothing but the atrophied crown of Melchisedech, so the Moralist of the Chinchas is one of them.

Claire lowered her head silently; she was beaten. I understood that her ignorance had crushed her. I took an innocent delight in her blush, but—not wanting to take the lesson too far—I turned to Césaire to talk about things more serious than "Literature" and "Music".

VIII. Spiritism

> When men dine, they tend to talk about
> immortality over dessert.
> E. & J. de Goncourt.

However, Césaire's intellect—the sum of his soul's faculties, in fact—appeared to me, for the moment, to be entirely absorbed by a plateful of "olives" of veal, The dish was his favorite, whose taste sensations he valued above all others. I felt sure, as I watched him, that they had stifled any notion of justice, human or divine. I judged it prudent to let the storm pass, as they say—and even to do my best to follow the excellent example of his stoical conduct.

In consequence, I thought that it was about time I brought into play the heroic apparatus of the masticatory and crotaphitic musculature, with which Mother Nature, in her foresight, had provided me. A moment later, our two sets of jaws entered into a silent competition with one another, with all due rapidity, efficiency and vigor, united in the trickery of discernment.

All of a sudden, in the midst of the intelligent silence which held sway over our distracted foreheads, Claire complained that the candlelight was too bright. It was, therefore, in discreet lamplight that Césaire, having decided that he was full, sank back into his chair in a classical pose. He thumped the table with both hands and the servants brought coffee and liqueurs. Raising his eyebrows he rolled his wild and satisfied eyes, and looked dazedly at Madame Le-

186

noir and myself. Then he savored the aroma of the fresh coffee, took a swig, put down his cup, twiddled his thumbs and looked at the ceiling.

"Perfect!" he said, letting the word fall in a guttural voice that was thick and hoarse with satiation.

His mouth, splayed like a policeman's helmet, attempted to sketch out a smile, and immediately launched into a "philosophical" discussion.

The thesis selected by the excellent Amphitryon was none other than this:

"Is this life the prelude to a further chain of existences, or is it definitive? Does the sum of our thoughts and actions constitute a new interior being soluble in Death?" In other words: "Does our miserable quotient immediately merit, after the dissolution of the organism and the disaggregation of its material form, the honor of being Unmodifiable?"

I leave it to the Reader's imagination to judge the effect that this topic—which would have confounded the patients in a lunatic asylum—produced in me. But the imperturbable Césaire gathered himself together and I saw to my horror that he was ready to set out, with all the complacency in the world, all the superstitions that had infected his mind.

Perhaps I should say now, so that the Reader is forewarned, that Césaire Lenoir was a haunter of solitary places, a man of dark theories and a vindictive temperament. Something rudimentary had gone astray in his fundamental nature. He pretended, laughing under his South Sea Islander's nose, that he had something in him of the *hairy vampire*. He was excessively fond of making jokes about cannibalism. It all seemed to be submerged within bourgeois innocence, but whenever he was carried away by his favorite themes—the form that the nervous fluid of a dead person might take; the physical and temporal power of the spirits of the dead over the living—his eyes burned with the flames of superstition. This savage spoke in a terrified manner of the great Devil of the inferno, and he had often succeeded in disquieting minds that were not as strong as mine, and making them ill with his bizarre and opinionated eloquence.

I have known him keep me on tenterhooks until morning with the tale of the captain of a certain Russian ship, taken prisoner by the islanders of the Malay Archipelago—a horrific story!—during the telling of which his face took on an expression of which I would not have thought it naturally capable. His true nature, his inner being, was possessed by a ferocity that subverted all his civilization.

As for what he called his "theological" ideas, they were for me the most ample source of hilarious gibes—unspoken, of course, but understood. Faithful to the prescriptions of the excellent authors that I had the honor of citing at the beginning of this memorandum, it is not my policy to censure people overtly. Lenoir, therefore, had no idea, when I expressed lofty and smiling approval of his stupid and fatuous theories, that I was privately nursing a disdainful, blind and almost sanguinary hatred for them. There was even something of that (ha ha!) in the way I had so pitilessly married him off some time before--for I always have a motive for doing what I do, and I alone, like Aeschylus' Jupiter, know what I am thinking.

Now, it was in that year, or thereabouts--according to those who knew him well—that faith in the doctrines of Magic, Spiritism, Animal Magnetism and, most of all, Hypnotism had attained their maximum intensity in my poor friend's mind. The suggestions that he claimed to be able to inculcate in passers-by were alarming and frightening. He backed up his theories with such aplomb as to raise gooseflesh by the utter monstrosity of their expression.

He took delight in the writings of Éliphas Lévi, Raymond Lully, Mesmer and Guillaume Postel, the gentle monk of Black Magic. He quoted the astrologer priest Trithemius. He swore by none but Aureolus Theophrastus Bombast, whom he called the "divine Paracelsus". Gaffarel and the popular Swedenborg threw him into delirious ecstasy, and he alleged that the Hell of purification, as analyzed by Jean Reynaud, was more than rational.

The moderns—Mirville, Crookes, Allan Kardec—plunged him into profound reveries. He believed in the risen dead of Ireland, in Wallachian vampires, in the evil eye; he quoted passages from the third volume of the mystic Görres to me in support of his propositions.

What was even more abracadabraesque was that Lenoir was a zealous and far-reaching Hegelian. How had that come about? Go on then, find an atom of good sense in the contradictions of men drunk on thought!—when it is proven that all of that leads nowhere, since one can never convince oneself.

As regards Animal Magnetism, he had boundless confidence in the very curious experiments of Dupotet and Regazzoni. On this matter, I was not so very far from sharing his opinions—although, it must be understood, in a more sedate and enlightened manner.

The old rascal was a firm believer in blows struck at a distance, in passions abruptly excited solely by the will of the magnetizer, in artificial wealth, in the pains of phantom pregnancy, in flowers poisoned by a glance and, finally, in condemnation by the formulaic signs of priestly Esotericism.

In his room, he had a pentagram of virgin gold and the apparatus necessary for the evocation of demons and the making of pacts. He understood the he-goat of Baphomet, the emblem lent, as everyone knows, to the ancient Templars. He spoke readily about the *Key of Solomon* and he believed in the "sidereal body" enclosed in everyone. And in support of these nonsensicalities, as cool as a Greenlander, he quoted texts which, rather surprisingly, appeared at first to be perfectly rational, logical, scientific and irrefutable--but which obviously could not be anything, at bottom, but the mischievous fruits of ignorance and charlatanry.

Such was the good doctor; and now he had posed the question—if it even qualifies as a question—that I have already mentioned. As we shall see, it led to an exceedingly strange discussion which it is necessary for me to describe in full, to illuminate the even stranger events which followed it.

IX. The Incredible Blunders, Indiscretions and Stupidities of my Poor Friend

> Philosophy commands; it does not obey.
> Aristotle.

We lit our cigars and went into the drawing-room. In order to be better able to enjoy the view through the open window of the distant shining waves Claire turned the lamplight down.

The night sky was a black chaos of horrid clouds, through which a few stars and a coppery crescent moon were visible, but the briny odor of the sea impregnated our lungs.

"Here we are at the theatre," murmured Madame Lenoir. "This evening's performance is the grand opera *The Sea*, with music by God."

"The fact is, if I dare put it in such terms," I replied, smiling, "that the swell of the sea provides a 'divine' bass-line to the harmony of of our thoughts."

I sank into the sofa. Madame Lenoir leaned on the balcony, turning her head to look out into the distance. The doctor installed himself in an armchair facing me, his singularly clear and bright eyes meeting mine with a profound and almost embarrassing fixity.

"My friend," I said to him, "my oldest and only companion-in-arms, I need your urgent assistance to cast light on a point of physiology that intrigues me."

"Spit it out, Bonhomet, spit it out!" Lenoir murmured, evidently flattered that a man like me should ask him to "cast light."

"To put it succinctly: have the health officials who serve in lunatic asylums thought of measuring, approximately, the proportion of reality contained in the hallucinations of their clients?"

By means of that incongruous question I hoped to make him understand the ridiculousness and poor taste of his own question.

"Before answering you," he said to me, emotionlessly, "I would be glad to know what you mean by the word *reality*."

"It is that which I see, that which I sense, that which I touch," I replied, with a pitying smile.

"No," said Lenoir. "You know perfectly well that man is condemned, by the derisory inadequacy of his sense-organs, to perpetual error. The discovery of the microscope was sufficient to prove to us that our senses are deceptive and that we cannot see things as they are. Nature appears to us grandiose and 'poetic', does it not? But if we were able to see it as it really is, in its all-devouring actuality, it is probable that we would shiver more in horror than enthusiasm."

"Of course!" I exclaimed. "We know that—but reality, for us, is relative, my friend; we must hold on to that which we can see."

"If the real is, by definition, what we can see," Lenoir said, "then I cannot understand why the hallucinations of a madman should not be reckoned realities."

I felt that I had my back to the wall, but I am one of those who is not driven back with impunity, because I don't like to be cornered.

"This is what I genuinely believe, my dear Lenoir," I said, after a pause. Then I added, hypocritically, to break through all the metaphysics: "the best thing is to kneel down before the Creator without seeking to penetrate the insoluble mystery of things."

"That depends," said Lenoir.

"How does it depend?"

"I could ask for nothing better than to kneel down before my Creator, on condition that it is actually Him before whom I am kneeling and not merely the idea of Him that I have formed. To admire God is exactly what I am asking for, but I am anxious to avoid adoring myself under that name, without knowing it—and it is difficult to recognize myself therein."

"But...your consciousness!" I exclaimed.

"If my consciousness has already deceived me once—as I have perceived with respect to my senses—who can tell me that it does not deceive me again in this matter? When I think of God I project my mind as far in front of me as I can, embellishing Him with all the virtues of my human conscience, laboring in vain to extrapolate them infinitely, but it always remains my mind, not God. I cannot get out of my own being. It's the story of Narcissus. I would like to be certain that it is actually God of whom I think when I pray, that's all!"

"Sophistry!" I whispered, smiling. "The sifting facility of the brain is, I believe, called objectivity. One is not created in isolation!"

"Are you sure?" Lenoir said, in a professorial tone that set my teeth on edge.

"You wouldn't deny, I hope, in the final analysis, that a God created us?"

"Lend me your ears. God? A mystery. Creation? Another mystery. To say that God created us is thus to affirm, simply, that our origin is mysterious: a point on which we are perfectly in accord, since it is precisely this mystery—or, to be more exact, this problem—that it is necessary to clarify, and which is only rendered more obscure by your personification. Now, every problem must have a solution. I can't get away from the thought that its solution might be possible today."

"Possible! God is good!" I exclaimed, putting my hands together. "With our poor limited minds?"

"Limited by what?" Claire asked, softly. "Can you conceive of a definite limit, when everything constitutes a *beyond*?"

A question like that, emerging from the mouth of a woman, would alarm people more prudish than me. I felt myself blush all the way to the whites of my eyes.

"Where do you see these 'limits' in the mind?" said Lenoir. "I am ready to prove that human understanding, by analyzing itself, must discover, in and of itself, the strict necessity of its reason for being: the law that produces the appearance of things and the principle of all reality. I'm only speaking from the viewpoint of this world, mind, setting entirely aside—if there is another—what my senses do not reveal to me."

I confess that the doctor's fatuity made my jaw drop. *Heavens above!* I thought. *Is there no end to this stupidity? He's just showing off, because of his wife.* "But, my friend," I said, aloud, "a simple Christian would ask you why humanity had to wait six thousand years, until you came along, before knowing the Truth...your truth...supposing that you had it."

"I would reply to the Christian: humanity had already waited four thousand years before knowing yours! Truth is not measured in years. As for me, isn't it necessary for me *to be* before I become a Christian? In order to be a Christian I must first be a man. I am, first and foremost, a man; a part of the human species; and when I am elevated by thought as far as the Human Spirit, I am the point at which the idea of Humanity-in-General is expressing itself at that moment. I cease to be a particular self; I speak in the name of the species that represents itself in me. Outside of the general idea, I would only be a madman experiencing the hallucination of the earth and the sky, chattering at random, like all the rest, about some base interest of 'practical' life."

I judged that the moment had come to lead Lenoir back to a better state of mind, and that it was necessary to bring him down to earth.

"Let me tell you what Cabanis said," I muttered. And I quoted him the passage in which the excellent officer of health lists examples of people bitten by rabid animals: wolves, dogs, pigs and cattle. *These individuals,* he states, *hide under the furniture, bark, howl, grunt, moo and imitate in their attitudes the habits and instincts of the animal that has bitten them.*" I added: "You must understand that the most perfect of human geniuses ought never to lose sight of the fact some such disaster might descend upon him, and that, in the face of the mere possibility of that humiliation, it is only with extreme and measured reluctance, and after mature consideration of the general point of view, that one ought to express such personal opinions.

"For me, Kant, Schopenhauer, Fichte and Baron Schelling are merely persons infected with a kind of natural rabies virus, and ought to have been treated in the appropriate manner." To humiliate him further I added: "And Hegel, whom you cited as your master, is no different from the rest of them in that respect. According to theology, when the Devil, in response to Michael's *Quis ut Deus?*, replied *Non serviam!*—a stupidity that was punished by all the celestial Virtues—he instructed us to beware of all precipitate enthusiasm." I smiled lightly. "Oh well, the werewolf Nebuchadnezzar gained little or nothing from the symbolic lesson addressed to his pride, and Hegel seems to me to be the Nebuchadnezzar of Philosophy, that's all!"

191

To complete the distress of the good doctor, I used the facets of my diamond to reflect a spark into his eyes.

While listening to this grandiose speech, Lenoir opened his eyes very wide, and I took great pleasure, secretly, in the difficulty that he would experience in trying to tie my disconnected statements together.

"You're not presuming to imply, I suppose," he murmured eventually, "that any disease limits us, since the species survives the individual. If Cabanis is bitten, Human Intelligence does not relieve his fever: it establishes it, studies and names the phenomenon, discovers the remedy and moves on. What are you trying to say?"

"I'm trying to say," I cried, "that if I place my thumb on a lobe of the brain, if I touch any part of the cerebral cortex, I instantaneously paralyze the will, the discernment, the memory or some other faculty of that which you call the soul. From which I conclude that the soul is nothing but a secretion of the brain, an item of essential phosphorus, and that the ideal is a disease of the organism, nothing more."

Lenoir started laughing, very softly.

"Then the problem reduces itself to knowing what the brain 'secretes' and what the 'phosphorus' is that serves as a Sun for the examining sense, the reflection of the Universe in thought, and why it is necessary that these 'secretions' exist, rather than not existing. It suits me well enough: as long as there *is* a question, the rest doesn't bother me. Arguments between physiologists and metaphysicians are only a matter of different vocabularies: science has its nations and its languages, just like the Earth. But what do you think you are saying when you affirm that you can paralyze the 'faculties' of the soul by touching the lobes of the brain? You are saying that you can paralyze the apparatus, the organs through which the faculties are exercised and externally displayed, not that you touch the faculties themselves, much less that you can annihilate them. It's as if you were to cut a man's legs off, saying: 'I challenge you to walk'—nothing more."

"A nice riposte," I murmured, feigning confusion—as if I had not learned these lamentably hackneyed banalities at my mother's knee. "Well, Lenoir, what conclusions do you draw?"

"I conclude that the Spirit makes the foundations and the functions of the universe. In the acorn of the tree, in the seed of the plant, one cannot say that the tree and the plant are contained *in miniature*: they have to be contained *ideally*. The true and the future plant are virtual in their seed, obscurely imagined therein. Through the medium of Exteriority, which is like the frame on which the eternally-changing Cosmos is embroidered, the Idea even denies itself, in order to prove itself, in the form of Nature, and I can reconstruct the process by employing the Hegelian dialectic.

"The Idea can only find itself in its own negation. Isn't the dynamic embodied by the growth of trees and blades of grass the same as that which makes vibrations surge forth from suns, throwing rings of matter across the sky to form other suns? As the fruits fallen from the tree or the flowers of the grass-stalks produce other flowers and other trees, as the wind carries away the pollen over the fields and through the valleys, so centrifugal force disperses astral pollen through the abysmal depths of space: that is the germination of the world, which Hegel—as you know—regards as a burgeoning plant."

X. A Philosophical Hotchpotch

Satan is a good logician.
Dante.

The servant brought in the tea.

Claire offered me a cup containing a hot infusion of Chinese tea, sugared and perfumed by kirsch. Her spectacles lent a sinister suggestion to her soft smile.

"Lenoir," I said, savoring a mouthful of the digestive liquor, "I ought to warn you that you are in contradiction with theologians and physiologists alike in stating that Idea and Matter are the same thing."

"No."

"What do you mean, no?"

"Don't the theologians propose that God is pure Spirit, and that he has created the world? Matter can therefore emanate from Spirit, just as the theologians say—so the difference is only apparent. As for the physiologists, are they not forced to affirm that the form of the body is more essential than its substance? Do you see?"

The thick armor of my common sense was impervious to Lenoir's sophistry; we were swimming in very different pools.

"Look here, my friend," I said to him, "are you abusing your rights as a host to the point of wanting to insinuate that this piece of wood, for example, isn't material?"

"Where do you see the 'matter' in that piece of wood?" he replied.

I hid my face in my hands: the wreck of that intelligence made me feel ill. He wanted to play the fool with me. With *me!*

"You're pretending that you can't see the matter in this piece of wood!" I said to him, dazedly.

"But, after all, that's elementary!" Lenoir exclaimed, who had finally become exasperated with the seeming ignorance of my words, and who was looking at me sideways. "I see a union of the attributes of form, of color, of polarity, of weight. I call a certain aggregate of these qualities *wood*, but what is it that sustains these qualities, which these attributes cover with their veil: the *substance*, in sum? Between your eyebrows! Nowhere else! You see perfectly well that its 'matter' is inaccessible to the senses, impenetrable and unrevealed, and

193

that its 'substance' is a purely intellectual entity, of which the phenomenal world is only a negative form, a reaction."

"But, my poor friend, what is an 'intellectual entity', or the 'reality of an idea'—a mere idea—compared with the evident reality, the fact, of this simple piece of wood, which you deny?"

"I have only to put that piece of wood on the fire to remove it from existence: your bush would then have disappeared and become something other than itself. What sort of reality is that, which is erasable, which is and is not at the same time, dependent on the dictates of chance? Can we honestly call that 'reality'? Go on! It is Becoming; it is Possibility, but it is not Reality, for what *might be* might just as well not be. Reality has to be something other than contingency, and we are therefore logically compelled to return to the question we posed to begin with: what is reality?"

"For myself," I murmured, pained by the doctor's paradoxical dialectic, "I insist, to the contrary, that whatever is solid and has weight cannot be merely an idea!"

"Recombine the idea of weight, since that dazzles you, with the idea of length, for example, and you will be better able to understand it all."

"In words, that's possible, but material facts do not lend themselves to such fusions and confusions as readily as ideas."

"You're joking, aren't you?" Lenoir said, after a momentary pause. "How can you think that a fact can demolish a logical idea, when the logical idea is the very essence of the fact?"

"Prove it, then! Try, try to apply the theory physically."

"But...it only requires me to slide a weight along the length of a bar of steel to enable the bar to lift a weight a thousand times greater. You must see that length and weight can be recombined with one another, in fact as well as in the realm of ideas."

"Wordplay!" I muttered, angrily. "It's specious. Fine! But in the final analysis, it's just words."

"How else do you want me to reply?" Lenoir said, with a smile. "How else can you question me? You deny the value of the word *word* with the word itself. Do you want talk to me in sign language? The wind blows, instinct howls, ideas express themselves."

"My dear Lenoir," I exclaimed, "let's get back to the question. I can conclude by affirming that as I can neither see nor touch ideas, I still prefer to apply the word *real* to things I can see and touch. And the entire human race would agree with me."

"No," said Lenoir.

"What do you mean, no?" I answered, for the third time, looking at the unfortunate Hegelian sadly.

"If things *are*, if the appearance of the Universe is *produced*, that can only be a matter of absolute necessity. There is a reason for it! Well, if that reason is the Idea, or something other than the Idea, it is preferable that the tangible entity should be in doubt, since all that it possesses of reality necessarily comes to it from that reason-for-being, from that Law-of-Creation—and that reason, that law, can only be grasped and understood by the Spirit. The Idea is, therefore, the highest form of Reality: it is Reality itself, since it participates in the nature of the ultimate laws and is intrinsic to the most elementary entities. From which it follows that if I study the logical consequences of the Idea I shall be studying the constitutive laws of nature, and my reasoning will coincide, if it is rigorous, with the very essence of things, since it will involve, in its contents, the necessity that is fundamental to everything.

"In a word, I am, when I think in this manner, the mirror, the reflection of the laws of the universe—or, as the theologians would put it, I am *made in the image of God!* Understanding is the reflection of creation."

I touched my forehead with a significant finger while looking at Madame Lenoir, who seemed to be listening silently, with profound attention, to the theories spouted by her pitiful spouse. I felt truly sorry for landing her with such a tub-thumper, so I poured myself another cup of tea.

"Ah, your God is not that of the theologians, my poor friend," I told him, with a heavy heart.

"That's beside the point," Lenoir said. "I'm talking Philosophy now, but—believing, as I do, only in the Black Sciences—I only attribute a doubtful, and entirely relative, importance to the principles I'm upholding at present. But since you mention it, let's see what your theologians have to say about God. According to Malebranche, God is the realm of the spirit, just as space is that of the body. According to Saint Augustine, God is the sum of everything, containing all that exists. Tertullian asks who could deny that God is body, just as he is spirit. Saint Thomas says that God is pure Action. The Nicene Creed says that God is the all-powerful Father. If I were to list all the so-called definitions of the Unconditional Being, whose conceptualization is inseparable from His existence, I would never get to the end! But the World-Spirit is not defined in that fashion. These glimmers and images are not so profound; the motto of Jacob Boehme, 'God is the eternal silence', is no more convincing to me—and I am sure that it is the result of an attempt to set aside all ulterior motives, the result of desperately filling out, so to speak, the dark side of the saying that Samuel Clarke never pronounced the name of God without suffering powerful physical symptoms of Terror and Deference.

"Anyway," Lenoir concluded, "I don't know whether the God of whom my spirit is conscious is essentially different, as a concept, from that of the theologians, but I do know one thing—and that is that I'm afraid of that dispenser of Absolute Justice."

I couldn't help laughing at this final sally.

"You have nothing to fear, Lenoir," I told him, "and certainly not that. Let's not exaggerate, or we'll make a mockery of common sense."

"That's true," said the doctor. "Let's bow down before this divine Common Sense, which changes its mind every century, and whose chief attribute is an innate hatred of the very word *soul*. Let's salute the Common Sense of 'enlightened' men, which insults the Spirit as it passes by, following the road that the Spirit has laid out for them and inspired them to run along. Fortunately, the Spirit takes no more heed of the insults of Common Sense than the Shepherd takes of the bleating of the sheep that he calmly steers towards the fold or the slaughterhouse.

Lenoir closed his eyes then, as if lost in a vision. "O Guiding Lights!" he murmured. "What would your glory be, after all, without the Darkness."

He smiled at me, and added: "It is a noxious Darkness which, incapable of enlightenment, extinguishes the Guiding Lights!"

After those words, I confess—yes, after that banal joke—the idea of losing my old friend seemed less frightful.

"All in all," I said, "what use are these fine speculations in the world of everyday experience?"

Lenoir looked at me gravely for a few moments, but made no reply.

XI. The Doctor, Madame Lenoir and Myself Are Seized by a Fit of Jollity

> And my heart was so joyful that I
> no longer recognized it as my own.
> Dante.[47]

Thanks to the evasive slant, the pretence of dullness and the learned frivolity that I had so far incorporated into my questions, Lenoir's replies—since he was upstart enough to value the ingenuity of his intelligence—had only made his incapacity in matters transcendental more obvious. I had evidently drawn him into terrain where, in spite of his best efforts, I would now be able to dig a ditch at my leisure in which to bury his illusions once and for all.

Meanwhile, he was collecting himself, leaning on his elbow with his head in his hand, probably mulling over some new enormity unworthy of submission to my criticism. His meditative silence proved to me, beyond a shadow of a doubt, the vacuity of his soul. If he had had anything to say, he would have come right out with it, like anyone else, without any need for futile reflection—which is the definitive indication of impotence and desertion.

"I won't conceal from you, my friend—I can even say my best friend—that I am already quite convinced of the vanity of your arguments as regards the practical side of your bizarre theories," I said. "I repeat: what possible use are they?"

---

[47] The citation is an epigraph from *La Vita nuova.*

He opened his eyes again and said, after a pause: "For you and your kind, no use at all. For others, disdainful of Death and anxious for Eternity, they serve to fight gloriously for Justice, with the certainty of victory."

At these words I could not suppress a slight gasp of fear, and my features took on such a fearful expression that Lenoir's jaw dropped. I had sensed—with a quasi-divine prescience, in fact—that he was about to count the interminable rosary of his socially subversive ideas. Without that instinctive gesture of reproach, he would undoubtedly have expounded at length on "the independence of the world" and would have given himself nightmares with the sound of his own voice. I saw that my gesture alone had laid waste to his resolutions and that he dared not persist in parading them before me.

Anyhow, what weight can the kinds of thoughts that are called grand, generous and enthusiastic have in the eyes of a serious man, when they only have to be reflected by my brain and dissected by my lips—shorn of all vain flourishes—to acquire an aridity capable of making the specters themselves yearn for the sarcophagus?

Lenoir stopped himself, and I took advantage of his silence.

"Yes," I said, "I understand you. It's a matter of peoples—of *the* people. You hope to make these dreams of liberty, dignity and justice accessible to them? But there's no way to carry out amputations on gangrenous souls; there are irremediable conditions for which one searches in vain for a scientific cure. The people? To be sure, no one cherishes them more than I, but just as my function is to complain, theirs is to suffer. If it were established that Science could make them good, who among us would not devote his soul, his life and his love to them? I'd be the first in line! Unfortunately, the victim, once his bonds are untied, has scarcely any other desire but to shackle the neck of his liberator—for the position of the poor cannot remain vacant in this world. You cannot redeem a single one without substituting yourself for him, and the benefits gladly accrued to him will be paid for in ruination, slander and death. It is a painful realization, my friend, very painful indeed!"

I resumed my paternal tone, and went on: "Progress and Enlightenment can only instill in these formerly unconscious and inoffensive creatures—who excite our pity, at least—the instincts of jealousy, hatred, envy and treason. Believe me, Lenoir, I am competent to judge these matters! I say this: *Woe betide the Benefactors if their actions can only have the result of making their victims disappear!* A curse on future republics, on ideal societies where sensible men would no longer have to shed tender tears, as I do, for the fate of the people! At the mere idea that I might be deprived of that satisfaction, my dear friend, it seems to me that my veins are flooded with bile instead of blood!"

That outburst generated a certain amount of gaiety, Lenoir and his wife having taken their mental alienation far enough to imagine that I was joking.

Charmed by their error, I felt obliged to go one better. Had they known me better I doubt that they would have been so openly contemptuous in that respect.

Indeed, I've noticed something rather bizarre, which sometimes puzzles me: that my pranks are always making me grow pale.

So I filled the room with one of those bursts of laughter whose repetition by nocturnal echoes, as I remember it, used to make dogs howl as I passed by. Since then, it's true, I have had to moderate their usage, because their hilarity even terrified me. I normally utilize their alarming manifestation in times of danger; they are my weapon when I am afraid, although my fear is contagious; they provide infallible protection against thieves and murderers, when I am in isolated spots. My laughter is better than prayers at putting phantoms themselves to flight—for I've never been able to contemplate the starry Heavens, myself, and the Spirits whose protection I invoke dwell in fainter astral bodies.

At any rate, it didn't take me long to perceive that what I had taken for a smile on Madame Lenoir's face was simply a trick of the light: a shadow that the lamp had thrown across her face. I recognized, too, that a certain nervous tic of the doctor's, accompanied by a fit of coughing, which I had taken for a burst of laughter, had caused me to make a similar mistake. He had merely breathed in the smoke of his cigar while listening to me.

And I realized that I had been the only one out of the three of us with sufficient party spirit to produce a fit of jollity.

XII. A Sentimental Debater

And Satan said: "Thoughts, whither have ye led me?"
Milton.[48]

We filled our teacups again and, between two spoonfuls of kirsch, I said: "My friend, what's the good of occupying yourself with all these airy-fairy things when you could live here in perfect tranquility, without ambition or speculative puzzles?" At this point I winked at him. "We'll never know the last word on all that."

I've said that Lenoir had a mania for philosophy, but I honestly never expected him to return to the insipid and idle discussion so enthusiastically and so suddenly.

"That's all very well," he said, "but it seems to me that we're part of 'all that' whether we like it or not. In which case, we're bound to occupy ourselves with it--and everything seems to testify, to the contrary, that we *can* discover 'the last word' on it. After all, note that the dialectic of Nature is the same as that of our brain: its works are its ideas. *The tree grows by syllogisms*, as Hegel said. Things are thoughts clothed with various exteriors, and Nature produces in the same way that we think. As soon as we recover the relations of a phenome-

---

[48] *Paradise Lost* Book IX, line 47.

non by means of logic, we classify it, we only have to call it by the name of Science and from that moment on we are its masters.

"We are able to trust, to some degree, in the value of our Reason—even regarding that which touches the final solution of the riddle of the universe. Why not? As for...God...let's proceed and act as if...Someone...ought to understand us--and as if we don't need to die. What I call 'fighting for justice' will still go on."

In response to these words, Claire murmured from her shadowed corner: "My friend, the definition of such a destiny is insufficient to the idea that we have of ourselves—and when I said just now that 'the Spirit of Man has no limits' I was implying, as you know, "if it is enlightened by the humble and divine Christian revelation."

I confess that I shuddered at those words, almost taking them seriously. *I see what you're getting at*, I thought. *Here comes Original Sin and the Vale of Tears, looming up on the horizon, extending their consequences into politics, religion, monarchy and social economics; present Property based in future Charity; in history the Bollandists, in Science, Joshua; if not, my dear brother, I shall imprison you, torture you, kill you, and cause your supporters to engrave HERE LIES A MARTYR on your tombstone. A system of desserts, for the use of women. Understood!*

I caught the ball on the bounce in order to spend a few moments sending Madame Lenoir a blistering return, Lenoir's rather careful paradoxes having passed me by—a humiliation that my wounded heart would never forgive. So, I performed a moral about-face; I changed tack without warning—which is to say that, without actually letting go of the idea of God, I set out to draw forth the consequences of atheism, in order to arrive at my own particular end: to shuffle the cards so thoroughly that we would all be arguing and shouting without knowing why.

"Allow me," I muttered. "Allow me—I believe there's a tautology here. Down here, Madame, we advance along a road that we cannot avoid. Why does this phenomenon occur? That is the question. Now, in order to explain this, many have started out by relying on Intuition—which is to say, Induction, with or without inspiration. But in order to be on top of a mountain it is necessary to have climbed the steps of which that elevation is the sum, one by one, and there is no spontaneous intuition. If Revelation is brought in to enrich the Problem, arbitrarily, with a new complication"—here I stood up and spread my arms wide—"there is no longer any means of understanding it! We must give up on it! I want to believe that a God has created the world, but if that means admitting that he cares enough about us to 'reveal' his intentions through some intermediary or other, how can anything be conclusively proven? I'm astonished that a mind like yours can still be soothed by such chimeras: they have had their day."

I believed that I had the right, as I sat down again, to savor the effect of my eloquence on my questioners, and my gaze wandered into the shadows, sliding towards Madame Lenoir. She had never left her impenetrable station by the window, and her silence began to disturb me slightly. I felt that her penetrating and inquisitorial eyes were watching me, their evil expression cloaked by her spectacles.

"Well, Claire!" the doctor murmured. "Have you no answer?"

"Oh, monsieur," the lovely Claire replied, smiling, "You know full well that the arguments which have sufficed thus far to confound the arguments of our friend are not absolute—and I don't want to complete his sad defeat."

Slyly, and with ill-concealed incomprehension, I studied the woman who was unafraid to aggravate my wounds to such a monstrous degree, but I could find no reply to her damnable words. I searched for a sally, a wounding epigram, an expedient; I appealed to bad faith; but all my brain's efforts remained fruitless; and when that wounding proof of my impotence had been adequately displayed to me I was overcome by indignation, spite and blind hatred. My heart shook and tolled a knell within my breast: fury, thirst for vengeance, vague ideas of murder—all the vilest sentiments, in sum—rose up dreadfully into my throat, and were abruptly reflected in my face by a complacent and approving half-smile.

Meanwhile, my gestures and my attitude encouraged her to go on.

"The fact is," I murmured, putting a brave face on it, "that Lenoir's statements would make Monsieur de La Palice jealous—if they did not make him blush."[49]

"But you made me sad," Claire continued, in her lovely and mystical voice, "when you declared just now that Science is sufficient for us to clarify the enigma of the world and that walking in its borrowed light is also sufficient for a just man to obtain an acquittal from God."

Lenoir lowered his eyes with a rather peculiar smile. I wanted to come to his aid, as I know how to do.

"You're repeating yourself, my good friend," I muttered. "You're scolding without cutting through the difficulty. What right has 'simple faith' to intervene in philosophy?"

"I know men who cannot be accused of repeating themselves, given that they have never said anything at all," the gentle creature replied to me—and then, turning to Césaire, went on: "When I think of Light, my very humble mind turns to the One who enables all enlightenment to be produced: the Spirit in which every notion and every essence is dissolved; penetrating and penetrated; irreducible, homogeneous unity. And when I think of the concept of God, when

---

[49] Jacques de Chabanens, Seigneur de La Palice (1470-1525) was killed in battle his soldiers made up a song about him containing the lines A quarter of an hour before he died/he was still alive, only intending to indicate the rapid effect of his wound, but the ill-chosen phrase was taken as a cardinal example of stating the obvious, and *une verité à la Palice* acquired that meaning in common parlance..

my mind reflects that concept, I genuinely penetrate the essence of it, in my thought; I participate, in effect, in the very nature of God, according to the degree to which he reveals his concept in me. God is the incarnation and ideal of all thought. And my Spirit, to the extent that I surrender my thoughts to God, is penetrated by God: an augmentation proportional to the living concept of God. The two terms, in the free expression of my desire to be good, are combined in that unity which is myself—and they are combined without ceasing to be distinct. Now, the Christian Revelation being the consequence and the application of this fundamental principle, I have not treated it as a 'chimera that has had its day' since it has the same nature as its principle—which is to say that it is eternal, unconditional and immutable."

"My dear Madame Lenoir," I replied, "I believe that you have made yourself too great an idea of God. If he is not only infinite but necessary, inconceivable and astounding, why is he always getting involved in conversations? Do you recall that Kant had an old servant named Lamb, who begged his master to reconstruct the proof of the existence of one God, which the great philosopher had utterly destroyed? We too have within us, every one of us, some old servant or other who asks for a God. Let us be more judicious than Kant: let us distrust our initial impulse; let us reply with a smile, albeit a melancholy one, and let us accept only such gifts as we may store to our benefit. The heritage of our first parents, to speak frankly, seems to me to warrant another expression entirely."

That was a drop of cold water.

Madame Lenoir, however, answered me placidly: "Why should we not ask Infinity even for a God? Must it not realize every thought—for what kind of Infinity could be so limited as to be impotent to realize a human thought? And as God, I assure you, is the most sublime thought we can conceive in our minds, it is an infinite insanity for us to set out to destroy it—and an impossibility as well."

I remained silent, unwilling to let them see what effect this had on me.

"That may be so!" Césaire replied. "But, my dear, no one nowadays can challenge the evidence of the evolution of man or refuse to take account of its seriousness. After all, Progress doesn't exclude Revelation: the initial punishment remains the same, although its intensity has diminished, thanks to the sweat of our brows, that's all. Revelation doesn't constrain us—myself, I see it everywhere!—you are quite free and very wise to confine yourself to it, but, in the realm of metaphysics, I am obliged to count only on Progress, achieved by man by means of Science."

"Ah!" she cried. How can it be sufficient for you, and your Humankind, to evolve only through that series of relative expressions whose sum constitutes your Science? In that case, instead of being perfect animals, we are only improving animals, forever trapped by an indefinite law of proportional progress. Even if the thing were absolutely true, there would be no point in being proud of it, for in a thousand years, according to this theory, we would still be digging like moles; what would the splendor, the grandeur and the depth of the hole matter, if we knew that it would be our destined tomb…if we are consecrated to Death, to which we march ever more rapidly? The very heavens, according to the affirmations of positive science, will sooner or later be consumed by fire or death. We can scarcely examine a past of six thousand years, and our appearance therein is hardly more than a matter of hours—and we dare to found our supreme hopes on a grain of sand, when we are bound, without remission, to return to dust, to darkness, to the Void."

"But the catastrophe of which you speak will not happen within a lapse of time so vast that it is almost absurd to think about it!" I exclaimed. "Let us first win our independence from Nature, and later, we shall see. Besides which: *Après nous, le Deluge!* Let's take what petty pleasure we can…that's my faith."

"But we shall always be dependent," she replied, "if only because we are forced to think. It's *necessary* to believe in Thought—even to deny it would be a thought. And that is why there is no single action, no single idea, nor any process of reasoning, that is not based in Faith. We believe in our senses, in our doubt, in our progress, in our annihilation, although all of it is doubtful, strictly speaking, since nothing can prove itself. The most profound skepticism of all begins with an act of Faith. Now, since it's necessary that we choose, we should make the best choice we can! And since Belief is the sole basis of all realities, we should prefer God! Science having explained to me, after its fashion, the laws of some phenomena, I want to go on, personally, to see in that phenomenon only what magnifies my soul, and not what might diminish it. If the mystics are deluded, what use is a Universe inferior even to their idea? In Death, can the logic of two abstractions restore to me my lost Divine Infinity? No!

"No—so I shall shut my eyes to the world in which my spirit seems to be a foreigner. It does not matter to me whether the laws of stellar mechanics are discovered, since they can only apprise me of certain destruction! That these stars might be extinguished is temptation! The 'scientific' future is an illusion! The history of modern times is the history of a humankind entering its winter season. The cycle will complete its revolution soon enough. As the sages of olden days have set me the sacred example, I shall not hesitate, as a Christian and a sinner, between your 'century of light' and the light of the centuries."

XIII. The Singular Remarks of Doctor Lenoir

> Ecclesiastes has said: "A living dog is worth more
> Than a dead lion." Save for eating and drinking, to be sure,
> All is naught but shadow and smoke, and the world is very old,
> And the annihilation of life fills the black tomb.
> Leconte de Lisle.[50]

---

[50] From "L'Ecclésiaste" in *Poèmes barbares*.

The furious spite that took hold of me during the course of this diatribe was so stifling that I had to adjust the knot of my cravat. Not knowing how to express my contempt for such doctrines in a sufficiently copious fashion, I contented myself with pronouncing the single word "Brava!" in a reedy voice eight times in succession, feigning enthusiasm.

One thing pleased me: the doctor had silently wilted under the withering glare.

I rubbed my hands. Their opinions differed, that much was certain. The particular point of dispute was of no importance; their convictions seemed equally absurd to me. The essential thing was to excite them against one another, in order that I might pose as a judge and have the final word. In the meantime, I left them to their quibbling while I devoted myself to my own thoughts with an air of profound concentration.

I nursed the fond hope that, if I were careful, this model household would soon come more or less to hand, and that they would hold their horses regarding "the immortality of the soul". I got ready to close in like a vulture on some choice carrion.

In this situation, I decided to take Lenoir's side—whatever it proved to be!—because his wife's theories had a unique propensity for irritating my brain until I almost lost all sense of myself. Also, the ever-tactful Reader will doubtless be expecting—as I was—some collision of the tiresome kind that spouses always have. Imagine my surprise, therefore—I might almost say disappointment—when I heard Lenoir murmur these strange words:

"Claire's intelligence is a profound and limpid mirror, where nothing is reflected but sublime verities, and I am proud to love her admirable being—forever."

On hearing these words I looked at Claire; it seemed to me that she had turned pale.

Césaire had risen to his feet. He took a step towards his wife and suddenly bowed down to kiss her hand, silently and for a long time, with a passion whose pent-up savagery and concentrated fervor astonished me in a man of forty-six.

Then he came back to sit on my right.

A few seconds went by during which I could hear nothing but the indistinct swell of the sea. I tried to use them profitably by gathering my scattered thoughts.

"Yes, the Ideal!" Lenoir said, abruptly turning traitor to the principles whose banal champion he had so far been. "Yes, invincible Hope. Faith. What could be more positive, after all? Wasn't it Swedenborg who said: *Belief is as far above thought as thought is above instinct?* Believe, then; it's enough. And when I insist on proclaiming the autocracy of some commonplace philosophy, of which there are as many as there are individuals—when I wag my tail in defense of the quibbles of Science, so proud in its troubling appearances and so vain in its real results—I agree, yes, I agree that I am always seized by an irresistible desire to laugh."

He turned towards me and went on: "If you only knew how surprising and terrible the living force of the Idea is in the realm of Faith! The power of an imagination, a dream, a vision, sometimes overcomes the laws of nature. Fear, for example. The mere idea of superstitious Fear, without any external motivation, can strike a man down like an electric shock. The things seen by a visionary are, in the final analysis, as solidly material to him as, say, the Sun itself—the mysterious lamp of this whole phantasmagoria of creation, disappearance and transformation! Have you ever thought about those monstrous humans with tiger-striped fur or grotesquely swollen heads, about conjoined twins and all the other horrible mistakes of nature produced by some sensation, some caprice, some sight experienced by a mother during pregnancy? Have you considered the infantile explanations offered on that subject by Physiology?

"If I were to open any medical journal, I would find facts like these, suggestive of the almost tangible reality of the Idea. I can quote the exact text: 'A woman whose husband had been stabbed to death gave birth, five months later, to a daughter who, at seven years of age, fell victim to fits of hallucination, in which the child cried: *Save me! Men with knives are coming to kill me!* That little girl died during one of these fits, and blue-black marks were found on her body like those of congealed blood, whose placement close to the heart corresponded, in spite of the sexual differences, to the wounds her father had received seven years before, while she was still unborn.'

"Call that what you like: I want to know exactly how the shadow, the idea, differs decisively from that which you call *tangible reality* if the mere reflection of an alien sensation has the power to infiltrate and instill itself, fatally, in the essence of our bodily being. A shadow—which is nothing but a shadow—can kill us in spite of being no more than a shadow. Let's think about that!

"Now open the works of the Physiologists. Béclard defines life as the organism in action and death as the organism at rest. Bichat's starting-point is this: Life is the sum of the functions that resist death. Consult the finest treatises produced since Harvey; reread Broussais' research on blood, and you will see that a physiologist as great as he was able to exclaim: *Without phosphorus, thought is impossible!* The majority, especially the most recent—who are the most rational—admit neither the idea of Life, nor the idea of Death, nor even that of the Organism. Now, returning from the divergent and contentious principles of Physiology, simply consider the fact—one of a thousand I could cite—of the phenomena produced by the deliria of the dying. It is then that visions begin to be a little more real...how shall I put it?...to be the only things meriting the title of reality. Death is impersonal; it is the reality of that which is now only vision. So far as I am concerned, it is certain that our actions then achieve a second incorporation, and that the Past is reaffirmed in Death as in the flesh.

"The Past is a shadow, and we sense instinctively that Death is the realm of shadows. Death and Life are nothing but the rigorous consequences of the eternal dialectic; by virtue of the fact that they are necessities, constituting the twin facets of Existence, their essence—like all the rest—is to be found in the Spirit. 'Thought being a given, Death is a given too,' as the Titan of the Human Spirit says, and it is that alone which can prove Immortality. 'Suppress Thought and the substances that remain might still be eternal, but cannot be immortal, for Death does not begin until Thought is extinguished and disappears. Death, created—like Life—by the Spirit, uplifts the Spirit.'

"And what we call Death is, in fact, no more than the median term—or, if you prefer, the necessary negation—posited by the Idea in order to develop through Thought into Spirit.

"I might even go so far as to say that we can catch—even now, on this side of Becoming—a few frightening glimpses of what awaits us, which our own pasts have put in store for us. Recall the thousands of individuals who, having been drowned or hanged, have been saved at the very last moment of their suffocation and brought back to life. All of them have affirmed that they had seen, on the point of death, all their previous actions and thoughts, including those long forgotten, pass before them, in a manner inexpressible in the language of living men. The real question is not whether or not 'the soul is immortal', since no item of evidence is worth more than any other as proof of it. The thing we need to know is what kind of immortality we might have, and whether we can exert any influence upon it from our present situation."

Utterly bewildered by this incoherent and preposterous flood of words, I said: "Then you believe"—I felt myself blushing as I pronounced the sentence— "you really do believe that the soul is somehow material?"

"I believe, at least," Lenoir replied, "setting aside all vain dialectical sophistry, that, for example, the force of Suggestion that a vengeful dead man might exert, *from the utmost depths of Darkness*, on a living being familiar to him—to whom, in consequence, he is attached by thousands of invisible mysterious threads—yes, I tell you, I believe that the force of Suggestion exerted on that person could become, over an indeterminate period of time, oppressive, irresistible, murderous and, in sum, *material*. For there are individuals so hardy that Death itself cannot entirely abolish their sentiments and passions."

I saw that it was necessary to put an end to these pranks, whose horror was beginning to make an impression on me.

"My friend," I said to him, "allow me to quote Voltaire, a man of intelligence, like yourself. 'When that which is said is no longer comprehensible, and when that which is heard is no longer conversational, this is what we call metaphysics.'"

Lenoir looked at me silently.

"That's true," said Claire, coming towards us. "But the same person also said, somewhere, in the tale of the Phoenix:[51] 'Resurrection is an entirely natural idea; it is no more astonishing to be born twice than once.'"

"Oh, resurrection" I said. "Voltaire was making a joke, you see. A clear thinker, he let nothing escape his mockery."

"Good!" said Claire, smiling. "If you call into question the persistence of the personality after death, I shall be able to show you that your argument is a futile waste of time. First of all, I should like to know whether it cannot be called into question even in life. When is the self really itself? At what time of life? Is your self of this evening the same as it will be tomorrow? Or at the age of fifty? No. We are the playthings of perpetual illusion, I tell you. And the Universe really and truly is a dream...a dream!...a dream!"

"A bad dream, even!" Lenoir added, thoughtfully. "Because—I can only repeat it dazedly—nothing that I have learned from philosophy has modified the disturbing and savage element of my nature, and I am afraid of becoming, once and for all, in some other visionary system, that which I am.

"Oh, if only I had Claire's trampoline of Faith to bounce me out of these dismal thoughts whose haggard prisoner I am! But there it is: I am too bound up in a world in which—I don't know exactly how to put it—two and two might be able to make something other than four. And yet..."

XIV. The Sidereal Body

> "Words! Words! Words!"
> Shakespeare, *Hamlet*.[52]

Lenoir pronounced these words in a tone which froze the smile on my lips. I was struck by the sudden impression that while we were talking Night had approached in person, and had taken the opportunity to mingle her own arguments with ours. The fact is that the mundane night outside, where cold winds whipped the waves into breakers, was now extending its starless void beneath thick clouds. The exchange of impressions was so swift that I thought I was experiencing a hallucination. It seemed to me that we were becoming very pale; the curtains stirred; we were under the influence of Midnight.

I felt my hereditary disorder awaken in the depths of my nature then. Unable to endure the sight of that desolate space, I leapt to my feet and shut the win-

---

[51] The "tale of the Phoenix" is presumably Voltaire's *conte philosophique* "La Princesse de Babylone" (1768).

[52] This quotation was added to the version of the story published in 1887 in the collection *Tribulat Bonhomet*, replacing a quotation from Friedrich Schiller used in earlier versions of the story.

dow, trembling with the sick apprehension which is, for me, the harbinger of hellish anguish.

Oh, that malady! How does it come about? Isn't it frightful?

Nevertheless, I concealed my sensations as best I could, and tried to seem indifferent as I replied to Lenoir.

"Are you daring to imply that you have another person within you, in addition to yourself, doctor? Damn it! That would be disconcerting, I confess— particularly for your peace of mind."

"But can you yourself, Bonhomet," Lenoir replied, after a pause, fixing his sparkling eyes upon me, "can you assure me that the external appearance that you present to us, manifest to our senses, is really the being that you know yourself to be?"

That unexpected question pricked my conscience. I looked at the doctor without making any response.

"And," he continued, "is not this exterior being—the only one accessible and perceptible—always accompanied within you by its spectator, its contradictor, its judge?"

"Yes," I said. "That's a theory the ancients held: *Homo duplex.* What are you trying to prove?"

That this interior companion—this occult being—is the only real one, and that it is what constitutes the personality. The apparent body is no more than a reaction to the other; it's a veil which thickens or lightens according to the translucency with which it is regarded, and the occult being only allows itself to be detected and recognized by the expression of features of its mortal mask. The organism, in the final analysis, is nothing but a pretext of the luminous body that suffuses it. One never thinks of one's body when one is alone—except, perhaps, to maintain its life. Think about this: if two people are bound together by some sentiment, they gradually forget the details of their appearance; they no longer see one another; they relate to one another in a more profound way, and it is the moral being that they perceive in one another; they know what really lies beneath the palpable simulacrum."

"That is specious," I murmured, feeling obliged to say something.

"And this is what provides the key to a wealth of mysterious contradictions," the doctor added. "The apparent body is so scarcely real that, very often, *it is not a man which inhabits the human form.*"

"Oh!" I exclaimed, with a nervous twitch—as if a crocodile had shivered inside me.

"What? Haven't you ever seen a human face taken over by some type of animal—or several animals at the same time? Well, carefully observe the habitual movements, the instincts, the tendencies of an individual who is predominantly bear-like, for instance, or tigrine, and you will come to see that there is something in him like a wild beast strayed into an alien envelope. How many men and women do you think there are, on Earth, who conform to their own concept of themselves? A man is merely a divine animal, differentiated from the others by the Ideal—and the man in whom the preoccupation with eternal things is not ceaselessly alert in the depths of his consciousness is still part-animal, not wholly emerged from the shadows; he isn't human, in reality, and the expression on his face betrays him continually, in spite of his apparent form. Similarly, the woman who conforms to her concept of herself is the one who, reflecting sublime hopes like a profound and clear mirror, elevates love and hope beyond Death. Do you think that such beings are numerous in our species? We must accept that towns are much like forests, and that it's not difficult to find ferocious beasts in them."

"You believe that the majority of living men..." I put in.

"Are still moved like puppets by the strings of base instinct," the doctor said, with a laugh that displayed two rows of teeth worthy of the jaws of a Carib indian. "They are invisible beasts, transfigured by their disguises, if you like, but they are actual beasts."

He went on: "And their facial features, through which the luminous essence of their true organism shines, offers superabundant proof of their innate hatred of Thought; of their deep-seated, insatiable, organic thirst to bring down, profane and annihilate every noble and pure inclination; and of their grotesque contempt for all sublime art, all disinterested charity, and everything else that is not as base and impure as their own preoccupations, actions and works! Whence comes their habit of demonstrating the justice of their opinions with violence and blood, and the impossibility of their ever understanding true Humanity, born of the Highest! Yes, I tell you—and you had better believe it—that the apparent body is not the real one; its constituent atoms change with every passing moment and it renews itself entirely in a cycle of six or seven months; properly speaking, it does not exist. It is only a process of becoming within the greater Becoming. It is its form, its idea, its impalpable unity that actually exists, and on which appearance is merely superimposed. And one of the physical proofs of this is that faces become bestial or light up at the approach of Death, in a striking manner, according to what the eyes can see there!"

"But you're just trying to talk about the soul, my friend," I put in. "which would, I suppose, require us to speak of *Homo triplex*!"

Lenoir's only response was a slight shrug of the shoulders.

"And me!" he suddenly exclaimed. "My self. Do you ever think about that? I sense predatory instincts within me! I experience black moods and furious passions, the hatred of a Savage, a wild insatiate thirst for blood. It's as if I were haunted by a cannibal! Yes, it's insane, but that's the way it is—and I know plenty of learned alienists who would be able to confess such things themselves if they weren't constrained to tranquility, dissimulation and silence by the need to earn their daily crust. And whenever I quit the realm of the Spirit I can clearly distinguish that infernal nature within me! It's the truth! And all the metaphysical speculations appear to me then like so many threads of sparkling nonsense, incapable not only of redeeming me from that horrible—almost diaboli-cal—intellectual form, but of giving me a single instant of reliable hope! That's why I dread this cloakroom that we call Death. That's why I can find no peace, I tell you! No, I know that I'll be this way forever!"

The clock struck one. I rose to my feet; I had recovered somewhat from my attack of nerves. Lenoir had gone way over the top this time—having over-stepped the mark, so to speak, by force of exaggeration. His superficial whim-sies were definitely becoming more and more inept.

"We'll talk about this another time," I said, smiling.

"Yes," he said, preoccupied and still rather somber. He took a portable edi-tion of the Bible from his pocket as he terminated his peroration by crying: "We should both pay attention to this book!" And he tapped the cover as if it were a snuff-box. He opened it, mechanically, as if at random. His eyes fell upon the passage in the Ten Commandments dealing with adultery and its punishment. Once he had read it out he blew his nose, with a noise that I found rather alarm-ing. There was a silence, during which he examined me as if to see what effect the quotation had had on me.

The only thing I had noticed was that as he pronounced the word "adul-tery" Madame Lenoir had shivered silently from top to toe in her armchair. But that was doubtless only a nervous tic awakened by the memory of some old love affair, inspired by the chill of the evening and the sea. The green thickets of Paphos always have their mysteries, and the malign petty god knows well enough what he is about--at least, that's my opinion.

As for the lieutenant, Sir Henry Clifton, the idea never even crossed my mind!

Lenoir closed the Bible abruptly, and added a low voice, as if to himself: "How to forgive adultery, indeed? O rage! I confess that the very idea makes me mad... Yes, I sense that I shall slake my lust for vengeance, even in the domain of Death—and that the loss of Paradise shall not stop me—if..."

And he turned his gaze towards his wife, as if to break himself upon her colored lenses and her leaden face.

Claire got up, and picked up a lighted candle.

"You're being inconsiderate," she said. "Our friend needs to rest." And she handed me the candlestick, smiling.

A minute later, I was in bed, falling asleep while laughing at that fantastic couple until the tears ran down my face.

XV. My Friend Gets a Chance to Offer a Conclusive Verification of his Mortifying Theories

> Death is a woman faithfully wedded to the human race:
> where is the man she has deceived?
> Honoré de Balzac.[53]

I shall pass swiftly over the charming and retiring existence that the three of us led for the next twelve days—after which my poor friend lay lifeless in his room with a shroud over his face, with a candle to either side of him.

Alas, he had been suddenly carried off by an overwhelming attack of apoplexy, caused by his immoderate over-indulgence in snuff. I had warned him many times about the dangers of that terrible herb, and the risks he ran, so to speak, in playing with it, but my pleas had fallen on deaf ears. Disdainful of the remonstrations of his loving wife, who threw herself at his feet more than once, begging him, in the name of the most sacred sentiments, to renounce his unclean passion, he did not even reduce the doses of the powder that he introduced into his nostrils, which agglomerated there until his sinuses were clogged with nicotine. The poison did not take long to spread from there to his entire body, bringing him to the point of delirium, and sometimes—let us whisper it—to furious madness.

As soon as I had arrived, having noticed his mania, I had resolved to save him and to cure him. In order to divert and diversify the demon of his habit I had tried filling his snuff-box with various substitutes: silver nitrate, mercuric chloroborate,[54] charcoal, calcium phosphate, the scrapings of old shoes, caustic soda, gunpowder and a thousand other inoffensive substances. In brief, I had looked after him as solicitously as his own mother. My efforts were useless: he took it all, his nose indifferent and its cartilages blinded. Nevertheless, I was determined not to be beaten. Deciding that I would cure him by applying homeopathic theory—the only one taken seriously by those whose good sense has not been obliterated—I shut myself up in my chemical laboratory.

I slipped into his snuff-box the most powerful sternutatory and revulsive compounds that human ingenuity could invent. It was necessary that he should be forced into submission or cured. I had decided to use explosives to bring his illness to an end. There is, I am content to hope, no ingredient known to any

---

[53] The slightly-misrendered quotation is from *"L'Elixir de longue vie"* (1830). Balzac actually likened death to a courtesan, but one who never deceives.

[54] Chloroboric acid and its compounds can be found in early nineteenth-century medical textbooks, recorded as a recent discovery, but has been undiscovered. Mercuric chloride, also known as "corrosive sublimate" was often used in the treatment of syphilis.

branch of medical knowledge with which I did not cleverly stuff his cavities. Putting my own life at risk, I heated crucibles were I pulverized concoctions of the deadliest plants, so useful in medicine when their doses are properly calculated. It seemed to me that the hand of God was at work in all that. I had temporarily neglected my dear infusoria; amity alone was my guide—and often, at night, when I awoke with a start from some nightmare, I perceived that my window-panes were aglow with the reflections of the laboratory where my alembics, retorts and test-tubes were boiling night and day. I took heartfelt delight in the thought that all that was accomplished there, under the protection of the good genius of true Science, would be deposited the following day in the olfactory apparatus of my unfortunate friend.

At the very moment when my treatment and care seemed about to be crowned by an unexpected recompense—I seem to recall that he had begun to look at his snuff-box, occasionally, with an indefinable expression—one Saturday evening about ten days after my arrival in the house, after a most enjoyable dinner, he suddenly turned pale during dessert. His eyes closed, his lips moved—and he was dead!

I had the presence of mind, during the general panic of Claire and the servants, to put my ear close to his mouth to hear what he was trying to whisper, and I distinctly made out the same bizarre phrase that I quoted above.

"How to forgive adultery, indeed?" he murmured. "I sense at this moment—at this very moment—that I shall undoubtedly incorporate the sentiment that I have always had within me...yes, I sense that, from the depths of external darkness, I shall slake my lust for vengeance—if..."

Those were his last words. You can imagine the grief and consternation into which we were plunged. How can one find words to express it? I give up. In any case, it would hardly be fitting to allow the public to intrude upon private pain.

XVI. What Might Be Called a Chaude Alarme[55]

> The cry of the outcast is but the translation of this thought:
> "Had I only known then what I know now!"
> Commentary on Theology

Ho ho! I too know how to be "poetic" when circumstances require it, when an event can be framed by a single word. Lyricism is not entirely useless; there are occasions to which it is suited, when it is forgivable. I could evoke it, when required, like almost everyone else in the world, if I deigned to lower myself to commit my ideas to print.

---

[55] A literal translation of this phrase with be "hot alarm," but it is a pun on the conventional phrase *chaude larmes* [hot tears], meaning to we copiously.

Yes, even I would have passed for a "poet", had I lived in an era when a feather in the cap could procure a fortune.[56] Honestly, I know a good number of pen-pushers who, if the trade brought in neither money nor women, would immediately cease to exploit the imbecility of others with their monkey-tricks and would get back to being just as normal as me—and who would, moreover, have better things to do, if it ever came to that.

Now, the Lenoir incident was, admittedly, of a kind to inspire me if not to epic prose, at least to "poetic" ideas and phrases.

The room where the dead man lay was situated on the third floor and had a high ceiling. A few drops of holy water, shining like funereal diamonds in the candlelight, lay on his waxy frozen face. Madame Lenoir was kneeling beside the bed, her head on the coverlet. I was kneeling there too, but further away, resting on my heels with my hands joined and my head lowered, staring at a red dot on the carpet in a dark corner at the back of the room, behind a chest of drawers. We were alone. The priest and the doctor had gone away an hour before, talking to one another in hushed voices, shutting the door behind them.

A large ivory crucifix hung between the curtains seemed to be pacifying the darkness.

Angrily, I berated the pitiless nature that had deprived me of my friend. I might almost have doubted Science, if I had not exempted it from my despair.

Suddenly, I don't know exactly what happened, but—to tell the exact truth—I felt something whose analysis, or even distinct enunciation, seemed to me to be beyond the terminology at the disposal of human vocabulary. It was, to put it simply, a thrill of cold in the eyes, the heart and the temples.

At that very moment, as I was asking myself what had happened to me, the young widow rose abruptly to her feet, her hair standing on end, candle-flames reflected in the lenses of her spectacles, her arms raised. She let out into the profound silence a terrifying cry, so deeply impregnated and saturated with mad horror that I felt myself flooded from top to toe with fear—fear unalloyed with any other sensation.

That fear inundated me, so to speak, quite unexpectedly. It paralyzed the play of my faculties for an appreciable interval. All I could do was blink my eyes.

Eventually, I managed to steal a glance at Madame Lenoir. Her attitude was not calculated to reassure a poor old man! It was devastating.

The result of this contemplation was a momentary shudder, and the instantaneous disappearance of my moral sense. And I began, without otherwise moving, still on my knees in that obscure corner, to emit long, slow and loud howls, progressing along a musical scale, whose volume increased proportionately as it descended towards the lowest notes in my baritone register.

---

[56] Another pun, *plume* meaning both "feather" and "pen."

At the third howl, I felt my fright shading into delirium, and I relieved my soul with a little laugh, scarcely distinguishable—which had the immediate effect of increasing the terror of the young woman to the point that she ran towards the door, seized it in panic, and ran down the stairs.

I followed her immediately, taking the stairs four at a time—without, as they say, wasting any time in idle commentary.

We only took two seconds to cross the landings and the flights of stairs to the garden door. In our simultaneous haste to get that execrable door open we neutralized one another's efforts. In my distress, I let out a stifled grunt, the sound of which caused me to fall into a faint in the poor woman's arms; her knees bumped into one another and we fell half-dead upon the floor.

Then there were shouts and lights and hurrying footsteps. The frightened servants came running; Madame Lenoir replied quietly to a question from an old valet. We were carried to our own rooms.

An hour later, feeling that I had regained possession of myself, I jumped out of bed, threw everything that I had into my suitcase, pell mell, and set myself to flee by way of the garden--silently escorted, s far as the door, by the basset-hound. I ran, breathlessly, to the coach-stop and jumped into the first one that came along. As the wheels began to turn and the coachmen cracked their whips to get the rig moving I experienced an immense pleasure. I felt that I was getting away from the Lenoir house--in which I promised myself, secretly, never to set foot again so long as I might live.

Oh yes, I resumed the course of my great discoveries; I saw new lands; I can even say that I made giant strides in the cause of Science! But the important thing is to complete this story. That which I have to tell is a thing so terrible that I have been deliberately prolix. I did not dare! I was putting off the fatal moment! But...tonight I have drunk excellent wines which have excited my brain, and I shall reveal all.

XVII. The Ottysor

There are more things in Heaven and Earth, Horatio
Than are dreamt of in your philosophy
Shakespeare, *Hamlet*.

A year later, I found myself in the South of France. I had been exploring in the Alps; I stopped at Digne. In accordance with my solitary habit, I took a room in a small hotel. I spent my days in the country, carrying my scientific instruments with me.

One night, fatigued by my research, I came back very late. I asked the bell-boy to send a fillet of fish, some pears and two liters of coffee to my room, to see me through the night. The waiter put on a show of regret. "Does monsieur not know that it is a public holiday? Except for one old lady ill in bed there's not so much as a cat in the house—no one at all in the kitchen! Everyone's gone off to see the fireworks. Monsieur will find some restaurants open if he cares to go along the road to the town centre—and there is a letter for you."

I took the voluminous letter from him silently, and read it by the light of the candle he was holding close to my face.

The letter was from England. One of my correspondents in London, a rather eccentric man—as all Englishmen tend to be—told me that he had won a lawsuit relating to his house, as he had hoped, that he was quite pleased. and that I should rejoice with him. A postscript added that "by the way," a young Englishman of my acquaintance, a naval officer, had perished in a most tragic fashion in the course of an exploratory mission to the remote regions of the Pacific. The steamship to which he was assigned was at 14 degrees south latitude and 134 degrees longitude, sailing south from the Marquesas to the sinister archipelago of Tuamotu. A boat was manned, under the command of the said officer to investigate places to land on one of a host of small volcanic islands: a black lava block rising to a prodigious altitude, balancing the storminess of the great equinoctial ocean with the vast green intensity of its forests.

"These latitudes are, in a manner of speaking, the most remote in the world," my correspondent wrote. "From the viewpoint of civilized nations, no potential commerce justifies the risk of sending ships through the innumerable reefs which bristle about the shores of these islets, lost in the flux of immeasurable waves, which thus remain totally unknown. This archipelago contains more than seven hundred of them, of which only a few are coraline.

"The frightful storms, the basaltic quicksands whose particles are like anthracite dust and the sudden falls of stagnant mist make these regions mortally hazardous to navigators, who have named these waters the Dangerous Sea. So many ships flying all kinds of colors have been lost there, that there has been a tacit decision not to stray into it. However, a band of Polynesian pirates, the Ottysors,[57] scavengers of shipwrecks, take refuge there on stormy nights, some squatting in caves while others wander across the rocks, awaiting their prey.

"Now, when it happened, the little detachment of explorers were making their way, as dusk fell, along the perilous sands at the foot of the island's cliffs. As they reached the water's edge, the young officer, who was perhaps fifty paces ahead of his escort, was attacked without warning as he rounded a rock. A huge black native—doubtless one of the piratical Ottysors—had already severed his head and was brandishing it horribly at arm's length before any defensive movement could be made or any gun fired. He had not even had time to cry out. As the squad rushed forward murderously, the native was seen to venture, with slow steps, into the deadly sands. A continuous salvo of shots was sent after him, lighting up the dusk, while the fantastic indigene, consecrating himself to death, was sucked down little by little into the fatal sands, before the eyes of his

---

[57] Villiers invented this term.

214

hesitant pursuers. He disappeared, choking to death, while his uplifted right fist still clutched the bloody head by the hair, as if displaying it triumphantly to the stars. Our unfortunate friend was none other than Sir Henry Clifton, who was serving on the vessel as a lieutenant, and with whom I believe you once travelled from Jersey to Saint-Malo."

I abstained, for the moment, from any reflection on Sir Henry Clifton as I digested this annoying news. I had heard talk of these extremely rare Ottysors, as black as jet, who lie in wait for shipwrecks. Norwegian and Dutch mariners also called these negroes the Demons of the Quicksands. These ferocious cannibals are shrouded in as-yet-unsolved mystery. Sometimes, on the reefs, they can be heard howling their somber war-cries by night. They are veritable ghosts. Not one of them has ever been captured, and in spite of the many volleys discharged at them, no one has ever seen them fall or flee. "No one knows what they do with their dead, if they do die," the Danish geographer Bjorn Zachnussën said, rather enigmatically.[58]

I resolved to banish this adventure from my memory, because it appeared to me to be of the kind that might trouble my sleep.

"Didn't you say something about an old woman ill in bed?" I said to the bellboy as I put the letter in my pocket. "Has she had supper?"

The bellboy, who was watching my face to see what effect the letter had, took some time to reply. "No," he said, eventually. "Her supper's there."

"Good," I said. "As she's ill, I'll have her supper. It'll serve her right."

And I laughed at this quip as I went up the echoing stairway.

I had got no more than two-thirds of the way through the habitual and regular duration of my laughter when the sound of my name, pronounced in an agonized voice, reached me from the nearest door on the landing that I was crossing.

I stopped short, feeling ill at ease.

"Who's that?" I said to the bellboy.

"What?" he said. "it's the old woman. I suppose she must know you."

"What's this woman's name?"

"Madame Lenoir."

"Madame Lenoir!" I whispered, after a pause. "What! The charming and incomparable Madame Lenoir, the widow of my poor friend?"

Then I asked myself: "But how does she come to be here?"

The bellboy put his tongue against his teeth and made a rude noise to display his indifference. "I don't know," he said, pretentiously.

---

[58] The invented name of Bjorn Zachnussën is suspicious similar to that of Arne Saknussem, the explorer whose manuscript guides the heroes of Jules Verne's *Voyage au centre de la terre* (1864), roughly contemporary with the first draft of *Claire Lenoir*, chapters of which Villiers read aloud in salons hosed by Leconte de Lisle and Nina Villard.

I greeted this neatly-turned phrase with one of my most gracious smiles, accompanied by an involuntary but vigorous kick up the young Mercury's backside. The candlestick fell to the floor. The bellboy, seized by an alarm for which I still search in vain for an explanation, took it upon himself to refamiliarize himself with the staircase in the manner of Hippomenes and Atalanta. I picked the candlestick up, and discreetly rapped the knuckle of my Saturnian finger three times upon the disquieting door while I held it in my other hand, together with my portmanteau.

"Come in," said a vaguely familiar voice.

I lifted the latch. A powerful odor of paint was the first sensation that assailed me, painfully. The walls, recently redecorated, were silvery white, absolutely uniform and glossy. They instantly put me in mind of those reflective metal plates which serve to augment the daylight in the studios of the worthy emulators of Daguerre.

In the bed, covered by white sheets and propped up on the pillow, was a woman. Her face was yellow and drawn, like parchment. She was dressed in mourning. An enormous pair of blue-tinted spectacles hid her eyes. Two or three flasks with pharmacist's labels stood on the mantelpiece, reflecting the light of the smoky candle on the night-table.

"I recognized your voice, doctor, in spite of the passage of time and my distress," the supine woman said, without moving. "Sit down by the bed; I have something to tell you. I have never lost track of you since Geneva, but this morning, as soon as I arrived...then I was sure of seeing you before dying."

I went towards the specter, compassionately. I could hardly recognize the beautiful Claire Lenoir as I studied her face, which had evidently been ravaged by some mysterious anguish. It was as if she had suddenly grown old.

I said all these things to her, delicately. She looked hard at me from behind her spectacles. The silence was profound.

"Yes," murmured Claire Lenoir, in a level tone, "you are a horrid old man!"

And she lapsed into pensiveness.

For the first time in my life, I understood certain tricks employed in farces on the Parisian stage; I cast my eyes around me, not knowing to whom she was talking. No one was concealed there; we were alone.

I took her arm and felt her pulse; it was irregular as well as faint. I took pity on her madness and sat down at the head of the bed.

XVIII. The Anniversary

> In which rejoice the swarm of evil angels,
> Swimming in the folds of curtains.
> Charles Baudelaire.[59]

"Tell me...tell me what Sir Henry Clifton confided to you," said Claire Lenoir, in a horribly low voice.

"Oh? Ah! Nothing," I replied.

"You know what happened while my husband, Monsieur Lenoir, was away. You do know!"

"I know nothing at all about it," I said.

"Oh, all right!" Madame Lenoir went on. "I won't tell you the outrageous circumstances of my miserable fall from grace. Just: I was beloved! I'm guilty!"

Infamous creature, I thought. Aloud, I said: "Oh well, what harm is there in that?"

"I know that a sin cannot redeem itself...but, after that, I remained faithful to Monsieur Lenoir until death—faithful even in thought."

"I'm not a priest, Madame."

"The priest has gone—and I'm dying, I tell you," Claire replied, in a preoccupied manner.

"Oh, my dear Madame Lenoir, can that be true? You're exaggerating! Your complexion isn't terminally bad, you're voice isn't whistling at all, and—save for the kind of attack that any one of us might suffer—you seem to me to be in relatively good condition."

"What about this, doctor?" she said, lifting up her spectacles.

I leaned forward.

"That?" I said, after a cursory examination. "Damnation! There are, indeed, certain symptoms of..."

"Of what?" she said, in a voice that set my nerves jangling.

"Of a malady that it would be absurd not to treat immediately," I added. "It's nothing much." Privately, I thought: *One thing's certain—it's too late.*

"Out with it, then!" she cried. "Do you imagine that I'm afraid?"

She shivered—more, I ought to say, because of a certain nervous wastage than fear of the imminent death of which she was evidently conscious.

"All right," I said. "Listen closely: apoplexy is a little rupture in the brain; I see now that the veins in your eyelids, your temples and your whole face are congested in a quite extraordinary manner. It's as if they were about to burst."

I rose to my feet in order to consult the labels on the flasks. "I'll go and find what's necessary," I told her.

---

[59] Slightly misrendered from "Une Martyre" in *Les Fleurs du mal*.

"It's useless! Stay! Death is one thing for which I've long been prepared. I know where I am—in a few minutes, at ten o'clock, it will all be over. So stay where you are! And trust that I'm still in possession of the last glimmerings of my reason. I've told you: I have something remarkable to tell you."

What remarkable thing could she have to tell me? Nothing, obviously. And yet I didn't want to hear it.

"My word!" I exclaimed, heartily. "My dear Madame Lenoir, I confess that I am lost in admiration! The fact is that you are very ill—and that you might be forced to part company with me at any moment! But I admire bravery, myself— I love the brave! To the devil with cowards! Speak, then—but quickly, for your voice is fading."

"Oh, shut up! Shut up!" she said, brokenly.

I was shocked and mortified; negligently, I took a toothpick and fell silent.

"Lean over so that I can talk to you," she said.

I obeyed, reluctantly.

"Alive," she went on, "he knew nothing! Nothing! Not ever! But understand this: I believe that he knows *now*. This is the evening of our anniversary— when ten o'clock chimes...yes, I believe that he will come to take me—by the *eyes!*" She pronounced the word with sudden force. "How can I resist him? My flesh was bound to his by an oath sworn at the sacred feet of God!"

Ah, what a truly bizarre thing! What mysteries the human organism contains! In spite of the place, the hour and the memory I did not flinch. *It's delirium*, I thought, *nothing more*. Never had I borne up so well, internally. Beneath the saddened appearance that the situation required, I felt brisk, alert, cheerful! I slyly popped a praline into my mouth and let it melt there, utterly delighted by my peace of mind. What had I to fear, anyway? Her husband could have counted himself lucky, at that moment, that he was dead.

"Don't be afraid—I'm here," I told her, to calm her down. "It's not every day that I have panics like the one that made me flee on the first night of your widowhood! That nervous excitement was, I confess, quite irrational in a man like me."

"Oh, you miserable wretch, I tell you that was the only unconscious glimmer of Reason—of true Reason—that you have had since the day of your birth," Claire said, still propping herself up. "Let's talk, and above all think, about that."

She had a kind of diabolical gurgle; her throat was choked with blood.

"Oh, the bleak breath of the outcast!" she said. "Do you remember the room? Your eyes were lowered. You were kneeling down! You saw nothing. As for me, I was slumped upon the bed, in my distress. I couldn't see anything either. But I shall tell you now what passed above our heads! Monsieur Lenoir reopened his eyes! He suddenly threw back the shroud and sat up, silently, his fists clenched and raised over me! He had the face of damnation! He ground his teeth—soundlessly, for us! Ah! Balefully, with two hellish gleams beneath his eyebrows, he cursed me as part of himself, in the name of the Godless night for which so many are bound. And we did not see him, because it was necessary that our heads were lowered at that particular moment!

"Then he lay down again, drew back the shroud with both hands and closed his eyes again; his face again took on that insensible mask that we shall all wear—that I shall soon wear myself. It was then that, without knowing what had happened, I got up and kissed him tenderly on his dead forehead, one last time, with tears in my eyes."

She fell silent; she looked at me fixedly.

"How...how do you know that's what happened?" I asked.

"I saw the scene played out the following night, in a dream, in a large mirror into which I was looking."

"Demons can indeed lurk in the depths of mirrors!" I told her, compassionately. Then, studying her with leaden eyes and scratching the end of my nose, I added: "But in real life...demons like that are not admitted into real life. How were you able to recognize me, in that mirror's reflection? My features must have been vague therein; I suppose it must have been the moral beauty exhaled, so to speak, by the sum of my features, that enable you to recognize me—isn't that so?" I paused. "A dream?" I repeated, almost to myself. "but Madame, in that case, why did you cry out, in the room, since you knew nothing of this, since you had seen nothing at all!"

"Once I had risen to me feet," Claire Lenoir replied, "as soon as I had embraced him, I put my ear to his mouth again and heard a dull laugh—a yelp that emerged from those furious lips! That was when I cried out, because I was overwhelmed by a boundless terror, a dreadful fear! And my cry came from so deep within my bowels that you understood its significance, as if by electricity."

This, I must confess, made me grow pale in my turn. The fact is that the deserted hotel, the candles threatened with imminent extinction, the idea of that anniversary and, above all, that bespectacled moribund woman in mourning-dress, were beginning to obliterate the soundness of my judgment. The malady of which I have spoken was invading me, moreover, little by little. I felt it rumbling inside me, like a vast distant ocean! go on! Go on! Spit it out! My teeth began to chatter madly, sweat ran down my brow; I became nauseous, my eyes protruding and rolling in their orbits; a frightful oppression weighed heavily upon my breast—and I cast off the mask.

"Vision and madness!" I howled, wildly, as I got to my feet.

XIX. Teterrima Facies Daemonum[60]

As the priest turned towards the cadaver
to read him the mass for the dead, on the
words *Responde mihi!* the dead bishop
was seen to sit up on the bier and cry in
a frightful voice: *Comparui! Judicatus sum!*
Justo judicio Dei, damnatus!
And he lay down again in the coffin.[61]
The History of Saint Bruno

"I have seen him again! Always in a dream!" said Claire Lenoir in the same hoarse and dull voice, without addressing herself directly to me. "three and a half months, or thereabouts, after his death. Except that, probably owing to the chance element in dreams, the external appearance which he then presented to me was different. It was definitely him. Oh, it was him!"

And the unhealthy, insane smile came to hover upon her lips like a will-o'-the-wisp over a tomb.

"You will pity my feeble mind because of these dreams," she went on, "but he had exactly the same bodily form, stature and color of those obscure beings mentioned—as you know—in the accounts of the explorers of the Pacific."

I thought of the letter; I jumped nervously, unable to believe my ears. I tried in vain to connect the two ideas: a lightning-flash, of a kind that is beyond the logic of human explanation, blinded my understanding utterly. I felt a cry of horror raise into my throat, hideously stifling.

"Yes," the dying woman went on, with a preternatural solemnly, "he was exactly like one of those monsters that haunt desert shores and evil seas. His body, wild and hairy, stood upright, smoked more deeply than ebony. The feathers of seabirds supplied his loin-cloth and other vestments. Emptiness extended all around him, populated with Terrors and the infinity of the imagination. The apparition was tattooed with fiery serpents; his hair, long and grey, fell in clumps about his shoulders. Oh, by what train of thought, by means of what ancient impression, was I able to come to transfigure him thus: to dream him thus, so crude, so different! He was standing alone among unknown rocks, looking into the distance, over the sea, as if he were waiting for someone. By his impenetrable manner, I felt rather than recognized that this was the dead man. He was

---

[60] "The Appearance of demons is loathsome." The quotation is from a work attributed to Saint Bernard.

[61] In the version of the legend of St. Bruno quote here the dead bishop responds to the word "answer me" by saying: "I have been summoned! I have been judged! I have been damned by divine justice."

furtively sharpening, behind him, a huge stone cutlass...his nocturnal eyes made my soul shudder with an anguish redolent with blood, the inferno and the agony of death; I woke up with a start, with a loud cry, steeped in cold sweat...

"Never have I succeeded in forgetting that dream."

She fell silent. How can I describe—are there word to express the frightful thoughts, which are, after all, born of funereal possibility—what paralyzed me from top to toe while I listened to these infernal sentences? I was knocked head over heels. The sentiments seething in my mind were unnamable.

Nevertheless, even though the sound of my own voice made me tremble, I spoke without taking account of the truth of my words. "No one! No one, fortunately—do you hear?—can determine the precise point at which the objective reality commences." And I added, with a forced laugh, that made my scalp crawl: "The lunatic asylums have not thought of it! Do you recall the lively discussion we had with that quibbler Lenoir?"

"Oh well, think that if you must," said the patient, with a mirthless smile, "and pray. Prayers, launched beyond Nature by the will, escape Destruction. I, who have never been ashamed to pray, even when my husband uttered his outrageous doubts—the cancer of our sad days—while feigning respect for my faith by love for my unhappy body; I, who want to repent of having committed a forbidden act—for it is not reason that can grant me absolution—I hope and I am sure that after an instant of agony God will not exclude me from all forgiveness."

Then, seizing her spectacles with both hands, she tore them from her face. She twisted the frame convulsively, and the lenses broke in her bloodied hands.

"I no longer need glasses to see it now!" she said. She spoke in a tremulous voice, but with a sort of smile redolent of truly infinite hope, by which her courage seemed to steel itself for some terrifying ordeal, imminent and supreme, after which her soul would be "saved."

The clock chimed ten.

There was a moment of silence, during which Madame Lenoir, having thrown back both halves of the long black shawl in which she had been wrapped, lay down exhaustedly on her back. Her head was slightly raised by the pillow and her staring eyes were wide open. She seemed to be studying, to be going gradually deeper, in spite of herself, into the blinding whiteness of the candlelit wall.

At that moment we heard the sound of the first fireworks, bursting in the distance; the national holiday was in full swing. Vague hurrahs were audible as the serious folk of the town took satisfaction in the sight of lovely rockets soaring skywards and exploding merrily in mid-air.

"Ah!" she cried, with a start. "Well, it's just as I said. *There he is!* Look! There! There! The monster of my evil dreams! There he is—just as he, Monsieur Lenoir, also dreamed! Must one, then, be a son of Ham to be *realized* thus, in Death? Why has he been sharpening that knife for so long, and so coldly, while looking out on the frightful sea? Ah! Vampire! Demon! Assassin! Get away from that wall! Let my poor eyes be!" The unfortunate woman was raving.

Her hands stiffened suddenly in an atrocious clench and her mysterious eyes grew wider still. Whatever she saw became, without any doubt, so dreadful that she could no longer muster breath enough to scream. She struggled, and then fell back with a kind of strangled sob, rigid. She was still staring at the wall.

She had undoubtedly given up the ghost—but I wasn't certain of it.

I threw myself on my portmanteau in order to take out a bundle of lancets; I rummaged around desperately; there was nothing but glass slides, instruments, collections of infusoria, lenses; I leapt across the room, without knowing where I was going! And I returned towards the bed, mechanically taking in hand a large magnifying-glass that I had found.

Then I took the candle and brought it nearer to the face of the dead woman. Trembling nervously, I studied the face through the magnifying glass.

Finally, it's over, I thought, with a sigh of relief. *She's definitely dead.*

Suddenly—I can't explain why—her stagnant eyes attracted my attention.

A most unusual idea suddenly came into my mind. Curiosity entered into my heart and swept all apprehension therefrom. I braced myself, shivering slightly; I wanted to examine the irises that had re-covered each of those dark pupils and plunge into the depths of the remaining disk! A demon took hold of my arms, leaned over my old head, applied the powerful magnifying-glass to my eye, directing almost forcibly towards the dead woman's eyes and the soul within. A whisper in my ear deadened my anguish:

"Look!"

From that moment on I became calmer; I felt that the old Science had taken hold of me again.

I moved my magnifying glass back and forth over her pupils.

The eyes presented no easily appreciable peculiarity, except for their extraordinary vitreousness. I was about to abandon my tentative examination when I observed that each pupil contained a point resembling a dark pinprick.

I immediately went to turn the key that locked the door, then I came back to the bed and crossed my arms, thinking about a means of experimentation.

I had an induction coil in one of my large pockets. *If I could excite the ciliary nerve...*, I thought, but I quickly rejected the idea as useless—futile, even. I took a little flask from my bag. *One drop of this alkaloid*, I thought, *might dilate the pupil.* But I rejected that idea too: the solution in question could not be fruitfully applied to a cadaver.

Suddenly, my eyes fell upon my ophthalmoscope.

"Aha!" I exclaimed. "There's the very thing!"

Grinding my teeth slightly, I took the corpse in my arms—a long nightgown served as a shroud—and stood it up against the wall, underneath a large nail. I was going to pass a cord under her armpits and knot the ends together to suspend her from the nail, but a thought stopped me in my tracks. Whatever might remain within those eyes would appear to me to be inverted, from top to bottom, the cavity behind the iris forming a *camera obscura*.

There was a means to obviate that difficulty, but I hesitated before having recourse to it. My colleagues will probably think the scruple puerile, but I was reluctant to dispose Madame Lenoir against the wall upside-down. They would say, I know, that it displayed an untimely sentimentality at the moment of a serious experiment, when no one should think about anything but scientific rigor. After all, many other people, even more famous than me, were practicing at every hour of every day, throughout Europe, upon at least fifty or sixty thousand female cadavers—drawn from the needy classes, of course—in amphitheatres, morgues, hospitals and so on. I would reply that it was only because I had always been on good terms, socially, with Madame Lenoir that the act seemed to me to be slightly sacrilegious.

It goes without saying that if the dear woman had, to the best of my knowledge, never been anything but poor and needy—my God, if she had been a laborer—the idea of hesitation would not have crossed my mind. At least, if some such silly scruple had momentarily crossed my mind, I would have stifled it with a blush, in order that I should not merit the derision of my colleagues. But I had, of course, always known Madame Lenoir as an honorable woman of means, and I confess that the knowledge instilled in me a certain respect even for her mortal remains. For that reason, I took up the body again, holding it at arm's length, and was wandering around the room, not knowing quite what to do, when I was struck by the perfect solution. It was so simple that I was truly astonished that I had not thought of it before.

This is what I did.

I simply replaced Madame Lenoir on her death-bed, with all due precaution, but I placed her *the wrong way round*, with her head and neck projecting over the edge of the bed, as if suspended above the floor. The waves of her chestnut-colored hair, already silvered, flowed over the foot of the bed. The face was thus presented to me upside-down, with the eyes at knee-height. They were still wide open, and I still could not help finding their solemnity slightly disconcerting. There was no doubt now that, if there were_ something within her pupils, I would be able to see the image in its normal orientation.

After that, I took one of the candles, whose dying flame was flickering, and placed it between the two of us.

I adjusted the large lens in the frame in front of the reflector and readied myself to direct the beam of light into the depths of Madame Lenoir's eyes.

As I shot my first glance into those eyes via the hole of the ophthalmoscope, however, I recoiled, without knowing why. I didn't want to know what it was that I had glimpsed!

I remained still for a moment. I cannot believe that Hell itself has ever reflected more hair-raising horrors than the ideas that drifted into my head in that interval.

Just then, the windows were colored by a distant sky-burst: one of the fireworks with which the exultant multitude of the men and women of the town was celebrating the national holiday. It made me shiver.

The candle was guttering out, though; I would soon be in darkness.

"No!" I exclaimed, flexing my knee. "I have to see! I have to see!"

And I brought my eye to bear on the luminous opening.

It seemed to me that, alone among the living, I would be the first to look into infinity *through the keyhole*.

XX. The King of Terrors

> The deep uttered his voice and lifted up his hands on high.
> *Habbakuk* 3:10.

Then: oh! fright of my life! oh! vision that has changed the world into a sepulcher for me, and installed Madness in my soul!

On examining the eyes of the dead woman the first thing I saw, distinctly outlined, as if it were a frame, was the strip of violet paper which ran around the top of the wall. And within this frame, like some kind of echo, I saw a picture which is beyond the expression of any language under the sun and the moon, alive or dead—and I say that without a single instant's hesitation.

Oh, how to describe it? What imagination could heap up the derisory inanity of the words that I am writing?

The paroxysm of ardent disquiet that seized me made the ophthalmoscope shake in my hands, and the beam of light danced in the eyes of the cadaver: in those huge inverted eyes, so vitreous, fixed, exorbitant and wide open.

And this is approximately what I saw:

Yes! The sky! Distant waves, a huge rock, the fall of a starry night! And upright on the rock, larger than life, stood a man like an inhabitant of the archipelagoes of the Dangerous Sea! Was it a man, this phantom? In one hand, lifted towards the abyss, he held a bloody head by the hair! With a howl that I could not hear, but whose horror I divined in the volcanic distension of the wide-open mouth, he seemed to offer it as a sacrifice to the darkness and the void! In his other hand, dangling down, he held a stone cutlass, bloody and loathsome. Around him, the horizon seemed boundless, the solitude eternally accursed! And, beneath the expression of supernatural fury, beneath the concentration of vengeance, ceremonious wrath and hatred, I suddenly recognized, in the face of the Ottysor-vampire, an uncanny resemblance to poor Monsieur Lenoir immediately before his death—and, in the severed head, the direly shadowed features of the young man of yesteryear, the lost lieutenant, Sir Henry Clifton.

224

Tottering unsteadily, like a little child, I extended my arms as I recoiled.

My reason fled; hideous, confused conjectures, maddened my stupefaction. I was no more than a seething chaos of anguish, a human rag, a brain as desiccated as chalk, pulverized beneath the menacing immensity! And Science, the smiling old woman with clear eyes, whose logic and fraternal embrace are a little too disinterested, whispered derisively in my ear that she too is no more than bait for the Unknown that lies in wait for us, patiently.

Suddenly, I hurled myself at the wall and held myself tightly against it, with my hands—the fingers of which were splayed by a nameless fear—flat upon the stonework.

"But...but..." I grunted, with a sidelong glance at the dead woman, "it must have been the case that in spite of the ancient lies of Extension and Duration...which all the available evidence proves to be lies...it must have been the case that the apparition was objectively real, to such an imponderable degree, perhaps within the living fluid, as to be projected in this way on your seeing pupils!"

I paused, and then concluded, in a low voice, with my hair standing on end and my fists clenched: "But...in that case...where are we?"

And as I leaned over the body—with the frantic rage of a sacrilegious tub-thumper—to re-examine the execrable but fascinating spectacle, the ophthalmoscope slipped from my hands at the sight of the dead woman's expression. As she suddenly lifted up her head I shivered, chilled to the bone; I saw two tears well up and run slowly and heavily down her livid cheeks.

And Death, veiling the Impenetrable, began to roll her profound shadows over *those eyes*.

Jules Hoche (1858-1926) became a prolific writer of popular fiction from the 1880s until his death, but he published his first book, Folles amours *in 1878 while he was still using the original spelling of his surname, Hosch—which he changed because of anti-German sentiments provoked while his native Alsace was under German rule following the fall of the Second Empire in 1870. "Le Docteur Quid" was first published in* Folles amours; *the translation first appeared in* The Maker of Men and His Formula.[62]

Jules Hoche: *Doctor Quid*

> All human actions are the fatal products
> of the cerebral substance
> Taine[63]

Omnia in mensura, in numero, et pondera disposuisti![64]

And Doctor Quid paced back and forth in his laboratory, his gaze somber and his head bowed, his upper body buckling under the weight of the enormous problem of which his cerebral lobes had just taken hold.

Here, a description would be *de rigueur*, in order to impress the reader suitably and not to be neglectful with regard to the constitutional elements of my story, but the task is beyond the scope of my pen, I humbly confess. There are mysterious bonds between Dr. Quid and his laboratory that I do not have the strength to disentangle. Both of them, although bristling with a thousand tangible or intangible asperities, encapsulated and completed one another so well that the abstract reasoning necessary to introduce them separately to the reader would destroy that secret harmony by its very essence.

The laboratory, in all respects similar to that of Wagner in *Faust*, the complex fluids saturating its atmosphere, the sticky, viscous floor furrowed here and there with grooves carrying crystalline residues toward nether regions, the bottles, flasks, retorts and alembics with disparate and uneven forms, the white-

---

[62] Available from Black Coat Press: *The Bad Dream*, ISBN 978-1-61227-904-6; *The Maker of Men and his Formula*, ISBN 978-1-61227-426-3; *"Future Paris"* (1895) in *On the Brink of the World's End*, ISBN 978-1-61227-474-4,

[63] The positivist sociologist Hippolyte Taine (1828-1893). The quotation is from *L'Intelligence* (1870).

[64] The quotation, more accurately rendered as *omnia in mensura et numero et pondere disposuisiti* is from the Vulgate Bible version of *Wisdom* 11:21: "Thou has ordered all things in measure, and number, and weight."

226

washed walls covered with cabalistic symbols testifying that coarse charcoal was sometimes placed at the disposal of the scientist's elucubrations, and finally, the scientist himself, the tenebrous Dr. Quid, who wears on his face and throughout his appearance the accusatory imprints of the chaos in whose bosom he consumes his existence, all form a single whole, utterly heterogeneous but perfectly indissoluble into its elements.

That isn't sufficient for you? So be it; I shall enter into a few details with regard to Dr. Quid. He is a scientist, as I have said. I will add that he is a modern scientist, for he is married.

Nowadays, scientists are divided into two classes: the ancient and the modern. Those two classes are completely different from one another in their manner of comprehending the usage of the natural attributes that Providence has granted them. The ancient scientist is celibate; the modern scientist is married. Between the two categories there is an abyss, which the former can only cross by means of the hymeneal tightrope. The ancient is still somewhat stained by alchemy; the modern has harnessed his chariot to the triumphal march symbolic of the rapid progress of chemistry.

Let no one be in doubt; it is marriage that has created modern science; it is matrimonial contracts that have extract chemistry from the bosom of alchemy, and the latter will only disappear completely when the last bachelor among scientists, or the last scientist among bachelors, ties the knot.

How can the influence of marriage on the progress of science be explained? I shall leave the care of that problem to those who cultivate the arid terrain of social physiology.

Dr. Quid had the fine and delicate features, the accentuated profile and the neat bone structure that characterize nervous temperaments. A wan pallor was spread over his entire face, the bloodless flesh denoting, in addition, an unfortunate predisposition to encephalic neuroses.

Thanks to those physical particularities, Dr. Quid could easily be taken into the possession of environments. His laboratory had gradually become indentified with him, and vice versa. His eyes had taken on a hyaline transparency; the proportions of his body had been slowly transformed. The slightest preoccupations were translated externally by implausible attitudes; his limbs were then grouped in accordance with certain geometrical shapes, borrowed from his bizarre instruments, and all his movements appeared to be the result of forces elaborated in his retorts.

Dr. Quid had been pacing back and forth in his laboratory for half an hour when he suddenly stopped and folded his arms—which indicated, in him, a violent nervous crisis.

"Well," he said, "this can't go on; either I emerge from this question victorious, or I consent to lose forever the faculty of solving problems. The spectacle of nature is sufficient in itself to demonstrate that everything in the organic realm, as in the inorganic realm, is submissive to the laws of number.

"Number is the first link that intelligence conceives between the phenomena of sound, light, heat, electricity, etc., when it studies them and seeks the common relationships that might unite them. Definite quantities intervene in every propagation, transmission or exchange of substance. The harmony that reigns in the world is, in consequence, immediate.

"Number is, moreover, an indispensable condition for the production of any harmony whatsoever. To take account of that, it's sufficient to consider audible phenomena such as music. All sounds are linked together by numerical relationships; such and such a note corresponds to such and such a number of vibrations, and consonances between chords can only take place if the numbers of vibrations in the notes have a simple ratio.

"Furthermore, phrenology informs us that there are such intimate relationships between the relationships of sounds and those of numbers that the organ of numbers in the brain is like a continuation of that of music, a sort of prolongation of the nethermost convolution of that organ. In all the branches of art, in its most varied forms, harmony is submissive to the same laws. A combination of colors, or an arrangement of lines forming a drawing, can only please if they're chosen or disposed in such a fashion as to emit vibrations whose numbers have a simple ratio.

"One thing is, therefore, to be posited in principle: number plays a supreme role in everything that is in movement; now, movement is the source of all like, so number plays an essential and preponderant role in life.

"Given that, if we pass from the physical domain to the mental by the insensible gradation that leads from physical events to psychic events, we will always find number playing the same role in actions attributed to the human soul. If we analyze sensations, the initial origins of ideas, we will find logarithmic relationships between their intensities and those of sentiments derived from them.

"Thus, certain psychological phenomena whose intensities increase in a geometrical progression correspond point by point with certain physiological phenomena whose intensities increase in an arithmetical progression. Number therefore links all the sensitive phenomena and ought to serve as the point of departure of a new way of envisaging them and studying them.

"People have often sought to explain why accord cannot be obtained between two people who have been brought together by an absolute conformity of character and seem to be made to understand one another. With the theory of number that is easily explained. It is known that a series of identical numbers of sonorous vibrations cannot constitute a perfect chord. In the same way, two characters represented by identical numbers cannot concord; to produce the desired accord it is indispensable that their respective elements are in a given relationship. 'Those who resemble one another assemble,' says popular wisdom. It is true, but it is necessary not to conclude from it that any confraternity can reign between peoples. Human attractions obey the same laws as electrical and magnetic attractions; contrary elements attract one another and similar elements repel one another. As soon as to similar numbers are in proximity a repulsion makes itself felt. That is why people who resemble one another can assemble as much as they like, but will never reach an understanding.

"In my opinion, these general considerations ought to permit the founding of a unique, clear and simple theory, which applies mathematics to the moral sciences, and in particular to psychology. Metaphysics, squeezed tightly by geometric reasoning and algebraic demonstrations, will then beat a retreat; all dubious questions will be formulated as equations, all the unknowns will soon be determined, and a new era will begin for human intelligence: the glorious era of number.

"Yes, but how can we assign to so many various and complex phenomena the same cause? How can we explain by one unique law all the anomalies of thought and sensibility, of human will? That's what I've been seeking for a long time, and will perhaps never find. There would be nothing new under the sun thereafter, because science could cross the eternal limits of the unknown!"

At this point, Dr. Quid's lower lip was elongated by bitterness, and he passed his hand over the anxious creases in his forehead. While his absent mind struggled in the grip of the problem that was obsessing it, his haggard eyes wandered over the immobile retorts that extended their curved necks into the air as if to listen to some silent sound or grasp something intangible. One of the gas lamps, which was burning almost above his head, with a shrill hiss, cast soft and vacillating gleams over his polished cranium.

Suddenly, he shivered.

His gaze had just fallen upon the opposite wall. A few hours earlier, at grips with his problem, he had despairingly scribbled in charcoal the famous dictum: *Nihil novi sub sole.*[65]

Now—he could not believed his eyes—the *Nihil* had been transformed into a majestic *Quid*, and above the vigorous period that he had placed behind the four words, as if by magic, an enormous question mark now floated.

Had the charcoal betrayed the internal preoccupations of the scientist when the latter had exhaled his despair and made it take form on the wall? No—he was sure that he had written *Nihil*. And then again, where had that question mark come from, which was trembling—for it could definitely be seen moving—as if it were afraid of being suspended over such a big question?

A slight smile now stayed over the scientist's lips. A part of the mystery was explained. The question mark was the shadow of a big hook curved in the form of an S and suspended from a curtain-rod in front of the gas lamp. The heat radiated by the flame was imparting an oscillation to it, very slight in reality but

---

[65] Nothing new under the sun; the substitution is a trifle ambiguous, it seems to be construed, in the context of the story, as "what [is]," although it could also be interpreted as "something."

whose amplitude was significantly augmented in the shadow. Nevertheless, the transformation of the *Nihil* into *Quid* remained a mystery.

After convincing himself that he could not account for that anomaly, the scientist ceased to worry about it, let himself fall into a chair and resumed his algebraic meditations.

Then a small, tenuous, crystalline sound, similar to the silvery plaint of a dropped pin, burst forth in the torpid sonorities of the laboratory. Unfortunately for him, the scientist did not hear it. If he had heard it, he would have darted a glance at the round-bottomed glass flask placed not far from his nose and would have recoiled swiftly. The flask contained nitrous oxide, and it had just cracked.

Slowly, the gas filtered through the fissure in the wall and spread out as far as Dr. Quid's nasal fosses.

The latter did not take long to feel its anesthetic virtues. His eyebrows fell heavily, like unbolted chassis, his head slumped forward on to this collar and he lapsed into a soporific state that affected the form of the most profound lethargy.

He might perhaps have remained like that for a long time but for the solicitude of his wife. Having become impatient with a wait that seemed to be extending indefinitely, and seeing that the time for dinner was long past, she decided to penetrate into the sanctuary of science. Her surprise was great when she perceived the god asleep in the midst of his retorts.

"Well, my love, you've forgotten dinner, then?"

The doctor did not budge.

His wife's anguished hands required a quarter of an hour to bring him round.

Finally, it was as if the scientist emerged from a dream, and his first words were: "What is it? What's happening? What's new?"

*

Judith Gautier (1845-1917) was the daughter of Théophile Gautier and was briefly married to Catulle Mendès in 1866-69. Her literary work frequently employed decorative Oriental settings in a highly stylized fashion, as in the collections include Les Princesses d'Amours *(1900),* Le Collier des jours *(1902) and* Le Paravent de soie et d'or *(1904).* "La Fleur serpent" *was serialized in* Le Rappel, *22-27 avril 1882 before being reprinted in* Isoline et la fleur serpent *(1882).*[66]

Judith Gautier: *The Serpent Flower*

In the short distance that separates Naples from Portici, while the boat that was carrying me cut soundlessly through the immobile azure of the gulf, my mind, leaping backwards some years, saw once again the day on which the woman I was going to visit had appeared to me for the last time.

Five years already? Or, rather, only five years—for that time, so full for me, seemed to have been much longer: empty days and months of idleness certainly slide more rapidly into the past, without leaving any memory, than times of toil, activity, and travel most of all. How many countries I had seen, in those years! Japan, Cambodia, all of India. What surprising mores! How much beauty, and how much ugliness! Beneath all those new visions, however, the image of Claudia Viotti had not been erased; rather, it had grown, looming over my memories from afar; she had become one of the attractive charms of the absent homeland—personifying it, so to speak.

I had been madly in love with her, in secret, without ever telling her so, without any hope, and although I had been cured of that love for a long time, it was not without some anxiety that I was going toward her again, about to confront once more the danger of her beauty.

Already I could perceive the Villa Viotti, whose grounds terminate, on the shore of the sea, in a long terrace from which once descends a long staircase of stone steps, between sculpted vases, bristling with misshapen cacti.

As I leapt from the boat on to the sand of the beach, I heard the sound of voices at the top of the stairway, and Claudia appeared on the edge of the terrace, accompanied by three people who were doubtless visiting her. I recognized her elegant silhouette without any hesitation, outlined against a dark green background.

I had left a young woman; I found a young wife. When I had left, Claudia was due to marry one of my best friends, Count Scala, but a few days before the

[66] Available from Black Coat Press: *Isoline and the Serpent Flower*, ISBN 978-1-61227-152-1.

date fixed for the marriage, my poor friend had perished during a crossing from Naples to Genoa, where he was going to settle some business matters and look for a few family papers. During a storm, it appeared, a wave had carried him away. Claudia waited in vain, and, on learning of his death, did not manifest any considerable grief. Six months later, she married a young Neapolitan, Leone Vitti, who had tried to compete with Scala for her, and who was, as they say, much dearer to her heart.

As soon as she saw me, Claudia rapidly came down a few steps, with a cry of joyful surprise.

"What! It's you, Doctor?" she cried, in that sonorous and slightly husky voice, which my ear remembered so well. "So you've finally come back. We would have sworn that you had become a Brahmin or that some jungle tiger had devoured you."

And she held out her ungloved hand to me, to which I applied my lips affectionately.

"You've become more beautiful," I told her, admiring her lovely face, so warmly pale, beneath the dark mass of her undulating tresses, brightened by a large red flower.

"Is that true?"

"One can see that the sun of love is shining over you," I added.

"Yes, I'm happy," she said, looking up at me with a gaze full of fire. "I know that Scala was your friend, but what do you expect? I didn't love him, and he behaved badly with me. I begged him to release me from the promise that my family and I had made him, to renounce the marriage; he didn't want to." With a truly terrible expression, she continued: "I believe, you know, that the anger he ignited in my soul brought misfortune to him; I cast the spell of the evil eye upon him, involuntarily. If he hadn't died, I don't know what would have happened." She changed tack, cheerfully: "But why are we talking about that? Come on, I'll introduce you."

The visitors, two ladies and a young man, of whom my memory retained no trace, had remained on the terrace; they both came toward us, and the introductions were made, followed by a moment of embarrassed silence, difficult to break between people who do not know one another.

"Look! Look! This is my son!" Claudia suddenly cried, showing me with passionate pride a delightful three-year-old child who had just hurled himself at her skirts.

The child looked at me, laughing, and then escaped, bounding along the pathways. He disappeared behind a large clump of flowers, crying: "Cuckoo!"

"Come on, Pepino, come back," said the young mother, drawing us toward the villa.

The residence soon appeared in the midst of lush vegetation, so darkly green as almost to be black. The sun, which was setting, projected its light upon the façade and turned it blood red from top to bottom. I don't know why, but I experienced a painful sensation, a sort of vague dead, as if some danger or dolor were threatening me.

Oh, I wish to God that I had fled at that moment, never to return, stuffing my fingers in my ears in order that no echo of that terrible house could reach me!

But I crossed the threshold with a tranquil tread, already forgetting the fugitive apprehension that had just assailed me.

We went into a large paved vestibule, and then into a small drawing room that opened into a conservatory where the mistress of the house preferred to sit. There were pretty birds there, rare plants and, attached to a perch by a silver chain, a little monkey that was frolicking in a sunbeam.

"You rarely come to Portici," I said to the young woman, after installing myself in a wicker armchair. "I'm very glad to find you here; I'm told that you're almost never in residence here."

That's true. Leone has a kind of aversion for this villa, and we rarely leave Rome. My husband is horribly sensitive, and the sea air irritates him. He decided to come because of Pepino, whose health prospers on this shore."

The visitors took their leave at that moment, and Claudia left momentarily to show them out.

During that minute of solitude I couldn't help thinking about poor Scala, who had died so conveniently, and was so little regretted by the woman who was to have been his life's companion. I remembered that he had been desperately in love with her, to whom he had been betrothed since childhood. Claudia had seemed to me to have an affection for him, but she had been very young then, and when her womanly heart had awakened it had, it appeared been given to another. To renounce the marriage would have been more that my poor friend could bear, and he had wanted to have the woman, doubtless hoping to win back her love. Who could tell, though? His death had been very strange—perhaps it had been voluntary; perhaps a devotion, all the more sublime because it had to be unknown, had driven the disdained and desperate lover beyond life. If that were the case, Claudia would doubtless shed a few tender tears for the man whom her rancor had not yet forgiven.

She came back and sat down with me, cheerfully.

"Well," she said, "tell me about India, giant forests elephants as tall as houses, fakirs with birds nesting in their eyebrows and apple-green gods with thirty-six arms. Speak, speak!"

I told her about my most outstanding adventures, my labors, my fatigues; then I interrogated her regarding her new life and her family. She was entirely orphaned now, her father having died shortly after the marriage; except for a few cousins, no one remained to her. Her husband and child were all she had to love henceforth, and that love filled her heart to overflowing.

She smiled as she spoke, sitting facing me on a low chair, her chin in her hand, in a pose full of grace and relaxation. I studied her with mute admiration, thinking that the man who had her love must be very happy.

Suddenly, she uttered a cry, and I saw her face change completely, her eyes widening in fear. I turned round swiftly.

A maidservant came running, holding Pepino in her arms, writhing in frightful convulsions. "Oh, Madame, Madame!" she cried. "What's wrong with him? His mouth is all black."

Claudia was breathless, as if petrified. "Doctor!" she cried, with a heart-rending expression.

I ran to the poor child, whose contracted features were no longer recognizable.

He was writhing in convulsive spasms, but he wasn't crying. The dark red tint that stained the corners of his lips immediately made me think that he had bitten into some poisonous fruit, and I thrust two fingers into his throat in order to make him vomit—but I obtained no result.

"My God," I murmured. "What can this poison be?"

"Poison!" cried the mother, in a shrill voice. "What are you saying? There's no poison here; children sometimes have these frightful convulsions—but you can cure him, can't you?"

I suppressed a shake of the head.

The poor child's condition was exceedingly strange; I rejected in vain an idea that imposed itself upon me. It seemed to me that I recognized the effects, almost overwhelming, of a poison known in other climes but unknown in Europe.

"It's impossible," I murmured, "Where could he have found that frightful plant?"

I undressed the child and tried to arm him up by friction, but I had very little hope. His tiny clenched fist dropped something, of which I took possession. It was the crushed pulp of a fruit or a flower, crimson in color. In spite of its shapelessness, I immediately recognized what I feared by its penetrating odor.

I could not suppress a exclamation. "The Serpent-Flower! It really is! Alas, the poor angel is doomed!"

Claudia uttered a howl that tore my heart, and I would certainly have given my life at that moment to be able to return the child to his mother; she had thrown herself upon him, covering him with mad caresses, calling to him, and launching ardent prayers to the heavens, mingled with imprecations.

The maidservant had fled, weeping, calling loudly for the master of the house, the father. He soon arrived, his eyes haggard, his lips tremulous and livid.

"Leone! Leone!" Claudia cried to him, through her tears. "He's going to die!"

I stood there, stunned by emotion, receiving the repercussion of that frightful despair full in the heart, distressed by my impotence. The soul revolts in the face of sudden catastrophes that surprise people in the midst of the most perfect happiness, which they destroy forever.

It was in vain that the distraught mother strove to reanimate her cherub and warm him up with her lips; the pretty laughter had fallen silent forever; that life, scarcely begun, ended there.

I drew away in silence, painfully embarrassed by being the banal witness of that grief.

It was still light; I went out into the garden and wandered along the paths at a rapid, mechanical pace. But while my body was, so to speak, abandoned, a singular memory imposed itself on my mind, reconstructing itself there like a vision of a strange clarity. At first, I could not make out any connection with the drama that had just upset me, and I tried to dispel it as an unhealthy suggestion of the fever.

I saw myself back in Calcutta, on the evening of a fiery day; I was sitting on the veranda of my Indian house, reanimated by the relative cool of the evening, in which I was delighting. All around, the tall trees and arbors were rustling faintly in the breeze, which was bringing me gusts of warm perfume. The blue light of the moon was competing with the red light of a lamp set on the table in front of me; I was finishing writing a letter, while lending an ear, intermittently, to the distant sound of a guitar accompanying a song.

No detail of that insignificant, long-forgotten scene was spared me; I gave way reluctantly to the obsession, and I saw once again the large moths and insects of every sort that my lamp attracted, and where even brushing my sheet of paper, the clouds of smoke that I was drawing from a long pipe in order to defend myself from mosquitoes, and the glass of iced lemonade from which I had sipped a few draughts by means of a straw. I was writing nonchalantly. The letter was finished, but, before closing the envelope, I carefully dropped a few seeds into it; then I sealed it and wrote the address:

To Count Antonio Scala.

Suddenly, the objective of that stubborn memory became clear; the seeds that I had enclosed in that envelope had been the seeds of the Serpent-Flower! Yes, that was it. I had forgotten the missive and its contents; memory brought them back to me cruelly. I had asked Scala to sow the seeds in a corner of his garden and to tell me whether the plant was able to grow in Italy.

I was then studying the properties of the poison, which I thought I might be able to use medically. It was shortly after receiving that letter that my friend had died; it had remained unanswered. Had he, then, given the seeds—of whose dangerous properties I had definitely informed him—to his fiancée, or sown them in her garden? Why had he not warned her to beware of the deadly poison? All that was obscure, but I sensed that it was true: the Serpent-Flower could not have arrived in a garden in Portici by any other means.

But if that were the case, I was the one who had furnished the weapon that had just killed that poor delightful child! On the mild and perfumed evening that had just passed before my eyes again, I had, without knowing it, prepared the despair of a family and the death of a child who had not yet been born! And I had returned from so far away just in time to witness the denouement of the tragedy whose first threads I had knotted.

If the poor mother knew that, would I not be a monster in her eyes? Her son's murderer! Ought I not to flee that house, in which I had given birth to desolation?

I continued walking nevertheless, in increasing agitation, wandering through the bushes and the thick-crowned trees in the grounds. The descending darkness made a painful impression upon me; the quivering of the leaves was extended in my nerves, and when the moon, enormous and red-tinted, emerged slowly from behind the branches, I thought I saw a phantom covered in blood.

I made vain efforts to react against that feverish state; I don't know what dolorous assault squeezed my heart; something prevented me from leaving, and told me that the drama was not over yet. I hastened, however, to get out of the covert whose dense shadow weighed upon me.

Hushed voices, and a noise that I could not explain, attracted my attention. In the darkness, I perceived an agitated group of people, and, desirous of not being alone any longer, I moved toward it.

They were the gardeners and servants of the villa, who, on learning of the death of little Pepino, whom they all loved, had spontaneously thought of taking revenge upon the unconscious plant that had caused the evil, which they credited with a kind of venomous soul. They had, therefore, armed themselves with spades and pickaxes, and where mounting a frenzied assault on the roots of a large bush growing, as if by hazard, beside the stairway to the water. They were heaping insults, reproaches and curses upon it, with all the impetuosity of the Neapolitan character, and, needless to say, I was not far from thinking that they were correct to heap execration upon that homicidal plant.

The moon had risen above the trees, and was shining full upon the bush. I really had, in front of me, the Serpent-Flower, the terrible and fantastic plant familiar to the dwellers on the banks of the Ganges.

In those lands of prodigious exuberance, where the vegetation, unruly and as if crazed, seems to expend its overabundant force in extravagant creations, such surprising products are not rare. The Serpent-Flower is among the most exotic, and it is difficult to form any idea of it when one does not have it before the eyes. It is like a clump of slender snakes standing on their tails, leaning their flat heads toward a little orange-red fruit quite similar to a small pineapple or, rather, a large strawberry, but velvety and reminiscent of a flower. It is the leaves that resemble reptiles, broadening at the tip in the form of a head, and those heads being dotted with two eyes and a sharp thorn, projecting like a dart. The resemblance to a snake is striking: all those eyes, staring at you, and all those darts that seem to be defending the red pompoms, upright on their stems as if turgid with blood, have the most extraordinary and disquieting effect.

The roots were profoundly plunged into the soil; evidently, the plant had already been growing there for several years. The gardeners persisted stubbornly, the moon casting huge gesticulating black shadows behind them, with fantastic elongations.

I had stopped near the laborers, my head bowed, singularly oppressed. I stared at the hole that was enlarging beneath the thrusts of the spades.

Soon, my ideas became confused; I thought that I was in a cemetery; the nocturnal light gave an appearance of tombstones to the rum of the wall and the first step of the stairway. The marble vases were funerary urns, the men gravediggers.

Poor mite! It was the same place where I had seen him a few hours earlier, his laughter still vibrant in the air, and they were digging his grave already!

"Oh, accursed plants! Diabolical flowers! Nests of vipers!" growled the gardeners, straining their muscles to extirpate the roots.

Yes, it was necessary to destroy it, that horrible plant, to burn it, crush it, to let no seed fly away to give birth to the red poison elsewhere.

Abruptly, a part of the bush gave way, and, drawn by the momentum, the men took a few steps backward; but they came back immediately and leaned over he uncovered roots. Then I saw their faces fall and their eyes grow wide. A clamor of fear went up, and then they all fled, making the sign of the cross.

What, then, had they seen?

I was alone. The cry of terror uttered by the men had caused my heart to race, and a dread of which I was ashamed sent a frisson through my flesh. The mad flight of the fugitives was no longer stirring the gravel of the pathways, to which I was still listening, deceived by the sound of my arteries, motionless, as if rooted to the spot.

What, then, had they seen?

Were informal flames emerging from that accursed hole? Were they mad? And was I mad myself, not daring to look?

I rushed forward, and as soon as my gaze searched that shifted soil, the same cry that had just startled my ears emerged from my own throat. I had not been mistaken; there really was a grave there, with a corpse inside.

Oh, the horrible, hideous, abominable vision! The roots, like claws, held a skull in their talons, and limbs convulsed in an atrocious pose. It was a skeleton, not yet completely stripped of flesh, with the remains of hair and a beard mingled with the filaments of the plant and shreds of cloth. The hollow eyes seemed to be looking at me, fascinating me, and my hair prickled in horror. A plaint seemed to rise up, to become distinct, and I clearly heard the words: "Avenge me!"

Then a sudden clarity was born in my mind. I started running like a madman toward the house.

The unfortunates were still in the same room, now lit by large candles, funereal in appearance.

"Scala! It's Scala!" I cried, as I came in, finding nothing else to say in my mental confusion, strangled by indignation and frozen by horror.

I no longer had any pity for the dolor of that mother; I could only see murderers ripe for punishment. However, the little cadaver was there, as white as a wax Jesus, and Claudia, drunk on tears, could not even see me.

Her husband had straightened up at my voice; he looked at me wildly, his eyes bruised by black circles.

"You killed him," I said. "I know. He still had my letter on him, and it contained the punishment, the terrible poison, the seed of that accusing plant; his death is avenged now; he is the one who killed your child; but it won't stop there—the crime has been discovered, the alarm raised; the murderer cannot deny his sin."

My voice was staccato, menacing; anger took my breath away.

The guilty man shook her head slowly. "Deny it?" he said. "Why deny it? I can see full well that it's all over. It's true, I killed him. I bought love at the price of a crime; fate wanted it thus—and had it been necessary to strew cadavers along the road that led to my beloved, I would not have hesitated. Doubtless you have never been in love; it's your right to condemn me—but love itself will absolve me."

I had my back to the wall, my arms folded; I remained silent, slightly disconcerted by that frankness.

He raised his profoundly agonized wife to her feet. She had not heard anything. He drew her to him, looked at her for a long time with ineffable tenderness, and dried the tears that were blinding the beautiful Claudia's eyes with his lips.

"Listen," he said to her. "Listen, my darling; your poor heart with be swollen by a further grief; silence your despair for a moment. It is to you that I owe my confession, and when I leave, I want to take your forgiveness with me."

"Leave?" she said. And her eyes widened. With an abrupt movement, she placed her hands on Leone's shoulders and gazed at him with anxious fixity.

Then he began the following narration, to which I listened without saying a word.

"Do you remember, my dear Claudia, that dolorous evening when all hope was lost for us? I wandered around your abode, not daring to go in, mad with anxiety. I watched the windows of your lighted rooms, the bright bay of the open door. You were making one last appeal to your fiancé. You wanted to beg him, to soften his attitude, to confess your love for me to him. How hellish those hours of waiting were!

"Abruptly, you appeared to me in the lighted doorway. You came down the steps of the perron, and I received you in my arms, icy and livid, grinding your teeth. 'It's finished,' you said. 'He refuses to release me from the promise made; the day of our wedding is fixed. Adieu! I shall die of it!' And you plunged back into the red gulf.

"I tottered at first, as if I had received a sledgehammer blow on my skull; then a sudden calm succeeded the horrible agitation that had been consuming me a little while before. It was like an unleashed torrent suddenly frozen by a polar wind. A hard, implacable resolution had frozen my fury. Laughter contorted my mouth, and I shouted after your disappearing form: 'The one who will die will be neither you nor me.'

"The lucidity of my mind was frightful; so confused a few moments earlier, it now appeared to me to be stainless crystal, the purest water crystallized. I took a dagger from my pocket that I always carried and took it from its sheath. The blade shone, and, my gaze fixed upon that cold clarity, I calmly planned my vengeance.

"I knew that the boat that had brought my enemy was waiting on the strand to take him to the midnight ferry leaving Naples that night. The Count was going to Genoa, his birthplace, to take care of the final formalities necessary to his marriage. It was on that circumstance that I based the entire plot of the drama that, for me, was playing out for the second time, so carefully had I foreseen and meditated all its details in advance. It unfolded before my eyes, so to speak, of its own accord; my mind, in a state of clairvoyant acuity that I only experienced that once, was like a mirror, over which passed with great rapidity all the scenes that were about to take place. All the dangers to be avoided, all the precautions to take to ensure the mystery, presented themselves to me and were resolved effortlessly. I experienced no dread or hesitation; I felt as if I were inspired, surely guided by an external force.

"I don't know how much time elapsed between the moment that you went back into the house and the moment when the Count came out—minutes or hours—but I suddenly straightened up within the shadow in which I was lurking, as loud voices became audible outside the house.

"Your father was escorting his chosen son-in-law to the perron. I heard a few phrases. 'Don't be upset by her caprices; they'll pass.'

"'I hope so,' the Count replied, laughing conceitedly. 'In the meantime, I have loved enough for two!'

"'Bon voyage!'

"'See you soon!'

"And my rival went lightly down the steps, his overcoat over his arm, and a cigar between his lips.

"I followed him, hiding in the shadows of the bushes, keeping low, as silent as a wild beast. When he set foot on the stairway to the water, I launched myself forward, gripped his throat with one hand to stop any cry for help before it emerged, and with the other hand, with a single thrust, plunged the dagger into his heart.

"Oh, no hatred can possibly equal that of a man in love, for I, who could not have cut the throat of a lamb without fainting, experienced no horror, no pity, but only a ferocious joy, a rage scarcely slaked.

"The stormy sky was very gloomy, the darkness thick. Even so, my enemy must have seen by whom he had been killed, for I leaned my face over his agony for a long time, without pronouncing a word, without my clenched hand letting a groan escape from the dying man's lips..."

"You merely anticipated me, Leone!" cried Claudia, who was drinking in her husband's words breathlessly. "I would have killed him on our wedding night."

Leone, whose narration had petrified me, darted a triumphant glance at me. His wife had not had an instant's hesitation in absolving him, and that forgiveness was sufficient for him. He clutched her to his heart, and continued, in a firmer voice:

"I stood up when the last quiver of life had ceased. Then I uttered a deep sigh, breathing with indescribable relief. The idea that had filled my nights with anguish, the thought beneath which I had writhed in rage and despair, was extinct forever. 'Claudia is his!' Those words could never be joined together now; I was finally free of him; they were rent asunder, scattered in all the winds of that tumultuous night. Punishment, separation, my beloved lost to me—those tortures were preferable to the one that had just shown me mercy. I was resolved, however, to do the best I could to conceal what people would call my crime, and in order to take full advantage of it, I neglected no precaution.

"I remembered—and it was a memory retained by my eyes rather than my memory—a wheelbarrow at the corner of a path, and in that wheelbarrow, thrown as if forgotten, a spade and a rake. I had noticed that while on my way to the furtive which we believed to be the last. If those tools had not chanced to be there, my situation would have been complicated. I ran to the path and, in my haste, collided with the wheelbarrow, whose implements fell out with a noise that frightened me.

"I drew nearer to the house. I looked at it as if in spite of myself. All the lights were out on the ground floor, but a few windows on the first floor were still illuminated; I looked for yours. Poor love! I divined the dejection in your tears, the wringing of your hands, as you cursed fate, and I had a desire to come and throw you a word of hope; but I resisted that desire; it was necessary that you be unaware of everything, in order that no fear could trouble your happiness.

"I went back to the dead man and dragged him into the corner of the balustrade, where the shadows were amassed with the greatest intensity. Then I readjusted my clothing, which the struggle with my rival had disarranged. I picked up his overcoat, which had fallen to the ground and I put it on. Then I went down the stairs rapidly.

"That overcoat was very distinctive and recognizable; it was an ample traveling cape with a loose belt that buttoned around the waist. It was a bright hazelnut-brown color, with large bone buttons. I was much the same height as the Count, and my beard was trimmed like his. The resemblance ended there, but on such a dark night, thanks to the recognizable coat, it might be sufficient.

"The boatman was asleep in the boat; he had not heard or seen anything— there was, in any case, nothing else to see but the dark night.

"I shook him as I leapt into the boat. He woke up immediately and stated rowing rapidly. The heavy atmosphere weighed upon the leaden, motionless water. On the other side of the bay the lights of Naples were reflected in long reddish trails. The rumors of the city were distinctly audible, but the sea was silent. We reach the quay and I headed for the ferry on foot, taking care to pull my hat down over my eyes and light a cigar.

"I knew that Scala's manservant was named Martino, but I had never noticed his physical appearance. I'd probably never even seen the fellow. That was something that made me anxious; Martino would surely be waiting for his master at the boat; he was bound to see me and mistake me for the other; what would happen then? The ship's lights spread a confused illumination; on the gangplank linking the boat to the quay there was the particular hubbub and bustle marking an imminent departure. I went forward bravely, enveloped by the smoke of my cigar.

"As I had hoped, Martino came straight toward the overcoat, raising his hat. 'I feared that the Signore might not get here in time,' he said.

"I replied with a kind of grunt, gripping my cigar in my teeth in order to mask my voice. 'I've reserved a god cabin,' he went on. 'The Signore's baggage is already there; here are the keys.'

"'Good,' I muttered. 'Let's see the cabin.'

"Martino went down ahead of me, and I followed him. It was a grave imprudence, for the entry-point as brightly lit and for a moment I thought I was doomed, but I had time to take out my handkerchief and plunge my face into it just as the lamp shone full upon it, and when the manservant stood aside to let me go into the cabin. I kept my back to him for the rest of the conversation, which I cut as short as possible but which seemed interminable to me. 'Perfect,' I said. 'You can go to bed. I don't need anything else.'

"He didn't go immediately, though. He made the bed, prepared a toddy and showed me the bag in which he had put provisions, listing everything he'd accumulated there; he also told me that the cigars were in the first compartment of the trunk. Those few minutes were full of anguish for me, but he finally went away without having conceived the slightest suspicion.

"Soon, I went up on deck, wanting to be seen by the captain. I went to greet him. 'Count Scala?' he said.

"I bowed. 'We're leaving in spite of the threatened storm?' I asked him.

"'We have to.'

"'How long will it be?'

"'Ten minutes.'

"I didn't have a moment to lose. I went back down to the cabin and opened the bags with a feverish haste. I took out the provisions and toilet items, which I set out in good order. I washed my hands in the basin, in case there was blood on them. I took off the overcoat that had provided me with such a good disguise and threw it on to the bed, which I crumpled; then I attacked the provisions, stuffing items of food into my pockets. I even drank an entire bottle of wine. Time was pressing. I cast one last glance at the cabin, which certainly seemed to have been occupied, and went out, carefully closing the door. I went back up and succeeded in leaving the boat unnoticed. A few moments later the engine's whistle blew, announcing the departure. The comedy was complete. Now it was necessary to get back to the more lugubrious scenes of the drama.

"I didn't want to take a boat to return to the villa; the boatman would have been a dangerous witness; I had to go the long way round the bay.

"The imminent storm rendered the roads deserted. I went part of the way at a run without encountering anyone.

"The first flash of lightning stung the horizon just as I set foot on the first step of the stairway, and a dull rumble rolled over the sea. I went up the steps slowly, vaguely frightened by the darkness, blacker after the flash of light.

"What if my enemy hadn't been completely dead? What if he were no longer there? What if it were necessary to recommence the murder of a wounded man?

"I couldn't find the spot where I had left the victim right away. I groped and groped in the dark, in vain, dreading finding the cadaver beneath my hand, and dreading even more that I might not. I was inundated by cold sweat.

"Abruptly, I touched hi icy face, and an involuntary start of alarm made me step back with a stifled cry. At the same time, a further flash of lightning showed me his horrible face, his eyes wide open, his mouth agape.

"Although I had maintained an extraordinary self-composure until then, I almost succumbed to the superstitious terror than invaded me at that moment. The storm burst with a frightful fury; the suddenly swollen sea added its groaning to the racket of the thunder; the wind was blowing tempestuously. I truly though that the heavens had been unleashed against me, and I had a desire to flee, to escape at any price that terrible face, which kept appearing and disappearing, and which seemed to be shifting in the intervals between the lightning-flashes.

"I had the strength to resist, however, and I set about digging in the ground.

"What point is there in telling you about the tortures inflicted upon me by that labor? Beneath the torrents of rain that were overwhelming me, in the tumult of the elements, beneath that furious sky, which the reflections of Vesuvius reddened at times like the fires of Hell...that almost invincible lassitude that paralyzed me...the hole that filled with water...the dead man watching me, with his staring eyes, hollowing out his grave! Several times, I saw myself as the victim of a frightful nightmare, and I wished that floods of lava might come to bury, along with all memory, the victim and the murderer alike!

"When it was all done, dawn was breaking and the storm had died away. The wan morning light rendered me slightly calmer, and permitted me to erase all trace of the murder. The storm had helped me by softening and furrowing the ground; the rain had washed away the bloodstains. I put the tools back where I had found them, and fled to my house, where I slept for twenty-four hours solid, exhausted.

"The rest you know. The Count's presence on the ferry had been firmly established by my audacious appearance. The discovered overcoat, the cabin in disorder, the remarks exchanged with the captain and the manservant, left no doubt. It was nothing but the disappearance of a passenger, easily explained by one of those accidents so commonplace at sea; the crossing had been difficult, the night very dark; given the awkwardness of the maneuvering and the noise of the tempest, a man might have been carried away by a wave without anyone seeing the accident and raising the alarm.

"Liberated by that death, your father no longer had any reason to refuse me; you became my wife, and the heavenly happiness of that union filled my soul completely, drowning the memory of the sacrificed rival.

"I avoided living in the villa in Portici—but when you talked about selling it, since it displeased me, I came back here in order to deflect you from that dangerous idea. The first time I saw the habitation again I was alone, I had to announce and prepare for our installation.

"Something always attracts us toward that which we ought to avoid. I wanted to go back to that corner of the grounds that I ought to have fled, the terrace on the water's edge. So I went there, alone, my head bowed, unable to help passing once again through all the anguish of that criminal night, seeking for the location of that furtive grave, forever unknown.

"Suddenly I uttered a cry of fright; on the very spot that I knew so well, that bare place, deliberately chosen because it was free of all vegetation, any clump where the gardener's spade might dig, through the white pebbles with which the ground was strewn, I saw that terrible bush standing, that medusal cluster, those bloody flowers with menacing darts, like the whips of the Erinnyes!

"What was that frightful growth? All of it seemed to be howling at me, writhing, denouncing me! How had that plant grown over the dead man? I tried to tear it up, but it was immovable, and I bloodied my fingers on the thorns.

"I was about to return to the assault when I saw a gardener arrive. He came toward me rapidly. 'Just what I wanted to ask, Signore," he said. "I dared not dig out that strange plant without orders, which came here I know not how, and looks at you in such a diabolical fashion."

"'Dig it out?" I exclaimed. "Dig it out? What are you saying?' And I felt myself going pale; but I understood that I was losing my head, and I was able to control myself. 'On no account dig it out,' I said. 'The plant is very precious and I'm very fond of it.'

"'We could put it somewhere else?'

"'No, no, it would surely die. I forbid you to touch it, and you'll answer to me for that.'

"I thought I would be able to forget that hideous plant, which fear had obliged me to conserve, but it had wounded my mind with all those poisonous darts, and it was lodged there forever. It was a vengeful hydra that was devouring me, and my happiness was now lined with terror. I avoided the part of the grounds where the blooming remorse grew, but I sensed it growing, becoming a bush, a thicket, a forest; I could see its menacing gestures, I believed that I could hear its cries for vengeance. Oh, I knew full well that it would reach us!"

Leone, who had gradually lost his initial calmness, and had become excited to the point of fever, stopped speaking, and fixed upon his dead son a gaze charged with distress. Claudia was weeping on her husband's breast. They seemed to have forgotten my presence completely.

During the narration I had passed through various sentiments. The horror and anger that had turned me upside-down had given way, gradually, to an involuntary interest, a culpable weakness that almost drove me to regret that the crime had been discovered. I was the one who had furnished the dead man with the means to make his vengeance surge forth from his tomb; I was not far from regretting the fact. Love is a very powerful excuse; an individual possessed by it is certainly no longer in control of himself; if he is threatened in his passion, he defends it even more than his life, and is not a man defending his life always pardoned? Loved by Claudia, of what would I not have been capable myself?

All those ideas were agitating confusedly in my head, and were far from having the clarity with which I have just expressed them. Almost involuntarily, however, I said aloud: "How can you escape the law? The frightened gardeners will have raised the alarm. Is there still time to flee?"

My voice made the two spouses tremble. They turned abruptly to look at me.

"Yes, yes—let's flee!" cried Claudia. "Come, let's take our poor child and go to the far end of the world."

Leone shook his head, and held his wife in his arms. A kind of rumor was audible in the grounds. "Listen!" he said, pricking up his ears. "It's too late—but at least they won't take me alive."

Claudia uttered a scream, and clung to Leone passionately. "Kill me first," she moaned. "I don't want to see you die."

The young woman's beautiful tresses were in disorder beneath her husband's kisses; in that undulating fleece, the redness of a flower burst forth; he was looking around, doubtless seeking for a weapon with his gaze.

Suddenly, at the same time as his, my eyes paused on that flower. He shuddered, and recoiled involuntarily, but immediately leaned over his wife, first kissed her hair, and then threw his lips over the flower, which he devoured.

"Stop! Stop!" I cried, launching myself toward him. "The Serpent-Flower! Again! Ah, how it takes its revenge!"

Leone looked up at me, his eyes full of tenderness.

"Thank you!" he said to me. "Look after her."

Claudia had straightened up, as pale as a specter. She saw her husband's face, which convulsed, his bloodied lips; she opened her mouth as if to scream, but without making a sound, fell unconscious on the floor.

A year later, almost at the same time of year, toward the end of autumn, a caleche was waiting outside the door of a lovely house that I had rented in one of the most tranquil streets in Naples.

It was there that, for more than a year, I had disputed with death for the unfortunate Claudia, whom a sharp fever had struck down on the terrible day that had robbed her of her son and her lover. I had had her removed from the deadly villa, but her condition had not permitted me to do more by taking her away from Naples.

It was with a fraternal devotion, perhaps mingled with a keener sentiment, that I had cared for her during those long, dolorous months. Many times I had thought her doomed, but then her youth, and perhaps the fervor I put into saving her, brought hope back again.

This time I had definitely triumphed; several weeks ago, convalescence had set in—but it was only the body that was commencing a rebirth, omnipotent nature hastening its work of repair, while the excessively enfeebled mind was still slumbering. It was not without a certain terror that I waited for the reawakening of sentiment.

What would happen when the soul's wound reopened?—when the fever that it had been possible to overcome was succeeded by a despair impossible to cure? Would I not be reproached for having snatched the prey from the jaws of consoling death? And, in sum, why had I done it? Had I not been guided by an egotistical sentiment, an unconfessed hope? Did I really have the right to impose life in that fashion on someone who no longer wanted it?

Those ideas had only occurred to me after the cure; during the battle with the malady I had no such thought. This time too, nature would doubtless aid me to triumph over the danger. I would take Claudia away—far away—to another clime, and gradually, the egotism of life would take hold of her again; she would thank me for having saved her...and who could tell what might happen thereafter?

The excursion she was about to make was the first I had attempted; if she stood up to it well, we would embark in a few more days.

I arranged the cushions in the caleche, made sure that the horses were not too lively, made a thousand recommendations to the coachman, and then went in search of my poor invalid. She came down mechanically, seemingly unaware, questioning nothing. She was no longer a woman now, but she was a very beautiful statue.

I made her as comfortable as possible, and we set out. A chambermaid was with us, at the front of the carriage. We went through the tumultuous city by the shortest route; I was in haste to be in the open country. The air as very calm, the sky resplendent; it was a true day of convalescence.

I kept watch on my companion's immobile visage; it was tranquil, expressionless. The eyes, however, were gazing with a kind of avidity; consciousness had not returned, but I divined that it was very close, and menacing.

As long as nothing precipitated the crisis! I don't know why I wanted it only to declare itself once we were at sea. That immensity seemed to me to be capable of diminishing human dolors to some extent, and then, it would be easier there to talk about hope, a future life, to summon God to my aid.

Claudia appeared to be interested in the play of the sunset; its gleams seemed to fascinate her—but I was in haste to return, not wanting dusk to catch us unawares.

Alas! As we came back into the city, a traffic jam stopped us. I leaned out to see what had happened. Scarcely had I turned my head than a horrible scream from Claudia cut through my heart.

A little girl had leapt up on to the footplate of the carriage, her hands full of flowers, and, laughing, she was holding out toward us a large red bouquet made up of those accursed, murderous, terrible flowers: a bouquet of Serpent-Flowers!

I uttered a frightful imprecation, while an abrupt gesture from the chambermaid sent the wretched child who had doomed us back on to the roadway.

It was too late.

Claudia had seen; Claudia had understood; that scream was the first and last of her reawakened soul. She had stood up, bolt upright, but she soon fell back on to the cushions, laughing atrociously. Her reason had fled forever.

The Serpent-Flower had finished its work.

I am writing these dolorous memories on the steamer that is taking me away, I know not where, forever.

Was it truly hazard alone that directed the events of that fantastic adventure? Personally, I can't believe that; I can clearly see the vengeance of the dead man in all of it.

I even think that Claudia's madness is due to one last weakness on the part of the lover disdained by the woman he adored, for, if I can judge the matter by the frightful void in my own soul, the impossibility of ever attaching myself to anything again, Claudia's dolor would have been irremediable, and the Serpent-Flower was merciful in taking away her memory.

Catulle Mendès (1841-1909) came to Paris in 1859, and was taken under the wing of Théophile Gautier. He began to cultivate a scandalous reputation when his short drama Roman d'une nuit *(1861) was prosecuted for obscenity, landing him in prison for a month. He fell out with Gautier over his marriage to the latter's daughter Judith, whom he left for the composer Augusta Holmes in 1869. He became a central figure in the Parnassian Movement, but proved extraordinarily adaptable and prolific thereafter, producing an enormous amount of short fiction for newspapers as well as producing significant contributions to the Decadent Movement in the novels* Zo'har *(1886),* Méphistophela *(1890) and* Gog *(1897). He was found dead in a railway tunnel, somewhat mysteriously.* "La Nuit de noces" *appeared in* Le Rose et le noir *(1885);* "Wedding Night" *was first published in* The Exigent Shadow and Other Strange Obsessions.[67]

Catulle Mendès: *Wedding Night*

A livid pallor of dawn slid through the curtains. I was not asleep, gazing at that sad light. A bell rang, violently, redoubled, echoing in the apartment, and a few moments later, Sylvain Brunel opened the door of my bedroom, followed by my domestic, dressed in haste, who picked up the lamp.

"You!" I cried.

My surprise was all the more natural because they day before, Sylvain Brunel had married a beautiful young woman with whom he had evidently been passionately smitten. What was he doing in my house at an hour when he ought still to be ecstatic in the delectable triumph of the wedding night?

My astonishment increased, and became a dolorous anxiety, when I had remarked the pale face of the visitor, his eyes injected with red bile and his lips trembling like those of a fever-victim.

As soon as we were alone, he put a hand on my shoulder and spoke very rapidly, stammering, with teeth that were chattering.

"Do you believe in the impossible? Do you believe in the prodigious chimera of the dead who live, like us, who love, hate, suffer and weep like us? In the miracle of the dead who accompany us in the street, take our arm, sit down at our table, lie down in our bed? If those things aren't true, well then, lock me up—I'm mad!"

While I considered him with an increasing stupor, he let himself fall into an armchair next to my bed.

---

[67] Available from Black Coat Press: *Don Juan in Paradise, ISBN 978-1-61227-848-3; The* Exigent Shadow, ISBN 978-1-61227-849-0; *The Little Fays in the Air*, ISBN 978-1-61227-846-9

"Listen," he went on, lowering his voice, his speech slowing, "you know how I love Gilberte, my wife! You can divine with what hectic desire, yesterday evening, I waited for the moment when the two of us would finally be alone? That moment came, so hopefully awaited. Heart melted in delight, I was outside the door of the nuptial chamber; my hand touched the key; I was about to go in...

"A frisson ran through me, from head to for, with the zigzag of an icy lightning bolt over all my flesh. What as the matter with me? At first, I didn't understand. The effect had preceded the cause. I had the symptom of terror before the terror itself. But the fear arrived very quickly, sharp and intense. Yes, I was afraid. Why? Because I thought, for no reason, about Madame de Mortales, the poor dead woman who had loved me so much, so close to the dear living one I loved so much! It was like encountering a tomb on the threshold of paradise.

"With the gaze of the spirit, which contemplates past things, I saw her, Laurencia, pale and motionless, in the big bed from which she was not to rise again, having no more life except in the depths of her eyes, where a wild and jealous amour burned; and I heard her repeating to me, with the harshness of her Aragonese accent the words that she had already said to me so frequently:

"'You will never love another woman, will you? No, never? Whether I live or die, you'll be faithful to me, forever? Oh, if you deceive me, Sylvèrte, beware! I'll avenge myself, treason for treason. Resolutely, coldly, if you prefer another woman, I'll deliver myself to another man. Even dead, for I believe that I shall wake from the eternal sleep to accomplish my vengeance.'

"I heard those mad and sinister words yesterday evening, my hand on the key of the nuptial chamber. I heard them confusedly, as if a specter were whispering in my ear. But finally, with a surge of will power, I drove away the chimeras and became master of myself; smiling at my folly, I opened the blessed door. Pale and trembling, in the lace of her peignoir, Gilberte was waiting for me, and became very pink when she saw me. I knelt down before her, like a pilgrim at the feet of a statue of the Virgin and I adored her, full of grace.

"Let those who boast of the vain joys of culpable amours say what they will; perfect intoxication, the supreme delight, is to contemplate the blush of a virgin soon to be a wife, who is frightened, but who wants it dearly. Gently, slowly, as one might touch the wings of Psyche, I had taken her in my arms, and on her lips, scarcely turned away...

"Extraordinary thing! To our kiss, it seemed to me that another kiss responded, also tender, distant, like a faithful echo. I looked at her; she smiled, more roseate; she had not heard anything. I was losing my mind, in truth. I hugged her more tightly in the crumpled malines; I felt through the lace the warm and smooth reaction of her delicate body...

"God! Who, then, outside that room, simultaneously so far away and so close at hand, had crumpled a peignoir as I had? I looked at her more intently: still smiling; this time, again, she hadn't heard anything; and that open garment allowed the sight of the frail pallor, scarcely blue-tinted by a pale vein, of her adolescent cleavage. The folly of being fortunate carried me away, redoubled by a strange rage—that of being prey, me, a man of sense and firm mind, to stupid reveries. I embraced her, I lifted Gilberte up, astonished by my rudeness, and in the alcove, I said ardent things to her, I bit her with frantic kisses, I enveloped her with insatiable caresses.

"Oh horror, horror! I tell you that those words, another voice pronounced them, down below, almost the same, heard by me alone, that those kisses, other mouths gave them, far away, and yet close by, that another body—where, then? where?—was enveloped by those caresses. There was around us an abominable parody of our amour.

"Have you, by some sad hazard, possessed your mistress one night in one of those dismal hotels near railway stations, where the neighboring rooms, only separated from yours by a thin partition, have welcomed other couples? Add to the annoyance full of shame of a dirty proximity, the irresistible conviction that the noises—the noises that were driving me mad!—were not coming from a bed that as too close at hand, but from some unknown, mysterious, terrible couch, a Sabbat camp-bed in which the damned ferment blood and blasphemy, and you will scarcely understand what I experienced!

"I struggled against the terror, always hoping to vanquish it, to drown it in amour, triumphantly to make the frisson of fear into a frisson of pleasure. In vain! In vain! I laughed with ecstasy, I gasped in horror. At one moment, while the words still repeated my words, the kisses my kisses and the caresses my caresses, I even thought, for an instant, that I saw, next to the recumbent Gilberte, so young and so beautiful, tenderly resistant—yes, next to her, in a narrow shadow—another woman, pale and cold, as Laurencia, embalmed in her tomb, must be at this moment, but loving, resisting poorly, like Gilberte!

"And when, from the vanquished modesty of the young girl-woman, I had extracted, in a redoubling of desire, the supreme confession of the sigh, a different voice, equally tender—alas, where did it come from?—died in the same sigh! Then I leapt from the bed, intoxicated by fear, seating in large droplets, and I grabbed my clothes, and I fled, and I ran through the streets, and here I am, finally. I'm mad, am I not?"

I think that there is no need to spell out the arguments by means of which I succeeded in calming the morbid excitation. I did not succeed in that without difficulty. However, after a long conversation, he consented to recognize that he had been, if not mad, at least hallucinated; that only the memory of Madame de Mortales, perhaps mingled with some remorse, had given rise to that singular aberration; and he left my house almost calm almost serene.

It is probable that I would not have thought about that adventure again, and that I would never have narrated the story, if I not read in a newspaper, two days later, a very horrible article. A warden at Père-Lachaise cemetery—a monstrous brute—had been surprised two nights before as he was violating a sepulcher abominably; and that tomb, said the newspaper was that of a young Spanish woman, recently deceased, Madame Laurencia de Mortales.

As for the abject wretch, he was tried by the Court of Assizes of the Seine, but he was acquitted, the reports of the alienist physicians having established that the monster was demented. What contributed above all to conciliating the clemency of the jury was the absurd but evident good faith with which he sustained during the trial that if he had lifted the marble slab it was because, as he was making his round, not drunk, shortly before midnight, he had been invited to do so by a soft feminine voice, which had appealed to him, sliding between the stones of the tomb, through the verdure of the yews.

Alphonse Allais (1854-1905) was a stalwart of Emile Goudeau's Hydropathes, making no small contribution to its members' reputation for prodigious alcohol consumption. A star of the Char Noir *cabaret, he also participated in the proto-surrealist Salon des Arts Incohérents in 1883-84 before going on to become the leading humorist writing for various newspapers, including* Gil Blas *and* Le Journal. *"L'Esprit d'Ellen" first appeared in* Le Chat Noir, *25 avril 1885; "El-len's Spirit" was first published in* The Adventures of Captain Cap and Other Stories.[68]

Alphonse Allais: *Ellen's Spirit*

That evening, I got home very late and utterly enervated. For the first time, in the year since Ellen had died, I had failed to honor her memory. On her deathbed, she had made me swear to remain eternally faithful to her. Mad with grief at the idea of the rightful separation, and feeling that, with her dead, every-thing would be finished for me, I had promised her what she had requested with a poor agonized smile.

Until that day, I had never broken my word; my worship of Ellen's memory had remained religious and exclusive.

Then, one day, at a wedding celebration, carried away by joyful compan-ions and beautiful girls, I had forgotten everything. My friends, wanting to chase away what they called my "black ideas," had plotted to get me drunk and throw me into the arms of some hussy.

Their plan succeeded. The girl was superb, quite expert although very young, with a red and fleshy mouth, and fascinating eyes, wide eyes like those of a grazing cow.

The image of the beloved dead woman never quit me, but became so vague and blurred on the blue horizon of my memory that I was not too cruelly ob-sessed by it.

The strong wine and the odor of women's perfumes had reawakened the beast in me—the brutal and dirty beast that, dormant in my being for such a long time, was finally compensated.

Then, in the morning, I was overwhelmed by a dolorous and irremediable nausea. The shame of my lapse caused me to leave the young woman's apart-ment so abruptly that she must have thought that I'd gone mad. All day long I walked feverishly, trying to forget my ignominy—a wasted effort. The pale

[68] Available from Black Coat Press: *The Adventures of Captain Cap*, ISBN 978-1-61227-218-4;

251

phantom of Ellen always loomed up before me, her heart-rending expression of cruel reproach brought me to the brink of tears.

When dusk fell, my anxiety became more terrible and more precise. I dared not go home, so sure was I that I would find my betrayed beloved there.

So, when I finally went into my apartment, I was less surprised than terrified.

Ellen was there, with her back turned to me, sitting in the armchair at my desk. Although it was quite dark, I saw that she was wearing the white peignoir that she had put on when she could still get up. Her favorite perfume was lingering in the apartment: a heavy and troubling scent dominated by wintergreen, which her sisters had sent her from America, and which she preferred to any other.

I stood on the threshold, mute with terror. Courage gradually returned, and, knowing full well that I was the victim of a hallucination, I struck a match and advanced into the room.

There was no one in the armchair. Nothing was out of place. But how had that perfume come to be spread around the room?

That odor, which delighted her, was odiously painful to me, and it had required all my love and patience to get used to it. Furthermore, I had put all her toilette apparatus away in a trunk, and since her death I had never touched them, so keenly did the sight of them revive my grief.

I opened the windows and went out on to the balcony until the door had dissipated completely; then my lassitude obtained the ascendancy over my enervation, and I soon fell asleep—but not for long.

There was a faint sound, as brisk and slight as the scampering of a mouse. At intervals, the sound was interrupted by a rapid click. The same perfume had resumed floating, with even greater intensity than before.

Again I struck a match and looked around. There was nothing abnormal in the room. For as long as the match burned, I didn't hear anything, but no sooner had it gone out than the faint sound resumed. Sometimes, there was a rustle of paper.

By listening attentively, I contrived to determine the nature of the sound: someone in the apartment was writing.

This time I lit my candle and got out of bed. Once again the sound ceased. Everything on my desk appeared to be in order. Trying to laugh at my hallucination, I went back to bd. As soon as obscurity was restored, the fantastic pen began to gallop over the paper again, only interrupting its flow to retrieve ink.

Crazed with fear, I dared not move under the bedclothes. I don't know whether I lost consciousness then or simply fell asleep again, but I don't know when the sound ceased.

I slept heavily until it was broad daylight. When I woke up, I remembered, and naturally attributed my nocturnal hallucination to a nightmare.

How terrified I was, however, when, driven by a curiosity that I thought superfluous, I went to examine my writing-desk.

The ink-well, which I always took care to close, was open. A pen-holder was lying there, still damp with ink. A sheet of blotting-paper had been taken out and used, certainly not by me as I always use powder.

The blotting-paper had evidently been used to dry a fresh page. The last lines and the signature were clearly visible there, although unreadable because of their reversal. Naturally, the idea of inverting the writing by means of a mirror occurred to me.

Immediately, I saw the signature *Ellen*, horribly distinct. It was definitely her signature, but with a hint of cruelty and precision that chilled me. Even with an effort, however, I could not reward any more, for the page, too dry when the blotting-paper as applied to it, had only left vague traces.

Since that moment, I've been unable to obtain a moment's sleep. Every night a strange perfume floats around me, dominated by wintergreen.

Desperately, I persist in trying to read the dead woman's illegible scrawl in the mirror, which has put an end to my repose—for Ellen will never forgive me for my base treason.

Guy de Maupassant (1850-1893) became the leading short story writer of the 1880s and made an important contribution, alongside Catulle Mendès, to the boom in newspaper short fiction, particularly in the pages of Le Figaro, Gil Blas and L'Écho de Paris. Although his primary reputation was for Naturalistic fiction, and the adaptation for the stage of his brutal "Mademoiselle Fifi" (1882) helped make the reputation of the Grand Guignol theater by virtue of the artful employment of a bladder filled with artificial blood, the sideline he maintained in contes fantastiques made him one of the principal contributors to that genre and one of the great artists of ambiguity. A version of "Le Horla" appeared in Gil Blas, 26 octobre 1886, but an expanded version (the one translated herein), deftly incorporating material previously published in Gil Blas on 17 février 1885 as "Lettre d'un fou," and was used as the title story of a collection published by Paul Ollendorf in 1887, and was rapidly established as a classic of the weird fiction genre. The present translation is original to this volume.[69]

Guy de Maupassant: *The Horla*

8 May. What an admirable day! I spent the whole morning lying in the grass in front of my house, under the enormous plane tree that covers, shelters and shades it entirely. I love this country and I love living here because I have roots here, the profound and delicate roots that attach a man to the land where his ancestors were born and died, which attaches him to what he thinks and what he eats, to customs as to nourishment, to local ways of speech, to the intonations of the peasants, to the odors of the soil, the villages and the air itself.

I love my house, where I grew up. From my windows I can see the Seine, which flows past my garden behind the road, almost in my home, the great and broad Seine, which goes to Rouen and Le Havre, covered with passing boats.

To the left, in the distance, is Rouen, the vast city with the blue roofs, under the pointed population of Gothic bell-towers. They are innumerable, slender or broad, dominated by the cast-iron steeple of the cathedral, and full of bells that ring in the blue atmosphere of beautiful mornings, hurling their mild and distant metallic hum as far as me, the brazen song that the breeze brings me, sometimes more loudly and sometimes fainter, according to whether it is alert or drowsy.

How good it is this morning!

At about eleven o'clock, a long convoy of ships drawn by a tug, as large as a fly, which scarcely gasped as it vomited a thick smoke, filed past my gate.

---

[69] Available from Black Coat Press: "*Martian Mankind*" (1887) in *News from the Moon*, ISBN 978-1-932983-89-0.

After two English schooners, whose red flags undulated against the sky, came a superb Brazilian three-master, all white, admirably neat and shiny. I saluted it, I don't know why, so much pleasure did it give me to see that ship.

12 May. I have had a slight fever for a few days; I'm suffering—or rather, I feel sad.

Where do these mysterious influences come from, which change our happiness into discouragement and our confidence into distress? One might think that the air, the invisible air, is full of unknowable Powers, to the mysterious neighborhood of which we are subjected. I wake up full of gaiety, with the desire to sing in my throat—why? I go down to the water, and suddenly, after a short walk. I return desolate, as if some misfortune were awaiting me at home—why? Is it a cold frisson that, brushing my skin, has jangled my nerves and darkened my soul? Is it the form of the clouds, or the color of the daylight, the color of things, so variable, which, passing before my eyes, has troubled my thoughts? How can one tell? Everything that surrounds us, everything that we see without looking at it, everything that we brush without being aware of it, everything that we touch without feeling it, everything that we encounter without distinguishing it, has rapid, surprising and inexplicable effects on us, on our organs, and via them, on our ideas and our very hearts.

How profound it is, the mystery of the Invisible! We cannot fathom it with our wretched senses, with our eyes that are unable to perceive either the very small or the very large, that which is too close or too far away, the inhabitants of a star or the inhabitants of a drop of water...with our ears, which deceive us, because they transmit the vibrations of the atmosphere in sonorous notes. They are fays who work the miracle of changing that movement into sound, and by means of that metamorphosis give birth to music, which renders the mute agitation of nature into song...with our sense of smell, feebler than that of a dog...with our taste, which can scarcely discern the age of a wine!

Oh, if we had other organs, which would accomplish other miracles in our favor, what things we might yet discover around us!

16 May. I am definitely ill. I was so healthy last month! I have a fever, an atrocious fever, or rather a feverish enervation, which renders my soul as painful as my body. I have incessantly the frightful sensation of a menacing danger, the apprehension of a misfortune that comes when death is approaching, the presentiment that is doubtless the affliction of an illness still unknown, germinating in the blood and in the flesh.

18 May. I have just been to consult a physician, because I can no longer sleep. He found my pulse rapid, my eyes dilated, my nerves vibrant, but without any alarming symptom. I have to subject myself to cold showers and drink potassium bromide.

25 May. No change! My condition is veritably bizarre. As evening approaches, an incomprehensible anxiety invades me, as if the night concealed a terrible menace for me. I dine quickly, and then I try to read, but I don't understand the words; I can scarcely make out the letters. Then I march back and forth in my drawing room, under the oppression of a confused and irresistible dread, the dread of sleep and the dread of the bed.

At about ten o'clock I go up to my bedroom. Scarcely have I entered than I give two turns to the key and I push the bolts; I'm afraid...of what? Thus far, there is nothing to fear. I open my cupboards, I look under the bed; I listen...I listen...for what? Is it not strange that a simple illness, perhaps a disturbance of the circulation, the irritation of a nerve-net, a slight congestion, a very slight perturbation in the functioning, so imperfect and so delicate, of our living machine, can make a melancholic out of the most joyful of men, and a coward of the bravest?

Then I go to bed and I wait for sleep as one waits for the executioner. I wait with the fear of its coming, and my heart hammers and my limbs tremble; and my entire body shivers in the warmth of the sheets, until the moment when I suddenly fall into repose, as one falls in order to drown oneself in a gulf of stagnant water. I do not sense it coming, as I did before, that perfidious sleep, hidden nearby, which lies in wait for me, which is going to seize me by the head, close my eyes and annihilate me.

I sleep—for a long time...two or three hours...and then a dream—no, a nightmare—grips me. I am well aware that I am lying down and that I am asleep...I sense it and I know it...but I also sense that someone approaches me, gazes at me, palpates me, climbs on to my bed, kneels on my breast, takes my neck between his hands and squeezes...squeezes...with all his strength, in order to strangle me.

I struggle, bound by the atrocious impotence that paralyzes us in dreams; I want to cry out—I cannot; I want to move—I cannot; I try, with frightful efforts, breathlessly, to turn over, to throw off the being that is crushing me and choking me—I cannot!

And suddenly, I wake up, panicked, covered in sweat. I light a candle. I'm alone.

After that crisis, which is renewed every night, I finally fall asleep, calmly, until dawn.

2 June. My condition has worsened. What is the matter with me? The bromide has no effect; the cold showers have no effect. A little while ago, in order to fatigue my body, which is, however, so weary, I went for a walk in the forest of Roumare. I thought at first that fresh air, full of the odor of grass and leaves, would pour a new blood into my veins and a new energy into my heart. I took a great hunting avenue and then turned toward La Bouille, via a narrow path be-

tween two armies of immeasurably high trees, which put a thick green roof, almost black, between the sky and me.

A shudder suddenly seized me, not a shiver of cold, but a strange shudder of anguish.

I hastened my steps, anxious about being alone in the wood, frightened without reason, stupidly, by the profound solitude. Suddenly, it seemed to me that I was being followed, that someone was marching on my heels, close enough to touch me.

I turned round abruptly. I was alone. I only saw behind me the straight, broad, empty pathway, high and redoubtably empty; and in the other direction it extended as far as the eye could see, exactly similar, frightening.

I closed my eyes. Why? And I started spinning on one heel, very quickly, like a top. I almost fell over; I opened my eyes again; the trees were dancing, the ground floating; I had to sit down. Then, oh, I no longer knew which way I had come. A bizarre idea! Bizarre! Bizarre idea! I no longer knew anything at all. I set forth in the direction that happened to be to my right, and I came back to the avenue that had taken me into the middle of the forest.

3 June. The night has been horrible. I'm going away for a few weeks. A little voyage will doubtless set me right.

2 July. I'm back. I'm cured. At any rate, I've had a charming excursion. I visited Mont Saint-Michel, which I didn't know.

What a vision, when one arrives, like me, in Avranches, toward the end of the day. The town is on a hill, and I was conducted into the public garden on the edge of the town. I uttered a cry of astonishment. An enormous bay extended before me, as far as the eye could see, between two divergent coasts lost in the mist in the distance; and in the middle of that immense yellow bay, under a sky of gold and light, a strange mountain rose, somber and pointed, in the middle of the sands. The sun had just disappeared, and on the horizon, still flamboyant, the profile was designed of the fantastic rock that bears a fantastic monument on its summit.

At dawn, I went toward it. The tide was out, as it had been the previous evening, and I saw the surprising abbey looming up before me, as I approached it. After walking for several hours, I reached the enormous block of stone that bears the little village dominated by the great church. Having climbed the steep and narrow street, I went into the most admirable Gothic dwelling constructed for God on earth, as vast as a town, full of low rooms crushed beneath the vaults and high galleries sustained by frail columns. I went into that gigantic granite jewel, as light as lace, covered with towers, svelte pinnacles, which twisted staircases climb, and which launch their bizarre heads, bristling with chimeras, devils, fantastic beasts and monstrous flowers, into the blue sky of the days and the black sky of the nights, linked together by delicately wrought arches.

When I was at the summit, I said to the monk who was accompanying me: "How well you must be here, Father!"

He replied: "There's a great deal of wind, Monsieur," and we started chatting while watching the tide come in, which ran over the sand and covered it with a steely armor.

And the monk told me stories, all the old stories about the place, legends, always legends.

One of them struck me forcefully. The local people, those of the mount, claim that voices can be heard by night in the sands, and then two goats can be heard bleating, one with a loud voice, the other with a faint voice. The incredulous affirm that they are the cries of sea birds, which sometimes resemble bleating and sometimes human plaints, but belated fishermen swear that they have encountered an old shepherd roaming the dunes between two tides, around the little town thrown so far into the sea, whose head, covered by a hood, can never be seen, and who guides, marching before him, a billy-goat with the face of a man and a nanny-goat with the face of a woman, both with long white hair, talking incessantly, quarreling in an unknown language, and then suddenly ceasing to shout in order to bleat with all their might.

I said to the monk: "Do you believe that?"

He murmured: "I don't know."

I said: "If other beings than us exist on earth, why have we not known them for a long time; why would you not have seen them yourself? Why have I not seen them?"

He replied: "Have we seen the thousandth part of what exists? Look, here is the wind, which is the greatest force of nature, which knocks men over, fells edifices, uproots trees, raises the sea in mountains of water, destroys cliffs, throws great ships to the breakers, the wind that kills, which whistles, which moans, which roars—have you seen it, and can you see it? It exists, thought."

I fell silent before that simple reasoning. That man was a sage, or perhaps a simpleton; I would not have been able to say exactly, but I fell silent. What he said then, I had often thought.

3 July. I slept badly; certainly, there is a feverish influence here, for my coachman is suffering from the same illness as me. When I came home yesterday I noticed his singular pallor. I asked him: "What's the matter with you, Jean?"

"I can no longer sleep, Monsieur; it's my nights that eat my days. Since Monsieur's departure, it holds me like a spell."

The other domestics are healthy, though—but I have a great fear of being afflicted again myself.

4 July. I am definitely afflicted again. My old nightmares have returned. Last night, I sensed someone crouching on me, and who, his mouth on mine,

was drinking my life between my lips. Yes, he was drawing it from my throat as a leech might have done. Then he got up, sated, and I woke up, so bruised, exhausted and worn out that I could no longer move. If this continues for a few more days I shall certainly leave again.

5 July. Have I lost my mind? What happened during the night is so strange that my heads reels when I think of it.

As I now do every evening, I had locked my door; then, being thirsty, I drank half a glass of water, and I noticed by chance that my carafe was full all the way to the crystal stopper.

I went to bed thereafter, and I fell into one of my frightful slumbers, from which I was extracted after about two hours by an even more frightful shock.

Imagine a man who is asleep, who is stabbed, and who wakes up with a dagger in his lung, gasping, covered in blood, who can no longer breathe, and who does not understand—that's it.

Having finally recovered my reason, I was thirsty again. I lit a candle and went to the table where my carafe was placed. I lifted it up and tipped it over my glass; nothing came out. It was empty! It was completely empty! At first, I did not understand it at all; then, suddenly, I felt an emotion so terrible that I had to sit down, or rather, I fell into a chair. Then I leapt to my feet again in order to look around. Then I sat down again, bewildered by astonishment and fear, before the transparent crystal. I contemplated it with fixed eyes, seeking to explain it. My hands were trembling. Had someone drunk that water, then? Who? Me? Doubtless me; it could only have been me. I was a sleepwalker, then; I lived, without knowing it, the mysterious double life that makes us suspect that there might be two beings within us, or that a stranger, unknown and invisible, animates our captive body at times when our soul is torpid, which obeys that other as ourselves, more than ourselves.

Oh, who could understand my abominable anguish? Who could comprehend the emotion of a man, sound of mind, awake and full of reason, who is looking fearfully through the glass of a carafe, from which the water has disappeared while he was asleep? And I remained there until daylight, without daring to go back to bed.

6 July. I am going mad. Someone drunk the whole contents of my carafe again last night—or rather, I drank it.

But was it me? Was it me? Who else could it be? Who? Oh, my God, I'm going mad! Who can save me?

10 July. I have carried out surprising trials.

Decidedly, I'm mad! And yet...

On 6 July, before going to bed, I placed on my table wine, milk, water, bread and strawberries.

Someone drank—I drank—all the water and a little of the milk. The wine, the bread and the strawberries were untouched.

On 7 July I repeated the same experiment, which gave the same result.

On 8 July I omitted the water and the milk. Nothing was touched.

Finally, on 9 July, I replaced only the water and the milk, having carefully wrapped the carafes in white muslin cloth and tying the stoppers. Then I rubbed my lips, my beard and my hands with black lead and I went to bed.

The invincible sleep gripped me, soon followed by the atrocious awakening. I had not stirred, eve my sheets were unstained. I ran to my table. The pieces of cloth enclosing the bottles were still immaculate. I untied the strings, palpitating with dread. All the water had been drunk! All the milk had been drunk! Oh, my God!

I shall depart at once for Paris.

12 July. Paris. I have, therefore, lost my head in the last few days. I must have been the victim of my nervous imagination, unless I really am a sleepwalker, or I have been subject to one of those observed but thus far inexplicable instances known as suggestions. In any case, my madness touched dementia, but twenty-four hours in Paris have sufficed to restore my aplomb.

Yesterday, after excursions and visits, which enabled a new and vivifying air to pass into my soul, I finished me evening at the Théâtre Français. A play by Alexandre Dumas *fils* was being performed, and that alert and powerful wit completed my cure. Certainly, solitude is dangerous for hard-working intelligences. We need people around us who are thinking and talking. When we are alone for a long time, we populate the void with phantoms.

I returned to the hotel very cheerful, via the boulevards. Rubbing shoulders with the crowds I thought, not without irony, about my terrors and suppositions of last week, for I believed—yes, I believed—that an invisible being was living under my roof. How weak and ready to take fright our head is, and quick to go astray as soon as a small incomprehensible event strikes us! Instead of concluding with the simple words: "I don't understand, because the cause escapes me," we immediately imagine frightful mysteries and supernatural powers.

14 July. The Festival of the Republic. I walked through the streets. The fireworks and the flags amused me like a child. It is, however, quite stupid to be joyful on a day fixed by government decree. The people are an imbecilic herd, sometimes stupidly patient and sometimes ferociously in revolt. They are told to amuse themselves; they amuse themselves. They are told to fight with their neighbor; they fight. They are told to vote for the Emperor; they vote for the Emperor. Then they are told to vote for the Republic, and they vote for the Republic.

Those who direct them are also stupid, but instead of obeying people they obey principles, which can only be stupid, sterile and false, by virtue of the very fact that they are principles—which is to say, ideas reputed to be certain and immutable, in this world where nothing is certain, since light is an illusion and sound is an illusion.

16 July. Yesterday I saw things that have troubled me greatly.

I dined at the home of my cousin, Madame Sablé, whose husband is in command of the 76th Chasseurs at Limoges. I found myself in the company of two young women, one of whom is the wife of a physician, Doctor Parent, who is much occupied with nervous maladies and the extraordinary manifestations to which experiments in hypnotism and suggestion and presently giving rise. He recounted to us at length the prodigious results obtained by English scientists and physicians of the Nancy school.[70]

The facts that he advanced appeared to me to be so bizarre that I declared myself utterly incredulous.

"We are," he affirmed, "on the point of discovering one of the most important secrets of nature—I mean, one of the most important secrets on earth, for there are certainly more important ones out there in the stars. Since human beings have been thinking, and able to speak and write their thoughts, they have made contact with a mystery impenetrable for their crude and imperfect senses, and have tried to compensate, by the effect of their intelligence, for the impotence of their sense-organs. When that intelligence was still in a rudimentary state, the haunting of invisible phenomena took banally frightening forms. That gave birth to popular belief in the supernatural, legends of prowling spirits, fays, gnomes revenants—I will even say the legend of God, for our conceptions of the creator, from whatever religion they come to us, are the most mediocre, the most stupid and the most unacceptable to emerge from the fearful brain of creatures. Nothing is more true than the saying of Voltaire: 'God made man in his image, but man has returned the compliment.'

"For a little more than a century, however, something new has seemingly been sensed. Mesmer and a few others have put us on an unexpected track, and we have truly arrived, especially in the last four or five years, at surprising results."

My cousin, also very incredulous, smiled. Doctor Parent said to her: "Would you like me to try to put you to sleep, Madame?"

"Yes, I'd like that."

She sat down in an armchair, and he commenced to gaze at her intently, fascinating her. I suddenly felt slightly troubled, my heart beating rapidly and

---

[70] The École de Nancy became celebrated in the 1880s as one of the two most important establishments—the other being the Salpêtrière in Paris—contributing to the study of hypnosis, and its development as a therapeutic method by Ambroise-Auguste Liébeault and Hippolyte Bernheim.

my throat constricted. I saw Madame Sablé's eyes become heavy, her mouth twisted and her bosom heaving.

After ten minutes, she was asleep.

"Place yourself behind her," said the physician.

I sat down behind her. He put a visiting card into her hand, saying: "This is a mirror; what do you see in it?"

She replied: "I see my cousin."

"What is he doing?"

"He's twisting his moustache."

"And now?"

"He's taking a photograph from his pocket."

"What is that photograph?"

"His own."

It was true. And that photograph had just been delivered to me that same evening, at the hotel.

"What is his position in the portrait?"

"He is standing up with his hat in his hand."

Thus, she could see in that card, in that blank piece of cardboard, as she would have seen in a mirror.

The young women, frightened, said: "Enough! Enough!"

But the doctor ordered: "You will get up tomorrow at eight o'clock; then you will go to find your cousin at his hotel and you will ask him to lend you five thousand francs, for which your husband has asked you, which he requires for his imminent voyage."

Then he woke her up.

As I returned to the hotel I thought about that curious séance, and doubts assailed me, not with regard to the absolute and unsuspectable good faith of my cousin, whom I had known since childhood like a sister, but regarding possible trickery on the part of the doctor. Might he not have been hiding a mirror in his hand, which he had shown to the sleeping young woman at the same time as the visiting card? Professional conjurers do far more singular things.

I went in, therefore, and went to bed.

The next morning, at about half past eight, I was woken up by my valet de chambre, who said to me: "Madame Sablé is asking to speak to Monsieur immediately."

I got dressed in haste and received her.

She sat down, greatly disturbed, her eyes lowered, and without lifting her veil she said: "My dear cousin, I have a great favor to ask of you."

"What is it, cousin?"

"It embarrasses me greatly to say this, and yet it is necessary. I need, absolutely need, five thousand francs."

"Get away—you?"

"Yes, me—or rather, my husband, who has charged me with finding them."

I was so amazed that I stammered my responses. I asked her whether she was truly not making fun of me with Doctor Parent, whether it was not a simple farce prepared I advance and very well played.

On looking at her attentively, however, all my doubts dissipated. She was trembling with anguish, so painful was that step for her, and I understood that there were sobs caught in her throat.

I knew that she was rich and I said: "What! Your husband does not have five thousand francs at his disposal. Come on, reflect. Are you sure that he has charged you with asking me for them?"

She hesitated for a few seconds, as if she were making a great effort to search her memory, and then she replied: "Yes...yes...I'm sure of it."

"He has written to you?"

She hesitated again, reflecting. I divined that the labor was torturing her mind. She did not know. She only knew that she had to borrow five thousand francs for her husband—so she dared to lie.

"Yes, he has written to me."

"When? You didn't say anything about it yesterday."

"I received the letter this morning."

"Can you show it to me?"

"No...no...no...it contains intimate things...too personal...I...I burned it."

"Your husband has debts, then?"

She hesitated again, and then murmured: "I don't know."

Abruptly, I declared: "It's just that I can't dispose of five thousand francs at the present moment, my dear cousin."

She uttered a cry of pain. "Oh! Oh, I beg you, I beg you, find them..."

She was excited, putting her hands together as if she were imploring me. I heard her voice change tone; she wept and stammered, harassed and dominated by the irresistible order she had received.

"Oh! Oh, I beg you...if you knew how I'm suffering...I need them today."

I took pity on her. "You'll have them soon, I swear."

"Oh, thank you, thank you!" she cried. "How good you are."

"Do you remember what happened yesterday at your house?" I said.

"Yes."

"Do you recall that Doctor Parent put you to sleep?"

"Yes."

"Well, he ordered you to come and borrow five thousand francs from me this morning, and you're obeying that suggestion at this moment."

She reflected for a few seconds, and replied: "But it's my husband who is asking for them."

For an hour, I tried to convince her, but I could not succeed.

When she had gone, I ran to the doctor's house. He was about to go out; he listened to me, smiling. Then he said: "Do you believe now?"

"Yes, it's necessary."

"Let's go to your relative's house."

She was already asleep on a chaise longue, overwhelmed by fatigue. The physician took her pulse, looked at her for some time, with one hand raised to her eyes, which gradually closed under the unsustainable effort of that magnetic power.

When she was asleep: "Your husband no longer needs five thousand francs. You are therefore going to forget that you asked your cousin to lend them to you, and, if he mentions it to you, you will not understand."

Then he woke her up. I took a portfolio out of my pocket.

"Here, my dear cousin, is what you asked me for this morning."

She was so surprised that I dared not persist. I tried, however, to reanimate her memory, but she denied it forcefully, thinking that I was making fun of her, and nearly became annoyed in the end.

There it is! I've just returned, and I haven't been able to eat breakfast, so much has that experiment disturbed me.

19 July. Many people to whom I have recounted that adventure have made fun of me. I no longer know what to think. The sage says: Perhaps...

21 July. I had dinner at Bougival and then I spent the evening at the boatmen's dance-hall. Decidedly, everything depends on the location and the environment. To believe in the supernatural on the Île de la Grenouillère would be the height of folly...but on the summit of Mont Saint-Michel? In India? We are frightfully subject to the influence that surrounds us. I shall go home next week.

30 July. I returned home yesterday. All is well.

2 August. Nothing new; the weather is superb. I spend my days watching the Seine flow.

4 August. Quarrels among my domestics. They claim that someone is breaking glasses in the cupboards by night. The valet de chambre accuses the cook, who accuses the laundry-maid, who accuses the other two. Who is the guilty party! It would require a fine mind to say!

6 August. This time, I am not mad. I have seen...I have seen...I have seen! I can no longer doubt...I have seen! I still feel a chill all the way to my fingernails, fear to the marrow of my bones. I have seen!

I was strolling for two hours, in broad daylight, in my rose-garden, in the path of autumn rose-bushes, which are commencing to flower.

As I stopped to look at a "Géant des Batailles" that bore three magnificent flowers, I saw, saw distinctly, at close range, the stem of one of the roses bend, as if an invisible hand had twisted it, and then break, as if that hand had plucked it. Then the flower rose up, following a curve than an arm would have described in bearing it to a mouth, and it remained suspended in the transparent air, all alone, motionless, a frightful red patch three paces from my eyes.

Bewildered, I threw myself upon it in order to seize it. I found nothing there; it had disappeared. Then I was gripped by a furious anger against myself, for it is not permissible for a rational and serious man to have such hallucinations.

But was it really a hallucination? I went back to look for the stem and I found it immediately on the bush, freshly broken, between two other roses still on the branch.

Then I went back inside, my soul disturbed, for I am certain now, as certain as the alternation of days and nights, that an invisible being is living nearby, which nourishes itself on milk and water, which can touch things, pick them up and move them, and is therefore endowed with a material nature, although imperceptible to our senses, and which lives, like me, under my roof.

7 August. I slept tranquilly. It has drunk the water from my carafe, but has not troubled my slumber.

I wonder whether I am mad. Sometimes, while walking in the sunlight along the river, doubts come to me regarding my reason; not vague doubts, such as I have had thus far, but precise, absolute doubts. I have seen madmen; I have known some who remained intelligent, lucid and clear-sighted, in all matters of life, save for one point. They spoke about everything clearly, with subtlety and profundity, but suddenly their thought touched the reef of their folly and was torn to pieces there, scattering and sinking in that frightful and furious ocean full of bounding waves, fogs and squalls known as "dementia."

Certainly, I would believe myself to be mad, absolutely mad, if I were not conscious, if I were not perfectly aware of my situation, if I were not fathoming it and analyzing it with a complete lucidity. I must be, therefore, in sum, a rational victim of hallucination. An unknown disturbance must have been produced in my brain, one of those disturbances that physiologists are attempting to note and specify today; and that disturbance must have caused a profound fissure in my mind, in the order and logic of my ideas. Similar phenomena occur in dreams, which take us through the most implausible phantasmagorias without our being surprised, because the verificatory apparatus, the sense of inspection, is asleep, while the imaginative faculty is awake and working. Might it not be that one of the imperceptible keys of the cerebral keyboard is paralyzed in me? After accidents, people lose the memory of proper names, or verbs, or numbers, or only dates. The localizations of all the parcels of thought is proven today. So, what is astonishing about my faculty of discerning the unreality of certain hallucinations being numbed at the present moment?

Gradually, however, an inexplicable malaise penetrated me. A force, it seemed to me, an occult force, paralyzed me, stopped me, prevented me from going any further, calling me back. I experienced the dolorous need to go home that oppresses you when you have left a beloved invalid in the house, and the presentiment grips you of an aggravation of her illness.

So, I came back involuntarily, sure that I would find, in my house, some bad news, a letter or a telegram. There was nothing, and I was more surprised and more anxious than I would have been if I had had another fantastic vision.

8 August. I spent a terrible evening yesterday. It is no longer manifest, but I sense it near me, spying n me, watching me, penetrating me, dominating me, and more redoubtable in hiding thus than if it were signaling its invisible but constant presence by supernatural phenomena.

I slept, however.

9 August. Nothing, but I'm afraid.

10 August. Nothing; what will happen tomorrow?

1 August. Still nothing; I can no longer remain in my house with this dread and the thought that has entered my soul; I'm going to leave.

12 August, ten o'clock in the evening. All day I wanted to go away; I could not do it. I wanted to accomplish that act of liberty, so simple and so facile—to go out, to climb into my carriage in order to go to Rouen. I could not do it. Why?

13 August. When one is afflicted by certain maladies, all the springs of the physical being seem broken, all energies annihilated, all muscles relaxed; the bones become as soft as the flesh and the flesh as limpid as water. I am experiencing that in my mental being in a strange and desolating fashion. I no longer have any strength, any courage, any self-domination or any power even to set my will in motion. I can no longer exercise my will, but someone is willing for me, and I obey.

14 August. I'm doomed! Someone possesses my soul and is governing it; someone is ordering all my actions, all my movements and all my thoughts. I am no longer anything within myself but an enslaved and terrified spectator of everything that I do. I want to go out; I cannot. It does not want that, and I remain, bewildered and tremulous, in the armchair in which it holds me seated. I only want to get up, to get to my feet, in order to believe that I am my own master; I

cannot! I am riveted to my seat, and my seat adheres to the ground in such a way that no force can lift us up.

Then, suddenly, it is necessary, it is necessary that I go into the depths of my garden to pick strawberries and eat them. And I go. I pick strawberries and I eat them. Oh, my God! My God, my God! Is there a God? If there is one, deliver me, save me, help me! Pardon! Pity! Mercy! Save me! Oh, what suffering! What torture! What horror!

15 August. Certainly, this is how my poor cousin was possessed and dominated when she came to borrow five thousand francs from me. She was subject to a foreign will that had entered into her, like another soul, a parasitic and dominating soul. Is that how the world will end?

But what is the one that governs me, this invisible, unknowable being, this prowler of a supernatural race?

Invisible beings exist, then. How, then, have they not been manifest in a precise fashion, as they are to me, since the beginning of the world? I have never read anything that resembles what is happening in my abode. Oh, if only I could quit it, if I could go away, flee and not return! I would be saved—but I cannot.

16 August. I was able to escape today for two hours, like a prisoner who chances to find the door of his cell open. I suddenly felt that I was free, and that it had gone away. I ordered the carriage to be harnessed quickly, and I went to Rouen. Oh, what a joy to be able to say to a man who obeys: "Go to Rouen!"

I had the carriage stop outside the library and I asked for the loan of Doctor Hermann Herestauss' great treatise on the unknown inhabitants of the ancient and modern world. Them, as I was about to climb back into my coupé, I wanted to say: "To the railways station!" and I shouted—I did not say, I shouted, in a voice so loud that passers-by turned round: "To the house," and I fell, crazed by anguish, on the cushion of my carriage. It had found me again and recaptured me.

17 August. What a night! What a night! And yet it seems to me that I ought to rejoice. Until one o'clock in the morning, I read! Hermann Herestauss, doctor of philosophy and theogony, has written the history and the manifestations of all invisible beings prowling around humans or dreamed by them. He describes their origins, their domain and their power. But none of them resemble the one that is haunting me. One might think that humans, since they have been thinking, have had a presentiment and a fear of a new being, stronger than them, their successor in this world, and that, sensing it to be imminent but being unable to foresee the nature of that master, they have created, in their terror, an entire fantastic population of occult beings, vague phantoms born of fear.

So, having read until one o'clock in the morning, I went to sit down next to my open window in order to refresh my forehead and my thoughts in the calm nocturnal wind.

It was good, it was warm. How I would once have loved that night!

No moon. The stars were quivering scintillations in the depths of the sky. Who inhabits those worlds? What forms, what living beings, what animals and plants, are out there? Do those who think in those distant worlds know more than we do? Can they do more than we can? What can they see that we do not know? Will one of them, one day or another, traversing space, appear on our earth in order to conquer it, as the Normans once crossed the sea to subjugate weaker peoples?

We are so weak, so unarmed, so ignorant, so small, those of us on this particle of mud that is spinning, circling in a drop of water.

I became drowsy while dreaming thus in the cool evening breeze.

Having slept for about forty minutes, I opened my eyes again without making a movement, awakened by I know not what confused and bizarre emotion.

I could see nothing at first; then, suddenly, it seemed to me that a page of the book that remained open on my table had just turned of its own accord. No breath of air had entered through my window. I was surprised, and I waited. After four minutes or so, I saw—yes, I saw with my eyes—another page rise up and descend on to the previous one, as if a finger had turned it. My armchair was empty, seemed empty. But I understood that it was there, sitting in my place, and that it was reading. With a furious bound, the bound of a beast in revolt going to eviscerate its tamer, I traversed my room in order to seize it, in order to grasp it, in order to kill it! But before I had reached it my chair was tipped backwards, as if something were fleeing before me...my table oscillated, my lamp fell and went out, and my window closed, as if a surprised malefactor had launched himself into the night, taking the battens in both hands.

So, it had run away; it had been afraid, afraid of me!

In that case...in that case...tomorrow, or some day, I might be able to hold it under my fists and crush it against the ground! Do not dogs sometimes bite and kill their masters?

18 August. I have been thinking all day. Oh yes, I will obey it, follow its impulsions, accomplish all its instructions, make myself humble, submissive, cowardly. It is the stronger. But a time will come...

19 August. I know, I know...I know everything. I have just read this in the *Revue du Monde Scientifique*:

"Curious news has reached us from Rio de Janeiro. A madness, and epidemic of madness comparable to the contagions of dementia that afflicted the people of Europe in the Middle Ages, is raging at this moment in the province of Sao Paulo. The bewildered inhabitants are quitting their houses, deserting their villages, abandoning their crops, saying that they are being pursued, possessed and governed like human livestock by invisible but tangible beings, vampires of a sort that nourish themselves on their life during their sleep and which also drink water and milk without appearing to touch any other aliment.

"Professor Don Pedro Henriquez, accompanied by several knowledgeable physicians, has departed for the province of Sao Paulo in order to study on the spot the origins and the manifestations of this surprising madness, and to propose to the Emperor the measures that seem most appropriate to recall the peoples in delirium to reason."

Aha! I remember; I recall the beautiful Brazilian three-master that passed under my windows, going up the Seine on the eighth of May last. I thought it so pretty, so cheerful! The Being was on it, coming from out there, where its race was born. And it saw me! It also saw my white dwelling, and it leapt from the ship on to the bank. Oh, my God!

Now I know, I have divined the truth. The reign of humankind is over.

It has come: the one whom the terrors of naïve peoples dreaded; the one whom anxious priests exorcized, whom sorcerers evoked on somber nights without yet seeing it appear, to whom the presentiments of the temporary masters of the world lent the monstrous or gracious forms of gnomes, spirits, jinn, fays and farfadets. After the crude conceptions of primitive fear, more perspicacious humans have had a clearer presentiment of it. Mesmer had divined it, and the physicians, for ten years already, have discovered, in a precise fashion, the nature of its power, before it had exercised that power itself. They have toyed with that weapon of the new Lord, the domination of a mysterious will over the human soul, become a slave. They have called it magnetism, hypnotism, suggestion—what do I know? I have seen one of them play like imprudent children with that horrible power! Woe betide us! Woe betide humankind! It has come, the...the...what is it called, the...? It seems to me that it is crying its name to me, but I cannot hear it...the...yes, it is crying... I'm listening...I can...repeat it...the...Horla[71].... I have heard...the Horla...that's it...the Horla, it has come...

Ah! the vulture has eaten the dove; the wolf has eaten the sheep; the lion has devoured the buffalo with sharp horns; humankind has killed the lion with arrows, with swords, with gunpowder; but the Horla will make of humans what we have made of the horse and the ox—its thing, its servant and its nourishment—solely by the power of its will. Woe betide us!

However, an animal sometimes revolts and kills the one who has tamed it...I too want to...I could...but it's necessary to know it, to touch it, to see it. Scholars say that the eyes of animals, different from ours, do not distinguish things as ours do...and my eyes cannot distinguish the newcomer that is oppressing me.

---

[71] i.e. *Hors là*: outside, or beyond.

Why? Oh, now I recall the words of the monk of Mont Saint-Michel: "Have we seen the thousandth part of what exists? Look, here is the wind, which is the greatest force of nature, which knocks men over, fells edifices, uproots trees, raises the sea in mountains of water, destroys cliffs, throws great ships to the breakers, the wind that kills, which whistles, which moans, which roars— have you seen it, and can you see it? It exists, though."

And I also thought: My eyes are so feeble, so imperfect, that they cannot even distinguish solid bodies if they are as transparent as glass. If an unsilvered mirror bars my path, I might throw myself upon it as a bird that has entered into a room breaks its head on the window panes. A thousand other things deceive sight and cause it to err. What is astonishing, then, in that it is unable to perceive a new substance, which light traverses.

A new being! Why not? One must surely come. Why should we be the last? We cannot distinguish it, like all the others created before us? That is because its nature is more perfect, its substance more refined and more complete than ours, because ours is so feeble, so awkwardly conceived, encumbered by organs always fatigued, always forced, like excessively complex mechanisms, because ours, which lives like a plant and like an animal, nourishes itself with difficulty on air, grass and meat, an animal machine prey to maladies, to deformations, to putrefaction, wheezy, poorly regulated, naïve and bizarre, ingenuously badly made, crude and delicate work, a sketch of a being that might become intelligent and superb.

We are few, so little in this world, from oysters to humankind. Why not one more, once the period is accomplished that separates the successive appearances of all the various species?

Why not one more? Why not also other trees with immense and splendid flowers perfuming entire regions? Why not other elements than fire, air, earth and water? They are four, only four, those nursing fathers of beings! What a pity! Why are there not forty, four hundred or four thousand? How poor, paltry and miserable everything is! Meanly provided, dryly invented, heavily made! Oh, the elephant and the hippopotamus, what grace! The camel, what elegance!

But what do you say of the butterfly, a flying flower? I dream of one that would be as large as a hundred worlds, with wings of which I cannot even express the form, the beauty, the color and the movement. But I can see it...it goes from star to star, refreshing them and embalming them with the light and harmonious breath of its course. And the peoples up there watch it pass by, ecstatic and rapturous...

What's the matter with me? It's him, him, the Horla, who is haunting me, who is making me think these foolish things. He is within me, he is becoming my soul. I shall kill him.

19 August. I shall kill him. I have seen him. I was sitting at my table yesterday evening, and I made a semblance of writing with great attention. I knew

full well that he would come to prowl around me, very close, so close that perhaps I would be able to touch him, to grasp him. And then...then I would have the strength of the desperate; I would have my hands, my knees, my breast, my forehead and my teeth with which to kill him, to crush him, to bite him, to tear him apart.

And I lay in wait, with all my sense-organs overexcited.

I had lit both my lamps and the eight candles on my mantelpiece, as if I were able to discover him by means of that light.

Facing me, my bed, an old oak bed with columns; to the right, my fireplace; to the left my door, carefully locked, after having left it open for a long time, in order to attract him; behind me, a very tall mirrored cupboard, which I use every day when shaving, when getting dressed, and I which I have the custom of looking at myself, from head to toe, every time I pass before it.

So, I was making a semblance of writing, in order to deceive him, for he also spies on me; and suddenly, I sensed, I was certain, that he was reading over my shoulder, that he was there, close to my ear.

I stood up, my hands extended, turning so quickly that I almost fell over. Well? One could see there as in broad daylight, but I did not see myself in my mirror! It was empty, clear, profound, full of light! My image was not within it...but I was facing it. I saw the large glass, limpid from top to bottom; and I looked at it with frightened eyes, and no longer dared go forward, no longer dared to make a movement, sensing that he was there but that he would escape me again, his imperceptible body having devoured my reflection.

How frightened I was! Then, suddenly, I commenced to perceive myself in a mist, in the depths of the mirror, in a mist, as if through a sheet of water; and it seemed to me that the water in question was sliding from left to right, slowly, rendering my image more precise from one second to the next. It was like the end of an eclipse. What hid me did not appear to have clearly defined contours, but a sort of opaque transparency, scarcely clarified.

I was finally able to distinguish myself completely, as I do every day when I look at myself.

I had seen him! The fear has remained to me, and still makes me shiver.

20 August. Kill him—how, since I cannot reach him? Poison? But he would see me mixing it with the water, and would our poisons, in any case, have any effect on his imperceptible body? No, no, without a doubt... Then what?

21 August. I have summoned a locksmith from Rouen and have ordered iron blinds for my bedroom, like those that certain private hotels have on the ground floor, for fear of thieves. He will make me, in addition, a similar door. I have represented myself as a coward, but I don't care.

10 September, Rouen, Continental Hotel. It's done...it's done...but is he dead? My soul has been turned upside-down by what I have seen.

Yesterday, the locksmith having installed my iron blinds and door, I left them all open until midnight, although it was beginning to get cold.

Suddenly, I sensed that he was there, and a joy, a mad joy, gripped me. I got up slowly and I paced back and forth for a long time in order that he would not suspect anything. Then I took off my boots and put my shoes on, negligently. Then I closed my iron blinds and, returning tranquilly toward the door. I locked it with a double turn. Returning to the window then, I fixed it with a padlock, the key to which I put in my pocket.

Suddenly, I understood that he was agitating around me, that he was afraid in his turn, that he was ordering me to open the door for him. I nearly gave in; I did not give in, but, placing my back against the door, I opened it just enough for me to pass through it, backwards; and as I am very tall, my head touched the lintel. I was sure that he had not been able to escape, and I locked him in, all alone, all alone. What joy! I had him! Then I went downstairs at a run; I took my two lamps into my drawing room, beneath my bedroom and I poured all the oil over the carpet, over the furniture, everywhere; then I set fire to it and ran away, after having locked the main entrance door with a double turn. And I went to hide at the bottom of my garden, in a clump of laurels. How long it took! How long it took! Everything was black, mute, still; not a breath of air, not a single star, mountains and clouds that could not be seen, but which weighed upon my soul so heavily, so heavily.

I looked at my house and I waited. How long it took! I thought that the fire had already gone out of its own accord, or that he had put it out, when one of the ground floor windows broke under the pressure of the blaze and a flame, a great red and yellow flame, long, soft and tender, rose along the white wall and kissed it, all the way to the roof. A gleam ran through the trees, in the branches, and a frisson too, a frisson of fear, The birds woke up; a dog started to howl; it seemed to me that day was breaking, Two more windows immediately exploded, and I saw that the entire ground floor of my house was no longer anything but a frightful furnace. But a cry, a horrible, shrill, heart-rending scream—a woman's scream—tore through the night, and two mansards opened. I had forgotten my domestics! I saw their crazed faces, and their arms waving.

Then, bewildered by horror, I started running toward the village, shouting: "Help! Help! Fire! Fire!" I encountered people who were already coming, and I returned with them to see.

The house was now nothing but a horrible and magnificent pyre, a monstrous pyre illuminating the whole region, a pyre I which people were burning, and in which he was burning too: him; him, my prisoner, the new Being, the new master, the Horla.

Suddenly, the whole roof was swallowed up by the walls and a volcano of flame sprang into the sky. Through all the windows open to the furnace, I saw the cauldron of fire, and I thought that he was there, in that oven, dead...

Dead? Perhaps...? His body? Was not his body, which the daylight traversed, indestructible by the means that kill ours?

What if he were not dead? Perhaps only time has purchase on the invisible and redoubtable Being. Why that transparent body, that unknowable body, that body of Spirit, if he too had to fear evils, wounds, infirmities, premature destruction?

Premature destruction? All human fear comes from that! After humankind, the Horla. After the one who can die on any day, at any hour, at any minute, by means of any accident, has come one who only needs to die on his day, at his hour, at his minute, because he has reached the limit of his existence!

No...no...without any doubt, without any doubt...he isn't dead. In that case...in that case...it will be necessary to kill myself...

"Jean Lorrain" was the pseudonym of Paul Duval (1855-1906), adopted at the insistence of his father, a Norman ship-owner, who wanted to protect the family name from the disgrace of employment by a poet, although his aristocratic neighbors the Maupassants had no such scruple. A flamboyant homosexual dandy, when he was forced to make a living from his pen after his father died ruined, Jean Lorrain became one of the most prolific and highest-paid journalists of the fin-de-siècle, and the personification, in his lifestyle as well as his writing, of Decadence. A story-series published in Le Journal *in 1900 as* Astarté *and reprinted in book form as* Monsieur de Phocas. Astarté *(1901; tr. as* Monsieur de Phocas*), provided a kind of retrospective summary of the Decadent world-view, penned immediately before he was forced to leave Paris because of health problems occasioned by his brief use of ether as a stimulant, which did not take long to kill him thereafter. "L'Égrégore" was first published in* Le Courrier français, *14 avril 1888, The translation was first published in* Nightmares of an Ether-Drinker *(2002).*[72]

Jean Lorrain: *The Egregore*

In the grandiosely designed park
Where the Cydalises lost their way,
Among the unexpected fountains
In the marble of the clear pond,

Iris followed by a young flock,
Phillis, Églé, nymphs in love,
With their indecisive plumage
Scantily clad, showing their breasts,

Lycaste, Myrtil and Sylvandre
Come through the fresh undergrowth,
Towards the great dormant trees.

They wander in the white morning,
All dressed in satin, as charming
And as sad as Love itself.

---

[72] Available from Black Coat Press: "Melusine Enchanted" in Tales of Enchantment and Disenchantment, ISBN 978-1-61227-838-4.

The young man sitting before the keyboard, struck a plaintive and charming chord as the last verse was completed. The woman who had added words to the melody took up the fan of feathers that she had laid down on the piano and brought it to her face, touching it to the corners of her lips as if she were stifling a yawn.

The large room decked out in blue and gold, with screens of soft Japanese silk depicting peach-trees in flower and great zigzagging flights of storks, was suddenly filled with the creaky rustle of stiff fabrics and the discreetly honeyed whispers of enamored women. Murmurs of "Ah! ah! delightful!" and "Bravo, brava" mingled with the patter of gloved palms: all the admiring and flattering chatter, sweetened by affectation, that was to be expected in well-mannered society.

Standing with the trains of their ball gowns gathered in straight-pleated tiers behind them, somewhat reminiscent of lovely serpents standing on their tails, bodices inclined to offer their breasts, women clustered around the performers, all of them conscious of being observed. Amid the incessant flapping of fans, the striking of pretty poses and the gracious movements of shoulders and bare arms, insignificant but exquisitely modulated questions were asked and answered.

"Adorable verses. Whose were they?"

"Monsieur de Banville's," the singer replied.

"Ah, Monsieur de Banville, my dear, author of *La Femme de Socrate*."[73]

"You remember, my dear, we went to see it three Tuesdays running, at the Française."

"Perfectly. Samary[74] wore a charming red dress."

"And the music?" chirped another voice. "By Messager, isn't it?"

"Messager, the author of *Deux pigeons*!"[75]

"I beg your pardon," the accompanist intervened, while wiping the sweat from his unusually pale brow, "but the author is here—there, at the back of the room."

And all the heads turn, blonde and brunette alike. Necks crane...oh, what a delightful turning movement that assembly in the music room contrives!

"The author! But that's Hermann, dear Hermann."

And all the dresses take flight as the women move to the other end of the room; it is an abandonment, a complete desertion. Others of a riper vintage, and more "in the know"—all accompanied by bald men of solemn appearance—are already there, showering compliments on a tall, slim and beardless young man,

---

[73] The Parnassian poet Théodore de Banville; the 1886 comedy in question is actually entitled *Socrate et sa femme*.

[74] The actress Jeanne Samary (1857-1890)

[75] The première of André Messager's ballet, knowing in English as *The Two Pigeons*, had also taken place in 1886.

who smiles and nods and tosses his head. His face is illuminated by two extraordinary black eyes. They are as lustrous and coldly black as his hair, which is thick with pomade, curled, combed and seemingly polished.

The singer is left behind, standing by the grand piano. The shrug of her shoulders is significant, as is the tight smile on her lightly-rouged lips. She whispers some secret impertinence to her companion, who raises his stool and smiles. His smile is as mysterious as hers. Then, taking up a sheaf of music from a scattered heap of scores, she opens it up and places it before her accompanist, pointing to a few bars at the bottom of a page. While he continues to mop the sweat from his brow with a cambric handkerchief, she sings the difficult passage in a undertone, while he accompanies her in muted fashion, barely touching the keys with the tips of his fingers. They are obviously rehearsing.

"Brother and sister," the physicist Forbster murmured in my ear. I had run into him again, purely by chance. "The Comtesse de Mercoeur and the Marquis de Sarlys. They share a passion for difficult melodies, symphonies in C and the operas of Wagner, as practitioners as well as connoisseurs. The Comtesse possesses one of the most beautiful voices in Europe; ugly as she is, with her prominent jaw and her dead face, she can bring the audience at the Opéra to its feet, even at a premier. Ah! if she wished, she could earn two hundred thousand francs a year with Gailhard—yes, with Gailhard himself![76] But as you see, she doesn't want it! The brother's talents as a pianist are conspicuously ordinary, but it's a family matter, a pathological case."

"Another pathological case!"

"Or a fantastic one, as you prefer. The macabre is all around us here: we are undoubtedly—you, at least, would not doubt it—on the fringe of one of the blackest tales of Hoffmann. The Marquis de Sarlys, whom you see there rehearsing with his sister—Charles Bertrand de Vassenage, Marquis de Sarlys and Comte de Baudemont, a landed gentleman afflicted with an income of a hundred and forty thousand francs a year, a member of the Jockey Club, the Imperial and the Union, the proprietor until six months ago of a racing stable, all of which he has now given up—is well and truly on the way to utter exhaustion, entirely likely to become extinct at the age of twenty-eight, in the full bloom of youth, under the influence of an Egregore."[77]

"What in God's name is an Egregore? I'm familiar with the reputation of the vampire, the lamia, the ghoul, the incubus and the succubus, but I have to

---

[76] The singer Pierre, or Pedro, Gailhard, was one of the administrators of the Paris Opéra from 1884 to 1903.

[77] The term "égrégore," derived from the Greek, where it means "watcher," and which is used in translations of various Old Testament and apocryphal writings, was employed rather enigmatically by Victor Hugo in *La Légende des siècles*, and else employed by the occultist who called himself Éliphas Lévi. Lorrain's adaptation of it to mean a kind of psychic vampire is original to him.

admit, to my shame, that the Egregore has escaped me. It rhymes nicely with *mandragore*—is it also something that flourishes beneath the gallows?"[78]

"Not exactly. Its foliage belongs to the vegetable-mold of the cemetery and its root to the interior of a sturdy coffin, but as regards the flower, that can bloom anywhere, from the underworld to the finest milieu. In this very room, for example, we can count two."

"Two Egregores! I can't stay here a minute longer—I must run to the cloakroom to get my coat. Society is becoming too dangerous."

"You're not in any danger; I'll protect you. But look at poor Sarlys. See those hollow feverish eyes, all a-glimmer and ringed in blue; that moist pallor of a perpetual cold sweat; that tortured physiognomy, breathless and bruised—the dolorously ecstatic mask of a hysteric. Well, six months ago I knew that fellow as a strong and sanguine man, in good health: an accomplished game-player, a very good runner, joyful and vibrant, seen at all the fêtes and all the hunts. For six months, though, the fellow has had no mistress, has never touched a playing-card. He, who was once a veritable centaur, scarcely mounts a horse; he no longer hunts, no longer dines out, and no longer maintains his circle of acquaintances. Instead, to put it bluntly, he consumes himself, empties himself, exhausts himself and murders himself in the scores of operas, symphonies and cantatas, riveted to a piano-stool between Hermann Barythine, the attractive young maestro, and the Marquise Annette de Mercoeur, née Sarlys, his sister."

"And the Egregore?"

"Is Barythine, that dear Hermann—the one those women are cooing over in their heady little voices. Look at him, now: slim, slender, svelte, with the supple form of a racing greyhound...or a fox. That rosy, almost adolescent beardless head perched on that elegant skeletal framework. Barythine is thirty years old. Who would believe it, eh? That youngster is older than the Marquis de Sarlys! I'll tell you the secret of that unnatural youth...it was known in the Middle Ages. Oh, the head is fine, even feminine; the nose is delicate, the mouth finely chiseled but narrow and incisive: a mouth made for murder, red as blood...oh, that tell-tale red!

"Hermann Barythine has no mistress either, and keeps his distance from fencing-rooms and clubs. He is invisible by day, cloistered in his splendid hotel in the Rue Bassano, where he sits at the organ, the piano or the cello writing bizarre compositions. During the evening and by night, smiling politely, he goes forth to the salons to gather the applause and the swooning cheers of women. The whole world is crazy about him; he is the maestro of the moment. Tonight here, tomorrow evening there, he goes triumphantly into society, towing behind him poor Sarlys, who is no longer able to leave him, imprisoned as he is by the power of an authentic charm. Sarlys stubbornly exhausts himself every night in

---

[78] Mandragore is the French term for the plant commonly known in English as the mandrake. Lorrain wrote one of his most colourful *contes* about it.

the interpretation, accompaniment and promotion of his works: Sarlys and the Marquise de Mercoeur, his sister. She is also an Egregore, after her own fashion, but is unconscious as yet of the fratricidal role that she is playing in this game of murder."

"A fascinating tale—but what proof do you have?"

"Proof...what more do you need? The sudden unreasoning passion that has derailed de Sarlys, the clubman, the muscular sportsman and rake, subjecting him to the alchemical talent of this Barythine, this unknown Pole of obscure nobility and fortune: this too young and too pretty Hermann Barythine; this enigmatic and no less disquieting creature of ambiguous sex and uncertain age."

"Then the Egregore..."

"Attaches itself only to its own sex, entirely in contrast to the ghoul, incubus or vampire. Their malevolent work is self-explanatory; it is with their kisses, with the accursed fire of their knowing caresses that they melt the flesh and the health of the living like wax. Their bedchamber is the Devil's crucible. The incubus drains and kills his mistress with sensuality; the succubus breathes in and drinks the wine of her lover. They are sent down here one after the other as accessories to the attraction of the sexes and the everpresence of lust. But the Egregore is another thing altogether. It is the unfeeling and deleterious influence of a creature of darkness, of a dead man or a dead woman that installs itself beside you in the guise of a living one, insinuating itself into your life, your habits and your admirations, meddling with your heart and taking odious root there, while its damnable mouth breathes a fatal passion into you: a commonplace madness; the folly of the artist or the amateur. And step by step, it increases the delusional and fascinating obsession, until you lie down one fine evening in the cold of the grave...the history of the Middle Ages is replete with the activities of Egregores. In Madrid, at least eight or ten of them were burned every winter; but the Egregore country par excellence extends across Austria, Poland, Russia and Bohemia—the fatherland of Barythine. Do you want to see an example of its work, here and now? Go ask the Marquis de Sarlys, casually, what the Comtesse de Mercoeur will sing next. Go on, I'll explain afterwards."

I went to the piano to enquire, as courteously as I could, the title of the next ballad the Comtesse would sing.

"The *Adieu* of Barythine," was the reply.

"Always Barythine!" Forbster smiled. "Now I shall walk over to the young maestro and offer my compliments. I will ask if he will do me the favor of letting me hear a certain ballad of his entitled *Eros*. If, after these few words of conversation that I have outlined to you, the Marquis and the Comtesse—after having announced *Adieu* and without having had any communication with Barythine—proceed to play Eros, what would your incredulity say then, Monsieur?"

"In that case, I would have to agree with you. It would be useless to protest."

Forbster left me, and went to intercept the young composer as he wandered from group to group, always surrounded by a crowd. The physicist and the composer exchanged a few words. At exactly the same moment, Princess Narmof, our hostess, called for silence.

Sarlys picked out on his keyboard a series of strange and very poignant chords. To this accompaniment, as dull and rumbling as a distant storm, the Comtesse de Mercoeur, very straight and very pale, added a superbly calm and poised contralto voice:

> *Standing in the fulgurant clarity of mountain peaks,*
> *The proud hunter Eros, the murderer of hearts,*
> *Shines, pure flame, above the abysses*
> *And hurls his sure and victorious darts.*

"Now," said Forbster, "watch Barythine, Sarlys and his sister. Look very closely at their lips."

Her staring gaze locked with that of the composer, who was directly in front of her, the Comtesse resumed:

> *A strike rings out across the sublime immensity,*
> *And under the glare of the implacable mocking sky*
> *A drop of blood, red produce of the crime,*
> *Falls at the naked feet of Eros, large as a flower.*

"Oh!" I exclaimed, clutching Forbster's right arm hard enough to make him gasp. I was frightened by what I saw while the ballad of *Eros* was completed by the third and last verse.

> *And the sun goes down and the immortal aurora*
> *Rises, Eros is there, in eternal glory*
> *Under the drops of blood, among the arrows of gold.*

Applause rang out.

I let out a sigh of relief. The strange vision, the terrifying nightmare, had come to an end.

While the Comtesse sang, as if hypnotized by Barythine, I believed that I could distinctly see—and was still convinced that I had seen—their lips swell up and redden, becoming scarlet. Meanwhile, the lips of the poor Marquis had whitened, becoming ghastly, in a face that was suddenly afflicted with suffering. His lips had whitened as if they were being emptied of all the blood that inflated the lips of the others.

When the ballad ended, the phenomenon ceased...but I had drunk so much Chateau Margot at dinner with the princess that evening.

Marcel Schwob (1867-1905) was sent to Paris in 1881 to study at the Lycée Louis-le-Grand, where he met the future writers Léon Daudet and Paul Claudel; he lived with his uncle, the librarian and novelist Léon Cahun. He became a professional journalist thereafter, working for L'Évènement *and* L'Écho de Paris. *His great admiration for Edgar Poe is very obvious in his story collections* Coeur double *(Ollendorf 1891) and* Le Roi au masque d'or *(1892). He also produced a book of fictitious biographies,* Vies imaginaires *(1896), but his health deteriorated catastrophically as a result of an undiagnosable chronic condition, which eventually killed him.* "L'Homme double" *first appeared in* L'Écho de Paris, *20 janvier 1890.* "The Double Man" *was first published in* Decadence and Symbolism: A Showcase Anthology *(2018).[79]*

Marcel Schwob: *The Double Man*

Footsteps sounded in the tiled corridor, and the examining magistrate saw a white-faced young man enter the room. He had glossy hair, with side-whiskers stuck to his cheeks, and his eyes were perpetually wandering or searching. He had the bewildered air of a man who did not understand what was happening to him. The municipal guards left him at the door, with a glance of commiseration. The gleaming and restless eyes seemed to be the only living elements in his ashen face; they had the lustre and the impenetrability of glazed black pottery. He was clad in a frock-coat and baggy trousers, which hung about his body as if suspended from a coat-hanger. His tall hat had been crushed by low ceilings. The collective impression, with the telling detail of the side-whiskers, was that of a wretched lawyer pursued by his colleagues.

The judge, seated beneath a lamp whose light fell upon the face of the accused, studied the pale grey flatness of that leaden visage, whose lines were traced by vague shadows. And while he thumbed mechanically through the documents which lay scattered on his table, the apparent respectability radiated by the man gave him—like one of those momentary explosions which illuminate the blame—the strange impression that he had before him another examining magistrate, with a frock-coat and trimmed side-whiskers, impenetrable and piercing eyes: a sort of unfortunate caricature, awkwardly sketched out in the charcoal-grey of the evening.

This indescribable respectability, which was certainly inferred from the cut of the beard and the clothes, confused the magistrate nevertheless and made him hesitate over the case before him. The crime had appeared banal at first: one of

---

[79] Available from Black Coat Press: "The Future Terror" (1891) in *The Germans on Venus*, ISBN 978-1-934543-56-6.

those murders that had become frequent in recent years. A woman of easy virtue, who lived in a little apartment in the Rue de Maubeuge, had been found in her bed with her throat cut. The cut, just below the thyroid gland, had seemingly been made by a hand accustomed to butchery; the carotid artery had been neatly severed and the neck laid half-open. Death had been almost instantaneous, since the blood had gushed out in a series of three or four liberal jets. The bedclothes, slightly disordered, were marked with extensive bloodstains, disposed in opaque patches, thick at the centre and fading gradually towards the edges to brown-flecked pink. The mirrored wardrobe had been smashed and wooden splinters scattered across the floor; the mattress had been torn apart and disemboweled.

The murdered woman, already of a certain age, was not unknown on the party circuit. She was out every evening at various theatres and restaurants. Her stolen jewelry had been valued, and when the goldsmiths and silversmiths recognized her distinctive rings and carefully-wrought necklaces, their testimony had been sufficient to direct the chief of police to the guilty party. The individual who stood before the judge had been unanimously identified. He was not in hiding; the second-hand dealers of the Marais and the petty shopkeepers of Saint-Germain knew his address. He had come to sell the jewelry with the same air of respectability that he had now: the air of a man who was inconvenienced and wanted to liquidate his assets.

When the magistrate interrogated him, he could not help employing polite expressions and sympathetic attenuations. The man's responses were manifestly mealy-mouthed and evasive, but they were as respectable as his exterior appearance. He was, he said, a solicitor's clerk. He gave the name and address of his employer. A word from the judge almost immediately brought back the reply: *unknown*. The man made a gesture of astonishment and murmured: "I know no more."

Files containing deeds and transcripts had been found in his room in a lodging-house in the Rue Saint-Jacques. When they were shown to him, he said that he did not recognize them. The magistrate, thinking that the files had been planted as evidence, was surprised. On pressing the interrogation, he ran into inexplicable contradictions. The man had the external appearance of a lawyer, but had no knowledge of legal terminology. He knew nothing about the solicitor who was said to be his employer except his name and address—and yet he persisted in his affirmations.

The jewels, he said, had come from an inheritance, and they had been entrusted to him to sell, to realize a sum of money. To the traditional question as to how he had spent his time on the night of the crime he replied: "I was asleep in my bed." When the landlord, called to give evidence, testified that the man had not returned home that night, only arriving the following morning, his face pale and in some distress, the accused looked at him in surprise and said: "No, no. Look here, I know perfectly well—I was in my bed."

The magistrate, nonplussed, summoned three shopkeepers, who recognized the man. They admitted without the slightest hesitation that he had sold them the jewelry.

"Look, monsieur," he said to the judge, "I've already told you that all that was entrusted to me by a person I met in the solicitor's office, to sell and then to take the proceeds to my employer."

What person?" asked the judge.

The man reflected for a moment, then said: "Well—listen—I can't quite bring it to mind . . . but it will come back to me."

Then the magistrate began to speak, showing him the inconsistencies in his story while maintaining a sort of respect for the external appearance that the man presented, as if taking pity on his crestfallen attitude and his idiotic reasoning. He called him "my friend" while gently pointing out his contradictions. He explained the crime the man had committed, since he seemed to be unable to understand it. He attempted to make clear its gravity and abominable nature, stressing the overwhelming sum of the evidence, and finished up with an eloquent peroration in which he said that the President often chose to exercise his supreme right to grant mercy to those who confessed their guilt.

The man appeared to appreciate the indulgence of the magistrate, and took his turn to speak when the judge had finished.

Until that moment the man's voice had been dull, monotonous and impersonal: utterly devoid of all nuances, as uniformly grey as his ashen face. The magistrate could not remember ever having heard one like it. But when the man replied to the judge's exhortation, he became exhortatory in his turn. The tones of his voice became accusatory, a pale imitation of the tones which the magistrate had employed in addressing him. The words that emerged from his lips were copies of the words that he had heard.

His discourse was negative; he limited himself simply to rejecting the contradictions and denying the evidence. He could not count on the clemency of the President, since he knew nothing of the crime.

When he came to this point, the judge had to stop him. The clerk of the court smiled as he wrote it down, in spite of the seriousness of the man and the horror of the crime. Standing before the examining magistrate's table was a singular being who mimicked the magistrate with a real talent, who colored his monotonous voice with the judge's tones, who impressed upon his own dull features the same expressive lines as those in the face of the man sitting opposite, who seemed to inflate his loose clothing with exactly the same borrowed gestures. He did this so well that the vague impression which had struck the examining magistrate as the accused made his entrance had now become the precise and distinct image of a man of law in conference with a colleague. It was as if the outlines of a grey, soft and blurred sketch had been reinforced to the point at which they attained the sharpness of an etching, or a white line set against a black background.

The judge went to the heart of the matter, authoritatively. He no longer talked of possibilities, but of facts.

The victim's throat had been cut by a practiced hand; the instrument in question had been found. The judge placed before the man's eyes a knife—a sharp butcher's knife—stained with blood, which had been discovered under his bed. The back of the blade was half as thick as a finger. This was the first evident connection established between the man and the crime. The effect was prodigious.

A tremor shook the accused from top to toe and his features convulsed. His eyes rolled, and became bright. His hair stood on end, as did the side-whiskers which seemed to be an extension thereof. His brow was furrowed and his mouth tightened. The man's figure now took on a painful rigidity, and with a strange gesture, as if he were waking up, he rubbed the skin beneath his nose two or three times with his index-finger. Then he began talking again, in a drawling fashion, his hands no longer stiff but following his words with gestures. These words were evidently addressed to people who were not there. The judge felt obliged to ask where he thought he was. At that question the man shuddered; his mouth opened without any effort on his part, as if it were overflowing.

"Where'm I at? Where'm I at? Why, at 'ome, o'course! This is what c'n 'appen t'yer, where I'm at!" He took up a pen from the table. "'Ere's *a dip-your-stick-in-the-blackstuff*[80], I allus help m'self. It makes a mess of yer bib, mind. They were good. I've gone afore the Red—'twas a merry dance, that. It's swalered what I writ wi' that there instrument. A good score! I'm a real showman when it comes t'jewels. Oh, they ain't cotton—see how they run!—like velvet. I've stuffed t'other pie, I've 'obbled'n'nobbled what 'e 'ad squirreled away. I've fooled 'im good'n'proper wi'a nice sham, summat beat. An' I don't fear macs what turn their coats, me. I work alone—an' I go t'sleep in me *gimme-yer-wood*."

The man lurched towards the judge's chair. The frightened judge got up, surrendering his position to the other.

Scarcely was the man seated when the reaction set in; his face became bloodless, his head lolled back and his eyes closed. His entire body collapsed into inertia.

---

[80] A literal transcription of this portmanteau word would be "dip-your-two-arms-in-the-black-vessel". The French "vase" has a double meaning, so "vase noire"—literally translatable as "black vessel" or "inkwell"—also implies "black mud", but the whole expression is obviously intended to carry at least two meanings—perhaps three if (as seems likely) there is a sexual innuendo as well as the obvious analogy between the clerk's pen and the butcher's knife. The problems of translation posed by the portmanteau expression extend even more acutely throughout the remainder of this colloquially slurred and delirious speech, but I have tried to capture the gist of it as best I can.

And the judge, standing before the other in his turn, felt that he was faced with a terrible problem. Of the two semi-simulated persons that he had had before him, one was guilty and the other was not. This man had two personalities, but the two were united in one: which was the real one? One of them had done the deed—but was that one the fundamental being? In the double man who had revealed himself, where was *the man*?

Anatole France (1844-1924) inherited the mantle of the greatest living French writer after the death of Victor Hugo, and won the Nobel Prize for Literature in 1921. Thaïs *(1890), a classical fantasy in the tradition of Gustave Flaubert's* La Tentation de Saint-Antoine *(1874), was followed by the collection* L'Étui de nacre *(1892), which laid the foundations for the more flamboyant collection* Le Puits de Sainte Claire *(1895) and helped pave the way for his final masterpiece of literary Satanism,* La Révolte des anges *(1914). "Leslie Wood" appeared in* L'Étui de nacre; *the translation is original to the present volume.*[81]

Anatole France: *Leslie Wood*

There was a concert and a comedy at the home on Madame N*** in the Boulevard Malesherbes.

While a flower-bed of bare shoulders was stifling in warm perfumes in the doorways, the rest of us, slightly grumpy old habitués, remained in the fresh air in a small drawing room where nothing could be seen, and where the voice of Mademoiselle Réjane[82] only reached us like the slightly strident hum of the flight of a dragonfly. From time to time, we heard laughter and applause burst forth in the furnace, and we were inclined to feel a mild pity for a pleasure that we were not sharing. We were exchanging jolly trivia when one of us, an amiable député, Monsieur B***, said to us:

"Wood is here, you know."

At that news, everyone protested.

"Wood? Leslie Wood? Impossible! It's ten years since he's been seen in Paris. No one knows what has become of him."

"It's said that he's founded a republic on the shored of the Victoria-Nyanza."

"That's a fairy tale! You know that he's fabulously rich and a great realizer of impossibilities. He lives in a magical palace in Ceylon, in the midst of enchanted gardens where bayaderes dance night and day."

"How can you believe such stupidities? The truth is that Leslie Wood had gone to evangelize the Zulus, with a Bible and a rifle."

---

[81] Available from Black Coat Peress: *"Honey Bee"* in *The French Fantasy Treasury (Vol. 2)*, ISBN 978-1-61227-545-1; *"The Story of the Duchesse de Cicogne and Monsieur de Boulingrin, Who Slept For a Hundred Years in the Company of the Beauty in the Dormant Wood"* in *Tales of Enchantment and Disenchantment*, ISBN 978-1-61227-838-4.

[82] The actress Gabrielle Réjane (Gabrielle-Charlotte Reju, 1856-1920) was at the height of her fame when the present story was written.

Monsieur B*** said, in a low voice: "He's here. Look."

And with a movement of the head and his eyes, he indicated a man leaning in a doorway, and who, dominating with his tall stature the skulls accumulated around him, seemed attentive to the spectacle.

That athletic frame and ruddy face with white side-whiskers, those bright eyes and that tranquil gaze: it really was Leslie Wood.

Recalling the admirable correspondence that he had given to the *World* for ten years, I said to B***: "That man is the foremost journalist of the era."

"Perhaps you're right," B*** replied. "At least, I can affirm that, ten years ago, no one knew Europe like Leslie Wood."

Baron Moïse, who was listening to us, shook his head. "You don't know what Leslie Wood is. I know him. Before anything else, he was a financier. He understood business better than anyone. Why are you laughing, Princess?"

Sprawled on a sofa, in the bleak ennui of being unable to smoke a cigarette, Princess Zévorine had smiled.

"None of you understand Leslie Wood," she said. Wood has never been anything but a mystic and a lover."

"I don't believe that," replied Baron Moïse. "But I'd like to know where that devil of a man has spent the ten best years of his life."

"Where do you put the ten best years of life?"

"Between fifty and sixty; one has made one's situation and one can enjoy life."

"You can interrogate Wood himself, Baron. Here he comes."

This time, the sound of applause announced that the performance had finished. The black suits, unblocking the doorways, spread out in the small drawing room and while the procession of couples headed for the buffet, Leslie Wood came toward us.

He shook our hands with a placid cordiality.

"A revenant! A revenant!" cried Baron Moïse.

"Oh." said Wood, "I can't have come back from very far. The earth is small."

"Do you know what the princess said? She said that you're nothing but a mystic, my dear Wood. Is that true?"

"That depends on what you mean by mystic."

"The word is self-explanatory. A mystic is a person occupied with the affairs of the other world. Now, you know the affairs of this world too well to care about those of the other."

At those words, Wood frowned slightly "You're mistaken, Moïse. "The affairs of the other world are much the more important—much, Moïse."

"That dear Leslie Wood!" exclaimed the baron, sniggering. "He has wit!"

The princess replied, very gravely; "You don't have wit, do you, Wood? I have a horror of witty men." She stood up. "Wood, conduct me to the buffet."

An hour later, while G***[83] was charming the men and women with her songs, I encountered Leslie Wood and Princess Zévorine again, alone before the deserted buffet.

The princess was speaking with an almost savage enthusiasm about Count Tolstoy, whose friend she was. She described that great man, who had become a simple man, donning the costume and the soul of a muzjik, and his hands, which wrote masterpieces, making shoes for the poor. To my great surprise, Wood approved on a way of life so contrary to common sense, in a slightly breathless voice, to which a commencement of asthma gave a singular mildness.

"Yes," he said, "Tolstoy is right. All philosophy is in the saying: 'Let God's will be done.' He has understood that all the ills of humankind come from having a will distinct from the divine will. I only dread that he might spoil such a beautiful doctrine with fantasy and extravagance."

"Oh," replied the princess in a low voice, hesitating slightly, "the count's doctrine is only extravagant on one point; it prolongs the rights and duties of a husband to the most advanced age and imposes on the saints of new days the fecund old age of the patriarchs."

Old Wood replied with a contained excitement: "That too is excellent and very saintly. Physical and natural amour befits all God's creatures, and if it is not mingled with trouble or anxiety, it maintains the divine simplicity and the holy animality without which there is no salvation. Asceticism is only pride in revolt. Let us have present in mind the example of the good Boaz,[84] and let us recall that the Bible makes amour the bread of old men."

And he was suddenly rapturous and illuminated, transfigured by ecstasy, appealing with his eyes, his arms and his entire soul to something invisible.

"Annie!" he murmured. "Annie, my beloved Annie, does not the Lord want his male and female saints to love one another with the humility of the animals of the fields?"

Then he fell into an armchair, exhausted. A frightful breath shook his broad chest, and he gave the impression of being more robust than ever, like those machines that seem more formidable when they have broken down. Without being astonished, Princess Zévorine wiped his forehead with her handkerchief and made him drink a glass of water.

For myself, I was stupefied. I could not recognize in that illuminate the man who had so often, in his study encumbered by Blue Books, talked to me so

---

[83] Perhaps Jeanne Granier (1852-1939), one of the best-known personalities of the Parisian social scene in the fin-de-siècle, although it is not clear why her name should be concealed while the equally-famous Réjane's is spelled out in full.

[84] In the Old Testament book of *Ruth* Boaz is eighty when he marries the forty-year-old Ruth, and although he dies shortly thereafter the marriage is not child-less.

lucidly about Oriental affairs, the Treaty of Frankfurt and the perturbations of our financial markets.

As I allowed my anxiety to be seen by the princess, she shrugged her shoulders and said to me: "You're very French. You consider all those who do not think exactly as you do to be mad. Don't worry; our friend Wood is rational, very rational, Let's go and listen to G***."

After having conducted the princess to the large drawing room, I got ready to leave. In the antechamber I found Wood, who was putting on his overcoat. He did not seem to be aware of his crisis.

"Dear friend," he said to me, "I believe that we're neighbors. You still live on the Quai Malaquais, and I've settled in a house in the Rue des Saints-Pères. In dry weather like this, it's a pleasure to go on foot. If you wish, we can walk together and chat."

I accepted wholeheartedly. On the perron he offered me a cigar and held out the flame of an electric lighter.

"It's very convenient," he told me, and he explained the theory of it to me clearly.

I recognized the Wood of the old days. We took a hundred steps in the street, chatting about indifferent things.

Suddenly, my companion placed his hand gently on my shoulder.

"Dear friend, some of the things that I've said this evening might have surprised you. Perhaps you'd like me to explain them to you."

"You interest me greatly, my dear Wood."

"I'll do so gladly; I hold your intelligence in esteem. We don't envisage life in the same fashion, but ideas don't frighten you, and that's a rare kind of courage, especially in France."

"I believe, however, my dear Wood, that for the sake of the freedom of thought..."

"Oh, you aren't, as in England, a population of theologians. But let's leave that. I want to tell you, in a few words, the story of my ideas. When you knew me fifteen years ago, I was a correspondent of the London *World*. Journalism is, among us, more lucrative and more considerable than it is here. My situation was good, and I extracted, I think, the best possible advantage from it—I mean in business; I made excellent deals and I conquered, in a few years, two very enviable things: influence and fortune. You know that I'm a practical man.

"I never marched without a goal, and I was preoccupied above all with attaining the supreme goal, the goal of life. Ardent theological studies, undertaken in my youth, had indicated to me that the goal in question is situated beyond terrestrial existence, but doubts remained to me as to the practical means of attaining it. I suffered cruelly from that. Uncertainty is utterly insupportable to a man of my character.

"In that state of mind, I paid serious attention to the psychic research of William Crookes, one of the most distinguished members of the Royal Society. I knew him personally and considered him to be, with reason, a scholar and a gentleman. He was then carrying out experiments on a young woman endowed with very singular psychic faculty, and like Saul of old he was favored by the presence of an authentic phantom.[85]

"A charming woman who had once lived our life and lived henceforth the life beyond the tomb, lent herself to the experiments of the eminent spiritualist and submitted to everything that he asked of her within the limits of propriety. I thought that such investigations, bearing on the point at which terrestrial existences connect with extraterrestrial existences, would lead me, if I followed them step by step, to discover what it is necessary to know—which is to say, the veritable goal of life. I did not take long to be disappointed in my hopes, however. The research of my respectable friend, although directed with a precision that left nothing to be desired, did not lead to a sufficiently clear theoretical and moral conclusion.

"In addition, William Crookes was suddenly deprived of the collaboration of the incomparable dead woman who had graciously accorded him several spiritualist séances. Discouraged by public incredulity and offended by the mockery of his colleagues, he ceased to publish any communications relative to psychic knowledge. I expressed my disappointment to Reverend Burthogge, with whom I had been in communication since his return from southern Africa, which he had evangelized with religious and practical mentality truly worthy of old England. Of all men, Reverend Burthogge was the one whose action had always had the most forceful and decisive effect on me."

"He's very intelligent, then?" I asked.

"He has a great doctrinal intelligence," Leslie Wood replied. "He has, above all, a great character, and you're not unaware, dear friend, that it is by means of character that one influences people. My disappointments did not cause him any surprise; he attributed them to my faulty method, and above all to the pitiful moral infirmity of which I had given evidence in that circumstance. 'Research of a scientific order,' he told me, 'can only ever lead to a discovery of the same order. Why have you not understood that? You have been strangely light and frivolous, Leslie Wood. Spirit seeks spirit, said the apostle Saint Paul. In order to discover spiritual verities, it is necessary to enter the spiritual path.'

"Those words made a profound impression on me. 'Reverend father,'" I asked, 'how can I enter the spiritual path?'

"'By means of poverty and simplicity,' Burthogge replied to me. 'Sell your possessions and give the money to the poor. You are known; hide yourself.

---

[85] The reference is to the medium Florence Cook, who notoriously manifested for the benefit of the myopic Crookes a seductive "spirit" name Katie King. Rumor has it that her communication with Crookes did not, as the story alleges, remain "within the limits of propriety."

Pray; accomplish works of charity. Make yourself a simple spirit, a pure soul, and you will have the truth.'

"I resolved to follow those precepts to the letter. I handed in my resignation as a correspondent to the *World*. I liquidated my fortune, which was invested, in large measure, in business, and fearing to renew the crime of Ananias and Sapphira,[86] I conducted that difficult operation in such a manner as not to lose a centime of that capital, which no longer belong to me. Baron Moïse, who saw me at work, concluded a religious admiration for my financial genius. On Reverend Burthogge's order, I poured the sums I had realized into the coffers of the Evangelical Society.

"When I testified my joy in being poor to that eminent theologian, he said: 'Be careful only to savor in poverty the triumph of your energy. What is the point of depriving oneself externally if one retains within oneself the idol of gold? Be humble.'"

Leslie Wood was at that point in his story when we arrived at the Pont Royal. The Seine, on which lights were trembling, was flowing under the arches with a muted moan.

"It's necessary that I abridge," the nocturnal narrator resumed. "Every episode of my new life could devour an entire night. Burthogge, whom I obeyed like a child, sent me to the land of the Basutos with the mission to combat the Slave Trade. I lived there in a tent, alone with that generous bedside companion called danger, in fever and in thirst, seeing God.

"After five years, Reverend Burthogge recalled me to England. On the boat, I met a young woman. What a vision! What an apparition, a thousand times more radiant than the phantom who showed herself to William Crookes!

"She was the poor orphan daughter of a colonel in the Indian Army. She did not have a particular linear beauty. Her pale complexion and emaciated face revealed suffering, but her eyes expressed everything that can be imagined of Heaven and her flesh seed to be softly illuminated by an inner light. How I loved her! How, at the sight of her, I penetrated the hidden meaning of creation entire! How that simple young woman revealed to me in her gaze the secret of the harmony of the spheres!

"Oh, simple, very simple, was my initiatrix, my beloved lady, sweet Annie Fraser! I read in her transparent soul the sympathy that she had for me. One night, one limpid night, when the two of us were alone on the deck of the ship, in the presence of the seraphic assembly of the stars, which were palpitating in chorus in the heavens, I took her hand and I said to her: 'Annie Fraser, I love you. I sense that it would be good if you were my wife, but I am forbidden to

---

[86] Chapter 5 of the *Acts of the Apostles* relates how Ananias and his wife Sapphira, who were supposed to have sold all their possessions when they joined the first Christian community, secretly held back a portion of their wealth, but failed to dupe Peter, and were both struck dead.

make my destiny, in order that God might make it himself. May he wish to unite us! I have placed my will in the hands of Reverend Burthogge. When we reach England, we shall both go to find him, if you wish, Annie Fraser, and if he permits it, we will marry.'

"She agreed to that. Throughout the remainder of the crossing, we read the Bible together. As soon as we arrived in London, I took my traveling companion to the reverend, and I told him what the amour of that young woman was for me, and with what a beautiful light it penetrated me.

"Burthogge considered her for a long time, benevolently. 'You may marry,' he said, finally. The apostle Paul said: 'Spouses sanctify one another.' But let your union be similar to the unions in honor among the Christians of the primitive Church. Let it remain purely spiritual, and let the sword of the angel remain between you in your bed. Go, remain humble and hidden, and let the world be ignorant of your name.'

"I married Annie Fraser and I have no need to tell you that we observed exactly the law that Reverend Burthogge had imposed upon us. For four years I delighted in that fraternal union.

"By virtue of the grace of the simple, simple Annie Fraser, I advanced in the knowledge of God. Nothing could any longer make us suffer.

"Annie was ill and her strength declined, and we sad to one another delightedly: 'Let God's will be done on earth and in Heaven!'

"After four years of that union, one day, Christmas Day, Reverend Burthogge summoned me. 'Leslie Wood,' he said to me. 'I have imposed on you a salutary proof. But it would be to fall into the error of the Papists to believe that the union of beings in the flesh does not please God. He has blessed the couples of men and animals twice, in the Terrestrial Paradise and in Noah's Ark. Go and live henceforth with Annie Fraser, your spouse, as a husband with his wife.'

"When I went home, Annie, my beloved Annie, was dead.

"I confess my weakness. I pronounced with my lips and not my heart the words: 'My God, may Thy will be done!' And, thinking of what Reverend Burthogge had just accorded to our amour, I sensed bitterness in my mouth and my heart filled with ashes. And it was with a desolate soul that I knelt down at the foot of the bed where my Annie reposed beneath a cross of roses, mute and white, with the pale violets of death on her cheeks.

"A man of little faith, I said adieu to her and I remained plunged for a week in a sterile sadness that resembled despair. How, on the contrary, I should have rejoiced in my soul and in my flesh!

"On the night of the eighth day, while I was weeping, with my forehead on the cold and empty bed, I had the sudden certainty that my beloved was near me in my bedroom.

"I was not mistaken. Having raised my head, I saw Annie, smiling and luminous, who opened her arms to me. But how can I express the rest? How can the ineffable be spoken? And ought one to reveal all the mysteries of amour?

"Certainly, when Reverend Burthogge had said to me: 'Live with Annie as a husband with his wife,' he knew that amour is stronger than death.

"In sum, my friend, know that since that hour of grace and joy, my Annie returns to me every evening, embalmed with celestial perfume."

He was speaking with a frightful exaltation.

We had slowed our pace. He stopped in front of a house of poor appearance.

"This is where I live," he told me. "Can you see that light in that second floor window? She's waiting for me."

And he quit me, abruptly.

A week later I learned from the newspapers of the sudden death of Leslie Wood, former correspondent of the *World*.

"Gaston Danville" was the pseudonym of Armand Blocq (1870-1933). He was the brother of the psychologist Paul Blocq, and declared that in his writings he was trying to develop a new kind of Naturalism based on contemporary psychological theories, especially those of Théodule Ribot. He was one of the authors who supplied the Symbolist periodical Mercure de France *with much of its prose during its first few years of existence, alongside Remy de Gourmont. Danville's contributions included a series of* Contes d'au-delà, *collected under that title in 1893, in which the "beyond" featured therein is not the afterlife but the unconscious, and the stories are steeped in ambiguity. "L'Ange noir" was first published in* Mercure de France, mars 1892 "The Dark Angel" *was first published in* The Anatomy of Love and Murder *(2013).*[87]

Gaston Danville: *The Dark Angel*

A flock of pink flamingoes traversed the capricious silvery clouds embroidered on the turquoise blue silk. Next to the exotic wall-hanging, a little Japanese skeleton slowly gyrated, hanging from a candelabrum by a slender thread that Pierre could not see from the divan where he was lying. Velvety and tremulous, the soft light of the candle, lit when he came home, was reflected in the two brilliants of his heavy shirt-front and ran sparkling streams of fluid gold over his frock-coat, in the lining of which a minuscule spring of heather had almost finished withering away. The palpitations of the flame died on the edge of the shadow in which the young man's face was placed.

Sitting in front of the fireplace on a scarlet cushion, in a grave, almost hieratic pose, his cat fixed the faint redness of the dying embers with her phosphorescent eyes: emerald crescents striated with jade. In the floating gloom, traversed by diffuse gleams, the fabric shade of a standard lamp overhung a broad lilac keyboard, heightened by bright sulfur-yellow.

Outside, the wind was playing a vibrant and lugubrious nocturnal symphony, entangled with long chromatic scales, inspiring with its furious breath the organ of grave chimneys, and, responding to the appeal of the plaintive harmony, sad, feeble, dolorous thoughts were evoked, and suffering too.

Pierre suddenly felt the return of the oppressive grip that had dug into his heart a little while ago, with the persistence of a terrifying clamp whose jaws were tightening relentlessly, without meeting.

Now, simultaneously, there is an intense, atrocious burning sensation in his breast, and a kind of slow tearing apart, fiber by fiber, of all his muscles. He

---

[87] Available frm Black Coat Press: *The Perfume of Lust*, ISBN 978-1-61227-580-2.

dare not risk a movement lest he exasperate the horrible torture. At the same time, his head becomes extremely heavy, to which is added the continuous fulguration of sharp, multiple, vacillating points suddenly plunging into it, assailing him indefatigably with their slender bite. His face contracts, he is suffering, silently and motionlessly—except that his teeth are digging into the bloodless lividity of his lips, and his fingernails are scoring the palms of his clenched hands.

At times, rushes of blood run beneath his damp, shivering skin in torrid waves, inundating his face, invading his forehead and then the skull, mounting a furious assault, while the unbearable pulsation of the arteries in his temples is like a beaten gong sounding the charge. It seems to him that his head is full of swarming beasts, whose innumerable and trenchant mouths and crazed muzzles are digging into his brain. Is it not about to burst? He is obliged to put the opaque and bloodshot veil of lowered eyelids between himself and his surroundings, so much does the slightest luminous vibration reverberate dolorously in his bruised being, multiplied tenfold by the fatiguing tension of his exacerbated nerves, excessively irritable in this moment of supreme and infinite anguish.

Then the paroxysm of anxiety is followed by a relative wellbeing, with occasional rapid twinges, commemorative of the terrible past traversed, like the last lightning-flashes of an easing storm, furrowing a purer sky still striped with somber shreds of cloud. The fugitive recollection of the evening, spent without any menacing presage at Madame de Prézilles' house, is sketched in his darkened consciousness, where foul odors of stupor float: an insignificant soirée, garlanded by the usual young women and the customary cortege of black suits, without the slightest memorable incident taking place.

The weave of painful sensations thins out, tears, and finally disappears.

Pierre breathes deeply, stretches his limbs, as if liberated from a nasty nightmare, glad to be no longer perceiving anything disquieting. Emboldened by the tranquility of relaxed nerves and corporeal serenity, he stands up, heads for an item of furniture with curious incrustations of malachite and jasper, and opens a drawer; it contains letters. He closes it gently, and finds the tobacco he was looking for on top. Meticulously, he rolls a cigarette between fingers that are still trembling.

Capricious arabesques form and break up, glittering milky blue spirals, rising up and fading away in a shifting design, stairways of candid dreams set in the sky. Pierre listens to the gusts of wind, the vibrant course of which is continuing. The racket is attenuated by the lowered blinds, the window-panes, around which the lead fittings snake irregularly, and the brown, rigid curtains, half-veiling the window with their copper-studded armor, the gaps of which take on a warm silky gleam of shiny new brass. The noise of the squall thus becomes a song, intoning distant melancholies, very softly, seemingly repeating the plaint of the waves on evenings when the tide is ebbing; and the feeble, excessively sad melody embroiders growling arpeggios over the monotonous purring of the drowsy feline, the gray furry ball of which is a palely-colored on the crimson satin on which it sketches an imprecise eclipse. The creaking of the dry wood-work forms sonorous breaches streaking the demi-silence.

Exhausted, not by the benevolent lassitude that summons sleep but by the arrival of discouragement, and the fear experienced upon emergence from danger, overwhelmed by the dismal and unstable host of ideas that are troubling him, the young man cannot make up his mind to go to bed, because he is all too familiar with the cruel insomnia in which agitated limbs refuse repose, the eyes wander in the darkness and the mind roams in the phantasmal night. Insidiously and perfidiously, however, a somnolent torpor numbs him, from which he tries to escape, fearing the advent of imaginary and terrifying visions, which bring dread, suffocation, intimidation and annihilation, with regard to a peril that is vain and derisory but nevertheless as dangerous as a real peril, and perhaps more so.

The lax and uncertain reverie retreats, fleeing through the free spaces of the vast field of memory and swerving into abrupt detours of association, which spur him along multiple pathways. At first he encounters insignificances, quickly neglected; then the landscape of fiction is animated, populated with characters, which take on a posthumous life; shadows, strayed from the utmost depths of memory, return to the light.

A face is finally detached from confused groups and divergent coexistences; black hair, nacreous shoulders of an ideal curvature and the tapering torso of a woman complete it. What caused that? Ah! The letters discovered just now! Pierre moves his lips involuntarily, from which a name emerges; then, without being aware of it, he pronounces incoherent words in a low voice, not hearing the words that translate, unconsciously, his intimate thoughts.

"She *must* be dead...I *sense* that's she's dead... When? That night, perhaps! Ah, the strange presentiment: my bones are icy...

"How come that absurd idea has struck me, and at the present moment, when, by a singular coincidence—very singular, to be sure—her image haunts me, as clear in form as on the first day of her apparition, when, in moments of intoxication, she penetrated soundlessly into this room?

"Why shouldn't she be dead? I can see her now, so pale; too pale for a living person. In particular, I don't like the dull, colorless hair that masks the nape of her neck; she had such beautiful hair.

"Eh? Someone just spoke, here, and *something* cold and fluid has come in...yes, *something*...that cat has woken up and is miaowing, sniffling, her hair bristling. Truly, something abnormal is happening: what?

"I don't observe anything...nothing at all...

"No noise. And I haven't been drinking ether![88]

---

[88] Danville's story series antedates the series of tales of hallucinatory hauntings that Jean Lorrain entitled "Contes d'un buveur d'éther" [Tales of an Ether-

"The supernatural force of this funereal conviction frightens me. I don't *want* to believe in this glacial revelation, suddenly surging forth, unmotivated; but it's impossible to withdraw myself from the strange evidence with which it's overwhelming me.

"In winter, the daylight is belated in its appearance; the hours only take flight heavily, and I'm alone, alone, always alone without any other company than that of evil thoughts! So, was I not cruel, cowardly and pitiless when the stupid voice of pride spoke within me? I let her go, nearly ten months ago now...oh, after a futile scene that I could have terminated with a single word. That word was burning my lips; out of imbecile vanity, stupid self-esteem, I didn't pronounce it. With one kiss, one gesture, I could have retained her; she was so good, so charitable to my easily-wounded soul. My arms, which I ought to have held out, remained inert, my mouth closed, my eyes harsh. During the fatal second, when she paused on the threshold of that door, and half-turned, still uncertain, the exact notion of a tomorrow empty of her, of the baseness of my conduct, frightened me. I let her go...

"That was ten months ago; was it not rather yesterday that I sought her svelte form by my side, that I thought I heard the accustomed rustle of her skirt, the faint patter of her footsteps?

"I'll never see her again, except in the chimerical countries of dreams...

"Dead!"

Desirous of escaping the emprise of sterile regret, Pierre decided on the ether.

Soon, he was smiling at prodigious, immeasurable marvels, looming up in the undulating mist of the Imaginary. A whirlwind passed by, swaying its great, dull vapor above the immense gulfs of Infinity, which extend all the way to mauve horizons, divined so distantly that a deliriant vertigo and a superstitious fear emanate from the enormous Space, mingled with attraction. The ground is strewn with the fleecy feathers of birds; it is agitated by slow convulsions, covered with pustules that swell to bursting point and then shrink to tiny bubbles; they vanish. Masses move, creep and change position with sinuous curvaceous deformations; a fiery incandescence floats over the chaos, which becomes more precise.

"You see: up there will scintillate crystal lamps, sparkling chandeliers, from which a sparkling cascade of green and red pendants falls. Painted bayaderes, like frail idols whose thin limbs will be dressed in muslin, run in mosaic frescoes around the rutilant vault. On the square, robust, powerful pillars

---

Drinker] (tr. in *Nightmares of an Ether-Drinker*), but Lorrain was a close friend of Rachilde, and Danville probably met him at the *salon* hosted by the Vallettes—in which case he would doubtless have taken a strong interest in Lorrain's anecdotes of his experiences drinking ether, just as Lorrain might have taken some inspiration from the "Contes d'Au-Delà."

constellated with bronzed nails, others stand up, columns of cinnabar, on which the sacred image of the Good Goddess is displayed!

"You see, my love, how the turbulent swarm of supple ballerinas dances, provocative wasps in corselets nielloed with light damascenes of shadow—so light! The tambourines groan and the flutes proffer harmonious modulations. At that spectacle, my limbs let go of terrestrial attachments, and I experience an inexpressible joy in no longer perceiving the greasepaint of life, of floating above forgotten human ugliness.

"So stay with me, my love...

"Oh, I once *sensed* that you came in silently, that I interrogated you...you didn't reply. You were cold, for the friction of your fluid vestment touched me...you aren't suiting by the fire...

"Stay close to me; tell me that you've forgotten the fatal moment when I was so nasty...

"If you knew, my love, how I have suffered, how I have wept, how I have cursed my absurd and baleful anger...now, I shall be so humble, so submissive, so tender, that you will love me; we were so happy once! Forgive me, please, forgive me! Beauty! You're still beautiful! Your long hair—how long your hair is!—still shines with an uncertain hint of amethyst or sapphire, which delights me when I see it shining there. And your eyes, your dark eyes—in truth, are they not even darker?—bring to my soul the repose that was once found there. You still have that virginal, alluring hue that your suntanned flesh possessed...

"But where shall I seek that flesh? It's getting dark; yes, it's getting very dark; and I can only perceive, in the darkness, vague pale floating islets...

"Why don't you speak to me? I adore your voice, I adore hearing its fresh and melodious timbre. You remain mute...and the veil enveloping you...? Are you going to take it off, to appear to me radiant and dazzling, dressed as for a fête? And what fête could be more joyful than that! For you're coming back to me, aren't you? You've forgotten you've forgiven? Say something to me; give me a kiss...

"Ah, here's the light, and that ray of moonlight, filtering discreetly, is worth more to me than the radiance of all the suns, since it permits me to see you better...

"You're laughing, I think, you're laughing, and your little pearly teeth are reflecting the light that illuminates them...Heavens! That's horrible! Am I dreaming? No, no, *she*'s doing me harm...those fingernails, those pointed fingernails, those dead woman's fingernails, digging into my neck...and that fleshless, bony head, gazing at me with its empty orbits...

"Ah!"

From a motif of weaponry, he snatches an open dagger and strikes at the phantom, desperately.

At the same time, he feels a sharp commotion in his breast; his shirt becomes sticky with a warm liquid.

Pierre staggers, bewildered, falls in a faint; and, having recovered an uneasy consciousness of the real, dies without understanding that he has killed himself, the victim of a deceptive hallucination, in the course of which, attributing his sensations to a foreign personality, he believed in the actual presence of the abandoned lover, in her macabre transformation, unaware that, in striking out at her, he has only afflicted himself.

The cat moans softly, sniffing the cadaver, while, near the exotic wall-hanging on which a flock of pink flamingoes is traversing capricious clouds, the little Japanese skeleton continues its slow gyration, hanging from the candelabra by a slender thread, which Pierre can no longer see.

Remy de Gourmont (1858-1915) was the leading literary critic of his era, and his studies of authors involved in the Symbolist Movement, many of them col-lected in Le Livre des masques *(1896) and* Le Deuxième Livre des Masques *(1898), provided a invaluable map of its extent and commentary on its ambi-tions. He became the principal theorist of Symbolism and Decadence, which he regarded as identical. He was one of the founders of the* Mercure de France, *and its most prolific contributor, developing his distinctively mannered short fiction in its pages. He collaborated with Alfred Jarry in 1893-94 on* L'Ymagier, *a pe-riodical devoted to Symbolist art, which developed a theory of archetypes simi-lar in many respects to Carl Jung's. Disfigured by lupus, he became a recluse before the century ended, and his health deteriorated steadily thereafter, alt-hough he kept on writing relentlessly while he could.* "La Dame pensive*" first appeared in* Le Journal, *22 avril 1894;* "The Pensive Lady*" first appeared in* From a Faraway Land *(2019).*[89]

Remy de Gourmont: *The Pensive Lady*

She resembled closely enough one of those dark-haired virgin saints, ar-ranged in an attitude of distracted melancholy. Her eyes, of a velvet blackness and a moist softness, always gave the impression of considering with astonish-ment a rare spectacle invisible for all other eyes; but she only ever gazed after-wards, when there was nothing more at which to gaze, at the beings and things that passed before her. Often, one could even speak to her, or touch her, without her perceiving it; she was one of those women who never know where they are, and never know where they are going.

She had married as if in a dream, less occupied with her husband than with the chimera whose flight she thought she was following, amid the possible land-scapes and the skies open to her imagination. Throughout her life she wondered how she had become a woman, doubtless initiated while a wind of inconceivable perfumes enveloped her with unconscious delights.

As she also spoke very rarely, her soul always remained obscure, even for the benevolent wills most determined to force the door of the tabernacle, and it was said of Aline that she lived like a flower, or the Daphne of the *Metamorpho-ses*, mute and verdant.

A creature made to be loved, she was loved, like an icon, with a religious respect. People brought her the small presents that please simulacra, and her chapel, like a renowned sanctuary, was ornamented with garlands an ex-votos

---

[89] Available from Black Coat Press: "*The Automaton*" (1892) in *The Germans on Venus*, ISBN 978-1-934543-56-6.

left by cured or consoled pilgrims. She was truly pacifying; her calm and her serenity soothed anxious hearts, and stained souls recovered their purity in being steeped in the dew of her soft black eyes.

By means of such gifts, she recognized love and compensated it; indiscreet desires stopped a few paces away from her, like superstitious brigands, and fell to their knees; the less fearful kissed the hem of her dress; not one of them had yet dared to lift it.

Every year, leaving her husband, a unique priest, to his affairs, the idol abandoned the sanctuary and went, a pilgrim in her turn, toward the dunes and the waves. Relatives welcomed her, proud of her imagistic beauty, and for months she ornamented the region, a Madonna on vacation.

She departed with her children, with the air of a Laure thinking about her Petrarch, the pensive Lady, and the train carried her away, unaware of landscapes, noises and the petty annoyances of travel. She arrived: the sea! The sea, fatherland of dreams! Aline, a living dream, found brethren among the melancholy pines rustling eternally in the sea breeze.

The dunes were her garden; all day long, she walked in the lukewarm sands, or, fatigued, lay down in the thin grass in the sheltered hollows. Violent or pacific, near or distant, murmurous or roaring, the sea sometime frightened the pensive Lady, by obliging her to pay attention to it; the sea wanted her to gaze at it, the sea wanted her to listen to it, the sea forced Aline to emerge from her dream, the sea was jealous, the sea wanted to be loved; Aline was frightened and fled into the dunes; crouched in the sand, like an ant-lion, but innocent, she remained motionless for hours, smiling—smiling angelically—attracting to her by means of her breath the invisible reveries, tiny creatures, of which the air is full.

Aline was happy, for she was alone. No matter how scantly she felt them, contacts made her suffer, at least afterwards, by reaction; the idea that someone had just touched her, or even spoken to her, caused her, if not a pain, at least an embarrassment. In the street, the gazes of "impure passers-by" had sometimes given her, on days of nervousness, the impression of a net of dirty cords that she had to break in order to pass through; here, enveloped by solitude, she was not soiled or touched by the desires of any individual, and in the absolute absence of sensations, folded entirely upon herself, sure that no contrary fluid would come to trouble the pure current of her eternal dream, Aline rose up almost as high as ecstasy.

A woman made to be loved—but above all to be divined, closed under the stone veils of the cloister; doubtless destined for the most intoxicating amours! Not to act, not to speak; sometimes to sing; that is the ideal of more than one person; it was Aline's ideal; and her veritable vocation.

In her phases of solitary ecstasy, Aline sometimes sang; it was a sort of joyful lament emerging from unconscious lips, a rhythmic chant, like that of the sirens, over the respiration of the sea.

She sang, and a fisherman coming back, chased by the rising tide, heard the song of the siren, the joyful lament of the pensive Lady; astonished, he pricked up his ears, accustomed to perceive the slightest nuances of the song of the wind in the pines; he had never heard such a song—he, who knew all the songs of the sea, for whom the foolish sirens had inflated their lungs and broke their conches; he got his bearings, he searched, and in a hollow in the dunes, he perceived Aline.

She was lying on her back, scarcely clad; her light white dress scarcely made a mist over her limbs, and her upper body was affirmed, held by her folded arms. Aline was charming, and a true siren thus posed on the sand, like a delectable wreck borne there by a caprice of the wind; her black hair spread out like wrack, truly similar to the algal tresses of sirens. The fisherman, still damp with sea-water, approached the apparition and caressed it with his heavy hand.

Aline was still singing, departed in a dream, ecstatic, her eyes closed; the fisherman, with his heavy hand, took possession of the wreck. Aline was still singing; the fisherman kissed the siren on the shoulder respectfully, as he had seen the priest kiss the altar before the sacrifice, because he was emotional and religious before such a beauty. Aline was still singing; the fisherman completed his work—and he saw clearly that she was not a siren, for no siren allowed herself to be approached so closely, and none ever risked conceiving of a man.

Aline stopped singing; the pensive Lady awoke, shivering, got up, her mouth bitter from the kiss that had stopped on her lips the flight of her dream song.

The fisherman fled, frightened; she seized him by the hand; he obeyed and listened.

"Why have you stolen me? I belonged to one alone, and his chain was gentle to me because I did not feel its weight. To belong to one alone is still to be free, for that one can love her—which is to say, to assimilate her to himself, to dissolve her in himself...but you, stranger, you have weighed upon my heart with all your weight, you have bruised me, you have been my master; from this moment on I am your mistress. Come, we shall wash ourselves together of the crime you have made me commit. Do you hear the voice of the sea—the sea that I love and of which I am afraid? She is calling to us and advancing to meet us; come! Why have you stolen me? I am one whom one does not steal twice; I am the treasure that is animated, that agitates, that twists and coils like an invincible serpent around the neck of the thief; come!"

And the pensive Lady, awakened from her dream, rose up, terrible, inhuman, implacable, and, taking the fisherman by the hand, she went with him toward the sea, dragging him like a little child.

The pensive Lady went into the sea.

Jean Richepin (1849-1926) was fined and imprisoned when his first collection of poems, La Chanson des gueux *(1876) was prosecuted for obscenity. His first collection of prose,* Morts bizarres, *was published in the same year. He became one of the most flamboyant literary Bohemians of the fin-de-siècle, to the extent that Sarah Bernhardt—opposite whom he starred in one of his plays—declared that he was a bigger ham than she was. Amazingly, he was elected to the Académie in a three-cornered contest against Henri de Régnier and Edmond Haraucourt. He was one of the most craftsman-like mass-producers of short fiction for newspaper feuilleton slots;* "L'Homme-peste" *first appeared in* Le Gaulois, *1 november 1895 and was reprinted in* Le Journal *as* "Le Yoghi," *1 mai 1897.* "The Plague-Man" *first appeared in* The Crazy Corner: Horrible Stories *(2013).*[90]

Jean Richepin: *The Plague-Man*

I shall tell the story as simply as possible, without seeking, by an excessively artistic expression, to make the singular adventure seem even more singular. I shall furnish the precise details, the names and the dates, that authenticate the memory for me, and which, for others, will render sound testimony as to my veracity.

In spite of everything, I have no great hope of being believed. But what right do I have to be annoyed? Even I, to whom the thing happened, to whom my sure memory and solid reason certify the exactitude of the facts making up the web, when I reflect upon the adventure, no matter how convinced I am that I really lived through, have all the difficulty in the world persuading myself that it was not a dream.

That is why I am offering it as a story and not as a history, preferring, in sum, the renown of the extravagant story-teller to that of the fallacious historian.

Few people know the English artist Michael Joshua Hawks, but the rare initiates of his strange talent retain an eminent place for him in their artistic esteem that is equally rare. They think—and I am one of them—that his talent is actually genius, and that Hawks will become famous on the day he decides to publish his visionary work, especially his "Illuminations of Horror."

It is, in ink drawings heightened by color, on blocks of talc, a complete account, phase by phase, of the frightful developments of the plague. Already terrible when one looks at them in daylight, placed flat on sheets of paper, those

[90] Available from Black Coat Press: *The Crazy Corner*, ISBN 978-1-61227-142-2; *The Wing*, ISBN 978-1-61227-053-1; *"The Metaphysical Machine"* (1877) in *News from the Moon*, ISBN 978-1-932983-89-0.

designs seem animated by a phantasmal life when Hawks shows them to you in transparency, in the fulgurant glare of his lamp, which emits an abrupt jet of incandescent magnesium.

It is impossible then not to utter a scream of fright, which is immediately followed by a cry of admiration—to which Hawks usually replies: "It's not me who deserves admiration; I've copied nature exactly, and nothing more."

But that response only astonishes you more, because everyone knows, and he admits it himself with a mysterious smile, that he has never left London and could not, in consequence, have studied in nature those tragic scenes of plague, always represented in his drawings as happening in India. And if anyone objects, he contents himself with accentuating his smile, and adding: "Of course—and yet, what is out there, I have seen here, although that wasn't there, in truth."

People gladly forgive him these eccentricities because they admire him and, at the same time, they love him. For, apart from that childlike desire to mystify you, Hawks is a charming companion, entirely as if he were not a great artist.

Having had an opportunity to render him an important service, and his gratitude having rewarded me with an increase in his good graces, I thought I was able, one day, to reproach him for his petty defect. Our Parisian argot lightened the accusation, and I didn't hesitate to offer him my criticism in the form: "Why the Devil put on this hoaxer act with your friends?"

He took on a serious expression, doubtless believing that I had insulted him by thinking him a hoaxer, and replied, with a forceful handshake: "You're right. I don't have the right, at least with you, to give that appearance. I need to prove to you that I'm not." Then, sadly, he added: "You're the one who wanted it."

An hour later, we caught a cab at the end of the street, in which we arrived, after tortuous detours, in the vicinity of Brompton Hill Road. During the entire journey we remained silent, at Hawks' request. He seemed ill at ease, morally as well as physically. In addition, the weather was frightful. Rain and sleet were falling in a yellow fog. We were shivering perpetually and stifling.

Drink a mouthful of cordial," Hawks said to me as we got out of the cab. He handed me a silver flask. I swallowed a mouthful of a warm and bitter liquid.

After fifty yards or so covered on foot we went into a small dark tavern. The proprietor was a Hindu. Gawks said a few words to him in a low voice. Then we went up to the first floor, where the Hindu installed us in a dark room, solely furnished with a large divan and lit by a night-light with a frosted globe.

Hawks had brought a box containing his "Illuminations of Horror." He told me to look at the transparent blocks of talc for a long time in that wan light.

"Commit the images firmly to memory," he added, "in order to ascertain their exactitude by comparing them to the reality."

When I had finished, he said: "Check the time on your watch, and write it down, as well as today's date, in your notebook.

I did as I was told. It was twenty past four in the afternoon on 12 December 1894.

When I finished writing in my notebook, as I raised my head, there was a man in front of us, although I hadn't heard or seen him come in.

He was on his knees, seated or rather folded up, including his heels; his face was ecstatic, his body entirely naked. That body was ascetically thin, the bones sticking out beneath the desiccated skin. The face, drowned beneath an enormous avalanche of white hair, the wisps of which were mingled with those of an equally white and no less enormous beard, seemed completely reduced to two eyes, haggard dilated and staring.

Hawks pronounced a brief phrase in an imperious tone, in a foreign language, in which I only perceived the word *yogi*.

Abruptly, the yogi's gaze plunged into mine. At the same time, the hot and bitter taste of the liquor I had drunk a little while before rose into my mouth again, and I felt simultaneously as if I were intoxicated by that liquor and hypnotized by that gaze.

Nevertheless, I was neither in the sleep of drunkenness nor that of hypnosis, for I distinctly heard Hawks saying to me: "Look at the models that I used to draw my 'Illuminations of Horror' from nature. You can and ought to see them as I see them myself. It's out there, and not here, and yet it's copiable here, and it is."

And I was so far from sleep that I replied to Hawks, reasoning with perfect lucidity: "Yes, indeed, I see. Undoubtedly your cordial is based on hashish, and by that means, the images I studied just now on your blocks of talc are being amplified."

For I saw them live, positively, and I was in a cold sweat of quivering horror.

It was in a village of bamboo huts, under tall trees with plumes of palms or large, flat leaves, near an immense river cluttered with monstrous plants, whose banks melted into muddy marshes—and all that amid the flamboyance of a harsh sun pouring out a rain of diamonds.

In the huts, whose walls seemed to me to be transparent, lay men, women and children, prey to the hideous disease, all the stigmata of with were manifest: crimson anthrax illuminating ardent embers on the black, the shoulders, the armpits, the groin; gangrenous pustules hardening into brown scars; pale red tumors and petechiae; faces convulsed and racked by stupor; fuliginous tongues and lips—in sum, everything that called forth cries of fright and admiration before the terror so magisterially expressed in Hawks' brilliant, visionary and exact "Illuminations of Horror."

Yes, yes, what I *saw* really was what he had rendered. I could not doubt it. But I saw it, myself, through hashish or hypnosis, undoubtedly, and according to his drawings. But where and how, before making his drawings, had he found the primary material necessary to his visions of hashish or hypnosis?

I asked him that, almost furiously. He replied, almost coldly: "I repeat to you that it exists, out there. The yogi is making you see it at a distance. But it exists. He releases it at will, in order that I can copy it. Do you understand, now? Do you understand? This yogi is known as *the plague-man*."

Here, in my memories, so coherent up to that point, there is a gap. Surely, under the influence of the liquor or the hypnosis, I lost consciousness for a while. Not for very long, though, for I found myself getting out of a cab at Hawks' door, and saying to him, angrily: "Definitely, my friend, you're a great artist, but also a poor friend. Your habitual mystifications were, strictly speaking, excusable. This isn't, any longer. You're making a fool of me now—it's too much. Goodbye!"

He tried to reply. He wanted to take my hands, to take me into his house. I refused. If he had admitted that he had wanted to take the hoax to its conclusion, I would still have forgiven him, but he was obstinate in his denials; he continued to play me for a fool. That really is intolerable, isn't it? It made me indignant.

Six weeks later I received an issue of the *Indian News*, in a band on which the address had been written by Hawks, in which an article had been ringed in red pencil.

The article related that plague had suddenly broken out in the village of Pendjah-Sloe, in the wake of a tornado, which had emerged unexpectedly, without any meteorological preliminary, in the midst of a serene sky. It had been possible to circumscribe the epidemic and prevent its spread. It seemed to have been caused, inexplicably, by the tornado, itself inexplicable. The reporter ventured curious theories on that subject, regarding the mysterious correlation of certain epidemics with atmospheric cataclysms. He offered statistics in support, including the exact date and time at which the tornado had surged forth and the first manifestation of the scourge had appeared.

That date was 12 December 1894. The local time corresponded with a London time of four-twenty in the afternoon.

So what? Had the yogi simply been seeing at a distance, having made me share hi vision in what occultists call the *astral mirror*? Or was he even more than that? Was he the formidable mahatma of evil that Hawks called the Plague-Man?

I have never dared to reach a conclusion, and you ought to understand now why, when I reflect on that strange adventure, that however convinced I am of having lived it in reality, I have all the difficulty in the world persuading myself that it was not a dream.

"May Armand Blanc" (1874-1904) was the nom de plume of the daughter of the sculptor Francis de Saint-Vidal and the writer Mathilde de Saint-Vidal. She published some work in the Mercure de France, *which published her only collection of short fiction,* Minutes bibliques *(1902), although most of her work in that vein was published in the feminist newspaper* La Fronde, *edited and written entirely by women. She wrote four novels, including* Bibelot *(1899),* Mila, roman nouveau *(1900) and* La Maison des roses *(1901), but died young of tuberculosis.* "La Grande fleur*" was published in two parts in* La Fronde, *11 & 18 mai, 1899;* "The Great Flower*" was first published in* The Last Rendezvous; Stories and Prose Poems *(2019).*

May Armand Blanc: *The Great Flower*

"Something strange is certainly happening in that little pot!" cried Dominique Privat one morning, while making the daily inspection of his "garden."

That garden, a wooden box solidly fixed to the external sill of the window, contained a dwarf rose-bush, two primrose plants, three dumpy crocuses, a hyacinth bulb in an old bottle of fruits-in-brandy and a second, minuscule, box forming a margin in the first, which was to be a lawn, and where Mahon grass was already pointing its fine green needles. Finally, in a corner, there were two or three pots without tenants, half full of earth, to which the "tools" were fixed—an old pewter fork, a wooden spoon with a broken handle, and a rusty pair of scissors—heaped up humbly. It was one of those pots that had attracted Dominique Privat's vigilant attention.

"Something strange is certainly happening in that little pot!"

And he drew it into the center of the garden, and leaned toward it with an anxious and happy solicitude.

In order to understand that sentiment on Dominique Privat's part, it is necessary to know that he had a soul fond of the unexpected.

At first glance, the person and existence of the worthy fellow did not allow any suspicion of that taste for adventure. A modest employment, feebly recompensed, delicate health and an uncomplicated mind certainly made him an undistinguished exemplar of humankind. He had always been sufficiently ignorant of passions to be scornful of them, and yet he believed he loved, and truly loved, the unknown.

Of that weakness, which he had to recognize, he accused himself, but that was the principle of his liking for horticulture. To hear him pronounce that slightly bristly and climbing word, armored with a thorny *r*, one might have thought that one saw in him a master gardener versed in the science of grafts and

306

the culture of cuttings, or a fervent amateur of audacious collections: orchids, tulips or ferns. However, his universe, Nature, his entire floral folly was contained in those half-dozen vulgar plants, and at the slightest manifestation of germination raising a bump in those four centimeters of earth deprived of juices, the shivered as if in expectation of the impossible, of a magnificent mystery.

O triumph of amour and imagination!

So, that little pot presented a singular appearance, at least in the prejudiced eyes of Dominique Privat.

The gray and dry earth that half-filled it, deprived of water—because it had not rained for days and Dominique did not include it in his irrigation—was slight swollen in places, seemingly inflated by new life...

But I haven't sown any seed in there, the worthy fellow meditated. *Perhaps it's a worm.*

But the supposition that it might be a miserable animalcule that was causing such a singular convulsion scarcely pleased him. Thus, he did not disturb the earth in the little pot, and resolved to wait. Oh, but this time it was no longer a matter of the usual wait for a germination—charming certainly, but foreseen.

All the heroic hours of life having as the inverse of their weave quotidian banality, Dominique Privat was extracted from his ecstasy by the shrill voice of his concierge's little daughter, who was bringing him a bowl of hot milk, as she did habitually every morning.

"Will M'sieur Dominique perhaps give me a flower this morning?"

And, feline, seductive, womanly, caressant and endearing, the child—eleven years old, with an amusing muzzle—added: "They're so very pretty, your flowers, and they grow so well in your garden!"

Flattered, the fellow could not contain himself, and said in a low voice: "What you can see is nothing much, but I believe I'm going to have an extraordinary flower—yes, truly extraordinary!"

"Ah! And what will your flower be?"

Monsieur Dominique did not want to compromise himself. "You'll see," he said. "You'll see!"

"Right away! I want to see it!"

With the superb faith of amour he leaned toward the little pot with the mysterious womb, half full of slightly inflated dry and gray earth, and said: "Look."

The child thought he was joking, and, being naturally cheerful, started to laugh; but Monsieur Dominique's gravity impressed her, and before nightfall, the entire quarter knew that Monsieur Dominique was going to have a magnificent flower.

That same evening, Monsieur Dominique believed that he might die of fright. With his lamp extinct and the moonlight paling the window, he saw a strange form behind the glass, half flower and half woman, with a beautiful smiling face, who tapped on the window pane with her five fingers splayed like petals.

Not naturally brave but impelled by an unknown force, Monsieur Dominique ran to the ensorcelled window, opened it—and saw nothing, except for his flowers sagely asleep under the moon's rays, and the little brown and gray pot, which kept quiet. However, he repeated, as in the morning:

"Something strange is certainly happening in that little pot!"

Having gone to sleep full of joy, emotion and uncertainty, Dominique Privat woke up prey to a vague sadness. His soul supported the weight of passions poorly, and doubts, expectations and hopes fatigued him rapidly.

In fact, the soul of Dominique Privat, somewhat weary, would have welcomed a salutary repose.

Living very quietly, from one trivial habitude to another—spending his time in the grave, futile occupations of a clerk at the ministry, and in the preoccupations devoid of dolor of biweekly nourishment—suited Dominique Privat's faithful nature admirably. But it is necessary to believe that he had a demon in his spirit, whose perverse pleasure consisted of knocking over like a house of cards the beautiful equilibrium of negative virtues, and Dominique Privat's first concern was to run to the window in his nightshirt, open it, at the risk of catching a cold, and examine the mysterious little pot ardently.

The cool morning breeze, the weak sunlight and the soft breath of the modest little neighboring flowers, open and respiring with full corollas: none of those charming realities touches the fellow's senses. The crocuses, like golden stars, the primroses, as fresh and round a children's mouths, were shining and smiling with all their frail petals, but he ignored them. The white filaments of the hyacinth, considerably elongated since the previous day, quivered in vain in the bottle in order to attract his benevolent attention, and similarly wasting their time, if they expected any affection in return, were the needlelike tips of the Mahon grass.

In his folly, Dominique Privat even forgot the dwarf rose-bush, his former pride, and did not see that the frail shrub had produced two buds, very delicate and pink, like miniature shells of floral nacre.

He was blind...

The swallows under the gutter mocked him—but he was deaf.

In truth, there was reason to be. Utterly absorbed, he compared mentally the secret condition of the little pot with that of a volcano before an imminent eruption. That image born of his excited brain enchanted him.

A volcano on a sixth-floor window-sill is already not banal. To anyone who had made the observation to Dominique Privat, full of the most deferential tact, that the present aspect of the pot did not differ sensibly from the aspect it had presented the day before, Dominique would have replied with the most profound scorn.

Now, scorn for reality, if it is not the commencement of wisdom, perhaps being that of happiness, Dominique Privat knew for a week all amorous deliria. He pretended to ignore nourishment, gave short measure to slumber and neglected every concern foreign to the object of his amour, and did so much and so well that by the end of the said week he was pale and thin—and his garden, by analogy, was in full decline. But what did it matter? The mysterious seed in the little pot was prospering magnificently.

It was not that its fruit had become visible to the naked eye. No, the earth was no longer gray or swollen, because Dominique Privat watered it with a jealous intoxication with the air of a florist's vaporizer. It had become a blackish-brown, even, unified earth similar to the soil in any pot in which nothing has ever been sown; but Dominique Privat knew now what was happening: before appearing in the light, the unknown plant was establishing profound roots.

However, by reaction, after a fortnight of fever, Dominique Privat felt very fatigued. He no longer knew the calm joy of eating well and sleeping well. His uneven and nervous humor surprised his colleagues, his concierge and his concierge's little daughter disagreeably. He became unbearable. He took society in hatred, and yet could not suffer the solitude that his unadmitted disappointment exacerbated further.

He was unable to renounce by free and forceful will the happiness that he had promised himself, but was no more able to give evidence of the patent and superb mildness of true faith, of veritable amour.

By virtue of an excess of misery and disgrace, he was subject to the vulgar allusions of envy and malice. His friends and neighbors, without modesty and without pity, heaped him with questions about "the great rare flower." Divining that he was unfortunate in that regard, they were ingenious in irritating his doubts and soiling his dead enthusiasm...

Anxious, maddened, hunted and desperate, Dominique Privat, in those bad hours, was unable to keep intact his still-vibrant but utterly unslaked passion for the cherished mystery, the unknown dream.

He floundered in hesitations and suspicions, he saw himself abandoned by the entire world; his "garden" was like a cemetery—and a single month had sufficed for such great disasters!

So, one evening, one mild moonlit evening, the soul of Dominique Privat, fond of the unexpected but utterly out of tune, became criminal, and, the prompt gesture following the fatal thought, he smashed the poor little pot and, angrily taking handfuls of the soil, scattered them to the four winds of the sky—but as there was not the slightest breeze that evening, the earth fell vertically, in little moist lumps, on to the neck of the concierge, who was sitting on the threshold of her lodge taking the fresh air. She flew into a terrible anger; there was an animated scene on the staircase, and Dominique Privat went to bed very agitated.

Scarcely was he in bed than his room filled with a strange light, as if the moonlight had established itself there as in open country. A subtle and exquisite odor floated, the window opened, and, trembling all over, wonderstruck and fearful, Dominique Privat saw, surging from the gaping frame, a admirable, tall flower, with a profound double calyx, similar to the twin gaze of two large velvet eyes, with petals of a dazzling whiteness, as bulbous and satiny as a woman's breasts, and the leaves and the stem tapered like supple arms, and that entire long, sinuous, undulating stem had an inexpressibly voluptuous allure…Dominique was greatly oppressed. He recognized *her*, the promise of his dream!

He spoke to her and appealed to her, but she remained distant and made a sign…immediately, a thousand flowers appeared, which invaded the room and the bed in hectic round dances, and began, the mad things, a frenetic and bewildering sabbat, emitting mortal perfumes.

The poor fellow thought: *I'm dead*! and he resigned himself to it stoically, by virtue of an excess of physical weakness.

Then the torture ceased momentarily, and the great flowers spoke—yes, truly, she spoke. She said:

"Your soul is cowardly, miserable creature, since, after having had the promise of my beauty, such as you saw me on the first evening, you have not had either the courage to wait or the strength to hope even so; you have been infidel by virtue of weakness, unworthy fellow, not equal to the proof; thus, you have lost me forever, and I am more than a flower, I am passion itself; you have withered it forever, but you will be punished, for you ought not to be unaware that, as the sage says, *it is necessary not to resist one's passions*…for they are women, and will avenge themselves…

Frédéric Boutet (1874-1941) arrived in Paris in time to hang out briefly at Le Chat Noir *and to encounter Oscar Wilde, whom he helped out of an awkward situation and befriended. His first collection of stories,* Contes de la nuit *(Chamuel 1898; second ed. 1903) was set very solidly in the Decadent Symbolist tradition, as were his collections of stories cast as horrific and melodramatic dialogues,* Drames baroques et melancoliques *(1899) and* Les Victimes grimacent *(1900). The two novellas* L'Homme Savage *et* Julius Pingouin *(1902) are also striking exercises in Symbolist fiction, but as the pressure of making a living forced his work to become more commercial the baroque aspects of his style and subject matter gradually faded away.* "L'Insistance de Lucie" *first appeared in the evening edition of* Le Matin, *known as* Le Français, *in 1903 before being reprinted in* Histoires vraisemblables *(1908);* "Lucie's Persistence" *was originally published in* The Voyage of Julius Pingouin and Other Strange Stories *(2013),*[91]

Frédéric Boutet: *Lucie's Persistence*

This happened in February 1901. The night was glacial and rainy, and I was hurrying home. I was amazed to find at my door, waiting for me on the pavement, a fellow named Canal. I knew him well, having been to college with him, but, given his mores and character, he was the last man I would have thought capable of stationing himself, in the rain, at three o'clock in the morning, at the door of a friend who might not be coming home at all. I ought to add that we had quarreled a couple of months earlier.

"Why," I said, "what are you doing here?"

"Waiting for you," he replied, a trifle nervously. "I...I wanted to ask you to come with me..."

"Go where with you?"

"Home...I'm worn out. I've been...exhausted for ten days. I need sleep. I have to..."

He raised his eyes and looked me in the face. I'd never seen him so pale, and he was agitated by a sort of tremor—or rather trepidation, like a steam-boat under pressure.

"But you don't need me to go to sleep," I said, by no means seduced by the prospect of not sleeping in my own bed, which was already waiting for me, I thought. "You have only to go home and go to bed. What's stopping you?"

---

[91] Available from Black Coat Press: *"The Valley Named Solitude"* in *Tales of Enchantment and Disenchantment*, ISBN 978-1-61227-838-4.

311

"Well...well..." He swallowed his saliva and his voice choked. "At home, I'm scared..."

At this point, certain items of information regarding the natural history of Canal are necessary. He was born in a respectable prefecture, to similarly respectable parents, who worked successfully in the notariat. Their only son had always given them pleasure, being of a robust and well-mannered temperament. After a reasonable adolescence and glorious studies, he had made a brilliant entry into the École Centrale, and begun to prepare himself a brilliant career as an engineer.

He was in his second year when destiny led him to encounter in the street a twin soul named Lucie, who was nineteen years old, a typist, and romantic. She was virtuous too, and her seduction cost Canal no less than four months of effort, but he loved her during that time, and was able to express his sentiments, even though the study of mathematics absorbed the better part of his faculties. The twin soul had ended up loving him too, for good and all, and had yielded.

They had moved in together, on the fourth floor of a tranquil house, she letting go of her family and typing, and he pursuing with his studies with only slightly less ardor: a course full of sagacity, which Lucie encouraged with all her might, while keeping house as best she could, in order get by on her beloved's allowance without going into debt. The latter allowed himself to be adored, and found it natural.

Things had gone on in that fashion for the duration of Canal's studies, and for some time after their glorious consecration: diplomas, certificates and qualifications of all sorts, for he was a capable young man. In the meantime, his love for Lucie was somewhat eroded, in spite of or because of the fact that he had nothing for which to reproach her.

Meanwhile, Canal's parents reasoned as follows: Now our son is completely grown up. He's a handsome fellow, intelligent and well-educated. With the six thousand francs of income that we'll give him and all his diplomas, he ought to be able to marry three thousand francs and expectations. Then he'll be able to launch himself in industry as a manufacturer and become a considerable man, which will be advantageous for everyone. Mademoiselle Bodin will fit the bill very well.

Young Lucie, too, was following a reasoning, which was incompatible with the preceding one from the practical point of view: When he met me, I was honest; he knows that. Since then, I've been faithful to him. I'm his wife before God and he's going to marry me before his fellow men now that he's an engineer and can live on his own income. I'm very happy because he loves me, and I'll love him for as long as I live. Should I not have consummated my marriage?

Canal, personally, was not reasoning at all, but he was unenthusiastic in contemplating the imminent day when the notariat and Lucie would come into conflict.

That day came, as every expected day comes, whether it be feared or desired, whether it brings dolor or joy. Canal *père* found out that Canal *fils* had a gilt-edged, and therefore dangerous, liaison, and recalled him to the prefecture in no time. There were a few family discussions, in which the highest questions of social morality were addressed, as well as the duties of children to their parents, and, by way of conclusion, an explanation of the essential perversity of vicious schemers who take possession of the hopes of family—all of it very moving.

The hope of the family began by standing up quite well to the familial objurgations and depreciations, but as he had a naturally egotistical heart, having never suffered, and organized his life according to what he believed to be the practical modern method. He convinced himself rapidly enough that the best thing for him to do was to please his family, and let go of the schemer in order to marry Demoiselle Bodin, already picked out, the daughter of the office's principal client.

That decision made, young Canal did not hesitate; he wrote Lucie a letter in which he "prepared the break," according to his own expression. He followed the letter three days later and continued to "prepare the break" in person, with all the usual considerations.

He prepared it so well that, after a formal explanation, Lucie—who clung to her plans and proved to be impulsive by nature, and denuded of philosophy—went to throw herself in the Seine, not wishing, as she explained in a pathetic letter, to become a ruined girl, nor to survive abandonment by the only man in the world she was capable of loving forever, and whom another woman was about to take from her, although she was his spouse before God.

She was found two days later, snagged on a pontoon, and brought back dead to the small apartment where she had lived with her husband before God—and for him there were painful hours, for he suddenly woke up from his ignorance of life and his ingenuous egotism. A few of his friends, of whom I was one, thinking that he had not acted well, took responsibility for communicating that fact to him, without indulgence, and he returned to the prefecture in a state of some distress.

The scarcely-concealed joy of his parents threw him into great perplexity, with intervals of satisfied indifference that followed bouts of the most cruel remorse. However, in view of his well-mannered character, he accomplished his duties as a fiancé scrupulously, and he was, all things considered, well on the way to forgetfulness.

He returned to Paris, having affairs to put in order and needing to obtain estimates for the construction of a factory. Doubtless, he plunged himself into work, and perhaps he retained a certain resentment regarding our observations, for he did not come to see any of his friends. Ten days went by, as I subsequently learned—and it was then that I found him, one night, waiting for me outside my door, in order to ask me to go home with him, because he was afraid.

"Afraid of what?" I asked, somewhat taken aback, because he was in a state of horrible anguish and I would not have thought him capable of such emotion.

"I'm afraid," he replied, distractedly. "Listen: I need to tell you everything. Since my return—which is to say, since the event, since I left straight away—I haven't be able to sleep at home...or stay there by night."

"Why, what's the matter?"

"This is it: when I came back, ten days ago, I had some difficulty going back into the apartment...you understand?"

"Yes, I understand."

"You told me that I'd acted badly, but I assure you that I had no intention of doing so. It was so new for me...I didn't know. My father always told me that when a student had finished his studies he left his mistress and got married..."

"That depends on the woman, and..."

"Yes, but I didn't know. Since...well, anyway, I went back home; it was ten o'clock in the evening and I had a candle. I put my valise in my study, which is on the right. The bedroom...her room...is at the end of the corridor, at the back. I went toward the door to go in. And then...then I fled along the corridor, down the stairs and into the street, running as fast as I could, to find people and light...and I could scarcely stop myself crying out, I was so afraid."

"Of what?"

"Of...of what as behind that door. *It* was waiting for me, I tell you...

"And since then, every night...

"In the daytime, I'm not scared, and I don't even understand how I could have been the night before, and I make the resolution to vanquish it. I work, I make preparations for my marriage, carry out my business calmly and make a firm resolution to go into my bedroom that night...and every night, I'm more scared than the previous one, and I flee, to wait for daylight in cafes, in all-night establishments, anywhere that there's people and light...

"Every evening. And I would never have supposed, before, that I was capable of suffering like this..."

He stopped, out of breath.

"Why don't you go back to the province?" I said. "You can tell your father everything and settle your nerves before getting married."

"No," he said. "I'm not ill and I shan't say anything to my father. I couldn't. I don't know how I can tell him. You know me well, you see; you know that I'm of sound mind...but is it me or a madman that's telling you this? This evening..."

"Well, what about this evening?"

"Well, I'd made a resolution to finish it. I went up to my apartment at about ten, and it seemed to me that I was better and that I'd be able to go into the bedroom... In the corridor, with the candle, I wasn't afraid, and I mocked myself... Well..."

He gripped my arm with all his strength.

"Well…the door opened in front of me. Understand this: it wasn't me who had opened it—it opened without me touching it. It opened of its own accord, you understand! And…*it*'s waiting for me behind the door…I know it! I thought that I was going to die without being able to get away. And you have to come with me in order for me to be able to go back in, because I'm now a ruined man if I can't succeed in vanquishing *it*. I've been worn out with fatigue, I tell you, for ten days, but I have to get over this if I want to become a man again. Understand this: it's my entire life! You have to come with me so that I can go back in. I need to sleep at home tonight, or I'll never sleep again. Will you come?"

"Yes," I said, "I will. I'll go into the bedroom with you, you can lie down, and I'll spend the night next door, in your study, on the camp-bed. You need to get out of this. After all, although you've been unjust to her…that's no reason for… As you told me, you didn't know. Let's go."

We soon arrived at his apartment. Canal didn't say anything more, but when we were in the corridor leading to the bedroom I saw that he was on the point of fainting. The door didn't open of its own accord and nothing remarkable happened. We went in. I opened the windows and the cupboard briefly; I shook the curtains and devoted myself to various reassuring exercises. I even cracked a joke, and Canal seemed much better. He lay down, and when I saw that he was quite calm and ready for sleep, with his permission, I went to establish myself in the study. I read for a while, then, everything being in order, I went to sleep.

The doorbell woke me up with a start. It was shortly after dawn. Workmen, accompanied by policemen, were bringing back Canal's badly battered corpse, which they'd picked up in the street.

He must have thrown himself out of the window to escape *the thing*, whatever it was, that was waiting for him behind the door, and had revealed itself after I had left the room.

"Renée Vivien" was the pseudonym of Pauline Mary Tarn (1877-1909), an English-born Symbolist poet, who was a member of a group of Parisian lesbian poets formed in the salon of the American writer Nathalie Barney; for some years she collaborated with Hélène van Zuylen, née Rothschild (1863-1947), who used the signature Hélène de Zuylen de Nyevelt, sometimes under the joint pseudonym Paule Riversdale, although it is strongly suspected that Vivien was the sole author of most of that supposedly-collaborative work. "La Saurienne" first appeared in La Dame à la louve *(1904, signed Renée Vivien); the translation first appeared in* Lilith's Legacy: Prose Poems and Short Stories *(2018).*

Renée Vivien: *The Saurienne*

The sun is terrible. The sun is more terrible than the plague, the wild beasts and the gigantic black serpents. It is more terrible than the fever. It is a thousand times more terrible than death.

The sun has burned my nape and my temples and my cranium; it is has desiccated and blanched my hair like the grass, during heat-waves. Another man than me would have gone mad after long marches in the desert. It seemed to me, at times that molten led was running over my brow and along my limbs. Ha ha! Another man than me would have gone mad, but I have a solid head and body. I've seen men howling and gesticulating like demons after long days of marching in the desert. The sun, hammering their imbecile brains, had given them strange ideas, But me, I've always been tranquil and reasonable.

The sun is terrible.

Toward the end of an afternoon, when long rays of light were still raining down, as sharp as javelins, I encountered a bizarre woman. I'm not a coward, but that woman scared me because of her frightful resemblance to a crocodile.

She had a rough skin, like scales. Her little eyes frightened me. Her mouth frightened me even more, being immense, with sharp teeth, also immense. I tell you that the woman resembled a crocodile.

She was gazing at the water when I had the courage to approach her.

"What are you looking at?" I asked her, curious as well as slyly frightened.

She posed her terrible little saurian eyes upon me.[92] Instinctively, I recoiled.

---

[92] The word *saurien* does not have the same implication in French as its English equivalent, referring to the order of reptiles that includes crocodiles, caimans, etc. rather than to dinosaurs, so a more literal translation would render this word as crocodilian and the artificial feminine derivative as crocodilienne, but it seemed more esthetically satisfactory to employ the transcriptions.

"I'm looking at the crocodiles," she replied. "I'm somewhat akin to them. I know all their habits. I call them by their names. And they recognize me when I go along the river bank."

She was speaking in such a simple tone, so naturally, that I shivered with glacial fear. I knew that *she was telling the truth*. I dared not stare at her skin, as rough as scales.

"The king and the queen of the crocodiles are my intimate friends," she continued. "The king lives at Denderah. The queen, who is as powerful and even crueler than him, preferred to go forty leagues higher up, in order to reign alone. She wants power without division. He also likes independence, which means that, while remaining good friends, they live separately. They only come together at rare intervals, for the act of amour."

I saw a gleam of libidinous ferocity in her pupils, which made my teeth chatter. I'm employing that banal expression deliberately, all the force of which, and all the horror of which, I understood at that moment. The frightful sun was oppressing me and crushing me, like the weight of a giant. Liquid fire, it was burning me. And yet me teeth were chattering as if it were winter, when the great frosts make your blood torpid.

"I believe you," I panted.

She drew closer to me, with a gauche movement that was heavily insinuating...

The simpering of that monster was even more terrifying than her deformity.

"No, you don't believe me. What is your name?"

"My name is Mike Watts."

"Well, Mike, I affirm to you that I can ride crocodiles mounted on their backs. Do you believe me?"

I was sweating even more abundantly, but this time it was a cold sweat that chilled my limbs.

"Yes, I believe you."

And, in fact, I did believe her. I'm not mad. I've never been mad, even in the desert, even when I was thirsty. But I believed her, and you would have believed her, as I did.

She sniggered odiously—which is to say that she opened her mouth. She opened her abominable caiman's mouth very wide, and showed me her teeth, silently. A frisson caused her body to undulate, and that was all. Oh God who invented Hell!

"No, you don't believe me," said the Saurienne. "But I'll prove to you the truth of what I'm saying."

She scrutinized the yellow river, which was carrying sand and mud.

"Here's one," she said. "Stand back."

I didn't wait for her to reiterate the order. I ran away as fast as I could. Some distance from the river, however, I stopped, suddenly fettered by something even more peremptory than fear.

At the moment when the crocodile unclenched its jaws I saw her hoisting herself up on to its back and, for the duration of a nightmare, I saw her riding on an alligator...

I'm not rambling. I have all my reason. Nor am I lying. Lies are for the civilized. We never lie. We hate complications.

The Saurienne came back toward me, leaving the crocodile thrashing around heavily in the brackish water. She came back, her eyes shining with triumph...and something else...

She was looking out for an exclamation of approving surprise. But I was tottering like a drunken man and stammering incoherent syllables...*ba...be...bou...bi...* And I was drooling like an idiot.

She looked at me with the libidinous and ferocious pupils of a monster in rut.

"Come," she commanded.

I tried to follow her. I could not. I made the strangled gestures of a lunatic restrained by a straitjacket.

A few paces from where we were there was a clump of very long grass, and trees whose branches resembled giant snakes. She squinted at that shelter from the corner of her eye. I had no difficulty divining what she wanted from me.

It would be difficult for me to explain to you what I experienced at that moment. All sorts of ideas were galloping through my brain, like an enraged dog-pack. I understood that it was necessary to kill the Monster, but how? How?

Bullets and blades would slide over her carapace without doing her any harm. Come on, isn't there even one vulnerable point? No...yes! The eyes...THE EYES!

I was seized by a joy of fever and delirium, the joy that is only known to shipwreck victims finally returned to land and invalids who see the dawn dissipating the night of their horrible hallucinations. I danced; I made my saliva hiss. I even stammered a few stupid amorous words to my redoubtable companion.

I emptied my water-bottle in a single draught. The thought of my imminent deliverance flowed through my veins with the beneficent warmth of brandy. I would thus have the strength to accomplish the murderous task...

And while the Saurienne, her gaze capsized beneath intoxicated eyelids, awaited the carnal satisfaction, I took my knife...

I took my knife and, striking the monster wallowing in the grass, I put out her eyes...

I put out her eyes, I tell you. Oh, that's because I'm courageous, me. You can complain on my account, but you can never claim that I'm a coward. Many

men would have lost their head in my situation. Me, I didn't hesitate for a second...

And as I went away I turned round to see, one last time, the yellow river
that was carrying sand and mud.

Gabriel de Lautrec (1867-1938) arrived in Paris from the Midi in 1889 and found employment as a schoolteacher while frequenting Le Chat Noir *and other literary cafés in the evening, befriending Paul Verlaine and throwing himself wholeheartedly into fashionable Occultism. He contributed to various periodicals before publishing a notable collection of* Poèmes en prose *(Léon Vanier, 1898) which he claimed to have been written under the influence of hallucinations induced by hashish, taken in pill form. Resident in Passy, he established a salon there where his guests included Jean Lorrain—briefly a neighbor—Alfred Jarry and Oscar Wilde. As the Symbolist Movement faded out and he lost his appetite for the Occult, Lautrec rebranded himself as a humorist, and became very successful, developing a quirky quasi-surrealist comedy.* "L'Ame de Sonia" *first appeared in* Revue des lettres, *6 juin 1906;* "Sonia's Soul" *first appeared in* The Vengeance of the Oval Portrait and Other Stories *(2011).*[93]

Gabriel de Lautrec: *Sonia's Soul*

It's impossible that I am mad. That will become evident. If I am in my right mind, why am I locked up? I think it's at the instigation of some demon that is pursuing me. We are all prey to larvae and elementary spirits. The physicians know nothing about that, and they laugh ponderously to hide their ignorance when anyone mentions the occult. They're like the priests of the Middle Ages who sprinkled the possessed with holy water. Today, they give cold showers. Scientists have a horror of novelty; it disconcerts and humiliates them.

So, I have been in this little rural house for several days. My cell is tidy. The food is tolerable. I have been given paper and ink. I will be able to work on my great work: *The Objective of the Subjective*. The book is destined to open the doors of the academy to me. Once elected, people will be obliged to admit that I am in my right mind.

Certainly, I have had an adventure. If the physicians had wanted to take the trouble, they would have understood my situation and they would have been able to take account of my condition scientifically. My case is novel, I agree, but, in sum, there's nothing extraordinary about it. It's one of those accidents that only happen very rarely, but which might occur at any time. Humans are bizarre and fragile beings. One moment of thoughtlessness is sufficient. I drank a soul, by mistake. It was Sonia's. With mine, that makes two, if I can count.

I'll say this very quietly: I'd repeat that thoughtlessness with pleasure. I can't forget the delicate and delightful sensation that I had at the time.

[93] Available from Black Coat Press: *The Sacred Fire*, ISBN 978-1-61227-876-6; *Vengeance of the Oval Portrait*, ISBN 978-1-61227-009-8.

But let's get back to the question. How did it happen? It wasn't planned. It was literature that doomed me. Poets employ an emphatic language; if one takes them at their word, one risks finding oneself in an absurd situation. I wanted to collect that soul on the lips, like a breath. Ridiculous idea! All it took to kill Sonia, and the first imprudence that I committed, in embracing her, was squeezing my hands a little too strongly around her neck. But what does it matter? All the regrets in the world won't change anything. It's necessary to consider the actual situation coolly. I have one soul too many, that's for sure.

Oh, at first it was perfect! I felt like another man. When I went through the streets, it seemed to me that everybody was looking at me with curiosity and admiration. I thought of that character of Edgar Poe's who had lost his breath, and the other one, who had found it.[94] What an implausible story, compared with mine! Besides, taking it seriously, I recall that they were as inconvenienced as one another, the first even more so. That's understandable. Two breaths! It would make one burst. But a soul…a soul isn't something material, in the relative sense of the term. A soul doesn't take up any space. There's nothing less encumbering than a soul. Mine, in any case, I'm sure of it, can't be very uncomfortable. It ought to fit in very snugly with Sonia's soul.

And the latter, since it's no longer anything but a soul, has naturally lost all its malice. It's too distressed. Children, when they're a little bit frightened, hardly ever think of being naughty. And souls, especially women's souls, are children in eternity.

It's necessary to suppose that it's huddled in some corner of my being, and that it's looking out from there with a flickering gaze, liked some sly and timid little beast.

The truth is that her presence doesn't disturb me at all now. The best moments, before, were those when she sat calmly and meekly in a corner of the room, reading beautiful stories while I worked. I wish the situation were different, but one gets used to things. It's nothing at all to have drunk a soul.

It's sufficient to know it, to take account, coldly, of the slightly abnormal situation and act in consequence.

A man who has two souls evidently can't live like everyone else, but it's easy to keep both ridiculous dread and exaggerated pride at a distance.

The important thing is the heart.

I fear, at certain moments, that it might quit its obscure corner and fly towards my heart, and collide with it again.

How is it made, a soul? I don't have the slightest idea.

Sometimes, though, I imagine that it's prowling around my heart, silently, like a mauve bat around a red lantern.

It's mauve! That's what I wanted to know. I'm sure of it now. What a sudden revelation! It's mauve. It's very important to know that.

---

[94] Edgar Allan Poe, "Loss of Breath" (1832).

And what does it see? What does it think? What impression has the change made upon it? Often, in the evening, when she was alive, we discussed the question of life after death. There was no other issue that preoccupied me as much. I remember long conversations in which we whispered in low voices, in the darkness, thinking about phantoms, until our voices were impregnated with terror. I was able to console her then—but now, I'm afraid that she might be afraid.

Then again, if one were sure that things will remain as they are—but I think about that. Suppose that the soul were to die, while lodged in my body. Perhaps there time comes when souls, too, die? After all, we don't know whether souls are mortal or not. Agreed, no one has ever seen one die—but that's not a peremptory proof, since one can't see souls at all.

At any rate, if that happened, I would find myself with the corpse of a soul, which wouldn't take long to putrefy. It would be necessary for me to get rid of it, no matter what the cost. Should I go to a surgeon? He'd look at me suspiciously. I'd have explanations to make. What good would it do to expose myself to difficulties? Wouldn't it be better to set it free right away? It would have the time to take advantage of that liberty. Then again, perhaps it's suffering, and finds itself constricted in its prison. So far as I know, this perpetual contact might not be pleasant for it.

In the end, it's a question of right.

Has one the right to keep a soul prisoner, profiting, as in the present case, from hazard or circumstance? I'm reasoning like a lawyer, but it's necessary to call things be their name. There has been an undue influence. The fact is undeniable.

It has, all the same, been lucky enough to have fallen upon an honest man. So many others would have no scruples and would keep it—but it's egotistical to want two souls. As if that were possible! Let's see!

One would remain to me. That's quite enough.

My God! I know full well…when one is in love…I could imagine extraordinary things. Two souls making one…just words, follies, at the end of the day. Besides, I didn't love Sonia. What I said just now was literary, for my amusement. I have to get rid of that soul, immediately.

For a moment, I thought of killing it, with one of those long pins that women put in their hats—but I'm afraid I might only wound it, and that it will suffer. Then again, I might not reach my heart.

Besides, why kill it? Isn't that precisely what I want to avoid—a dead heart? Isn't it better for it to live and be happy, if it can? It will go out into the world, as light as a bird, a perfume or a musical note, and when it has found some beautiful form—a flower or a woman—it will take that for its home.

I need to give it a way out. That's easy. The slightest opening would suffice.

There's no point thinking about a revolver. They've taken mine away, on some ridiculous pretext. On reflection, I'm glad about that. In a case like this, a revolver isn't what's needed at all. It would surely be taken by surprise, and the noise would frighten it. It would start fluttering madly around my breast, bumping into the walls, without finding an exit. A dagger is better. Here's exactly what I need—they've left me the slender knife with a narrow blade that I use to cut the pages of books, to liberate the souls of thinkers enclosed therein.

Sonia's soul will fly out through the wound, and I'll keep mine, tranquilly. It has no reason to leave—provided, dear God, that the other doesn't want to persuade it and take it away! But I'm not worried. I know my soul. There's nothing to fear.

I shall set Sonia free.

Lucie Delarue-Mardrus (1874-1945) was a prolific poet, sculptor, novelist and journalist who was a regular contributor to Le Journal *for forty years, having initially made her debut supplying short fiction regularly to the* Contes du Journal *slot. She was married to the physician and Oriental scholar J. C. Mardrus between 1900 and 1915 but was also an intimate member of Natalie Barney's circle, along with Renée Vivien, and was awarded the first Renée Vivien Prize for poetry in 1936. "L'Archange au cabaret" was first published in* Le Journal, *24 juillet 1906; "*The Archangel in the Cabaret*" first appeared in* The Last Siren and Other Stories *(2019).*

Lucie Delarue-Mardrus: *The Archangel in the Cabaret*

She was some child in a garden, a little Marie or a little Berthe, who was playing silently in the corners, who never had the cross, and whose large ringed eyes, when they dreamed, prompted people to say: "She's idle." People also said: "She's a liar." And people repeated to her every day: "Your guardian angel is watching you!"

But she smiled mysteriously at that, because she knew full well that her guardian angel did not have the soul of a schoolmistress. And without being able to explain such a complicated thing to herself, she knew, with the certainty of instinct, that the unpleasant faults that made her a shameful and scolded child could not trouble in any way a certain place in her soul, a place unknown to all, chaste and cold, where seraphic whiteness held sway.

In any case, and although she was often told that one could never see him, she often distinguished her angel. She was not unaware that, on Sunday, he mingled with the children of the choir and gazed at her from afar with luminous eyes, magnificently changing, and which understood everything. Other people mistook him for a sunbeam or confused him with the ornaments of high mass, the gold of the censers, the linen of the surplice or the statues of saints, but Marie was ecstatic, immobile. Then someone jabbed her severely in the ribs, and whispered to her: "Read the mass!" And her poor little face rapidly plunged back into the open book. Thus she was forced to the boredom of the Roman parishioner, instead of being allowed to follow her own liturgy.

Now, as the unpleasant faults and the punishments actively pursued their parallel work, it happened that, from school to apprenticeship and from apprenticeship to the sidewalk, the little girl, mutated into a prostitute, became the same Marie or the same Berthe and walked in the bad places of Paris, her large eyes a little more ringed.

In order to arrive there she had passed through many chagrins and many humiliations, but she had not complained. because she was very meek. Furthermore, those things had simply seemed to her to be the continuation of the idleness and lies, the scoldings and punishments over which her childhood had wept so many warm tears. All in all, she did not find the life of grown-ups very different from that of little girls...

And then, what it is necessary to say above all is that the supernatural that had flowered in the soul of the culpable little girl had not abandoned the woman of ill repute. Without her experiencing the need to talk about it to anyone, wings continued to beat around her heart. Her child angel, who had once been no taller than a petty clerk, with the wingspan of a swan at the most, had grown with her in proportion to her height. He had become an archangel, of tall stature.

In the evening when she chanced to be alone in her poor prostitute's room, he came in with the sunset through the closed windows and, standing in a corner, gazed at her.

His wings, although furled, filed the entire room. Their great cumbersome and white pinion feathers trailed around him, stretching as far as beneath the furniture. And doubtless the odor of high masses of old remained in his hair, for his head, when he moved it, smelled good, like a censer. As for his face, it was perfectly handsome. But how would Marie have had the leisure to study him in detail? Since she had known him, she had never been able to detach her gaze from his eyes. Their formidable and charming gaze entered into her, and there was, without terror, without embarrassment and without even a blink of the lashes, an absolute communication with the mystery. There was also something simple, like the gazes exchanged between animals, and something pure, discreet and honest, like a sharp dagger plunging into the soul all the way to the hilt.

When someone knocked on the door, the winged adolescent flew away with the loud noise of a fan that frightened seagulls make. And Marie, opening the door to the monsieur, tottered a little, because the archangel's eyes had left her with spots in her eyes, as when one has looked at the sun. And the monsieur thought: "The kid has had one absinthe too many!"

One evening, for the first time, Marie spoke to her archangel.

She had come back from a little cabaret on the edge of the Seine, where she habitually touted for custom in summer. Her heart was beating with a great emotion because of what had happened. Some kid with made-up eyes, one of her comrades, with whom she was chatting, had suddenly started weeping on her shoulder; and Marie had felt at close range the spasms of the great feminine sob that, without one knowing why, always in reserve, waits even in the depths of those who are only prostitutes, as if all women were born with a heavy heart.

She had interrogated the child delicately, and had found out what was doing harm to her life. But she had perceived that neither she, nor the others, nor any of those in whose midst they moved had, as she did, a white relationship with some vesperal friend, in the eyes of whom to recover intact the immaculate conception of the interior soul. Then, an idea had come to her, as spontaneous and simple as those that are born in humble hearts. That was why, that evening, she waited, quivering, for her archangel.

He came. She greeted him respectfully as she was accustomed to do; then, without looking at him, for fear of absorbing herself immediately in his eyes, she said: "We've never talked. But this evening, it's necessary that I tell you something. You must know what I do with my days and my nights, since you've often been obliged to fly away to leave the place to clients. So I'd like to ask you this: Would you like to come with me this evening to the café. It's on the edge of the Seine, under the arbors, and although there's a fête today, it won't be very well-lit. No one will recognize you. But there will be a lot of people there, and I'd like to have you with me, solely because of your eyes. A great desire has come to me for you to gaze at my comrades. They're unhappy, even though they make merry. And if your eyes open even once in their midst, they'll be consoled for the rest of their lives. Do you understand? I'd like to lend them your eyes..." she uttered a little intimidated laugh and added "What is your name?"

There was something like a harp arpeggio in the room when he replied: "Domination."[95]

She clapped her hands.

"Domination! What a lovely name! My name's Marie. So, Domination, would you like to come with me this evening?"

The archangelic voice spoke like a song; it said: "But what are we going to do with my wings?"

Abruptly consternated, Marie lowered her head. "That's true! What are we going to do about them? We can't walk in the street like this; we'd be taken to the police station right away."

Suddenly remembering the days of her apprenticeship, rediscovering the gestures of a seamstress, she advanced tranquilly, with neither fear not effrontery toward the innocent and brilliant being, and her hands manipulated the giant wings with hasty movements.

"Perhaps by turning them like this..."

---

[95] This name might have no significance other than the literal meaning of the word, but it is probably not irrelevant to observe that that Lucie Delarue-Mardrus' name was often coupled by contemporary observers of the Belle Époque with that of the notoriously beautiful poet Comtesse Anna de Noailles, one particularly notable coupling being in Robert de Montesquiou's essay "Deux Muses" in the significantly-titled *Professionelles beautés* [Professional Beauties] (1905). Anna de Noailles' novel, *La Domination*, was also published in 1905, featuring the exploits of an exceedingly handsome and perverse young man, a model of contemporary ennui. Delarue-Mardus and Noailles apparently loathed one another—Montesquiou's coupling was deliberately mischievous— but they surely kept a sharp eye on one another's work.

But there was no means of dissimulating them. The great plumes always overflowed, fluffing up like the white wheel of a peacock-tailed pigeon. The archangel mingled his fingers, like lily buds, with Marie's poor hands. They both shook their heads like embarrassed young women.

In the end, Marie had a sudden inspiration.

"I'll put one of my dresses over them!"

And then, without laughing, she fastened a wretched skirt over the sacred body puffing it up complaisantly. Then, as the plumes still overlapped, she went to look for her beautiful stole with three long tippets and arranged it over the winged shoulders.

It doesn't suit you very well," she said, while adjusting a boater and a veil on the head embalmed with incense, "but there's no means of doing otherwise. As for these few long feathers that are still trailing, they'll be mistaken for the lace of your petticoat."

And they both went out into the black night, in quest of the train that would take them to the little cabaret of vicious nights.

Marie made recommendations: "Above all lower your eyes, Domination! Lower your eyes. You understand that if you only open them slightly, everyone will come to look into them, and there'll be five hundred people around you right away, like moths around a candle. When we've arrived, only then will you open them, suddenly, and you'll gaze. And, you see, it will be as if happiness were letting two stars fall into the middle of all those people..."

They went. The nocturnal cabaret, because of the nearby Seine and its grassy banks, had a simultaneous smell of fish and hay. Oil lamps were hanging here and there, with a few Venetian lanterns, and under the arbors, amid two or three sunflowers, there was a great noise of diners finishing their meal. The immeasurable shadows of the diners moved behind them against the walls, amid the coming and going of a few waiters in blue aprons. A rusty piano was tapping out a waltz.

And as soon as she went in, Marie shouted in a clear voice to everyone: "I've brought you a new kid!"

She shouted with the soul of the Precursor in the desert. And because people had been drinking adulterated alcohol, their eyes were shining and they were ready, on no matter what pretext, to become overexcited. That is why they quickly flocked around Marie and her companion. And people also came through all the doors of the little guinguette, regulars and others, rich monsieurs and well-dressed women who had come to amuse themselves on that festive evening with the poverty and the vices of the poor. All the classes were there, rubbing shoulders, hoisting themselves up on tiptoe in order to see. And the hats of the socialites quivered with all their plumes between the reflections of top hats, the kepis of soldiers, the hair of the prostitutes and the white berets of apprentice bakers.

Then Marie removed the veil from the head of her archangel. Glorious and prophetic, with the great tremor of those who make revelations, she murmured: "Open the eyes."

And, the archangel having lifted his eyelids, the fulguration of his pupils spread around him like a burst of sunlight in the middle of the night.

But in the circle of people there was neither a surge nor a recoil. The majority, having not noticed anything, were already going away, thinking about something else. A few men and a few women sniggered. Some came, with a dirty gesture, to look at the supernatural face at close range. Alone, the child with the made-up eyes who had wept on Marie's shoulder formulated the vague sentiment of the crowd. She stopped behind the wings hidden under the double and unusual protrusion, crossing over beneath the cloth of the stole and deforming the three capsized tippets; and gently, in order not to disturb Marie, brushing the archangel's back with an eloquent finger, as she might have done that of a hunchback, she muttered between her teeth:

"You know, she has rather pretty eyes, the kid, but it's a pity that she's crippled..."

OTHER ANTHOLOGIES OF
FRENCH SCIENCE FICTION & FANTASY
by Brian STABLEFORD

The Aerial Valley: Five utopian fantasies by Jacques Fabien, Victor Hugo, Gustave Marx, Jean-Baptiste Mosneron de Launay and Turrault de Rochecorbon.

Automata: The Imaginative Legacy of Jacques de Vaucanson; Fourteen scientific romances by Charles Barbara, Jacques Boucher de Perthes, Frédéric Boutet, Didier de Chousy, Léon Daudet, Emile Goudeau, Arnold Mortier, Henri Ner, François-Félix Nogaret, Jean Rameau, Romain Rolland, Ralph Schropp, Marcel Schwob and Edmond Thiaudière.

The Bald Giants: Thirty-Nine scientific romances by Alfred Capus, Louis Champeaux, Gustave Geffroy, Edmond Haraucourt, Albert Keim, Pierre Mille, André Monselet, Maurice Montegut, Joseph Montet, René Morot, Maurice Renard, Gabriel Tarde, Louis Ulbach and Adrien Vély. (*forthcoming*)

The Conqueror of Death: Eight scientific romances by Alphonse Brown, Paul Combes, Camille Debans, Emile Gautier and Georges Price.

Funestine : Five *contes de fées* by Guillaume-Hyacinthe Bougéant, Pierre-François Godard de Beauchamps and Catherine de Lintot.

The Germans on Venus: Thirteen scientific romances by Alphonse Allais, Rémy de Gourmont, Jules Lermina, André Mas, Eugène Mouton, Louis Mullem, Charles Nodier, Nicolas-Esmé Restif de la Bretonne, Adrien Robert, X.B. Saintine, Marcel Schwob, Louis Ulbach and Théo Varlet.

The Humanisphere: Four utopian fantasies by Paul Adam, Victor Considérant, Joseph Déjacque and Fernand Giraudeau.

The Incredible Adventure: Three interstellar excursions by Louis ForestPaul Gsell and François Léonard.

Investigations of the Future: Seven scientific romances by Pierre-Simon Ballanche, Victor Fournel, Alfred Franklin, Théophile Gautier, Arsène Houssaye, Jean Jullien and Maurice Spronck.

Journey to the Isles of Atlantis: Seven scientific romances by Pierre Billaume, Félix Bodin, Gaston Derys, Pierre Grasset, Gustave Guitton, Pierre Hégine, Julie Lavergne and Louis Lemercier de Neuville.

The Man With the Blue Face: Eight scientific romances by Alfred Assolant, Camille Debans, Arnould Galopin, Charles Guyon, Ernest d'Hervilly, E.M. Laumann, Bernard Lazare and Gaston de Pawlowski.

The Mirror of Present Events: Ten scientific romances by Georges de La Fouchardière, Henri Lanos, E.M. Laumann, François-Félix Nogaret, Jean Rameau and Régis Vombal.

Nemoville: Twelve scientific romances by G. Bethuys, Alfred Bonnardot, Alphonse Brown, Emma-Adele Lacerte, Claude Manceau, René du Mesnil de Maricourt, Pierre Mille, José Mosellli, C. Paulon and Emerich de Vattel.

The New Moon: Four fantastic voyages by Henri Delmotte, Alexis-Jean Le Bret and Edmé Rousseau.

News from the Moon: Nine scientific romances by Georges Eekhoud, Stéphane Mallarmé, Guy de Maupassant, Louis-Sébastien Mercier, Eugène Mouton, Fernand Noat, Jean Richepin, Adrien Robert and Albert Robida.

The Nickel Man: Eleven scientific romances by Jacques Boucher de Perthes, Pierre Bremond, Léon Daudet, Georges Espitallier, Louis Gallet, Pierre de Nolhac and Ralph Schropp.

On the Brink of the World's End: Seven scientific romances by Raoul Bigot, Jacques-Antoine Dulaure, Charles Epheyre, Jules Hoche, Joseph Méry and Colonel Royet.

The Origin of the Fays: Thirteen *contes de fées* by Louise Cavelier, Charles-Antoine Coypel, Catherine Durand, Marianne-Agnès Falques, Marie-Madeleine de Lubert, François-Augustin de Paradis de Moncrif, Charles Pinot Duclos, Jean-Jacques Rousseau and Carl Gustaf Tessin.

The Queen of the Fays: Twenty-seven *contes de fées* by Catherine Bernard, François Fénelon, Louis de Mailly and Jean de Préchac.

The Revolt of the Machines: Eight scientific romances by Michel Epuy, Emile Goudeau, X. Nagrien, Gaston de Pawlowski, Jules Perrin, Edouard Rod, Jules Sageret and Louis Valona.

The Supreme Progress: Eighteen scientific romances by Paul Adam, Charles Cros, Charles Epheyre, Eugène Mouton, Louis Mullem, X.B. Saintine and Victorien Sardou.

Tales of Enchantment and Disenchantment: A History of Faerie, with an Exemplary Anthology of Forty Tales by Marie-Catherine d'Aulnoy, Charles Baudelaire, Catherine Bernard, Frédéric Boutet, Nicolas Bricaire de Dixmerie, Charlotte-Rose Caumont de La Force, Louise Cavelier, Philippe de Caylus, Charles Duclos, Catherine Durand, Marie-Antoinette Fagnan, Marianne-Agnès Falques, François Fénelon, Anatole France, Marie-Jeanne L'Héritier, Édouard Laboulaye, Jeanne-Marie Leprince de Beaumont, Catherine de Lintot, Jean Lorrain, Marie-Madeleine de Lubert, Louis de Mailly, Catulle Mendès, Henriette-Julie de Murat, Charles Perrault, Pierre-Alexis Ponson du Terrail, Jean de Préchac, Nicolas Edme Restif de la Bretonne, Marie-Jeanne Riccoboni, Sophie Rostopchine de Ségur, Jean-Jacques Rousseau and Carl Gustaf Tessin.

The World Above the World: Nine scientific romances by S. Henry Berthoud, Michel Corday, Alphonse Daudet, Camille Flammarion, Henri Lanos, André Mas, Jules Perrin, René de Pont-Jest and Charles Recolin.